ACKNOWLEDGEMENTS

Special thanks to:

Paul & Mandy Sigaloff, James & Kate Meikle, Marten & Kristen Foxon, Hiroshi & Julia Sheraton, Eric Bader & Hilary Love, for vowing to make your partnerships much more than a technicality in 2003 and for inspiring me to turn my attention to the question of marriage.

The Reverend Freda Evans—for talking me through the "I do's" and don'ts.

Charlotte, Kate, Louise & Alice—for always being there, for better, for worse....

My family and friends—for their continued enthusiasm, support and encouragement, for richer for poorer, in sickness and in health....

My agent, Carole Blake,

Sam Bell, for insightful editorial input.

And,

Mr. Day... Thank you for making mine.

Technical Hitch

Jane Sigaloff

RED
DRESS
INK™

First edition January 2005

TECHNICAL HITCH

A Red Dress Ink novel

ISBN 0-373-89508-9

www.RedDressInk.com

Printed in U.S.A.

Marriage is a wonderful invention; but then again,
so is a bicycle repair kit.
          —Billy Connolly

I hate it at weddings when old relatives tell me,
"You'll be next, love." I get my own back at funerals.
          —Mandy Knight, British comedienne

People take shorter honeymoons nowadays,
but they take them more often.
          —Sally Poplin

Vivian: I just want to know who it works out for.
          You give me one example of someone that
          we know.

Kit: You want me to name someone? Like name
         someone. Like give you a name of someone?
         Oh, God, the pressure of a name.

PAUSE

          Cinderfuckinrella

          —*Pretty Woman*, 1990
           Writer J. F. Lawton

THE SMALL PRINT

The wedding vows used in the course of this book are generic and based on the Christian marriage vows. Obviously there are almost as many different versions of vows as there are designs of wedding dresses, and each varies by culture and by couple. The selection incorporated in this book are by no means better or worse, richer or poorer than any other. They are just, thanks largely to the mass media, based on the best known of them all, and reading them aloud will not make you any more or less married than you were when you started this book.

Get Hitched:

Get married.

See also: Tie the knot. Do the aisle thing.

Technical Hitch:

i.   A breakdown (mechanical) or breakup (human) resulting in delay or temporary failure.

ii.   A problem.

iii.   An unexpected or unforeseen obstacle or snag, usually unpredictable and often at the worst possible moment.

See also: Cock-up. Balls-up. Cold feet.

Technical Hitch

DEARLY BELOVED,
WE ARE GATHERED HERE TO JOIN TOGETHER
THIS MAN AND THIS WOMAN
IN HOLY MATRIMONY...

one

Jess inhaled deeply in an attempt to calm her galloping heart rate, but adrenaline had seized the moment and the more she tried to reason with her nervous system, the more it chose to ignore her. It was now or never. Not that Elvis was asking. And never was far too risky. Maybe it would sound better out loud than it did in the confines of her mind.

'I can't do this.' Petulantly Jess flung her necklace back onto the table in a flourish of general frustration, just as a cloud passed across the sun, casting a momentary shadow across the bedroom and proceedings in general. She couldn't have choreographed it better herself. Pure Hollywood in West London. A sign. Disappointingly, though, no Hammer House of Horror thunderclap.

'Here, let me. It's just a tricky clasp…' Standing behind Jess, Fi grinned at their joint reflection in the mirror. While Fiona was resplendent in full dusty pink bridesmaid regalia, Jess only resembled a bride from the neck up, her favourite black cotton cardigan, faded jeans and flip-flops diluting the overall effect. Never the girliest girl on the block, there had been a

time when Jess had joked about getting married in white
jeans…but that had been in the 1980s, when they were still
socially acceptable in countries other than the Caribbean.
'And then, madam, I think it's about time you got changed…'

Jess's dress was currently hanging in a room of its own lest
a splash of coffee, kamikaze Biro or eyeshadowy finger accidentally strayed. Careful not to dislodge the veil that the
hairdresser had attached to Jess's now perfectly tamed hair
only moments earlier, Fiona rotated the necklace into its op-
timal position before standing back to admire her handiwork
and coo her approval. Jess looked on silently. Apparently
today was for everyone else's entertainment. She felt like an
extra in a film, and unknown to the rest of the cast there was
a major plot twist just around the corner.

'It's just perfect.' Fiona swallowed a sigh. One day someone would design a piece of jewellery for her and have it
delivered on a breakfast tray. Hopefully a couple of years before she had stopped ovulating.

'I mean I can't marry him.' Jess shuddered. Nope, out loud
it sounded just as bad—and Fiona was definitely the wrong
person to be telling first. But time was running out, and at
least—at last—the sentence that had plagued her all night,
all week, was now in the public domain. Not that she felt any
better.

Fiona paled. Her blue eyes had never been any wider, her
pupils dilating and contracting in turn as her brain did its best
to digest this breaking news. Jess was her best friend. And
Nick was her brother. In the Battle of Allegiances this was
the Third World War waiting to happen—and she was a natural born pacifist.

'Of course you can.' To Fiona's relief, Sarah's voice wafted
out of the bathroom in a tone usually reserved for soothing
a child on the verge of a shoelace-tying tantrum. 'This is no
time for runaway bride talk. You and Nick are practically
married already.'

'I'm not joking.' Jess wished that her veil would double as an invisibility cloak. If only she'd gone to Hogwarts for her education instead of an ordinary day school. She could hardly algebra her way out of this situation. She was still waiting for the moment in her life when all that $x=y$ stuff was going to come in useful.

Fiona and Sarah exchanged a look—one that suggested neither of them knew what to say next. But Sarah refused to be thrown by her older sister's attempt to alter the course of events. Six years as a kindergarten teacher and she could handle anything. Under-fives were rarely predictable. As, she was learning, were over-thirties—although at least they could go the toilet by themselves.

'What on earth are you talking about? Why not?' Sarah's question was as direct as the eye contact she was forcing Jess to make. Maybe Montessori teachers and the Gestapo received the same training.

Jess paused to gather her thoughts—which, at the moment of truth, had suddenly started to blur around the edges. Along, apparently, with her ability to construct sentences.

'One hundred and seventy guests at £80 per head says you can.' Financial blackmail, emotional blackmail, Fiona had her brief. Get bride to aisle. And nothing was going to stop her now. She was on the verge of having a sister for the first time in her life. Her brother was about to become the happiest man in the world. And bridesmaids always pulled at weddings.

'I don't even know one hundred and seventy people.'

'*We* don't even know.'

'What's it got to do with you, Fi?'

'No, I mean "we" as in you and Nick. Mr and Mrs.' Fiona sighed. 'And right now it's got everything to do with me. Wedding phobic wedding planners can't exist. It's inconceivable.'

Enviously, Jess stared out of the window at a pigeon sitting contentedly in the window box of the house opposite.

She could feel colour rising in her cheeks. She wished she could be anywhere else, be anyone else, just for today. 'We're a rare breed.'

The blushing bride knew this was all her fault. She'd been perfectly happy living with him. Yet from the minute she'd said yes to marriage she'd been panicking inwardly. And silently. Then the Carlisle wedding had come along, and for six months she'd been living and breathing their plans, just going through the motions with her own. And now, if she didn't follow her gut, in a couple of hours she'd be Mrs Seaton.

She listened to the muffled chorus of normality outside. Strains of just another Saturday morning in the rest of the world. People collecting dry cleaning, braving supermarkets, watching cartoons, administering failsafe hangover cures... Maybe if she tied her veil to a radiator she could leap out of the window and abseil down to freedom.

'And what about the honeymoon?' Fiona was covering all angles.

'What? So now I'm supposed to marry him because we've got a holiday booked? It's only money. Love and marriage might once have gone together like a horse and carriage, but they don't necessarily go hand in hand like a house and mortgage.'

Sarah watched her sister carefully. She was beginning to get a feeling in her stomach that she rarely had these days. The one that had started five minutes before the end of her A-level history exam, when she'd realised she had answered the wrong number of questions from the second section. Jess simply didn't do drama queen. It wasn't in the James genes. But—Sarah glanced at the alarm clock on the bedside table— Jess was still in her Levi's.

Pausing for a moment to ensure she had the full attention of her ladies-in-waiting-and-in-denial, Jess needn't have worried. Four eyes studied her intently. Four ears pricked to attention. 'It's just, well…' She cast her gaze floorwards and addressed her big toe. 'I've been having my doubts for a while now. And, I mean—well, what if Nick isn't in love with me…?'

Fiona jumped in to defend her family name. 'Now you *are* being ridiculous…'

Jess held her hand out to silence her bridesmaid. This was a sentence she definitely needed to finish.

'I mean not really in love with me. But more—well, I guess more with the idea of being married and having children.'

'Is there someone else?'

Sarah had to ask. Fiona, meanwhile, was still taking in the last couple of points. Apparently she was having trouble understanding English this morning.

'Don't be ridiculous. I haven't got time to get my legs waxed these days, let alone have a bloody affair. I barely even see Nick that often. Sleeping next to each other doesn't count as quality time. I mean this is the first weekend I haven't been working in…in months.'

'Well…' Fiona searched for something positive to say. 'Life's like that sometimes.' Surely people didn't really call off weddings. Not to her brother. And not on her shift.

Sarah leapt in before Jess could. 'Fiona's right. Ups and downs. Give and take. Getting married is a stressful business. They say that along with moving house and—'

'You don't need to tell me.' Jess shook her head as she interrupted. It probably hadn't helped that the Carlisle wedding had demanded so much time and energy. But, going on column inches and magazine covers alone, Emma and Jack were the hottest newlyweds of the moment—and she had played a high-profile part in that. Indeed, the extent of the media buzz around the taming of heart throb actor Jack Carlisle was trademark Patrick Robson. PR by name, PR by nature, he was the master of the invention of tradition. What he touched, people aspired to be part of.

The headshake had been taken at face value.

'I don't know what you think you're disagreeing with.'

'I wasn't. And I know I've been hiding from myself for the last few weeks. The trouble is, I see too many couples throwing themselves at their Big Day only to find that when the confetti settles the cracks they were trying to paper over with their marriage certificate start to reappear.'

'What are you trying to say?'

The million-dollar question.

'I don't know… That I was merely in the right place at the right time…that he's hung up on being married…and I'm not.'

Fi rolled her eyes in an attempt to discredit her best friend. However, it was sounding more and more as if Jess had really thought about it. Not good at all. 'Have you discussed any of this with him?'

'I don't want the happy ending…'

'Of course you bloody do.'

'I want the happy beginning…not the beginning of the end.'

Fiona couldn't believe she was hearing this. It was like listening to an echo. *She* was the one who'd spent years worrying about letting a man into her life and heavily mortgaged flat to pee on her Habitat toilet seat and to connect his PlayStation to her hard-earned wide screen plasma television. But then she hadn't met a man she'd take on holiday, let alone contemplate spending a lifetime with, in ages—make that *ever*.

'…and then there was the map thing.' With every confession Jess felt her horizons widen.

As Sarah listened to her sister a pain gripped her chest. Probably heartburn. She didn't normally have a bacon sandwich for breakfast. Should have stuck to the usual muesli. Unless, of course, she was having a heart attack… Passing out was probably not a bad idea. She checked her watch. Just over an hour until they were due at the church. And to think she'd actually been excited about today.

'The map thing?' Fiona's impatience wasn't even thinly disguised as she searched the dressing table. 'Sarah, have you seen the Rescue Remedy?'

Jess ignored their attempts to belittle her crisis. A few drops of flower juice steeped in brandy were hardly going to provide a solution.

'Well, it was probably just a catalyst, but…'

'What bloody map?' Fiona started opening drawers increasingly urgently. 'And you of all people should know that marriage is for life, not just for Christmas, or autumn, or Sep-fucking-tember.'

She resisted the urge to stamp her foot or burst into tears—this might have been her first call-up as a bridesmaid but she wasn't eight years old. A pity, because for the first time in over twenty-five years she felt like throwing a tantrum. She did her best to regain at least a smidgen of composure before continuing. No mean feat, bearing in mind that it appeared Jess had taken the lot.

'You think the need for direction is the problem here?' Finally she spotted the little bottle in her handbag and, unscrewing the lid, bypassed the dropper and took a swig before proffering it to Jess, who waved it away dismissively, the carefully teased tendrils of her dark hair itching her neck.

'You should have seen the look in his eyes. For that moment he hated me.' Jess's voice was steady.

'He was probably just stressed, worrying that you might be having second thoughts—you know, something ridiculous like that…' Fi stopped herself. No one could muster a smile, let alone a laugh.

'I missed a turning, not a period. In fact the latter would probably have been less of a big deal.' Jess turned to face her sister. 'Since you and Simon had Millie, he is obsessed with having children.'

'For God's sake, Jess, don't try and blame your hang-ups on me. And you know he'll be a great dad.'

Jess nodded. That much she knew. It would just be so much easier if she could buy him a baby.

Sarah sensed a fleeting weakening of resolve. 'Seriously—come on, Jessie. Just swap the civvies for the dress, we'll apply the finishing touches, and I'll buy you a leather bound road atlas for your first anniversary—a real road map for peace. Or better still one of those in-car GPS navigation systems—impossible to get lost whether you're in the middle of the Atlantic, halfway up the Himalayas or in the centre of London. Bloody marvellous what they can do these days.'

'It's not that simple.' Jess's normally robust voice was becoming softer and softer. 'You know it's not like I've ever *wanted* to get married.'

Fi drained the small bottle and chucked it in the bin. 'That was years ago. Wasn't it? Can I just remind you that you were never going to drink coffee either, or alcohol, or kiss boys…Thatcher was still in her first term. Britain still had a Conservative party.'

Jess refused to get sidetracked by a list she had made at a sleepover party over twenty years earlier. A list which Fiona was clearly never going to forget. 'I still don't know why things had to change. It's not like I need to marry him for his money, and I have an identity I really quite like, and then yesterday… I don't know—it triggered something. It reminded me of an argument my parents had.'

'You think our parents got divorced because of a map?'

Jess nodded, apparently mute.

'Not because our father couldn't be faithful?' Sarah did her best to mask her exasperation. 'I mean, their sense of emotional direction was probably a little off, but…'

'It had already gone wrong by then. And they always used to argue in the car. You must remember…'

'All parents argue in the car.' Sarah wasn't budging.

'It was symptomatic of a bigger picture.'

'It was symptomatic of a family outing.'

'Come on, guys…' Fiona could sense a family stand-off and went for conciliatory '…this is probably a classic case of pre-wedding nerves.'

'Don't try and lump me in with every other bride out there. Besides, this is my first wedding. The others are just a day job.'

Fiona shrugged at no one in particular. At least she'd tried. Sarah stepped up to the plate.

'Jess, you're my big sister. You know I love you very much, but this is really not the time or the place for semantics.'

'But it *is* the time and place for getting your dress on.' Outwardly Fiona was trying to keep it light. She wasn't sure how to handle the alternative. And she certainly didn't want to have to even *think* about how she was actually feeling in public.

Jess sat herself down cross-legged on the floor, her back resting against her bed—their bed—and looked around the room. Lucy, their black cocker spaniel, was lying by the door, doing her best impression of a draught excluder. Her head was resting on her paws, her eyes begging her mistress to reconsider. Pure anthropomorphic guilt-inducing Lassie behaviour. Jess refocused her eye contact on the bipeds in the room.

'Look, don't think this is easy for me, but all you two can think about is the ceremony. What about the rest of our lives? The "until death us do part" clause—or at least until alimony us do part?'

Sarah sighed as she sat down opposite Jess. 'If you weren't sure, what on earth were you doing saying yes the second time…?'

Jess didn't dare answer. She couldn't. Yes, she'd turned him down once—but then they'd recovered; he'd said he understood. And then, nearly eight months ago, the quintessential weekend away, a whole bottle of red wine, a perfect open-air moment, a shooting star…

'I don't mean to belittle your entire career, but this is exactly why Simon and I decided to elope.'

'A decision about as popular as the introduction of the poll tax as far as your families were concerned.' Jess couldn't help it. Since Sarah had been born she'd expected to be at her wedding.

'It's what we wanted. This big white dress bollocks doesn't mean anything.'

'Try telling the vicar that.'

'Look, when it comes to nuptials, size isn't everything. It isn't about feeding two hundred people. The scale of the day doesn't have to be a direct reflection of the intensity of a couple's feelings for each other. It's what you have the rest of the time that's important, and I've never felt better about life than I do as a Mrs.' Sarah was done. Her high horse had completed its lap and was heading home.

'I just don't know any more.' Tears pricked Jess's eyes. 'Sometimes it's good, we're great, but then other times it's—we're not. Statistically, long-term cohabitees who get married get divorced. And if he's the one I *am* meant to marry, why have we waited nearly seven years?'

'Nick would have married you years ago.' Fiona gave up trying to pretend she was OK and sat down on the chair at Jess's dressing table.

'I'm sorry. I can't really explain. But I know me and—well, I know something's not right.'

Fi allowed her head to fall forward into her hands without a second thought for her eye make-up. 'Fuck. You're serious, aren't you?'

'Maybe I'm just not the marrying kind.'

Fiona snorted nervously.

'Whereas Sarah definitely is…' Jess focused on her sister. It was easier. 'I mean, where were your doubts?'

'I didn't have any.'

'None at all?'

'OK, Simon slurps his tea, never cleans the shower, leaves his socks in sweaty balls next to the laundry basket and visits his mother a little too often—but nobody's perfect. I love him; he loves me. Nothing is insurmountable. My reservations were not about my choice of life partner but about the day itself…' Sarah trailed off. Nearly three years later, it was still an inflammatory topic of conversation. Luckily Jess was far too pre-occupied with herself on this occasion.

'And you don't think this getting married thing is all about timing?'

'What *isn't* about timing? Shopping, travelling, careers, relationships—it's all about seizing the right moment. Life happens when it happens. You can't predict it and you can't plan the big stuff…'

Fiona was grateful that Sarah had retained total articulacy in the face of a crisis.

'…And if you were nowhere near a relationship at this thirty-two year-old moment, I bet you would be *totally* the marrying kind. You've just got the choice. Look at Fiona…'

'Hey, her time will come…'

Fi bristled. 'There, there.'

Jess raised a hand at her best friend apologetically. 'That wasn't meant to sound patronising.'

'Well, it did. And if my moment does arrive, you can bet I won't be waiting seven years before deciding to tie the knot…I might not wait seven months….or seven weeks.' Fiona laughed a little too quickly. 'Look, it's no secret. I have no desire to die alone. I want a husband, I want children, I want a garden, I want matching wine glasses. I want the next life-stage while there's still time to enjoy it, and if it all goes tits up I'll handle it. I admit I'm fussy, and that—Catch 22—nice boys seems to move seamlessly from one relationship to the next with barely a moment on the open market. But I'm still hopeful. My parents will have been married for forty years next year…'

'Well, my parents were barely happy for four.'

'Be negative. It's your prerogative. Just bear in mind there really *aren't* plenty more fish in the sea. I blame global warming. And then there's the overfishing…all these women who get married two, three, four times. Trouble is, Jess, you're suffering with twenty-first century too-many-options syndrome. Don't look a gift horse in the mouth.'

'A gift horse… Damn, we only had a gift list…'

An inappropriate attempt at a joke from the almost-bride, who was determined to return the focus to *her* crisis. Fiona's was hardly breaking news.

'Next you'll be telling me to just go through with the ceremony and get the marriage annulled if I still feel the same after the first dance. Believe me, I of all people know what today means.'

Jess's gum ached where she'd stabbed herself with the electric toothbrush earlier, in an overzealous attempt to brush her doubts away. Worse still, today wasn't even nearly over.

Sarah sat down next to her and manually unclenched the fists Jess had subconsciously formed in her lap. 'Are you sure you're sure? You know this will change everything?'

Jess nodded slowly. 'No. I mean yes—I think.' She was a living, breathing contradiction in terms. 'I mean, yes, I'm sure. And, no, I can't marry him.' A tear. Another tear. A whole queue of tears. The monsoon season had just arrived in West London.

'OK.' There was nothing OK about it, but Sarah needed a beat to compose both herself and the next sentence. 'The bottom line is it's your day and it's your call.' She was on the verge of tears herself. Nick was already part of the family, vows or no vows.

Jess sniffed and wiped her now streaming nose on her cardigan a second before she saw Fiona proffering the tissue box.

'I can't even visualise myself at the reception, let alone at the altar.'

Fiona took a deep breath. 'But you do love him?'

Jess shrugged, then nodded. Imagining life without Nick was like imagining life without a mobile phone—she knew it was possible she just couldn't remember how. 'Of course. And I know this is going to sound trite and naïve, but I really don't want to hurt him. Trouble is I can't do this…not today…maybe not any day…'

'I'm not sure he's going to be quite as interested tomorrow…' Fiona sighed. This had been going to be so perfect.

'I should never have said yes. It was just—he was so happy and excited. And I was…' Jess exhaled slowly. She had been going to say drunk. But while that might have been an accurate statement physiologically speaking, this was far more complicated than a case of one drink too many.

'My guess is he still is. You need to talk to him.' Sarah looked at her watch. 'He's due to be leaving Chris's flat around about now.'

'It's unlucky.' Nick got annoyed when she didn't call to say she was running late in general, so a no-show at the altar was definitely going to merit a phone call at the very least. Maybe it would be easier to get married after all. How bad could it be? Everyone had doubts, didn't they? Apart from Sarah, of course.

'Not as unlucky as his bride not turning up.'

Of all the siblings in the world, Sarah had to be hers. 'I did sit up last night and write him a letter.' Jess castigated her inner wimp.

'A letter? Who the fuck writes letters any more?' Fi was incandescent. 'One minute you're going to be together for the rest of your lives and now you don't even want to talk about this. Why don't you just send him a bloody text message and be done with it?'

'Look, Fi, believe me—I know this situation is going to

be hardest on you, and I truly am sorry.' Suddenly Jess was terrified. Not marrying Nick was one thing, but losing Fi in the process was incomprehensible. She closed her eyes for a second, but when she opened them again, nothing had changed. Maybe if she tapped her heels together three times? Only she was at home already. Bugger.

Fiona wasn't interested in apologies. Her voice had soared an octave and her delivery was becoming increasingly rapid-fire. Words fired from her mouth like a volley of machine gun bullets. 'Top tip—bit late now, I realize, but maybe useful for next time—probably best to mention doubts/letters/intentions to call off a wedding, like, even the day before. I mean, perhaps at the point where everyone hasn't already set off for the venue, before I've spent an hour having my hair curled…'

Jess started picnicking on a manicured nail as she waited for the storm to pass.

'Jesus, Jess, the caterers have probably already shaved the butter and put it on ice,' Fiona went on.

'Shaved the butter?' Sarah's hostess with the mostest gene had been piqued. Not only had she been happily married for nearly three years, and produced a perfect baby, but she was one of the only twenty-eight year olds Jess knew with a butter dish to her name.

'Hello? Surely my future happiness is more important than the physics of butter curling?'

'Curls…that's it. I knew shavings was wrong.'

'Is anyone listening to me?'

'We've been trying not to but it hasn't worked…' Fiona's voice started to crack. Suddenly she was sounding very Elkie Brooks. 'Look, of course we're bloody well listening. We're just both in denial. Just tell me you didn't post this letter…'

'Of course I didn't post it. I hadn't definitely decided until right now. Actually, Fi, I think it's best if you give it to him.'

'No way.'

'He's your brother.'

'A fact I have never been more acutely aware of. My life has just hit a fucking hot spot.'

Sarah attempted to calm things down. 'So you don't think there's any chance, even an outside one, that he'll be relieved?'

Jess could have kissed her sister. Absolutely no chance whatsoever, but good to see she was thinking positive—or had at least taken her decision on board.

'Relieved? *Relieved…?*'

As opposed to his sister. 'He's been waiting for his wedding day for most of his twenties.' Fiona was speaking faster and faster.

Jess let her head flop back onto the bed. 'I rest my case.'

'Jess, you have to talk to him. You two are good together, you love each other, you own a house together…' Fiona insisted.

'We can't stay together for the sake of the mortgage…'

'And what about Lucy?'

'…or the dog.' Although Lucy's timely head-raise at the mention of her name was making Jess feel even more guilty than she had a moment earlier, and she hadn't thought that was humanly possible.

'You can't just walk away. I mean, you have to talk about this. Maybe we can just push the ceremony back by an hour or so…' Fiona mused.

Jess closed her eyes momentarily. And if he succeeded in talking her round? Then she'd be married with doubts… This was supposed to be the happiest day of her life. So far it was definitely the most stressful. She had to keep her nerve.

'I'm not getting married because the alternative is too scary.'

'Nick's one in a million.'

'But what if he's not *the* one?'

'The one? The bloody one? He's about to be the one who got away.'

Sarah interrupted the battle of the best friends. 'Hang on. I thought this change of heart was about you not wanting to get married.' Sarah was pacing distractedly.

Change of heart. Maybe a heart transplant was what she needed. Female logic and double standards were in the building. One rule for her, another for the rest of the world. And in Sarah and Simon's case she genuinely did believe that they were soul mates.

The doorbell rang. Three heads swivelled in unison.

'Coming.' Sarah threw her voice in the direction of the stairwell. 'Nobody move.' She was definitely in charge. Checking her watch and the schedule, she ran her fingers through her cropped hair agitatedly. 'Damn. It must be Michael. Five minutes early for fifteen minutes of "getting ready" pictures. Just brilliant. You really had thought of everything.'

Jess pulled her knees up to her chest. 'I can't see him. This is hardly the time or the place for a wedding photographer.'

'Roger that. Fi, nip downstairs and tell him there's been a change of plan and he's to go straight to the church.'

'Me?'

'I can hardly send Jess, now, can I? And don't say too much. Just in case—you know…'

'But what about—?'

The doorbell rang again. This time more impatiently. Shortly followed by a manual rap on the door.

'Quick, before Dad gets off the sofa.'

Fi inhaled noisily. 'Fine. Just remember I'm not that creative when there isn't a balance sheet involved. I work with numbers, not people.'

There was total silence in the bedroom as Jess and Sarah listened to the conversation taking place in the hall. Something about having her hair redone. Disastrous eye make-up, all hands on deck, Fi promising to take a few photos of her own and then laughter. As if it was just another happy, if chaotic, wedding day.

'Right.' Fi closed the bedroom door as she returned to the fray.

'Genius performance. Thanks.' Sarah was feeling quite guilty about having sent Fi.

'Whatever. OK, we don't have much time. Where were we?'

To their dismay, Jess hadn't lost her place—although she had finally removed her veil. 'Just say Dan was the one.'

'You and Dan split up—what?—ten, twelve years ago?'

'But we were really good together.'

'And there was less pollution, children had more respect for their elders…You were, like, fourteen…'

'We were nineteen, Fi.'

'And didn't I hear on the grapevine that he's living with a guy now?'

'Who asked *you* to be the details person?'

Sarah bent down and grabbed Jess's ankle.

Jess shook and reclaimed her lower leg before her sister managed to shackle her to something. 'What the hell are you doing?'

Sarah looked up. 'Just as I thought. Cold feet.'

'Very bloody funny. And I'm sweating. Is it just me, or is it hot in here? Do you know, statistically this is the warmest, driest week in September? I plan an excellent wedding…'

'When you're not the one who has to get to the ceremony on time,' Sarah added.

Fiona was just staring into the middle distance as the two sisters continued. Aside from introducing her brother to the woman who was now going to call off his wedding at the eleventh hour, she was wondering if this could in any way be her fault. She really didn't want to have to take sides. She needed them both. And they needed her back. And who cared if blood was thicker than water? As far as she knew neither of them had H_2O flowing through their veins. She'd known Jess much longer than Nick had. Long enough to know she wouldn't be doing this on a whim. Damn. Damn. Damn.

Sarah paused for a quick recap. 'So, you're calling the whole thing off on the basis of what? Lack of a sense of direction?'

'And he doesn't like dancing.'

'Doesn't like dancing? Short fuse with maps? Sounds like grounds for divorce to me.' Sarah paused. 'What's Nick supposed to tell everyone?'

Jess brightened a little. 'Maybe that's it. Maybe my phobia has got nothing to do with marriage. Maybe I'm just scared of divorce. Or children? I mean not children in general, but, you know, childbirth, parenthood…'

Older sister maybe. Less mature sister definitely. Sarah forced herself to keep cool—well, tepid. 'I thought you said you'd thought about this.'

Fiona had had enough of sitting on the sidelines. 'Look, our mothers were all married with children at our age. I would be if there was a decent man on the horizon. Face facts. You're just a marital retard.'

'I'm not.' Jess felt like stamping her foot.

'Well, listen to yourself for a minute…'

'Hang on,' Jess interrupted Fi. 'Our mothers were living in a different world. They had twenty-one-inch waists…'

'Allegedly.' Fiona couldn't help believing this was a conspiracy amongst women in their early sixties. She was sure her thigh was approaching twenty-one inches in diameter.

'Plus they couldn't support themselves on their incomes. They didn't have mortgages or pensions. They had to get married.' Jess was doing an excellent job of convincing herself she was doing the right thing. 'Maybe I'm not cut out to be a Mrs. Maybe I'm too selfish, too demanding…'

Fiona nodded, perhaps a little too vigorously. 'Right now, sweetie, neither one of us is going to disagree with you.'

A moment of silence as everyone tried to absorb the magnitude of the last few minutes.

Sarah, ever the pragmatist, was the first to snap out of it. 'Last chance to change your mind. Take a few minutes. Have a coffee. Go for a walk.' She consulted her watch. 'We can probably release you for seven…make that ten minutes, if you promise to come straight back.'

To the disappointment of her bridesmaids, Jess didn't move. 'You're really going to do this, aren't you?'

Jess nodded. 'Yup. I am.' Her voice was quietly calm.

'I'll get the phone.' Sarah disregarded the slightly absent look that always came over her sister when faced with something she didn't want to do. 'You'd better call him now.' Silence from the bride. Sarah didn't care as long as she rustled up enough words for Nick. 'Meanwhile, someone had better prise Dad away from the newspaper. Maybe Simon should take him to the pub?' Sarah really needed a hug from her husband right now. And a stiff drink. 'It's time to get this show off the road.'

Jess's shoulders slouched in her cardigan. 'I'm sorry, you two.'

Sarah nodded numbly as she went to fetch the phone and the father of the no-longer bride. Fiona, meanwhile, had given up trying to blink back tears. 'You're not the only one.'

Nick couldn't stop humming wedding tunes. It had started with a couple of hymns and processionals round the golf course first thing, moved on to a rendition of Elton John's 'Kiss the Bride' in the shower, and now, much to Chris's amusement, a unique version of Billy Idol's 'White Wedding' was reverberating off the bathroom tiles.

Chris was waiting at the bottom of the stairs, not altogether patiently. Jess's schedule was very detailed. They were currently eight minutes behind. And counting…

'Come on, mate,' Chris shouted up, interrupting the chorus. 'We need to get moving. You were ready ten minutes ago, so whatever it is you're doing in there, stop. And if you've touched that wet-look hair gel, it's got glitter in it.'

'Glitter gel? You poof.'

'It was an eighties party. And the bad news is you don't have time for another shower.'

'What I would I be doing with hair gel these days?' Nick smiled at his reflection. 'Flyaway hair ceased to be a problem when my hairstyle became limited to a number two all over. I'll be right out.'

One final comfort pee later, Nick washed and dried his hands and adjusted his cufflinks for the twentieth time in as many minutes. He rarely wore a suit these days, let alone a waistcoat, but he definitely looked the part—and he felt it. Freshly showered, shaved, and a glitter-free zone. He opened the door and resisted the urge to slide down the banisters.

'Mr Seaton, look at you. No jeans. No Timberlands. In fact, there's a high chance that she might not recognise you. And…' Chris mimicked the Bisto kid as Nick descended the stairs in a cloud of Jess's favourite aftershave '…you smell so good.'

'Shut up.'

Chris helped Nick into his tailcoat—no mean feat, given that Chris was a good six inches shorter than his best friend who, at six foot four, could have played basketball if he'd grown up in a country that had taken it seriously as a sport. As Chris tossed him his top hat Nick felt he should be tap-dancing to the church. A pair of spats, a cane and a syncopated beat and he'd be ready to give Fred Astaire a run for his money—if he'd had any natural rhythm, that was. Playing air guitar and air drums were about as close as he ever got to dancing. He couldn't help feeling that he and Jess should have been practising their first dance a lot more. Hopefully everyone would be too pissed to notice.

'Quick beer for the road? Or a Bloody Mary?'

Nick grinned. Chris must have spotted his momentary change in demeanour.

'Are you trying to get me drunk? I thought we had to leave?' Now in the hall, Nick was eager to get to the church as close to 'on time' as they could manage.

'Don't think you'll be popping out for a beer at midday on Saturday any time soon.'

'Nice try, but you and Mel are far too happily married for me to believe a word of that ball and chain bollocks.'

Chris smiled sheepishly. 'OK, it's definitely all it's cracked up to be. Doesn't mean I wasn't nervous on the day, though. All those people watching. All eyes trained on you. All that attention. It's enough to drive a man to the bar.'

Nick held his hand out horizontally in front of him, rock-steady. 'It's high time she made an honest man of me.'

'It's about bloody time you stopped your miscreant bachelor ways.' Chris punched Nick's arm jocularly. 'You've been a serial monogamist for as long as I can remember. In fact, Mr Seaton, I think you had your first relationship before I even had my first shag.'

'Just because you couldn't spell commitment until you were twenty-six.'

'Isn't that the number of years you and Jess have been together?'

'Very funny. Look, as long as I'm not the oldest dad on the block, always complaining about having a bad back or needing an afternoon nap…'

'Something you and Jess haven't been sharing with the rest of us?'

'No, no. But I hope it won't be long. It would be great if our kids could grow up with Sarah and Simon's.'

'I thought they only had Millie?'

'They're bound to have another one soon.'

Chris raised his eyebrows. 'Well, I hope Jess has scheduled time for all this breeding.'

'Two weeks in paradise away from her bloody office and without her mobile phone should get the ball rolling…'

'Surely you mean the balls…?'

'Promise me that's the last testicle joke I'm going to hear today. Now, then—got the rings?'

Chris pretended to search his trouser pockets urgently. 'Of course I have.' Chris opened his front door with a flourish. 'Your chariot awaits.'

Nick peered up and down the road, scanning the parked cars. 'Chariot?' He spotted a newish silver Mercedes, idling, with a driver, but that was as close as it got.

Chris locked the door behind them and led the way. 'OK, so it's an executive car. But no one sees you arriving, and you're leaving the church in a Rolls.'

Nick had at least been hoping for a bit of ribbon.

They'd barely been on the road for two minutes when Chris's inside pocket started ringing. Chris had organised his ushers with military precision. Best man for the job—today and every day. He couldn't believe it was now. Finally. Already. Opening the window in search of fresh air, he rested his elbow on the door frame and, grinning at the blue skies and sunshine, reached for his shades as two girls in the next car tooted him. Raising his hand, he waved and smiled. Today he was invincible.

'Hi, Sarah. What could I possibly do for the matron of honour? You know it's traditional for us to… Well, if we weren't married ourselves, of course.' His tone was buoyant.

Behind his own sunglasses, Nick closed his eyes and tuned into his best man's end of the conversation.

'Yup, we've left already. ETA twenty minutes. Should be able to make up five minutes on the road, so all on schedule. Si called earlier. Apparently the florist has surpassed herself. He's distributed the buttonholes and he'll give the corsages to the mothers as they arrive— What? Pardon? Hello? Listen, you're breaking up… Hang on—that's better. Yup, of course he's here. I'll just pass you over. Drumroll, please, for the man of the moment, Mr Nick Seaton—AKA the Groom…'

★ ★ ★

Jess stared at her reflection in the bedroom mirror. Salty tear trails had carved a path through her make-up, her lipliner was incomplete, and her hair was eerily overstyled. Pulling the pins out, Jess felt the tension ease and allowed her tresses to fall onto her shoulders, releasing the fragrance of the salon's expensive shampoo. Patching up her face as best she could, she reached for her sunglasses. She wasn't ready to look herself in the eye. Jessica James had turned her world upside down in less time than it took most people to take a bath. Fifteen minutes of fate. Finally she was an adult, with a proper life-changing decision behind her. The rules of disengagement were blurred, but she'd stumbled through and now her whole life was in her hands. She had an ex-boyfriend, but at least she didn't have an ex-husband.

Removing her platinum engagement ring, Jess placed it carefully on the dressing table next to Nick's selection of aftershave bottles gathering dust. Catching a ray of sunlight, the diamond appeared to wink, and without thinking Jess rotated the band so all she could see was the diamond's less sparkly underside through the claw setting.

The house was deadly silent, apart from Lucy's erratic breathing as she twitched her way through a dream. Everyone else was at the church. The silence hadn't come a moment too soon after the mayhem that had erupted as the news broke. Applying moisturiser to her hands, Jess celebrated their nakedness.

The doorbell rang, piercing the karma as Jess wheeled her suitcase to the top of the stairs. For the first time in nearly seven years she was single. Yet only seven days ago she had been organising the society wedding of the year…

two

Normally a sleepy road to nowhere except the garden cen-tre, the level of excitement in the village high street was pal-pable. A high-pitched air of expectation emanated from the gaggle of teenage girls camped on the grass verge to the left of the gates of Manor House, while older residents huddled in small groups staring disdainfully at the press photog-raphers, the outside broadcast trucks and everyone dressed in jeans and trainers clutching polystyrene coffee cups and bacon sandwiches. The media circus had come to town.

A young blond reporter, leaving nothing about her ample cleavage to the viewers' imagination, had stolen prime posi-tion at the gates to the stately home and was intermittently recording pieces to camera. Items which Jess was watching on a small television screen inside the kitchens, a mere half-mile on the other side of the boundary walls, as she ran through her checklist one more time and remembered to breathe.

Sipping a glass of water, Jess kept one eye on the ongoing attempts to broadcast today's big celebrity news. Stating the

Obvious Television—one rung further down the cerebral ladder from Reality TV. Yes, they were in Somerset. Yes, Jack Carlisle was getting married. In the presence of guests. To Emma Hunter. Who—yes, it was highly likely—would be wearing a white dress and clutching a bouquet of…flowers.

Jess scoffed at Philippa Preston's 'exclusive' report, as she started to speculate as to whether the bouquet would be hand-tied. Now, foot-tied—that would have been something to report. Philippa was desperate to get her carefully manicured finger on the pulse, but to Jess's relief she had no more information at her disposal than the handful of so-called facts which the papers had run with that morning. According to the *Somerset Standard*, an 'inside source' had revealed that the cake had gold leaf decoration and a water feature and Emma was going to be followed down the aisle by swans. As if.

'On the day that a thousand hearts are breaking, we are here to bring you the detail that the others can't. Live at Jack Carlisle's wedding…'

Jess smiled. 'Live', maybe, but 'at'? Definitely not.

'…this is Philippa Preston outside Manor House, proving that dreams can come true…'

Jess grimaced as Gabrielle's hit of the same name started to play with a soft-focus montage of relationship-so-far photos of Jack and Emma mixed to the music. She reached for the mute button just as her walkie talkie crackled into life. Gerry's gruff Scottish tones were only just intelligible amongst the static. In a world where mobile phones the size of matchboxes worked all over the world, radios still crackled.

'Jessica? Final security sweep complete. All clear. Bride five minutes away. Bridesmaids three. Rosie with them. Over.'

Maintaining celebrity privacy had become a competitive sport, and Jess was proving to be a gold medallist.

Security was tighter than Kylie's hot pants, and it needed to be. One of the guards had found a photographer sleeping in a tree first thing that morning. He'd been escorted from the grounds, but no doubt his 'My-night-in-a-tree-almost-at-the-wedding-of-the-year' story would be headline news in one of the Sunday tabloids tomorrow.

It didn't get higher profile than this. Not since David Beckham married Posh Spice had the nation been quite so interested in a groom. And this fairytale had been spun with the added element of accessibility.

Emma was just your average girl next door. An only child orphaned at nine years old by a drunk driver. And the public had taken her to their hearts. The reality was much less 'Annie' than the feature articles suggested. It hadn't exactly been a hard-knock life, but after the death of her favourite uncle she'd set out for London—actually only forty miles from where she had been living in Sussex, and no red bandanna of possessions on a stick over her shoulder or a knapsack in sight, but her decision had been pure Dick Whittington as far as the papers had been concerned. The tabloids believed that Jack had 'rescued' her, but Jess had spent enough time with the two of them over the last seven months to know that the reverse was much closer to the truth.

Everything had been checked and double checked. Lists were her not-so-secret weapon. The groom was in the chapel, as were the guests, and Rosie had been briefed not to let Emma out of her sight. Good assistants meant you really could be in two places at the same time.

The TV coverage returned to the studio, no doubt having given Philippa a moment to reapply powder and lipgloss in advance of the arrival of the bridal party. A couple of vacuous presenters were now speculating over the choice of champagne. People needed real hobbies and the world needed fewer television channels. Turning the set off assertively, Jess ran a brush through her hair and set off for the chapel. She'd learned a long time ago that wedding planners didn't run anywhere, for risk of causing panic amongst the rank and file. And it was showtime.

The screams of Jack's fans faded into the distance as the Bentley S-1 crunched its way up the gravel drive towards the entrance to the private chapel, and Emma Jane Hunter leant back against the red leather upholstery and prepared to surrender her surname. Staring out of the window of the classic car she wondered if her parents would ever have understood. In the highly unlikely scenario that they had secured ringside seats to her life, she could picture her mother's face—a figment of disapproval.

Unlike her fiancé, Emma hadn't done any acting since she'd left school, yet today she felt unreservedly as if she was playing a part—in full costume, on a world stage, with the shortest of rehearsals. Expectation was everywhere. The morning had vanished in a blur of ablutions, and if Amy hadn't been there, and Patrick wasn't sitting next to her right now, she might have believed it was all an elaborate hoax.

Of course she could have held out for true love for ever. As a little girl she had fantasised about the Ken to her Barbie with no thought of joint bank accounts or pre-nups. Posters of squeaky clean unattainable bratpackers had been carefully torn out of magazines and Blu-tacked to her bedroom walls in a collage of aspiration. She had imagined herself as Mrs Lowe, Mrs J. Fox and Mrs Estevez before moving on to pop stars and finally boys of her own age. But never had she dreamed she'd be Mrs Jack Carlisle…

Emma unwound last season's stripy chunky knit scarf, the aggressive central heating playing havoc with her body thermostat. It was a bitter cold January morning in Soho, and Club Tropicana inside their office. 'I've got the cuts you wanted on Carlisle's latest antics…'

'Great.' Patrick kept reading as Emma dropped a clear

plastic folder on his desk. To her amusement he was pretending to be immersed in *The Times* editorial.

'And you'll never guess what…'

He looked up. 'Any chance of a coffee before we get down to a few e-mails?'

Emma pulled a cappuccino out of the brown paper bag she was holding. 'Skinny, wet, with a shot of caramel?'

'Excellent work, Hunter. You'll make someone an excellent wife.'

Emma produced one of her wryest smiles. Thirty-three and not even a sniff of a relationship in five years.

Patrick sucked his first sip of coffee through his teeth and swilled it around his mouth as he transferred his interest from the broadsheet to the tabloid cuttings—much more his style. Finally he swallowed, the taste of stale toothpaste removed and the rest of his drink far more appealing.

'You'll never guess what…' Emma attempted to jump-start their conversation whilst reminding herself he was a man. Single file concentration. Essential if you were a racing driver. No time or spare processing capacity for composing mental shopping lists or planning what to have for dinner when you were taking corners at up to 150mph. In an office chicane-free environment, however, it could get quite wearing. Hopefully this time he was listening.

'What?' Placing his fingertip on the line of text he was reading, Patrick looked up. She had his attention.

'Guess who just smiled at me in the queue?'

'Who?'

'The verb was "guess".'

'Nearly eight million people in London and I'm supposed to guess?'

'Think big…'

'Sharon Stone, Michelle Pfeiffer, Kim Basinger…?'

Emma sighed as Patrick rattled off his fantasy date list. Forty-something men could be a real cliché. At least this forty-eight year old could be. He'd even owned a red Ferrari—until his second divorce.

'OK, take it from the top. And this time make it someone I might be interested in…'

'Brad Pitt?'

'Much better. Now, someone who isn't happily married. And who lives in London.'

'I give up.'

'Think relevant.'

'Em…' Patrick sat back and ran his hands through his hair, the light brown of his younger years now only detectable via his eyebrows. It wasn't white, or off-blonde, but pure John Major grey, and it gave him gravitas—an air of sophistication. 'I said I give up. I really don't have time for this. We need to reply to some e-mails, and I've got the meeting of the week in a couple of hours with my friend Jack…'

'He shoots, he scores.'

'I'm sorry? I don't get it.'

Her elation was waning. As Patrick's PA she lived and breathed his appointments diary. She knew when he was at the dentist, when it was his mother's birthday, when his car insurance expired, what he liked in his sandwich, how often he went for a pee in the average afternoon. So she was hardly likely to forget when one of the most attractive and eligible men in London was coming to the office for a meeting. But, thanks to a night out and the faint edge of a red wine hangover, she had. Damn.

'That's who I saw. Jack. But your *friend*…?' Emma transferred her irritation to Patrick. 'You sat next to him at a Cancer Research dinner for—what?—an hour?'

'Actually, it was more like three. And we got on very well. Plus he called me. Isn't that what friends do?'

'It's what clients do. Friends don't exchange business cards.' Emma rubbed her eyes. She would have been feeling a lot fresher if she'd remembered to eat last night. Her no drinking in January resolution had lasted precisely four days, and she hadn't made it to the gym since before Christmas either, so her next visit was going to effectively cost her nearly sixty pounds.

Emma sighed silently. It had been just another fragile morning in comfortable jeans and Adidas shell-tops, with a slightly washed out black polo neck and her favourite (make that *only*) winter coat completing the ensemble. And then there he'd been, ordering a double espresso and an apple Danish as she'd waited for her much needed coffee. Her still-drying hair had been in a scrunchie, and she'd just stood there wishing she'd found time to take her coat to the dry cleaners since September. Her security pass had been dangling around her neck like a medallion, her pens protruding from a coat pocket, and *his* press clippings had been in a file in her hand. Lady Luck was clearly out of the country.

Her first impression had been that Jack Carlisle looked even better in the flesh. Her second impression was that he knew it. Just the way he stood, head slightly cocked, his jeans perfectly not too new and not too old, his hair a little too long—fashionably unkempt. It all screamed carefully constructed couldn't-care-less. Her third impression was that behind the veneer of confidence, and despite the sidelong glances he was deflecting, he was just a guy ordering coffee in Soho.

Allowing her small black-mood-cloud to move on, Emma sat at her desk ready for Patrick, posture-perfect. She managed 1950s deportment for at least five minutes every day before secretarial slump kicked in. She had a top of the range chair; she just hadn't adjusted it properly. Besides, shoulders back meant breasts out, and she didn't need to attract more attention to her chest. She'd been on dates where men had spent the entire evening addressing her jumper. And this morning in her haste she had, of course, selected the wrong bra. Nothing minimising about this one. But Patrick was oblivious to her underwear crisis as he looked up, ready to start.

'Jesus, Jack Carlisle needs to watch himself. His looks alone aren't going to keep him in the public's good books for ever. And he really needs to temper his passion for married A-list women with young children—although I guess at least that means the suggestion he might be gay is off the radar.'

'Just because he went on holiday with a male friend. If that's all it takes for rumours to start, I've been a lesbian for years.'

Patrick laughed. 'It's hardly the same, Em.' He flicked through the pile in search of a specific fact. 'When was the last time he was in rehab?'

Emma silently praised herself for having read the articles on the way up in the lift when she clearly should have been taking the stairs. 'Last year. He was in for three months and rumour has it he's been clean ever since.'

'Still smoking and drinking?'

'In moderation. Which, incidentally, makes him human.'

'And he only really got into a serious drugs downward spiral after his brother died?'

Emma murmured confirmation as she scanned a newspaper article Patrick had left on her desk. Fucking marvellous. Apparently twenty-first-century men were intimidated by witty, capable women. In a strange twist of Darwinism her greatest strengths were also apparently her greatest weaknesses.

'Er, thanks for this, Patrick.' Looking down the page for the name of the journalist responsible for this latest nail in her relationship coffin, she was distracted by another headline. 'How to look like a Bond girl in only thirty minutes a day...' Now, that was a plan. But were they talking for a couple of months or perpetuity?

The phone interrupted before she'd had time to memorise even one of the exercises—although the *Licence to Grill* message was coming through loud and clear. Patrick cleared his throat as she let the phone ring a third time before remembering it was her life's work to answer it. She was sure she could spare half an hour a day. She could probably spare three hours a day if she was guaranteed to look like Halle Berry at the end of it.

'Good morning—Patrick Robson PR.' Emma turned the article over, forcing herself to concentrate on the voice at the end of the line.

'Good morning. Is he there?' Perfect enunciation. Pure RADA—and, Emma suspected, more than a little Prada. Not to mention a double espresso.

'Who's calling?' Despite the fact she knew precisely who it was, Emma had been trained by Patrick to treat everyone exactly the same.

'Jack Carlisle.'

'I'll just put you through.'

It was a nanosecond of power that Emma relished. 'Patrick—Jack for you. Is now a good time?'

Patrick nodded and dipped his finger into the froth of his cappuccino, determined to mop up every last drop.

'Patrick…'

Bloody Bond Girls weren't allowed mocha lattes. Apparently they contained as much fat as your average sumo wrestler. Ignorance was bliss, or at least it had been. Maybe this would be one occasion when she didn't believe what she read in the papers.

'Patrick…' Impatient, Emma did her best not to convey her disgust as he slurped his finger clean.

'OK, let me have him.'

Patrick's extension rang thirty feet from Emma's phone and he picked up, leaning back in his chair and putting his feet on his desk. 'Morning, Jack. My apologies for the delay, but I was just wrapping up a conference call.'

Emma smiled as she logged on to the Internet. They talked a good office. Most of their clients had no idea that the great Patrick Robson worked out of premises the size of a small but perfectly kitted out studio flat in a serviced office building. But they had the right postcode. Location, location, location.

'Yup, just looking at them now… Well, the room is booked…'

Emma mouthed 'Two o'clock' and waved two fingers across the office without looking up from checking her Hotmail account.

Patrick nodded his gratitude as he continued his sentence without skipping a beat '…for two p.m. But of course if you want to make it earlier…In half an hour? I'll just check my diary.' Patrick flicked through some papers on his desk, forgetting that in this electronic diary age no rustling was required. 'That'll be perfect. Do you want to come to the—?'

Emma waved at Patrick and moved her head from left to right and back again vehemently. Half an hour? That didn't even give her a chance to nip out to Gap.

'Indeed.' A slightly sycophantic laugh. 'No, you're right. Morning coffee at Claridges it is.' Patrick tossed his empty cup into the bin. He owed his career to caffeine.

Emma exhaled. Makeover moment over. She'd had quite enough excitement for one morning already.

A peacock screeched from the top of the balustrade as Jess tucked a stray tendril of hair behind her ear. In at the deep end, and with less time than she would have liked, they'd toyed with a number of venues. But Jack had been adamant: heritage over hotels. And as Emma didn't have a couple of stately homes at her disposal, and the Carlisle family pile at Greenhill needed a lot of work, it had been Manor House all the way. The estate was the consummate mix of formality and intimacy plus, over three hundred years old, it had once been the seat of Jack's great grandmother's family. With quite enough tradition to go round, it came complete with an amenable (and now even wealthier) owner, and an existing chapel in its grounds. Russell Crowe eat your heart out.

Jess emitted an inaudible sigh of relief as the bridal car came to a halt under the canopy shielding Emma's entrance from the rest of the world. The bride had arrived, the groom was *in situ,* and from here on in everything that could go wrong was down to her—much the way she preferred things.

Jack Carlisle clenched his toes inside his shiny new Gucci brogues and stared at the stone floor slabs, focusing on the organ music and trying to ignore the faint high-pitched whining and staccato growl of helicopter rotors chopping through the Somerset airspace as the media swooped and circled overhead. Privacy was a red rag to the paparazzi, and, to be honest, he still couldn't see the problem with a quick photo opportunity. Rumour had it that a picture of today was worth in excess of half a million pounds, but then again it was only understandable that the world's press needed a bit of proof that the media's favourite wild child was tying the knot. Yet both the wedding planner and the PR guy had been adamant: if he really loved his wife then this was their moment, to be cherished in private.

If he really loved his wife.

Jack rocked backwards and forwards in his shoes. It felt like ages since he'd had a cigarette, and it wasn't like he could nip outside for a quick puff now. In which case he really wanted a piece of chewing gum. But years of public schooling had taught him that chewing in church wasn't something that either God or the vicar would appreciate. Trying to contain his cravings, he consulted his watch. Five minutes late.

Spotting the time-check, his father patted him on the shoulder from the pew behind.

'Bride's prerogative. Your mother kept me waiting all her life. And then she bloody well left early.' His voice was the perfect stage whisper. Just loud enough to elicit a ripple of laughter from the guests seated nearest to them, followed by a murmur of sympathy.

Jack did his best to smile at his father's attempt to put him at ease. Physically they might only have been inches away from each other; emotionally they were miles apart.

'She'd have been so proud of you today...'

James's voice was a portal to a bygone era, to the days when monogrammed handkerchiefs and leather driving gloves had been *de rigueur* amongst the upper classes. Formerly one of Britain's best loved actors, now practically retired, he'd received an Academy Award in the 1960s—although Jack wasn't convinced it had been awarded for anything other than enunciating clearly and looking dapper in a motion picture. He had always been showstopping in Burberry—in the days before the brand had been hijacked by the hip-hop generation.

'As would Charlie...'

As he heard his father rummaging in his trouser pocket for a handkerchief, Jack could almost feel his brother's arm on his shoulder.

'Emma's a delight, and it's high time this family got its house in order.' James blew his nose noisily.

Jack sighed. His father talked about the Carlisles as if they were Montagues or Capulets, Kennedys or Windsors. And Charlie might have been the number one son, but he'd also been the ultimate brother and his only sibling. He would never be able to replace the only person who had truly understood what being his father's son meant.

The sun was shining brightly as Jess opened the car door for Emma. The clunk of the door mechanism on the Oxford Blue vintage Bentley was immediately followed by the mechanical chorus of a hundred telephoto shutters opening and closing urgently, as desperate photographers blindly held their cameras aloft, pointed over the wall, and the choppers circled overhead like a shoal of sharks.

Francesca B, dress designer of tomorrow, wafted out of the

porch of the chapel to ensure her creation was fulfilling its potential whilst the Carlisle family jeweller, flanked by a Securicor guard, fastened a diamond choker around Emma's neck. On loan from the Carlisle family vault and hers to keep only until after the official photos had been taken.

Patrick grinned, masking his nerves. *In loco parentis* was not a role he was familiar with. 'Well, Em, this is novel. I don't normally do weddings unless they're my own. I've always been the one waiting at the end of the altar.'

'Then this should give you a whole new perspective.'

'Indeed.' Remembering his duties, Patrick proffered his arm and Emma took it gratefully.

Leaning in for an air kiss of support, Emma muttered out of the corner of her smile. 'This was all your idea, remember?'

Patrick winked at Emma. 'As if I could forget.'

Thanks to her fateful morning coffee run, they hadn't even had to lie. Well, at least there'd been a kernel of truth in the fairytale they'd concocted. Patrick was just waiting for someone to write the screenplay and hire Sandra Bullock to do the honours. It had been one of his more inspired lunches…

Five hours since Patrick had left for his meeting and counting. Emma's in-tray was empty, the filing was up to date, she'd drafted a couple of press releases, eaten her sandwich, plus a special promotional five-finger Kit Kat, and worked out she had consumed at least eight hundred calories versus the fifteen she'd probably burned going out to fetch them.

According to Patrick's paper, marriage was fashionable once again. Passport sized photos of celebrity couples framed the article, which trumpeted a minor increase in the British marriage rate. She couldn't help thinking this was careful manipulation of the statistics, probably by the people who charged nearly a thousand pounds for three tiers of fruit cake. Since she'd worked in PR she had a conspiracy theory for everything. Emma was bored. Time to phone a friend.

The call was answered almost immediately, and apparently mid-sentence. 'Georgie, put that down—now. Hello?'

'Bad time, Amy?'

'I'm warning you.'

'I'll call back later.' Emma prepared to hang up.

'Not you, Ems. We're baking. And to think I chose to give up a career in recruitment to bring them up. So what if my father ran off with the nanny when I was twelve? Frankly, Tim doesn't have the energy. Or I'll employ one with a moustache and body odour. I miss personal space. And silence.'

Emma laughed. Amy was exactly one month younger than her. And exactly two life-stages ahead of her.

'Georgie, I saw that. Stop pinching Pippa. So, Ems, how can I help? Listen, G—last chance. No Tweenie treats if you do that again. I don't care. She's two and you're five. God, Emma, please entertain me with tales of the city before my brain becomes one hundred per cent preschool puree.'

'I was just calling for a chat before I'm tempted to buy more comfort food instead of embracing the Bond Girl diet. January sucks.'

'Look, if you're feeling too sedentary just come and look after the girls for a morning. Who needs Pilates to tone your upper body when you're picking children up all over the place?'

'Unfortunately I've got to sit here in case Patrick decides to come back from morning coffee...'

'But it's...'

'I know. It became a lunch meeting...and if I wasn't talking to you I'd be trying to bludgeon myself to death with the stapler. Some bright spark has had a chocolate machine installed in the kitchen. Waistline suicide.'

'Well, if it makes you feel better, I've had two more rejections from publishers.'

Emma regretted her selfish rant at once. 'Oh no, Amy. I'm so sorry.'

'Don't be. It's their loss.'

'You were supposed to keep me fully updated.'

'I know, and I am. Witness my new attitude. I'm tired, and actually I haven't got time to get upset. I know it's a great proposal. It's not my fault they have no idea what children really want to read. And I've got another career anyway. Two if you include this parenting malarkey.'

'You go, girl.' Emma had always envied Amy's self-belief and ability to take everything in her stride: husband, babies, baking…

'We'll see. Maybe that was it. Something I had to get out of my system. Why should I lose sleep over letters from editors who reject people for a living? I bet they even send out letters to end relationships, stating that the potential object of their affection lacked a certain special something that separated him from the rest of the pack.'

Emma giggled. 'Your time will come and I'll dine out on your success—use your name to book myself into fancy restaurants, do your filing…' And stop sitting around in her swivel chair waiting for a man to need her.

'Someone needs to do a study on the psychological effect your job has on your life. I bet it would be really interesting.'

'Then surely I should be a self-publicist?'

'Not necessarily. But PR has made you cynical. How is the cut-and-thrust world of spin surgery today?'

'Today is definitely a slow burner. I've read two newspapers already.'

'Anything I need to know? I haven't had time to read more than a couple of lines of newsprint since Pippa started walking. It's like she's magnetically attracted to hazards. Maybe I should lease her out to Health and Safety…'

'Well, apparently you've met the man you're going to marry by the time you're thirty, and according to latest figures marriage is on the up.'

Amy laughed. 'So for once I was just so ahead of myself.'

'It's ridiculous, though.'

'Not really. I mean, you spent most of last summer at weddings,' Amy reminded her.

'So, what? I'm the exception to the rule?'

'You're the one that gave up on love.'

'Can you blame me?' Emma sighed. 'After six months with me Peter realised he was still in love with his ex. Dave wasn't ready for commitment but only two months later he was engaged. And Henry forgot to mention he had a girlfriend in another city—until they got married, that is.'

'So you've had a bad patch.' Amy was in full diplomatic mode.

'More like an era. I have officially taken myself off the market before I pass my sell-by date and I feel much better as a result.'

'Of course you do.' Amy couldn't have sounded any less convinced.

'I do.'

'Look, maybe you've met your future husband and you just don't remember.'

'Marvellous. How many guesses do you think I get? The man in the sandwich shop has always been quite smiley... Oh, my God. I almost forgot to tell you...'

'What?'

'I met Jack Carlisle in Starbucks this morning.'

'The actor?'

'Yup.'

'Apparently you'll never see the left hand side of his face in publicity photos, although that could be an urban myth. He's not bad-looking, either.'

Not bad-looking? Compared to Amy's husband, Jack was a god—or a demi-god at the very least. Emma typed his name '+photo' into Google and pressed enter.

'Well, he's even more attractive in the flesh. And he's in a meeting with Patrick right now—' Emma stopped herself. She was sure that was meant to be confidential information.

'Pippa, darling, if you put your hand in that bowl one more time Mummy is going to be very cross. His film was on television the other night—you know, the one where he's a tennis coach.'

'*Game, Sex & Match*.' It was his only leading role to date. He'd been resting on his reputation ever since.

'I've always thought he was a bit smug. Personally I've always preferred his dad. Not doing much these days, but a good old-fashioned gent.'

'You pension-snatcher.'

'Careful. Tim's forty-three, remember?'

'James Carlisle has got to be late fifties at the absolute youngest.'

'So when you say you *met* him, I bet you didn't even talk to him.'

Amy knew her far too well. 'Erm, no. And by the way, I didn't tell you he was meeting Patrick.'

'Of course not.'

'And there are photos of him from every angle on the internet.' Emma clicked on the link to Jack's page on celebritybutts.com. 'Blimey, he's won Rear of the Year twice in a row.' He was a client. It was research.

'So it's official. He's an arse.' Amy laughed at her own joke. 'There's even a rumour that he bats from the pavilion end.'

'He plays cricket?'

'No, that he's gay, you idiot.'

'Look, gay or not, he's a pretty impressive specimen, and there are no calories in eye-candy.'

'Hey, honey, I'm home. Right.' Patrick sat down at this desk. 'Let's get cracking.'

Coffee had clearly been replaced with something a little more alcoholic. It wasn't that he was particularly flushed, or slurring his words, he was just determined to work at a greater pace than normal to prove to himself and to his PA that he wasn't pissed—which he definitely was.

'Ames, I'm going to have to go.' Out of the corner of her eye, Emma noticed they were not alone. Jack Carlisle was propping up the doorframe while Patrick rummaged around for something. Hurriedly minimising her Internet Explorer screen, Emma wondered how long he'd been standing there. She definitely should have stayed in bed this morning. 'I'll call you later.'

'Come over and play soon. Fresh cookies in about two hours. And let me know if Jack Carlisle turns up at the office with flowers.'

'No flowers, but…'

'He's not there now? Em?'

Hanging up, Emma focused on her employer, smiling esoterically as she imagined Amy's current expression in Chiswick. 'Good meeting?' Her professional persona was in the house.

'Excellent lunch.' Jack replied. He had sunglasses on the top of his head. In London. In January.

'Where did you go?' Emma closed her mouth and ran her tongue across the outside of her teeth in an attempt to freshen up. She was ninety-nine per cent sure you couldn't see her screen from the doorway. Or at least she had been. Now sixty-five per cent and dropping rapidly.

'MATV…'

Meat And Two Veg was the hottest lunch venue in town. Part and parcel of the carbohydrate-free revolution.

'A friend of mine runs it. I don't know if you know Julian Royal…?' Jack paused.

'No.' Strangely enough, Emma didn't have many young, rich restaurateurs in her phone book. 'I know *of* him, of course.'

'The food there is so fresh—and delicious. Make sure you go some time. Mention my name if you're struggling to get a table.'

Emma nodded. A meal at MATV or a pair of new boots? No competition.

Patrick rescued her from obscurity. 'Emma, have you seen the piece on the engagement of Mitsy Motown?'

Emma plucked the relevant folio out of the cabinet. She'd only filed it two hours earlier. And it had been pending for two weeks.

'Now, that's what I call efficiency. Every man should have an Emma.'

'I'm sure.'

There was an easiness about Jack which was making Emma feel slightly awkward and more than a touch guilty about the whole gay moment—which she was really, really hoping he hadn't heard.

'My apologies. Jack, meet Emma Hunter, my PA. Emma, this is Jack…Carlisle.' Patrick remembered office protocol just in time.

Jack proffered a perfectly moisturised and manicured hand for shaking. Sure enough, his right cheek was forward. 'Are you sure we haven't met before? You definitely look familiar.'

'I queued with you in Starbucks this morning.' Patrick cocked an interested eyebrow as Emma snorted and then blushed. The snort had started life as a giggle but her body had let her down at the last minute. 'But aside from that, no, I don't think I've had the pleasure.' The pleasure, eh? If Amy had been there she would have been making retching noises, but, while Emma was loath to admit it, so far it really *was*.

'That must be it. I don't forget faces.'

Jack reached for his copy of the cutting and shook Patrick by the hand. 'Thanks for lunch. I'm going to shoot off now. Look forward to meeting up in a few days' time.'

Patrick escorted his new best friend towards the door. Jack turned and performed a mock salute. 'Good to meet you, Gemma. See you again.'

Emma nodded and smiled inanely. He might be good with faces but he was crap with names.

The office door had barely closed behind them before Emma had hit redial, but this time Patrick was back before she'd even been connected. Hanging up for a second time, she glared at her boss. 'You could have called to alert me to our visitor. I'd have at least…'

'What? Nipped out for a blow dry? He was only here for two minutes. Anyway, wait until you hear this…'

For a man in PR, Patrick could be a real gossip behind closed doors. He looked left and right in the manner of a cautious child crossing his first main road. Nothing was coming.

'He wants to settle down and get married.'

'Jack does?'

'Think about it. It's just what he needs. Credibility. Maturity. Commitment. An heir.'

'That's quite a shopping list.'

'And it's perfect. Marriage is in.'

'I read that article too,' Emma dismissed.

'Apparently married men live nearly ten years longer than single men.'

'And the women?'

'Don't know.' Patrick half-heartedly searched for the article amongst the papers on his desk.

Emma produced the relevant page, neatly folded, from her in-tray. 'It didn't say, but I can tell you the answer.'

'Look, before you get your Women's Lib head on, women live longer anyway. Maybe it's just nature's way of ironing out the difference.'

'There is nothing natural about spending your whole life with one man.'

'Hey, do you think the life expectancy thing works for divorced men?' Patrick mused.

'I don't think you get an extra ten years per wife, if that's

what you mean. But you definitely lost weight after you and
Laura split up, so maybe what they really should be saying is
that divorce is good for your health.'

'The few pounds I lost in weight pale into insignificance
alongside the hundreds of thousands of pounds that relationship cost me—definitely not good for my health or my life
expectancy. Anyway, I don't think Jack's motive is longevity,
but now that Charlie is no more it's down to him to tow the
family line and extend it.'

'I'm loving your compassion. An arranged marriage.'

Patrick hesitated. 'I guess—in a way. But this has got to
look like the real deal.'

'Surely Jack could have anyone he wanted?'

'Really? He's been so busy rebelling he's become trapped
in a social circle of carnivores—and married ones at that.'

'So what's in it for him?' Emma sat back and waited to be
enlightened.

'Hey, this was his idea.'

Emma frowned at her boss.

'OK, I admit I didn't discourage him…'

Emma folded her arms.

'And I ordered another bottle of wine when the subject
came up… But look, this is what we do. He desperately needs
to be taken seriously. He needs more than a new leaf. He
needs a new garden. He's tired.'

'He's *tired?* Who isn't tired?'

'He's just chasing his tail sustaining his reputation. He's
started doing adverts and he hasn't had a decent audition in
months. He needs stability. He wants a family. And, ideally,
a son.'

'And what does the rest of the world do when they want
to settle down? Call the king of spin or get out there and
start dating?'

'He's had enough of being the media fall guy, of making
mistakes…'

'I know how he feels.'

Patrick took no notice of her. 'He wants to be in the papers for all the right reasons, and if he's married maybe people will leave him to have at least something of a private life. People love giving celebrities a second chance.'

'Or a third or a fourth. Enter Patrick, fairy godfather, and a match made in Mayfair.'

'It's all about selecting the right woman. Whoever marries him won't have to worry about anything ever again.'

Emma shook her head. 'You're suggesting he *buys* a wife? Just imagine if this ever got out…plus marrying for money just seems so tacky…so old fashioned.'

'Or so modern. Think about it. It's honest. A heartache-free zone. A business partnership. And Jack Carlisle has more assets than most. He told me his father met his mother through a family tie. They didn't fall in love over a red rose or a sunset. They grew to love each other. And they had a marriage that lasted over thirty years.'

Emma interrupted 'And then they divorced?'

'And then she died.'

'Oh.' Bugger. Emma wished she'd read all the cuttings instead of flicking through them.

'Romance is just there to make us all feel better. Throughout history marriage has been political. I married people I was in love with and look what happened.'

Emma sighed. She could see his argument clearly enough, but if it was true it made the world a much less exciting place. 'OK, so say that we are arranging a marriage here—secretly, of course. To who?'

'Good question. This afternoon you and I are going to draw up a shortlist…I'll be Mr God and you can be Mrs God.'

Suddenly Emma loved her job.

An hour and a half later they had dismissed at least sixty single eligible women of varying public standing.

'Right—that's it.' Emma clipped the lid onto her pen assertively.

Patrick brightened. 'Who?'

'No, that's it I need to pee, and I need a drink.'

She was only out of the office for five minutes, but when she returned Patrick's entire demeanour had changed. He'd even opened a bottle of Pinot Grigio from the office fridge. Behaviour strictly reserved for Friday afternoons and winning moments.

'I've got it!'

'Who?'

'It's so bloody obvious. It's been staring us in the face all afternoon—or at least it's been staring me in the face.' Patrick raised his glass. 'You.'

Emma didn't even look up from her paper-shuffling. 'Exactly how much did you drink at lunchtime?'

'Seriously—why not? He needs to get married, you want to get married, and you like him.'

She shot him an exasperated glare. 'I like him like I like Harrison Ford, like I like Hugh Grant, Ben Chaplin, George Clooney…'

'Exactly.'

'My attraction to them has no basis in reality.'

'He smiled at you this morning…'

'It might have been wind. He might have been thinking about Cindy Crawford. He might have been reacting to the special blend of the day chalked up on the board…'

'And he liked you.'

'He did?' Emma sat up in her chair, aloofness forgotten.

'Well, you were chatting in the office.'

'And now, if I'm not mistaken, you are suggesting I marry a client? I think you'll find Clause 56(b) of my employment contract states—'

'It's perfect. It's a girl-next-door masterstroke. And what is there about you not to like? You're attractive, witty, articulate. Plus you understand the press. You don't take drugs. You make a great cup of tea. You have curves in all the right places, You're a size—' Patrick screeched to a conversational halt before rerouting. 'Well, what does it matter? I mean whether you're a size ten or a size sixteen it really doesn't...'

'I'm a twelve.' Emma bristled. 'Well, most of the time.'

'Perfect. Plus, you don't go to the gym. You can barely spell Pilates. You've faced tragedy and bounced back...and you wouldn't have to worry about not having a pension again—ever.'

'Well, there you go. My phobia of financial planning could have been a blessing in disguise. As to the "faced tragedy" part—I'd never seen losing my parents as being a unique selling point before.'

'Forgive the tact bypass. But you know what I meant...'

Emma nodded. Unfortunately she did.

'You've always said you had a feeling things would work out in the end.'

'In the end. Not the day after tomorrow.'

'Come on, Emma. It's a great idea.'

'An idea is all it is.'

'Think about it. Emma Hunter, this is your life. You only get one chance.'

Emma laughed derisively. 'You're crazy.'

'Why not?'

'Aside from the fact you're not holding a big red book, Jack and I have nothing in common. I doubt he's ever had an overdraft, he sleeps with the most beautiful women in the world... Do you want me to go on?'

'You're beautiful.'

'You're drunk.'

'Well, you're very attractive,' Patrick conceded.

'Stop now, before you tell me I've got a great personality and a lovely pair of tits.'

Patrick was about to confirm both of the above, but

stopped himself just in time. 'Come on, Em. You've always said you wanted a big white wedding.'

'Great. I've just gone from beautiful to desperate in under twenty seconds. I had been hoping for the whole package. Women say things in the abstract that they don't mean all the time—for effect, for hormonal reasons…'

'Maybe you can't have it all.'

Emma raised a silencing eyebrow.

'Come on. I've done it—twice. Two of the happiest days of my life. And there's nothing that will get you out of bed and into the office faster in the morning than two divorces.'

'Your trouble is you're married to your career.'

'Now you're sounding like both of them.'

'And you're still paying for it now.'

'No, I'm paying for *them,*' Patrick corrected.

'OK, but presumably you were in love at the time. You don't select a partner by adding "find soul mate" to your to-do list for the weekend, between collecting the dry cleaning and washing the car.'

'OK, let's do pros and cons.'

'Are you ignoring me?'

'We need to build a backstory for the press release.'

'For a start, *I* do press releases.'

'Not when you are the subject.'

'Besides, I'm sure he'll have someone more glamorous in mind.'

'Is that a yes?'

'A definite no. Marrying for money is so…so Anna Nicole Smith. I like my life. Well, it's OK. And it's mine. I don't want to be on his payroll.'

'We're talking society pin-up, eligible bachelor—not infirm Texan oil octogenarian. He says he's ready to settle down. You'd be good for him.'

Emma paused. Against her better judgement she was just wondering…

'A maybe?' Excitement flashed across Patrick's eyes. He was incorrigible.

'No.'

If she put herself in the running for Jack's plaything could it do any harm? Maybe he would only ever be in love with himself? But it wasn't like she had any men on her horizon at the moment. And January was always a non-starter of a month.

'Are you seriously going to turn Jack Carlisle down without even meeting the guy for a drink?'

'Meet Jack for a drink?' Emma knew she was playing with fire.

'Now you're talking…'

Amy kissed the air just adjacent to Emma's fragrantly powdered cheek before lowering the veil over her best friend's face. 'Can you believe this place? And you look amazing.'

Emma cast a glance over her bridal posse from behind her designer net curtain. 'We all look pretty good…and the girls look very still. What have you done to them?'

'No refined sugar since yesterday afternoon and a touch of bribery. Don't tell Tim. He seems to think you can just be rational with fives and under. Ready?'

Emma nodded. Amy had been the hardest to convince during the deluge of 'Hurricane Jack' and 'Storm in a Coffee Cup' related headlines. But Emma had succeeded in peddling Amy a mix of pure faction, and once she'd met Jack she'd been much easier—even a little sycophantic.

'Just as long as you're happy.'

'I am.'

'Then so am I. Talk about falling on your feet. Mind you, if I had Jack on bended knee in Central Park I'd probably say yes, and I'm already married. Amazing. One day you're a confirmed maiden aunt, and then a week later you're in love with a man half the world has lusted after on the big screen. And watched in bed at least twice in ninety minutes.'

'I know.' Emma decided to tiptoe past the maiden aunt reference.

'I mean, if you'd said he'd run into you, spilt orange juice on your white T-shirt and invited you back to his place in Notting Hill to clean up, it would have been more believable than meeting in the queue in Starbucks. Do you even *know* how many women have started spending days drinking coffee in the Soho branches? I'm surprised they haven't sponsored today, or at least developed a new blend in your honour…'

'Blame him.' Emma squeezed Patrick's arm. 'He's the one who sent me out that morning.' Time to interrupt before her nose started growing and ruined her profile.

As the bridal party stepped into formation Emma focused on her escort for the aisle.

'Come on, then. Time to give me away.'

Patrick smiled at her fondly. With no children to his knowledge, this was not a role he had been prepared for. 'I'm ready. And by the way, you look exquisite. I'm beginning to wish I'd kept you for myself.'

Emma blushed. Winding the blue ribbon that he had insisted on giving her for luck between her fingers, she approached the door to the church. Patrick hesitated.

'Ready?'

'As I'll ever be.'

Smiling at her wedding planner, Emma took her final position. In the absence of a mother, Jess had been there for her from day one. Nothing seemed to ruffle her feathers. She came, she listened, she understood and she executed…and right now she was waiting to give the head of music his cue.

'Thanks Jess. For everything.'

'Hey, you just get in there and remember to take it slowly up the aisle.' Emma had been a dream client. A woman with a clue about what she wanted and not a hint of the Bridezillas. Professionally, Jess hadn't needed to take her fake smile out of its box in months.

Emma nodded as she recalled the rehearsal. She'd practically sprinted to the altar long before the piece of music had finished—but then she'd been in trainers, not Gina couture sandals. She tested Patrick's arm. Solid as a rock.

Jess simultaneously dipped her head and pointed at the organist. A beat, and then a trumpeter could be heard. The vicar and the choir entered, setting the pace, and then Emma put her best foot forward and entered the rear of the church.

The congregation coughed and rose as one and the hairs on the back of Jack's neck stood nervously to attention as the Trumpet Voluntary echoed through the chapel and his bachelor days flashed before him. Gingerly he turned to catch a glimpse of his bride. She was surprisingly beautiful. And real. From the minute she'd ordered a Guinness the first time they'd gone for a drink he'd known they'd get along. Catching her eye, he gave her a smile in the hope it would calm him down. She'd charmed everyone so far. Even the press. His popularity was soaring. Cheque mate.

Jack ran his fingers through what was left of his hair, his dark, normally unkempt mane having been tidied for his latest role as a husband. He was looking forward to some time out. Paris and New York had been great, but it had only been a few days—a bit of hand-holding in public, enough to get them press coverage. Now three whole weeks at an ultra-luxury resort on an exclusive Caribbean island beckoned. And the wedding ring would look even better when he had a tan.

Jess allowed herself a moment of silent self-congratulation as Emma set off down the aisle. Judging from the expression on his face, Jack Carlisle genuinely liked what he had just seen. The moment was perfect. His trademark blue eyes were highlighted by the turquoise embroidery on his waistcoat, the scented candles and pink roses in the chapel were working their magic. Money might not be able to buy you love, but it could certainly inject a little romance where needed.

Phase one was underway. Leaving Rosie behind, in case of an unforeseen emergency, and gently pulling the doors to the chapel closed behind her, Jess hurried across the manicured lawns to check on the tables. Her phone vibrated in its holster. Quick on the draw, she pressed 'read' on the newly delivered message without breaking her stride.

Here comes the bride…in exactly seven days it'll be our turn. Hope today going well. Love you. Nx

To her surprise, a wave of absolutely nothing passed over her. He was so excited. And she was sure she would be. Jess pressed 'reply' but then stopped. First she needed a whole minute to herself.

three

If paradise was coconut-laden palms, pure white fine sandy beaches, green hills and iridescent clear waters in every conceivable shade of green and blue, Jack mused, then this was it. Relishing the intensity of the sun on his bare torso, the light breeze ruffled his chest hair, providing the perfect amount of convection. Absently he absently licked the sweat off his top lip and swallowed hard, the accumulation of sea salt from his earlier snorkelling session burning his throat. He was thirsty enough to consider walking along the beach to the bar. Soon.

Drifting in and out of consciousness, he stretched on his sun lounger. The only intrusions into his blissed-out state were the waves sifting the sand a few metres away and the occasional crash of a pelican dive-bombing the sea's surface in search of a snack. Jack's left hand itched and, grabbing at his third finger to strip it of the ant or mosquito causing the moment of irritation, he smiled when he realised his mistake.

Noticing her husband's apparent return to—or at least pit

stop in—reality, Emma looked up from her magazine. 'Hey, do you want a drink…?'

Even better. His new wife was telepathic. Jack nodded from somewhere between asleep and awake and watched the kaleidoscope show playing on his eyelids as the sun danced through the tips of the palm fronds overhead.

'There's a waiter on his way—what do you fancy?' He usually had a beer. Sometimes a Sprite. Or a lime and soda. She didn't know his holiday routine yet at all. 'In fact I might wander over and save him half the trip. I mean, I must have burnt at least three calories in the last hour.'

Emma had never been more lethargic. It was too damn hot. And her sunbed was too damn comfortable. Five stars bought you the sort of beachside comfort that package holidaymakers could only dream was possible. Her cushions—note more than one—were calico covered, not too hard and not too soft. She was in baby bear heaven.

Assisted by the promise of a cold drink, Jack eased himself onto his elbows and forced himself to open his eyes. Reaching for his shades, he peered along the perfect crescent of semi-deserted beach as the mirage became reality. 'It's his job, Emma.'

'He's wearing long trousers. He must be about to melt.' Her concern voiced, her conscience was appeased and she had no intention of going anywhere.

Light-headed with dehydration, Jack sat himself up, clenching his stomach muscles and smiling at his wife. Self-contained, but not self-centred, Emma was an easy person to be around, and to his amazement three weeks had flown by. He hadn't even finished a book yet. Surveying the scene, his gaze came to rest on the object of her attentions.

'Excuse me, Mrs C…' Emma stiffened at the use of 'Mrs' in a sentence addressed to her. She definitely wasn't old enough. Or was that mature enough? 'Have you bought another glossy without telling me?'

Jack was Just Gay Enough when it came to reading matter. And there were very few magazines to feed his habit on this island. He was a feature junkie. Yesterday she'd caught him reading *Oprah* magazine in the bathroom. Zeitgeist, it would appear, was available in all good newsagents and resort gift shops—at a price.

Emma smiled sheepishly. 'I just found it next to the *New York Times* in the lounge area. Another guest must have left it. It's a couple of weeks old, but…'

Jack squinted at the familiar masthead and caught the date of publication. 'Hey, have they got our…?'

Emma nodded. 'Oh, yeah.' Eight months ago she, like the rest of the single female population, had been on a diet, at the sales, about to go to the gym, and about to buy a flat. Now her wedding was in a magazine. She wondered if she could get away with keeping a scrapbook?

Jack leapt up to snatch the pages but the sand had apparently reached the same surface temperature as the sun. Sitting down again, he lifted his singed soles and peered under his sunbed in search of his Havaianas while Emma tried and failed not to laugh.

'You're just sitting there looking at our wedding photos and you haven't told me?' Jack was indignant.

'You were reading, and then when I got back you were asleep. Snoring away, as usual.' Maybe his reputation was a mistake of media proportions. Maybe his chronic snoring problem was the reason he'd had so many one-night stands.

'You snore too.'

'I do not.' Actually, Emma couldn't be sure that she didn't.

'You do. Well, it's more of a snuffle most of the time.'

Damn. Princess Emma she was not. Earlier she had emerged from the sea—as graciously as you can in flippers—hoping to emulate Ursula Andress in *Dr No.* But she suspected her exit from the water had been rather more Big Bird in *Sesame Street.*

'So…' Jack craned his neck. 'How are we looking according to *CelebriTee?*'

'The guy only got a couple of shots before Gerry realised what was going on. And, by the way, Jess was furious that you let him keep the film.'

Jack stared into the blue. 'I know, I know. You've only mentioned it three or four times. A week.'

'If Jess had her way, she'd have pressed charges.'

'It wasn't her call. And I'm not sure I believe in all this secrecy.'

'But these pictures have probably been sold around the world by now. Someone out there is dining out—literally— on the exclusive,' Emma reminded him.

Jack couldn't have looked less bothered. Emma, on the other hand, was far less nonchalant.

'I still can't believe someone managed to get in. Can you imagine if his interest in you had been less passive?'

'It's just a business…' Jack folded his arms behind his head as the waiter arrived and took their drinks order before disappearing as unobtrusively as he had arrived. 'Look, we're fully clothed, and—' Jack reached over and angled the magazine so as to avoid the sun reflecting on the page, which was stiff with sun baked sweat and salt water and had the consistency of a stale popadum '—excuse me, but are we or are we not looking pretty fucking fantastic? You looked stunning in that dress.'

Emma blushed and self-consciously wrapped her sarong around her thighs a little tighter. She was having a strange day. A slightly empty feeling had engulfed her first thing that morning, and as yet she hadn't been able to shake it off.

'Doesn't it all seem like more than three weeks ago?' Jack was still staring at their photo.

'I guess.' It had been a perfect day. Everything Emma had ever wanted and more—or less.

'Can you believe that I, of all people, am married?'

'*We're* married.' Emma was still struggling with the concept. 'Jack and Emma Carlisle. It sounds good, though, doesn't it?'

'Jack?'

'Yes, honey….' Jack had no trouble with terms of affection. In fact they tripped off his tongue so easily and frequently that Emma wasn't sure how much of it was for her real benefit or just out of habit. She probably shouldn't have cared, but she did.

'Aren't you looking forward to getting home?'

Emma was missing her support system. Nothing ever seemed real until she had shared it with Amy—and, in fact, Patrick. Not that she was going back to the office. Apparently wives of A-list celebrities didn't work. She wondered if they were allowed to watch daytime TV. Maybe she was going to have to run a charity or something—between facials, of course. As long as she didn't have to release a single or pose for a nude portrait… Suddenly her old supermarket and sofa Saturdays seemed positively enticing.

'Charming. Thanks very much.'

'You know what I mean.' Emma smiled.

Either Jack was having a good time or he was a better actor than the critics believed. There'd been little touches she hadn't been expecting—unless, of course, months of lying to the press had resulted in her starting to believe her own rhetoric. Analysis aside, it had been a great holiday. And realistically it would have been hard not to feel loved-up in a setting like this. But they both knew the deal. Emma just had to remind her sun-baked hormones every day. She was sure it would get easier in time. It was just that she hadn't expected to feel so relaxed.

Jack had read and re-read the few lines of copy and was now studying the photos intently. 'Did we really have lucky lavender on our napkins?

Emma nodded.

'Nice touch.'

'Jess and I thought so.'

'And does she do other parties? Or just weddings?'

'Why? Thinking of having another one?'

'No way. Carlisles marry for life.'

'Yeah, right.' For better for worse—but for ever? Suddenly her bikini top was feeling a bit tight in the halterneck area. She didn't know what she wanted any more. The world had been her oyster and now it was Jack's.

Oblivious, Jack was still poring over the pages. Quite a feat, considering there were literally only three photos to look at. 'Do you think my hairline is receding?'

'No.' Emma inspected her French manicure for flaws.

'But there…' Jack handed her the page, his thumb almost obscuring his head in the photo.

'There's hair there.'

'And a lot of forehead.'

Emma held the magazine at arm's length to get an overall view. 'If your hairline was further forward you'd look like something out of *Planet of the Apes*.'

Jack smiled and put the magazine down, moving himself over to the edge of Emma's sun lounger. 'If you don't mind, you're talking to *FHM*'s Man of the Month.' His tone was playful.

'And don't I know it? You've got more beauty products than I have…a union of hearts, minds and moisturisers.'

Jack hadn't felt this chilled out in years. Leaning across to return the magazine, to Emma's surprise, he gave her a kiss, his senses overwhelmed by a heady cocktail of sea air, Lancaster sun products, approaching ice-cold lager and good old-fashioned sweat. Admiring her glistening cleavage, he traced the strap of her bikini from her neck to the line where her tan ended and her breast began. Raising his gaze to meet Emma's, he kissed her again.

She kissed him back. Maybe this being married thing was agreeing with him. Maybe he was falling… Emma's thoughts dissolved into her desire… And then there was a roar as a cigarette boat raced across the bay on the other side of the reef.

Instinct seized Jack, and as he whipped his head round, squinting out to sea at the perfect view of the uninhabited islands opposite, he saw it—the tell-tale glint of a lens as the boat raced out of sight.

'Bingo.'

Emma tensed as she wondered if her thighs had been pressed unflatteringly against the sun lounger. 'You love being in the public eye, don't you?'

Jack shrugged as he stared approvingly at Emma's red string bikini. 'You're looking pretty hot today.'

Jack Carlisle thought she was pretty hot. She should feel like she had died and gone to heaven. But she didn't.

He lay back on his bed. 'Do you know, I think we should try and do this once a year? No skiing.'

Skiing? Not one of the strings Emma had ever managed to attach to her bow. Sun had always beaten snow hands down when it came to holiday destinations.

'No partying, no golf….'

A sport she had been saving for her fifties—and only on the condition that women were allowed into all the bars in all the clubhouses all of the time. Now, crazy golf—that was fun…

'Just a real do-nothing holiday.'

Emma smiled. That she could handle. She could potter for hours. For Britain, in fact. 'Definitely.'

Silently, the psychic waiter returned. To Emma's amusement there was almost more condensation on the outside of the glasses than there was liquid inside them.

Jack took his glass and raised it to his wife. 'Cheers.'

'Cheers.'

'To us.' Jack took a large sip of his beer without taking his eyes off her.

'Really?' Emma did her best not to flinch as a drop of ice cold water landed on her stomach.

'Why not?'

They clinked their glasses. A couple on the last afternoon of their honeymoon. Then back to reality—or surreality. But right now a Kodak moment. Why not indeed?

four

Jess was in a tropical emotional state—short, unpredictable, intense bursts of precipitation suddenly giving way to absolute calm and prolonged periods of sunshine. She hadn't spent this much time alone since she'd been hanging out in an amniotic sac. And twelve days of honeymoon with no honey, no moon, no husband and the sort of Sex on The Beach that came in a glass with a straw definitely left a girl with too much time to think. And too much time to eat. The Fat Lady within was waiting in the wings. Wings… Jess scanned the menu for her favourite drinking snack.

Finally she understood the true meaning of Blue Sky Thinking. She'd always thought it was an excuse for blokes to swap their pinstripes for their golf clubs, but, difficult as the last two weeks had been, she'd definitely needed the break. Having spent the last decade of her life in perpetual motion—constantly running late, chasing her tail, gulping down coffee and barely fulfilling her commitments to everyone else, let alone to herself—it was as if she'd been granted a fortnight of headspace. For the first long week, every time

she'd looked up she'd been expecting to see Nick on the horizon, wandering over in his surf shorts and the old faded
light blue T-shirt he always wore on holiday. Now in two
days she'd be home. And things were finally starting to slot
into place.

Sitting at an empty table outside the Bath & Turtle Bar, Jess
ordered lunch and a Carib beer as a lone chicken strutted and
walked-like-an-Egyptian around the palm- and cactus-filled
courtyard. She probably should have asked for a Painkiller, but
her hangover this morning had required a fistful of the more
traditional ones, and she was off coconut cream and rum for
life—or at least the next twenty-four hours. Here, cocktailing
was a verb and a way of life—yet today she would have killed
someone for a Starbucks frappuccino, and if that made her a
slave to capitalism then so be it. She missed newspapers, she
missed Twix bars, she missed Nick. There, she'd said it. But
he'd backed her into a corner. He'd stopped listening to her
and she'd panicked. Nobody's perfect.

Making herself as comfortable as she could on a plastic
chair in eighty per cent humidity, she stared at the Weather
Channel, muted on the television suspended high in the
corner. In the background the Beach Boys gave way to
UB40, then Mr Marley. The perfect soundtrack for gazing
into the eyes of the man you loved and had just married. Perfectly irritating if you were hungover, thirsty, sweaty, alone
and had forgotten to bring a book into town.

Having slept through most of the first week, she found
minutes now took hours. No mobile phone to check for
messages, no e-mail, no deadlines. Yesterday she'd clambered
over rocks in search of a deserted bay, only to end up in the
front row for a destination wedding. Here two, not three, was
the magic number. Pairs of sunbeds, of towels, tooth mugs,
even drinks were coupled up for Happy Hour. Maybe the
guidebooks were wrong. Maybe Noah had been behind the
construction of these luxury resorts, not Rockefeller.

Jess had been hoping to lose herself in the hustle and bustle of Spanish Town, only there was no activity. Virgin Gorda was a corner of the Caribbean that enabled overworked, overpaid newlyweds to remind themselves why they'd got together, before jointly purchasing souvenir mouse mats, oven gloves, shorts, T-shirts, baseball caps and shot glasses as an *aide-memoire* as they headed back to their separate offices. Incidentally, Gorda translated meant fat. Like A Fat Virgin. Jess forced herself to smile.

Wondering why she hadn't ordered a salad, Jess watched as an armada of clouds effortlessly paraded across the sky in a breeze which hadn't made it to ground level, where the humidity was playing havoc with her hair. Ironically, she looked like she'd just tumbled out of bed after an hour of frenetic sex—probably all part of the appeal for honeymooners. A tropical island where post-coital chic ruled.

'Jessica? Jessica James?' A weathered black woman in her fifties, almost as wide as she was tall, was bearing down on her personal space.

'I thought it was you.'

Jess had never seen this woman before in her life.

'It's Ella, from Villa Rentals…'

Or at least she couldn't recall having met her before. Thanks to the time difference and the complimentary drinks on the plane, check-in had been a blur.

Jess's beer and lunch arrived. Her day was looking up. Jess proffered a chicken wing, but to her relief her new friend declined. Jess knew her suspicion of over-friendly semi-strangers was one hundred per cent London, but she wished that Ella would piss off—or at least sit down.

'I saw you sitting here all on your own…'

Tact was not an island trait. Jess nodded, her mouth full of chicken.

'So you're leaving tomorrow?'

'Yes.' The novelty of having a real-time conversation had faded fast.

'Anyhow, you've had a call.'

'A call?' Jess's social vacuum was over and she could barely contain the rush of excitement. 'So you came to find me?' Suddenly Jess was all in favour of small communities.

'You weren't home, so it diverted to the office.'

'Nick?' Jess's heart leapt, and before she could stop herself her gaze darted to all four corners of the square. He was there. She could feel it.

'I don't know, dear…' Ella shook her head benevolently.

Jess bet she'd been the anecdote of the week after she'd arrived on her own.

'Donna took that one, and she'll be dropping the message round at the house for you.'

'Thanks.' Jess left a suitably large dollar bill on the table and, clutching her open bottle of beer, set off at a pace that made Ella smile. You could take the girl out of London, but you couldn't take London out of the girl. Or at least not in twelve days.

Despite her taxi driver's laid-back attitude to acceleration, Jess made it back to the villa in record time and, sweat pouring from areas she hadn't previously realised had pores, she scoured the surfaces for a note or traces of a fiancé. Nothing. Ten minutes and one large incline later, Jess was still looking for the Villa Rental-reception. Clearly exclusivity here was synonymous with a total lack of signage and patience had never been her virtue. Finally she found the office—closed for lunch—and, light-headed with frustration and exertion, headed back to her safe haven. And her message. He was still in London. But nevertheless Nick was the man. In every respect.

Grabbing the phone, Jess walked out onto the balcony that wrapped itself around three sides of the house, offering breathtaking views of the sea. She dialled the familiar number hurriedly, impatiently waiting for the international connection, almost breathless as she waited for him to pick up. She'd been thinking about him all day and now he'd called. The power of transatlantic telepathy. It was a sign.

Seven-thirty p.m. in the UK. Jess pictured Nick in their cluttered sitting room, Lucy sprawled on the floor beside him as he lay on the sofa in jeans, his socked feet hanging over the armrest. Jess watched a Frigate Bird riding the thermals. She couldn't wait to hear his voice.

'Where were you…?'

And then she could.

'Where was I?' Jess's stomach knotted. Three words were all it had taken to bring her temporary euphoria crashing down to earth. In her clearly sun-baked imagination this had been going to be a very different call.

'I called hours ago…'

Jess went for light-hearted over defensive. 'Hey, "instant" and "communication" aren't two words that come in the same sentence over here. I might be a mere five hours behind Greenwich Mean Time, but the Virgin Islands are about ten years behind the UK technologically. "Urgent" here means same-day.'

'You were out?'

'I was rehydrating in town—if you can call it that. More of a village by our standards. I was snorkelling this morning—one of the dive instructors told me about an amazing bay—and…' Jess edited herself. It sounded like she was having far too much fun—which she really wasn't. A stony silence greeted her. 'And then I stopped for some lunch.' Why couldn't he have called yesterday, when she'd been at the villa all day?

'Sounds tough.'

'I don't have to be sitting in a dark room staring at the wall to feel shitty.'

'Try waking up in our bed in our bedroom.'

'I'm sorry.'

'Yeah, well, me too. So, how is it?' His tone was listless.

'So beautiful—the views from the villa are even more fantastic than those pictures suggested…' Jess took a breath. The excitement in her voice was purely because he had called, but she was sure Nick wasn't getting that impression. Time for a change of tactic. 'But to be honest it's not much fun being here on my own.'

'At least it's your choice.'

Jess berated herself. Nick was definitely the wrong person to be expecting sympathy from. He sounded so different. His voice was clipped, grim, sarcastic. The kindness that always prevailed, the buoyancy, was absent. And this was all her fault.

'Jess?'

'I'm still here. I'm sorry. I just didn't think.'

'Something it would appear you're making a habit of.'

'I miss you.' An overture to normality, to the future.

Nothing.

As her optimism disappeared into the ether, Jess held the handset at arm's length and peered at it. It was difficult to see in direct sunshine, but the 'talk' light was definitely still on.

'Nick?' If Cable & Wireless had cut her off at that moment they would be facing serious legal action.

'I'm here.'

'How are you?'

'Oh, you know. Not so bad. I mean, emotionally crushed, but fine.'

No ambiguity there, then. Emotionally crushed? Jess hoped that was a reversible condition.

'I really wanted to talk to you. I need to talk to you.'

'I've been here the whole time.'

'I wanted to wait—you know, to talk face to face…' What had she been expecting? So she was a bit lonely in the Virgin Islands. He was a bit stood-up at the altar and still in London. 'I'm back in two days. Maybe you should have gone away—you know, to get away from everything…everyone.'

'Strangely, I haven't been in the mood. Bit busy here, what with presents to return and all these people feeling sorry for me. Plus I've had things to sort out. Main reason for calling, actually.' He was so perfunctory and businesslike a chill ran through Jess, despite the fact that the ambient temperature was eighty-five degrees.

'I'm so sorry.' Jess's voice cracked. Suddenly she hated telephones. And 'sorry' had never seemed such an inadequate word.

'Bit late now.'

Jess took a deep breath. Time to put her cards on the table.

'I think I might have made a mistake.'

'You only think…?'

Only to pick them up again and give them a shuffle while buying some time. 'You're cross.' She'd never been good at cards.

'Oh, come on, Jess. What the fuck do you expect? "Cross" doesn't even begin to cover it. You're there on our honeymoon and I'm here in our ex-home. You're everywhere I turn. Only you're not.'

A pause as Nick stopped to pull himself together—and Jess wondered how soon she could get home. And to think she'd been half expecting him to arrive to patch things up. Clearly that was her department. All this time to think and she hadn't been able to see the other point of view. She needed to go on a course in empathy. She'd always hated selfish people who thought the world revolved around them, yet now… But he hadn't finished yet. She braced herself for the next bullet.

'We had a wedding planned, only you didn't feel like it— you had a headache or something. There wasn't even someone else. You just didn't want to be with me. I wasn't enough. I got the gist of it, I think.'

Jess could hear Nick battling to stop his voice from crack-ing. Put that way, she didn't sound very nice. But she *was* very nice, if a little confused.

'So, what? You'd rather I'd been having an affair?'

'At least I might have understood. You love me, you love me not. You weren't the one who had to stand up and tell our family and friends that you weren't coming. You should have seen their faces. It even took a few attempts to convince them I wasn't joking. I've never been more humiliated.'

Jess grimaced at the thought of Nick having to labour the point. 'You could have asked Chris to make the announcement.'

'I don't sprint from responsibility. I don't leap on the next plane to the sun.'

'Come on, Nick. You told me to go.'

'I told you to come to the church. It's not like you listen to everything I say…'

Jess was silent. Speechless. More than 130,000 words in the *Concise Oxford English Dictionary,* and not one of them seemed appropriate.

'I mean, how many weddings have we been to?'

'Together?'

'I repeat: have *we* been to?'

Jess pretended not to recognise his combative tone and proceeded as normally as she could. 'Around thirty?' No wonder she didn't have any savings.

'Exactly. And how many have you planned?'

'Probably the same again. Maybe even forty.'

'And how many couples do you know who have called it off on the day?'

Jess paused. She was getting the picture. 'None?'

'Correct, Girl Wonder.'

Apparently she had almost married The Riddler.

'So, as you can imagine, it's not like there's a well struc-tured Plan B. Chris and I invited everyone back to the marquee for a drink or two—wedding insurance doesn't cover a change of heart—but the atmosphere was pretty strained. There's only so much sympathy and wide-eyed tacit concern that a guy can take in one afternoon.'

The Technicolor of Jess's view was feeling increasingly inappropriate. 'I'm sorry. I really am. I just couldn't—I mean, it wasn't...' In the heat of the marital moment, her nagging doubts had become nagging truths. To marry or not to marry, that had been the question.

'Please, spare me. I know. I mean, I don't know—I'll probably never know—but I know... I just wished you'd talked to me about it all earlier.'

'I didn't know. I did and then I didn't. I panicked. I've been doing lots of thinking while I've been here.'

'Yes?' Nick's voice was tight. Controlled.

'And I think we still have things to talk about. I mean, it doesn't have to be... I would really like to see you when I get back. Maybe we should go away for a weekend? I owe you so much more than you know, and I think there's still so much...'

'That sounds like a brilliant idea.' Only from Nick's chilled delivery it was clear it didn't.

'Well, at least let's have dinner or lunch or something.'

'Classic knee-jerk panic. Fear of being alone.'

'It's not that. I promise. I really think we have things to sort out.' So, her Get Nick Back plan was still embryonic.

'Which is why I called in the first place.'

'It is?' Jess stopped in her tracks. She hadn't even given him a chance to tell her how he was feeling.

'Yup, I can't find Sarah and Simon's new number anywhere.' Hope sailed off into the horizon.

'That's because it's in my head and on my mobile.' Both with her at the moment. Not that her mobile worked there. All part of the attraction of isolation, apparently.

'You never did keep our address book up to date.'

Jess resisted the urge to bicker. Who even *had* a paper address book that they used any more? 'You could have e-mailed her.'

'I wanted to call her. I want to drop some stuff there tomorrow for when you get back...'

'Stuff?'

'I'm presuming shorts and flip-flops won't work in London at the end of September...' He was sounding like a weary, irritated, inconvenienced parent. 'We can arrange for you to come and get the rest as and when.'

'Oh.' The reality of her decision was starting to dawn. She wasn't going home. A hot tear ran down her cheek as she dashed off the number.

Nick's voice was flaccid and devoid of any emotion. 'Unless you want me to move in with Fiona?'

'Of course not.' Did she? Fi only had a one-bedroom flat, with a very uncomfortable sofa-bed which was only a double if your house guests were Oompa-Loompas or you'd drunk more than your weekly allocation of units in one session. 'I just hadn't really—I mean I didn't...'

'I don't know if you remember, but you called off our wedding?'

'Is that supposed to be funny?'

'I didn't think so.'

'But you're still happy to meet and talk about things?'

'"Happy" is a long shot, but...' Nick sighed '...I guess we can meet. God, Jess, I can't believe this is happening to us...'

Jess swallowed to prevent her saying anything she might regret later. Her thoughts were roaming far and wide and needed shepherding. 'Well, thank you. I really appreciate it.' Seven years reduced to extreme courtesy. Outwardly calm and rapidly becoming less positive, she couldn't wait to get off the phone and burst into tears.

'Call when you're back.' He hung up.

Diving into the pool, Jess relished the muted version of

her life as she completed a length underwater. And to her added relief it was impossible to cry immersed in water. Coming up for air at the far end, suddenly she couldn't wait to be back in England. She needed to face the music before it petered out completely. And she was sure life would all seem more manageable with straight hair. Jess swam over to the steps. Time to pack up her troubles—or at least return them to their mother country.

five

'Anything else I can get for you, Mrs Carlisle?'

The flight attendant removed her plate.

'Mrs Carlisle?'

Jack cleared his throat.

Emma looked up from her book mid-sentence. Ah, yes, that was her. Mrs C.

'Sorry?'

'A drink? A DVD, perhaps? Another neck and shoulder massage?' Sandy was determined to tout her wares, her ample bust currently at Emma's eye level.

'No, thanks.' Emma couldn't quite get used to first class. The miracle of air travel hit her every time she fastened her seat belt, yet it would appear that the more money you paid—or, more accurately, the more money someone paid for you—the less it was cool to want to press your nose up against the window. And people-watching was a definite no no. Even earlier, during a tea-spillingly turbulent moment, no one had so much as made eye contact in the first-class cabin.

'I, on the other hand, will have all three of those.' Jack was almost horizontal, his tan set off perfectly by a pale pink T-shirt—an item of clothing for which—if you were male— you either had to be gay, colour blind, or famous.

'Certainly, sir.'

Emma smiled to herself as she wondered if the offer of a massage had come from short dark, gay Michael, as opposed to tall, blond, I-wish-they-all-could-be-Californian Sandy, Jack would have been quite so keen.

'I think I'll stretch my legs. I take it it's OK if I go for a walk?' Emma gestured to the curtain of exclusivity.

'It's fine with us if it's fine with you.' Sandy failed to hide her surprise. 'I can offer you a foot and lower leg massage, if you'd prefer?'

'No, a walk is what I need. I won't be long.'

'I'm sure you won't…'

Emma was sure she saw Sandy wink at Jack esoterically.

'…It's a jungle out there.'

Jess couldn't wait to land back in civilisation: socks, *BBC News* and no more bloody mosquitoes. As she peered out of the window, scratching absently, she was mesmerised by the sea. From 32,000 feet the water looked solid, the waves wrinkles on a surface that had the dermatological texture of an elephant. Or skin on a rapidly cooling rice pudding. Jess smiled. So now she was clairvoyant. Apparently she could see surface tension everywhere.

'Tea or coffee, madam?'

'Coffee, please.' Jess placed her micro-cup on the tray for a split second before removing it again. And only just before the pouring had started. 'Actually, could you make that tea?'

Three weeks ago she'd known exactly what she wanted. Now she couldn't even decide what to drink. Pretending to immerse herself in her book, she just wanted to be at home.

★ ★ ★

Emma walked the length of the plane and tried not to think about the lack of solid ground beneath her feet. Economy was full. Rows full of freshly sunburned people trying to sleep, all with a little bit too much body in not quite enough space. Tucking herself into an empty seat to allow a trolley to pass, Emma peered nosily at the novel that the adjacent incumbent was reading. And then to her embarrassment the woman looked up.

'Jessica? Jess?' She was a bit browner and less well-kempt, but it was definitely her.

'Emma?' Subconsciously Jess rescraped her hair into her scrunchie and removed a couple of crumbs of eyeliner from the corners of her eyes—but she was delighted to see a familiar face.

Emma couldn't believe her luck. A friend. Out of the blue. Or at least in the blue. At around 30,000 feet. 'What the hell are you doing here?'

'I was about to ask you the same question. Jack isn't flying you economy, surely?'

Emma laughed. 'No, I just needed a moment to myself. I thought I'd take a walk on the wild side…'

'So, how was Little Dix Bay?' Forgetting that the seat wasn't hers to offer, Jess patted the space next to her, determined to keep on the offensive. Of all the rows in all the planes in all the world, she should have known that Emma was going to walk into hers—and, of course, when she was reading something decidedly lowbrow. She never ran into anyone when she was clutching a Booker Prize winner.

'Fantastic.' Emma realised she hadn't even had to lie. 'Although, between you and me, I'm ready for London. I don't think I'm cut out for island life—or twenty-four-hour five-star hotel living.'

'I'm trying to feel sorry for you.' Jess paused for a moment of empathy. 'Nope. Not working.' She smiled.

Emma grimaced apologetically. 'I know—I know I sound like a spoilt child. But I can't wait for a cool evening, a home-cooked meal, plates that don't match and a night on the sofa. We didn't even have a television in the room. Something to do with resort karma...'

Jess raised her eyebrows at the thought of her fortnight without cable. She must have watched over twenty episodes of *Friends*.

'But how was yours? Apologies—that would be self-centred bride syndrome. Where is it you were staying? I think Jack would like to go back to that area every year.'

A man started walking down the aisle towards them and Emma took her knee off the seat. 'I'd better leave you to your private life. I'm sure Nick wants you all to himself.'

Jess blushed. 'That's not Nick.'

Sure enough, the man passed them by—and to Emma's embarrassment she noted he wasn't even a vaguely attractive specimen.

'Nick's not here, in fact.' Jess realised how much she really wanted to talk to someone.

'He's not? You mean, you...' Emma struggled to assemble a list of scenarios, from worst case to best case.

'Called it off.'

'You did not?'

Jess nodded sheepishly. 'Less than an hour before.'

'Oh, my God. That's terrible. Isn't it? I mean, good for you...if that was the right thing for you to do...' Emma was floundering.

Jess sighed. 'I don't know now.' But she was relishing the opportunity to be telling someone who hadn't been directly involved.

The occupant of 29B returned and aligned himself with his seat. A large man, impatient to get back to his movie. But Emma couldn't leave Jess now—or at least she didn't want to.

'Hey, why don't you come up-front for a drink?'

Jess hurriedly stuffed her book into the seat pocket in front and then hesitated. 'I'm not sure that's allowed.'

'Well, I'm not leaving you here. We're mid-sentence and mid-Atlantic…'

Jess couldn't have agreed more.

'Why didn't you call me? You knew where we were staying. You booked it, for God's sake.'

'Emma, you were on your honeymoon. I am your wedding planner. I'm not your sister.'

'Well, in the absence of one of those, I could have improvised. We could have picked you up for lunch on the boat Jack chartered.'

'Lovely—just the three of us.'

'It wouldn't have been like that. Although I can't really believe that I'm married.'

'I can't believe I'm not.'

Sensing that there was more to come, the man waiting coughed in a concertedly conscious fashion before attempting to tuck his tummy into the waistband of his trousers.

Emma turned to him. 'Sorry. All my fault. And it's OK. She's coming with me.'

A bead of sweat formed on his temple. 'I don't care where she's going, I just want to sit down.'

Emma squeezed out of his way as Jess shoehorned herself out of her seat area and followed her down the aisle. Indeed, Jess was just marvelling at how long planes were when Emma stopped just before the curtain and, immersed in a world of her own, Jess walked into the back of her.

'Sorry.' Jess did her utmost to retain her dignity, and turned a blind eye to the sniggers of the Business Class section.

'Excuse me?' Sandy's twenty-a-day purr became positively shrill as she stepped out to block Jess's path to the nose of the plane.

'She's with me.' Emma continued to her seat.

Sandy rooted Jess to the spot with a look, before following Emma. 'I'm afraid you can't bring guests up here without prior arrangement. We don't have any spare dinners.'

'She doesn't want dinner. She just wants company and maybe a drink. She can have one of mine.' Emma wasn't going to take no for an answer. She was determined to filibuster Jess into First Class. And in a moment it was going to be easier for Sandy to let them both in than to encourage a conference on the borderline of Business and First. 'She's a close personal friend.'

Emma transferred her attentions to her husband. Time to flex her new Carlisle muscle. 'Jack…' Emma caught her husband's eye and he unplugged himself from his i-Pod. 'You won't believe who I found in Economy.'

Sandy balked. Not even Business Class.

Jack leant out of his seat. 'Hey, Jess. How's it going? Come and have a drink with us. I didn't realise wedding planners came on the honeymoon too, but I guess that's real service for you…'

Jess hovered uncertainly, doing her utmost to disregard the surreptitious glances of the other passengers, unsure whether Sandy would let her get so close to the cockpit. Emma leaned in, screened by her seat, in an attempt to have an at least partially private conversation with her husband.

'Don't be ridiculous, Jack. She's supposed to be on her *own* right now.'

'Well, you're the one who invited her up here.'

'I mean she's on her own *honeymoon.*' Sometimes he could be very obtuse. Maybe ten years of substance abuse had taken its toll.

'How do you know?'

It might just have been Emma's imagination, but it felt as if Jack was behaving differently already—and they hadn't even entered British airspace yet. His patience was thinner than it had been since the wedding.

'We spent a lot of time together in the run-up. She was getting married the following week. We sent flowers.' Emma had made sure of it. Which meant… She smacked herself on the forehead. How tactless. Not that she had known.

'Women chat too much.' Jack smiled at Jess before muttering to Emma through his upturned mouth. 'Well, you could at least have asked *him* up here, too.'

Emma hissed into his ear. 'She's on her own.'

'So you keep saying.'

'I mean she didn't get married after all. Not that you need to know. But just be sensitive, OK?'

Jess was loitering, doing her utmost not to inadvertently invade the personal space of any of these prized customers, but it was difficult to blend in when she wasn't wearing even one linen item. Economy might have been cramped, but even with Emma's unconditional support she was much less comfortable up here.

Jack beckoned for her to join them, and suddenly Sandy appeared to unfold a spare chair for his table. Jess walked over as expensively as she could. Emma smiled encouragingly. She might have been sitting in First Class, but she still felt fairly average.

'So, good trip?' Jess was doing her best to take the right to roam in her stride.

'Superb.'

Jack wasn't a man of many words this afternoon.

Jess smiled. 'I'm so glad.'

Emma decided to help him along. 'Thanks again for the perfect wedding day.'

'Hey, it's what I do.'

'It's what you do best.' Jack smiled. 'Unless, apparently, it's your own…'

Jess blushed, and Emma wished she had kept her mouth shut as she glared at her husband. He did his best to make amends. 'I mean, I'm sorry to hear…'

'These things happen. And I'm hoping it's not the end of the road—just a ditch, or a sleeping policeman…'

'You ditched him to sleep with a policeman?' Jack laughed at his own joke while Emma wished she'd married someone more sensitive—or at least a man who hadn't drunk a bottle of wine with dinner.

'No, that would have been a lot simpler, actually.' Jess laughed a little too hard.

'Oh, right. Well, good luck, I guess. If that's what you want, of course.' Jack was doing his best to say the right thing.

'It's what I need. And once again I'm so sorry about the whole photographer debacle. I see *CelebriTee* got hold of the UK rights to the photos, and I think *Star* published them in the States.'

Jack nodded seriously. '*Star*? Really? That's huge circulation.'

'I can't apologise enough. The guy appeared to have a genuine invitation. I just can't quite fathom how… I intend to have a full security review when I get back.'

'Really, there's no need. Accidents happen.' To Jess's relief he looked concerned rather than upset. And that was more for her benefit. There were moments when she really didn't understand celebrities, and this was one of them.

'Not to me. Not at work, at any rate. My career depends on the confidentiality of my clients. I can only thank you both for being so magnanimous about it all.'

'Look, I've grown up with the paparazzi, and nothing surprises me as far as they're concerned. Plus, the photos were great—the party looked fantastic, the venue was awesome. I'm sure your phone will have been ringing non-stop.'

'If they want a wedding planner who gets cold feet.'

'Don't take this the wrong way, but no one will care about your own situation.'

'I hope you're right.'

'They'll just want Jack Carlisle's wedding planner. Oh, and the happy-ever-after for themselves—'

Emma interrupted. 'Well, that's easy then…'

They all laughed as quietly as they could, but judging by the blindfolded stare coming from the man in the next seat in his sleeper suit, not silently enough.

Jess got to her feet. She wasn't feeling that sociable, and was certainly not in the mood for a threesome. 'Great to see you guys again. Good luck with everything. I really need to get back…'

For what? A plastic glass of chilled red wine? Next to no legroom? A microscopic bag of pretzels?

'…to watch the next film. And I don't want to miss the duty free trolley.' Jess had never bought anything from that trolley in her life.

Emma waved from her seat. 'Great to run into you. Really.'

Jess nodded emphatically.

'I'll give you a call next week. We should have a drink or lunch or something.'

'Brilliant.'

The polite we'll-meet-again cruel-to-be-kind fob-off, practised the world over. But in the case of Emma Carlisle, Jess hoped it might be true. She had a feeling she was going to need all the friendly faces she could muster.

six

'I can't believe it gets light at six a.m. on a Sunday. I mean, really—what's the point…?'

Fi had never been a morning person. If she'd been in charge of creation the dawn chorus would have started around eleven. Weekend mornings were a precious commodity and today she was the queen of self-sacrifice.

'I don't even feel very well. I think I'm coming down with something.'

Nor was she a confrontational human being. Plus, for the first time in recent memory—or certainly in this year's diary—she had left a warm-bodied, warm-hearted man asleep under her duvet.

Bemused, Simon shook his head. 'You don't think your acute nausea might just be down to the fact that you have new news…?'

Fiona was silent. Trust her to have met someone just at the time when being chirpy about that loving feeling was going to be off the agenda as far as her best friend was concerned. A wave of exhaust fumes somehow penetrated Sarah and Simon's VW Golf and turned her stomach over.

'It's only been a few dates…' Fiona raised the sleeve of her jumper to her nose and attempted to breathe through a Persil-infused lambswool filter, continuing in a slightly muffled tone. 'Anyway, all news by definition is new—isn't that the whole point?'

Simon smiled at Fiona's attempt to divert their conversation. 'I was thinking more about your brother's situation…'

Swallowing hard, Fi rubbed her eyes so hard that they squeaked in their sockets. If Simon was insisting she was in the upright position at the crack of dawn on a Sunday morning she was going to need the biggest coffee money could buy—and maybe a Get Out Of Jail Free card. To go.

Sarah yawned in the passenger seat, and to Fiona's amusement, directly behind her in her baby seat, Millie did the same. Sarah exhaled noisily. 'I still don't understand why we *all* had to come and get her.'

Simon took his hand off the gearstick and rested it gently on his wife's thigh. 'Well, first of all she doesn't technically have anywhere to go. She might own half a house, but Nick's made it perfectly clear that—'

'We agreed she was coming to stay with us before she left.' Sarah was beginning to wish she'd kept her mouth shut. Their mother had far more spare room, and whilst it might have been an awkward commute, selfishly she loved their set-up. It was so relaxed. So comfortable. Or at least it had been.

'Come on. There was a lot going on that day. And we owe her. Don't forget who came to collect us when we got back from Bali,' Simon reminded her.

'That was nearly three years ago.'

'It was still a big deal.'

'It was her decision.'

'And she ended up in the middle of a situation she didn't volunteer for,' Simon concluded.

Sarah looked out of the car window at the planes stacking up across West London, queuing to land. 'Hey, you have to hand it to her. She's always the first with the breaking news...'

Fiona remained silent in the back seat, wishing she'd made time to wash her hair instead of reaching for a scrunchie. A greasy-hair-related dip in self-confidence was the last thing she needed today.

'I just wish I'd double checked her arrival time before suggesting this. Even Millie's still normally asleep—aren't you, darling?' Sarah's voice became a rhetorical coo as she burbled at her year-old daughter.

'Look, she's going to have enough to deal with in the next few weeks without having to win you over too.'

As usual, good old Simon was making total sense—and somehow Sarah had inadvertently placed herself on the shortlist for sister-from-hell. Simon ended up with the full quota of Brownie points every time. Not that life was a competition. Yeah, right.

Fiona stared out of the window. She hated being present when couples argued. From his rear view mirror Simon noticed her trying to lose herself in the non-existent view.

'Don't worry. She's always like this if she hasn't had two pints of coffee before she leaves the house...'

'Don't talk about me like I'm not here.'

Simon patted his wife on the knee. 'Then start behaving like you are. If you aren't capable of being civil, I think I'll leave you in the car...'

Sarah pulled a face worthy of one of her kindergarten pupils. If he wasn't careful she was going to steal his lunchbox and matching flask. Instead, she wrestled to create enough slack in her seatbelt before leaning across and giving him a kiss on the cheek. She never could stay cross with him for long.

'Look...' Simon included Fiona in the conversation by turning his head fractionally towards the back seat. 'It's been a difficult couple of weeks for all of us, but we can't just let her wander through Arrivals into an airport devoid of a friendly face. For all we know she's conjured up some half-baked fantasy of a *Love Story* reunion with Nick.'

Sarah nodded grimly before turning to Fiona. 'He's just so infuriatingly…good. Most husbands would be complaining about having their sister-in-law to stay indefinitely, but mine insists on driving to the airport to fetch her. I mean, really…'

Most husbands. Not an accessory that the majority of Fiona's peers had managed to acquire as yet. Or at least not one of their own. Twelve years of being chained to their office desks had taken its toll, and she still wasn't convinced the chemistry of attraction could be transmitted via a Broadband connection.

Her mobile beeped.

Off to Brighton for day with R to have some fun. Two weeks of non-marriage already. This is going to get easier right? Thanks for great lunch yesterday. You're one hell of a sister. Nx

One hell of a sister who hadn't mentioned she was on her way to the airport. Not that he'd asked. Guilt was a bloody inconvenient emotion.

Simon raised an eyebrow at her via the rearview mirror. 'Everything OK?'

'Just perfect.' Nick didn't know whether he was coming or going and Jess was arriving any minute now. Watching Millie gurgle innocently in her baby seat next to her, Fi wondered what on earth had possessed her to agree to this jaunt. Safety in numbers, Sarah had said. More like piggy in the middle. But apparently twenty years of friendship meant warts and all.

Jess stared out of the window as the plane broke through the grey fleece blanket of cloud covering Sussex. London

Gatwick indeed. As close to the centre of town as London Stansted. She wondered how long it would be before they had London Leicester. Her stomach lurched as they dropped a few thousand feet.

A new day. Five hours lost somewhere over the Atlantic. It was no wonder people got jet lag. At least if she'd kayaked across the ocean she'd have had time to get used to the time difference. Jess chewed her gum as fast as her jaws would allow, hoping for at least a sliver of spearmint freshness as they landed.

She needed a shower and a toothbrush. She shouldn't have had a second half-bottle of wine with dinner. Especially as now, a mere few hours later, apparently it was the morning. She wondered who on earth had got away with suddenly informing half the world that they had an afternoon again while the telling other half that they'd already had their day? And they said time travel would never catch on. It really didn't help that she'd never mastered the knack of sleeping on planes. Maybe if she'd been given a bed and a sleeper suit… Idly Jess wondered if Jack and Emma had been woken with a kiss and a cuppa—and whether she'd ever be woken that way again.

Touchdown. Jess was back in Nick country. As she transferred her travel trust into the tiny wheels on the undercarriage and the engines roared into reverse thrust, an electronic dawn chorus filled the cabin. Anxious not to miss a single moment of potential communication, everyone had turned on their mobiles, against specific orders, as they taxied towards the gate.

Jess rummaged for hers and, power restored, glared at the screen. Her neighbour was steadily working his way through his messages and, to her relief, finally Jess's phone joined its peers. Excitedly she dialled her answering service. Three new messages. She frowned. That was only one and a half a week.

Two from her mother and one from Sarah. Nothing from

Nick. Not even a text. Jess waved her phone around in her seat area in the vain hope that there was a localised problem with network coverage. And to think she'd entertained the thought, albeit for a split second, that he might have decided to come to the airport to meet her. There were high standards and then there was the fantasy league. The Hollywood edition. She'd even managed to convince herself that Nick's telephone manner had been an index of his feelings for her: he was hurt therefore he cared.

After a moment of delay as the First Class passengers disembarked, Jess impatiently followed the herd of holidaymakers to reclaim her baggage and her life.

'Woo-hoo! Welcome home.'

Oblivious to her wan welcome committee, Jess stared ahead blankly as she entered the Arrivals hall, trying not to see the happy reunions taking place all around her and wrestling with her inner accountant over whether to go for the expensive but easy cab option or to take the tube.

'Over here…Jess.'

Squinting along the rail, wondering whether she was hearing things, she gave the crowd a cursory glance and there they were. Jess felt tears prick the back of her eyes as she waved and wheeled herself over, wanting to point out her gaggle of friends to all the people who'd been feeling pity for her a few moments earlier. Purgatory was over and it looked like she had survived judgement day—even if, to her amusement, Fi was almost green with the early-morning effort.

Jess smiled, realising she was using a set of muscles she hadn't exercised much over the last fortnight.

Ducking under the bar, Fi gave her best friend a hug. 'Well, you missed the paparazzi. Mr and Mrs Married came through about twenty minutes ago, looking very relaxed and happy I have to say. A job well done, missy.' Fi realised her mouth was running away with itself. One enormous latte later, she was firing on more cylinders than she'd known she possessed. When caffeine meets adrenaline… Time to change the subject…

Sarah got there first. 'Just look at the colour of you.'

Jess answered almost apologetically. 'To be honest there was nothing else to do. It's not like I was lingering in air-conditioned boudoirs.'

Sarah gave her little big sister a restorative squeeze. *In situ,* it was far harder to be tough on her.

Simon reached over and pecked her on the cheek. Jess did her best not to squash Millie while returning the gesture and giving her niece a kiss too.

Simon took the baggage trolley from her. 'You're looking great. A break was probably just what you needed.' Jess thought she was definitely going to cry. They were all being far too nice.

'Or a break-up, of course.' Sarah could always be trusted to be totally honest.

'We'll see…' Jess's smile was esoteric, enigmatic and hopeful as three pairs of eyes fleetingly examined the state of the arrivals hall lino. 'I can't believe you came to fetch me. That's so great. And it's so…'

'Early?' Fiona hazarded a guess…

'I was going to say kind.' Jess laughed. Back on British terra firma things felt a lot more manageable. 'So, who's seen Nick, then?'

Simon barely let Jess finish her sentence. 'Anyone fancy a coffee before we head to the car?'

Saved by the bean. Sarah and Fi couldn't have been any more enthusiastic—even though, Jess noted, they were still clutching paper cups from the last round.

'So what's new?' Jess took a sip of her coffee and waited for the caffeine hit as they sat round her baggage trolley, small-talking at speed.

'Not much, really…' Fiona could feel her cheeks getting rosier. 'It's been a quiet couple of weeks: political party conference season in seaside towns starting with the letter B, and I know I should care more about the domestic economy and the future of our health service than I do about international flight prices and the new season of *Six Feet Under,* but I don't. What else? Tim Henman is still our greatest tennis hope, the Tube has been totally buggered, I'm thinking about buying a scooter…'

Jess listened for the kernel of interest she knew would be sandwiched in there somewhere amongst the shoal of red herrings.

'…I'm sort of seeing someone…'

There it was.

'…French Connection have got the most amazing coats in for autumn…'

'Fuck that.'

'Don't you mean FCUK that?' Simon was one coffee ahead of the rest of them.

Jess wasn't going to be distracted. Her tone was a combination of interest and incredulity. 'Fi, you jammy little whatsit. Come on, who is he?'

'Just a guy I met at your non-wedding.' Fiona smiled. She couldn't help it. Just thinking about him resulted in the syrupy grin normally reserved for watching the closing scenes of romantic comedies.

Jess tried to recall the eligible bachelors on their guest list—to no avail. Detailed recall had clearly been lost in the aftermath as self-protection had stepped in and wiped any difficult files off her emotional hard drive. 'Who?'

One, two, three…Fi wanted to count to ten to help her keep calm, but she didn't have time. 'Michael.'

Michael, Michael, Mick, Mikey, Mike. 'My *photographer*?' Jess was incredulous. Over two years of working together and she hadn't even known he was single.

Fi nodded. 'We've only seen each other a few times—well, quite a few times. But I have a good feeling about this one…although now you'll tell me he's gay, used to be called Michaela, is married, or a transvestite…'

Jess paused and Fiona panicked.

'What?'

'I'm sure he said he was living with his girlfriend,' Jess said hesitantly.

'He was. But that ended six months ago.'

'Are you sure?'

'Of course I'm sure.' Was she? Fiona racked her brains for any female touches in his flat.

'Cool. And at least you know he is capable of a long-term relationship.'

The girls giggled together. Fiona had a history of picking the more dysfunctional specimens from the dating pool.

'Can't say I'd have put you together myself, but…'

'But…?'

Jess struggled with the truth.

'Well….it's just…'

'Accountants do have a creative side, you know.'

Jess nodded and laughed defensively. The only problem being that laughter seemed to be bringing her very close to tears of a non-specific nature at the moment.

'He's a lovely guy. A bit young for you, perhaps, but…'

Fiona paled. If that was possible at this time of day.

'A toyboy?'

'You didn't know?'

'I didn't ask. I just assumed. I mean, he doesn't seem… How young are we talking?'

'It's very fashionable at the moment. Every Hollywood woman worth her salt has a younger man.'

Fi did her best to smile. Hollywood actress, maybe. City accountant, definitely not. 'How old?'

'He's twenty-nine I think. Yup, pretty sure his thirtieth is coming up, so that's only two and a bit years. Nothing.' Jess laughed gaily.

Relief swamped Fiona. Not ideal in the abstract, but he hadn't missed any cultural references so far and he had quite a few grey flecks in his hair. She was so right-now-this-minute. 'And you don't mind?' Fiona still couldn't quite believe it. Just when she'd started to mentally prepare herself to compromise in order to reduce her risk of dying alone, and now maybe she wouldn't have to.

'Mind? You're practically family.' Jess smiled. 'And you know I only employ the best a bride can get.'

Silence. Maybe it was too soon after the whole jilting thing to be making bride jokes—she wasn't sure of the etiquette—this was all brand new to her.

'OK, it is typical that we have never managed to be single at the same time in fifteen years, but…' Jess clapped her hands childishly. 'Brilliant. I must give Mike a call and congratulate him on his frankly excellent taste. The only trouble is…'

'What?'

'Well, it's obvious, really.'

'What is?'

'Well, who will take the photos at your wedding? I mean if your boyfriend…'

'Jess…' Fi's tone was as firm as her circuit trained abs.

'What?'

'Boyfriend?'

'Well, from where I'm standing…' Jess teased.

'He's just a guy I'm dating.'

'Whatever makes you feel better, my love.'

'Please, Jess, promise me you won't stir?'

'*Moi?*'

Three pairs of eyebrows raised gently and Jess noticed that Sarah and Simon were lightly holding hands. Good to see marital bliss did exist. And they were just so natural together. Or nervous.

'It's just, well, I know I've only known him for ten minutes but I really like him.'

'Got it.'

Fi's brow was still furrowed.

Jess placed her hand on her forearm. 'I promise. Right, so, come on people—what is it?'

Simon smiled pseudo-calmly as Fi, mouth full of coffee, concentrated on not spraying milky foam across the table as she attempted to swallow and exhale simultaneously. Jess watched their display of synchronised sipping and waited for them to take a breath.

'Come on, guys. A lift from one of you would have been marvellous—but three for the price of one? I've only been away for two weeks, and I know Fi having been on a couple of dates is newsworthy but it doesn't warrant quite so much tension.'

'We didn't want you to come back to an empty arrivals hall.' Sarah was talking as fast as she could think. 'I mean, we knew the homecoming thing was going to be tough, and so we just thought it would be nice for you.'

Jess wasn't even nearly convinced. 'Nice thought, but honestly... Come on—spit it out. I mean if Fi had been dating Nick, then obviously that would have been bad... Hypothetically, of course. I mean, if they weren't related... You know...'

Sarah rescued her from her whirlpool of inarticulacy. 'Speak of the devil—Nick dropped some stuff off for you at our place yesterday...'

'How was he?' Jess felt her stomach knot as she pictured him starting his Sunday in the knowledge that she was home. She'd been debating the merits of popping in to see him later. Strike while the iron was hot, while she still had a tan, that sort of thing...

'Oh, you know Nick. Fine. Well, fine considering...'

A three-way exchange of glances. No one wanted to be the one with *this* item of news.

'What?' Jess did her best to make eye contact with her nearest and dearest, but even Millie wasn't playing. 'You can all chill out. I spoke to him on Friday.'

Sarah was nodding unconvincingly 'You did?'

'Yup, he called, and we've arranged to have a chat about things.'

'Really?' Fiona's tone was mockingly incredulous.

Jess was only one step away from pinning Fiona up against a wall. Something had happened.

'We *were* together for nearly eight years.'

'Bloody hell, you haven't changed your mind, have you?' Sarah momentarily forgot whose side she was supposed to be on. Things had always been complicated when it came to Jess and relationships. Nick was her first serious relationship, and it wasn't just men she hadn't been able to make her mind up about. Teenage shopping trips had been torturous as by the time she had decided she really liked something it had inevitably sold out.

'Well…' Jess hadn't wanted to have to admit this out loud so soon after landing, or lose the support of her Arrivals posse, but there was no time like the present and this *was* exciting news. 'Well, maybe, yes…'

Jess was rewarded with the blankest of stares in triplicate. She carried on.

'I needed to take a step back. I was confused. Obviously we're not going to be able to fix things overnight, but I'm hoping that—' Everyone was stony-faced. Jess's pulse started racing. 'What is it?'

Simon was the bravest. 'Slight problem with your plan, perhaps.'

Jess swallowed and nodded for him to continue.

'The thing is…look I'm just going to come out with it straight, you're a big girl. Nick's been seeing someone.'

The information entered and exited Jess's brain without taking hold. 'What is this? Shag a Seaton month?'

'Excuse me?' Fiona was indignant. 'Michael and I haven't had sex.'

'You haven't? Why not?'

Fiona blushed. 'OK, we have. But I wish I could hold out for more than two or three dates…I'm such a slapper.'

'Maybe in a world where slappers don't have sex more than once a year or two. You're in your thirties. You're hardly going to hold hands and snog for two weeks first.'

'So speaketh the expert. You were single in your twenties for—what?—three months?' Fiona pointed out.

'How you like to mock me.' Fi was almost one hundred per cent accurate. 'Please, stop beating yourself up about everything and just relax.'

Sarah giggled. She couldn't help herself. But Jess telling Fiona to relax? Now, that was entertainment. Jess was tensing up by the second.

'How the hell can Nick be "seeing someone" after two weeks?' If she was honest it wasn't the *seeing* bit that Jess was worried about. It was all the other senses on offer. 'I mean, that's a bit fast, don't you think?'

'You dumped him at the altar. Pretty final, I'd say.' In a sea of women, Simon was determined to present the male perspective.

Jess felt dizzy and disorientated. 'It's classic rebounding all over the place behaviour.' Jess paused. 'And two weeks plays eight years. I mean, surely there's no contest there?' She gripped her cup a little tighter.

A round of wishful nodding.

'I mean, who on earth…? Don't tell me. It's that blond estate agent from Fulham.'

'Nope.' Fiona's denial preceded a silence which, despite the ambient noise and bustle around them, appeared to cocoon them all.

'Then where did he meet someone…?'

Jess watched them all postponing the now inevitable.

Even Simon. Apparently cuticles were fascinating this season.

'Not at our wedding, surely?'

Sarah licked her lips nervously. It was enough.

Jess shook her head in disbelief. Clearly her wedding had been the place to be. If only someone had told her. 'So, someone we know?' Her pragmatic gene was working overtime as a line-up of all the female guests started spooling through her mind.

'I don't know her very well.' It was Fi's straw and she was determined to clutch at it—for as long as possible.

'So, come on—who?'

Sarah had been through enough in the last twenty minutes. All this tension couldn't have been good for Millie. 'Rosie.'

'Rosie?' Jess swallowed hard as she tried to take everything in her stride. 'As in my assistant Rosie?'

'No, as in Cider With Rosie. How many Rosies do you know, for goodness' sake?'

'One less now.' Jess's mind was racing. And to nowhere in particular. A series of emotional bombshells began to detonate inside her skull. Either that or she was getting a headache.

Simon intervened. 'It's bound to be a case of geography…'

Jess grimaced. It had never been her favourite subject. Too many maps, too much rainfall.

'She was there. She probably just listened and made him feel human at a time when he didn't know which way to turn. I'm afraid it's a genetic weakness. Men don't like coping alone. In fact, most of us can't…'

Jess could hear Simon. Or at least she was standing there and her fingers weren't in her ears. But after thirty-two years of practice her brain was having trouble with the interpreting bit.

'Jess, you can't even imagine what he must have been

going through…it probably means nothing to him. It's just a male reflex defence mechanism.'

Jess would have married Simon there and then if he hadn't already been married to her sister. And if she'd fancied him even an iota and if she'd been the spontaneous marrying kind. She couldn't have been any more grateful for his sanity under fire.

'Rosie.' Jess sucked her next breath in over her teeth as she addressed the middle distance. This was bad. Not only was Rosie petite, slim and beautiful, but she always seemed to have time to pluck her eyebrows, reapply her lipgloss and always carried a handbag to match her shoes, plus, worst of all, she was on *her* payroll.

'Well, she's fired.' Jess thought she'd feel a release, but she only felt bitchy. It might once have been a free country, but not any more—not today.

Simon leapt in again. 'I think you'll find she's resigned.'

Rosie wasn't the only one. Jess concentrated on breathing…in…and out. So now she was manless and assistantless. Probably best to get on another plane and start again. Time to open a bar on a tiny island and disappear into a bottle of rum.

'Fuckity fuck. Bollocks.' Jess's thoughts were gathering. 'Talk about shitting on your own doorstep—or at least mine. He bloody well could have looked a bit further afield than my office.' Composure was on the way—if running a couple of seconds late. Terrible traffic, no doubt. 'I guess you can't really blame him for grabbing hold of the first available woman.' Jess was thinking aloud. 'I mean, I did a pretty awful thing to him.' She allowed her head to rest in her hands for a nanosecond.

Fi studied her best friend for cracks in her veneer and closed her mouth, which was somewhere between ajar and gaping. Jess didn't really do philosophical. There was no way this phase was going to last long. If only she'd never introduced Jess to Nick…

A) She'd have had a flatmate for the last eight years and would be better at sharing and at compromise.

B) She'd have had a partner in crime to go and flirt in bars with.

C) Today wouldn't be happening.

D) She'd be having hot sex instead of cold coffee.

E) She wouldn't be risking alienating the best thing that had happened to her in years by: i) setting an alarm for an ungodly hour on a Sunday morning and ii) getting up and leaving him—thereby risking him snooping around her flat and finding 1) Phil Collins' *Greatest Hits* or, 2) her Rampant Rabbit vibrator— she wasn't sure which was more embarrassing.

Jess forced herself to carry on. 'Well, I think we can still work it all out. Really I do.' She paused for a moment of thought. 'So, do you think he's liked Rosie for ages?'

'Jess.' Simon, Mr Sanity, intervened. 'He loved you for years. He was about to marry you. I doubt Rosie has been a long-term prospect or pin-up…'

Pragmatic, funny, sensitive and *hers*. Sarah had never loved her husband more.

'Right…' Getting to his feet, Simon had endured enough. 'Let's get going. And you, Jess, can talk us through your holiday romances in the car…' A group laugh at this, the nearest they were going to come to a joke, and then a return to content-free diet conversation.

Jess wasn't used to the silent treatment, or at least the talk-about-anything-else treatment, but there was nothing she could do until she got to a phone and a door that locked. This was between her and Nick. Dating by committee never worked.

Jess lay on the sofa-bed in her temporary bedroom, staring at the ceiling, wondering why on earth she had been in such a hurry to get back to London. With the bed open, the room was basically a spare mattress, with barely enough room for Jess to shimmy round the corners. Her shins had already taken a bashing. Her case was still in the hall, along with the few boxes Nick had delivered. The accompanying note was still in her hand. An instruction to give him a call about removing the rest of her stuff and a request from him to buy her share of the house 'the sooner the better, so we can both move on and put this all behind us'. Brilliant. So now she was going through a divorce without even having been married.

And now a knock at the door. Alone in love, but not in life.

'Yup?'

'Are you awake?'

'Well, I'm talking, which should give you a pretty clear idea.'

Sarah overlooked Jess's sarcastic tone and would have walked into the room if there'd been space. Instead she stood on the threshold.

'OK, I just thought…you know, with the time difference and everything…. Anyway, I've brought you a cuppa.'

'Great. Thanks.' Jess's gaze was still fixed firmly on the ceiling rose. Rose. Rosie. Rosie Lee: tea. That woman was everywhere.

'I'm sorry, Jessie. I guess you thought it would all be different.'

'I think I did far too much thinking far too late.'

'Your tea?' Sarah proffered the great British cure-all.

Jess realised there wasn't an available surface that wasn't sprung. Battling against jet-lag and nascent depression, she forced herself into the upright position and took the cup, grateful that at least she had one permanent ally—even if the decision to move in with her younger, happily married and babied sister was somehow only magnifying her current feelings of emotional failure.

'This room is tiny.' She'd been meaning to say thank you—

it had just got lost in translation. It must be a blood relative thing. Fi rarely got the same treatment.

'You can always stay with Mum.'

'Like I've got two spare hours a day.'

'Or with Dad. He did offer.'

Jess took a wobbly sip. Amazingly kind of him, under the circumstances. The circumstances being that he had recently paid an awful lot of money for a party that had never happened. But moving in with him was not an option. Henpecked and semi-retired, with far too much time for attention to detail, his latest penchant for military history made interesting anecdotes even less likely and quick conversation impossible.

'Sorry. I didn't mean to be grouchy. Thanks for putting me up—or at least for putting up with me.'

Sarah smiled as welcomingly as she could. 'It's our pleasure.' Having to lock the only bathroom door, no noisy sex— no sex anywhere except the bedroom—a queue for the shower in the morning... Really, it was perfect.

'How is Daddy anyway?' Her doting father. The first man in her life. And, once again, the only one.

'Ah, yes, the father of the bride—or at least the father formerly known as the father of the bride, now father of the almost-was-bride... Apart from pretending he's going to have to come out of semi-retirement and saying that you should have had a McWedding, he's fine. I did point out that I didn't think Ronald McDonald nor the Hamburglar were licensed to perform the ceremony.'

Jess did her best to smile as she visualised suitcases opening to release bundles of twenty-pound notes swirling through a breeze. She'd pay him back eventually. Or at least buy him an enormous Christmas present.

'I'll give him a call.' It was all she could afford at the moment.

'Good plan.'

'How about Mum?'

'She'd love you to stay with her.'

'You know that's not what I meant. Look, you'll hardly know I'm here. It's only for a bit, and I can babysit a couple of nights a week if you like.'

'I'll hold you to that. As to Mum, put it this way—the attention is finally off me and Simon now.'

'At least something good has come of all this, then.'

'I think she's loving the drama,' Sarah confessed.

'That's a terrible thing to say.'

'Well, it sure beats *Coronation Street* and *The Archers* at the moment. And, surprisingly, she's on your side.'

'There had to be a first time.' Jess paused. 'It's all going to be OK, though, isn't it? I mean, eventually. You know—my life and all that.'

'Of course it is.' Sarah perched on the edge of the bed and hoped she sounded convincing enough. 'Just don't expect too much too soon.'

FIRST I AM REQUIRED TO ASK
ANYONE HERE PRESENT WHO KNOWS
A REASON WHY THESE PERSONS MAY NOT
LAWFULLY MARRY TO DECLARE IT
NOW OR ELSE HEREAFTER FOR EVER
HOLD THEIR PEACE...

seven

'More wine, Anna Nicole?' Patrick started pouring before Emma could give him an answer. Tucked away in their high-backed booth, their wine glasses were out of the sight of most of the waiters.

Emma laughed indignantly before leaning across the table carefully, so as not to dirty her new Joseph jacket. She wished she was wearing jeans, but Patrick loved his traditional old-boy restaurants, so instead she felt as if she'd come to lunch in fancy dress—as a grown-up. 'I didn't marry Jack for his money…'

'Of course not. Love at first lifestyle.' Patrick drained his glass.

Emma wasn't going to rise to his goading 'Anna Nicole loved J. Howard Marshall…' She'd always hoped that she had. Even just a little bit.

'Absolutely. Although I'm sure it didn't hurt that her final settlement from his estate worked out at more than a million dollars for every year they were married. At least Jack has youth on his side. And looks…the bastard.'

'Hey, that's my husband you're talking about.' Emma drowned her conscience in another mouthful of red wine. 'Anyway, this was your idea.'

'I'm hardly going to be taking the moral high ground, now, am I?' Patrick fiddled with his silver cufflinks.

'Instead it would appear that you are trying to get me drunk…'

Wrong tense. Emma might have been doing her utmost not to display any outward signs of inebriation, but her next loo trip was going to be interesting. The last time she had managed a Beyoncé-esque arse-swinging strut to disguise her unsteadiness, but that was almost a bottle of wine ago. She should have eaten more bread instead of the olives. Her half-hearted attempt at the Atkins diet wasn't going well, but at least she didn't have to work later. She let her head rest on the back of the booth and smiled.

'As if…'

So his master plan wasn't exactly an original one. To be fair it wasn't really a plan. It didn't have a beginning, a middle or an end yet, but he wasn't ready to get the bill either.

'Look it's only recently that we've all been blinded by the concept of true love. You're just one step ahead of the rest of us.' Patrick raised his glass in a mock toast.

Emma sighed. 'The myth has always been for sale. I'm no trailblazer. I just want what everyone else has got—or at least natural conception and a child born in wedlock.' As she ran her fingers through her freshly highlighted hair a few strands got stuck in the claw setting of her engagement ring. She couldn't even do agitated glamorously. There was no hope.

'Correction. What everyone else would like to have and thinks everyone else has got. They're peddling love on a multimedia scale now.'

'*You're* peddling…' Emma pointed a recently untangled finger at Patrick.

Patrick covered her finger with his hand. 'There's no escape. Red is the new black.'

'Sorry, spin king, but love hardly needs rebranding. Before Richard Curtis and the Ephron sisters were the Brontë sisters. Before Julia Roberts there was Jane Austen. The human condition is much the same, it's just the accessories that are different.'

Patrick pretended to look wistful. 'The fantastical quest for true love.'

'You don't think it can ever be a reality, do you?'

'I thought so twice.'

'See—you married for the ideal.'

'And divorced for the reality. Which is why you've got it spot-on and Jack's turned out to exceed expectations so far, has he not?'

'Yes. I guess.' The more wine she consumed, the more sense Patrick seemed to be making. She'd never even noticed he had a softer side before. 'I think it's time we ordered coffee.'

'So it might not be true love; it's certainly got to be an improvement on your old lifestyle.'

Emma thought back to the woodchip walls and brown fitted carpet of her rented flat, mentally comparing and contrasting it with the mezzanine bedroom, floor-to-ceiling windows and exposed brick and stainless steel kitchen of her new home. No competition. But, while she wouldn't be admitting it to anyone soon for fear of being whisked away by a brigade of men in white coats, she did miss the office. Yes, Emma Hunter—make that Carlisle—craved an inadequate salary, a little filing, e-mailing and inconsequential chit-chat with the man across the table, who had always made her feel needed, if only for the mundane things in life.

'Who says it's not love?' She knew she was a hopeless case. A cynical exterior masked a slushy core.

'Do you think he's falling for you?'

Suddenly embarrassed, Emma went on the offensive. 'What's it got to do with you?'

'That's no way to speak to the man who gave you away.'

Emma twiddled her earring distractedly. 'Maybe…'

'Really?' Patrick was far more interested than he dared to admit.

'Of course. Wouldn't you be?'

'Of course.' Patrick didn't skip a beat and stared into her eyes.

Unnerved, Emma looked away and focused on realigning her dessert spoon with her fork. 'Look, he's an actor. It's hard to know what to believe.'

'Well, if I had you waiting for me when I got home…'

By giving Emma to Jack he had made the ultimate sacrifice for his career…or at least that was how it was starting to feel…

Emma balled her napkin and threw it across the table. 'Stop setting the cause of women back hundreds of years. The day I am at home waiting impatiently for Jack to come back so I can serve him a meal, is the day you know I've been married too long. He's not a bad cook himself anyway. Not all men think home-cooked food comes from Marks & Spencer.'

Patrick didn't like being laughed at. At least not by Emma. 'Look.' He folded her napkin and passed it back to her. 'The Naked Chef was still in nappies when I was growing up. Plus, M&S even sell perforated clingfilm. No more wrestling with the whole roll, and you can microwave almost anything.'

'Pathetic.'

'I'm busy running a company.'

'Pathetic.'

'Single.' Patrick looked across the table at his former PA. Katy didn't have an eighth of Emma's personality. 'And please stop. I don't think my ego can take much more.'

'So, anyway, what did you want to discuss over lunch?

I'm beginning to think that meals with you are probably dangerous.'

'I make some of my best business decisions over lunch,' Patrick boasted.

'Exactly. That's how I got into this mess in the first place.'

'Mess?'

'I mean this Mrs Carlisle ruse is all very entertaining and, hey, the last few months have been a blast—really, they have—but who I am kidding? I don't even *like* having facials, and I hate the idea that he's scrutinising what I spend.'

'Not to worry. I'm expensing this. Wife of client, you know…'

'It's farcical. We have joint credit cards and we don't even have a joint CD collection.'

'Come on—think of the advantages. And it sounds like you had a fabulous honeymoon…'

Emma hesitated. Somehow with Patrick she couldn't just give the glossy overview.

'Nice little bikini number, too…'

The photos had, of course, made it home long before they had.

Emma was already starting to tire of the two-dimensional aspect of her new life. 'I still don't really know what's going on in his head. Only what he tells me—and to be honest that's not much.'

'It'll take time. It's about trust. And habit.'

'It's just he talks to the media so much, and yet if you read it all he doesn't really give anything away.'

'Then he's cleverer than you think.'

'Maybe.' Emma was disappointed. If she couldn't have a no-frills bitching session with Patrick, who could she talk to?

'Anyway, you haven't actually known each other very long.'

Emma smiled. 'True.' She'd owned goldfish that had lived longer than her relationship with Jack. 'A whirlwind romance…or maybe that should be *faux*mance. We'd be crap on that show *Mr & Mrs.*'

Patrick took another sip from his glass. 'Anyway, enough about him. The reason I invited you out for lunch is…I have a proposition.'

'Can I just remind you that I am married?'

Patrick smiled. 'You are?' He'd been thinking of little else since she'd arrived. 'It's just…the office isn't the same without you.'

'Much quieter, I'll bet.'

'Much less fun.' Understatement of the afternoon. 'We were a good team.'

'Katy not responding to your charms, eh?'

'It's not like that. And she's positively anal when it comes to keeping the filing up to date.' Patrick stopped himself. A secretary who loved filing anything other than her nails, was hardly cause for complaint.

'Sounds like a keeper. So, what's the problem? Not pretty enough for you?'

'She's gorgeous. In a very obvious way.' Her legs were mesmerising.

'Of course. So you don't fancy her at all, then?' Emma raised her eyebrow goadingly as she downed a long overdue glass of water, before realising it was only going to make a trip to the Ladies more pressing.

'Nope.' Well, not as much as he fancied Emma.

'And you didn't welcome her to the company with a bottle of champagne and lunch for two at the Ivy?'

'That's tradition.' Patrick knew his defence was weak.

'That's attempted seduction. So maybe you'll have to do some real work for a change now, instead of stealing Cupid's.'

'I suppose.'

His office wasn't the same, his life wasn't the same. And she was playing with him.

'But I guess this is what happens when you sell your PA to the highest bidder.'

'Come on, an hour ago when you told me that your honeymoon surpassed all expectations you didn't sound like you were complaining.'

'I hadn't had a three-week holiday since I was at university. And, yes, it was great. But what happens next? Now we're married, I mean. I don't have a purpose any more.'

'To love and honour? To produce a son and heir?' Patrick was doing his best.

'That's not a full-time job. Besides, I need to do something for *me*. I guess I could do some charity work.' Emma sat up a little straighter, encouraged by the thought of more responsibility, more social interaction and less free time in a week.

Patrick sniggered. 'That didn't take long.'

'Pardon?'

He took another sip. 'You just said you could do some *charidee* work. You're so *Hello!* already.'

'Well, I could. What?' Emma knew Patrick well enough to notice the flash of something in his eyes.

'I might have something for you.' He congratulated himself. He was a genius.

'I wasn't thinking of the Patrick Robson Ironing Pile charity.'

'What do you take me for?' Patrick didn't allow her time to respond. 'Seriously, I've been asked to publicise a comedy night. It's a stand-up charity benefit for single mums… Damn, what are they called…?'

'Sleep-deprived busy people? Mums on the open mike?'

'Bugger. Erm…'

Emma could almost see the cogs turning as Patrick did his best to prove he still had a memory.

'Lone parents. That's it.'

'So, what? You help raise a ton of money so one day they can afford to go out and have a night as good as the one *you* are having to generate some cash for them? Surely it would be easier if people just volunteered to go and babysit for a single mum so they could pop out and enjoy the show instead?'

'Yeah, yeah.'

'I'm being serious. I can see it now. "Stand-aLone Comedy presents: Give Mum the night off…"' Emma reached into her new Furla handbag and, plucking out a gleaming Mont Blanc rollerball, started scribbling on a napkin.

'Hey, I like that…' Patrick rubbed his chin. 'And, more to the point, I think the media will love it. Especially if we get a few celebrities on board. I know you won't like this, but…'

'No.'

'I haven't said a word.'

'You don't have to. Don't tell me—Jack would be perfect?'

Patrick loved the way that he didn't even have to finish his sentences whenever Emma was around. It was a wave-length thing.

'So basically you're using me to get to my husband?'

'Hardly. Look, we could do two nights. A gala fundraiser and then… Are you sure you don't want to come back to work?'

Emma wasn't listening. As she scribbled away she provided a voiceover to her thoughts. 'Obviously it should be sit-down, not stand-up comedy. Much more popular. A bit like sitcoms.'

Patrick tried to keep up with her thoughts. 'Which of course is an abbreviation for *situation* comedy…'

'Oh, I always thought it was comedy you sat down for—usually on your sofa at home.'

'Emma…'

'It could be. It *could.*'

'Come on—come back to work. You know you want to. I miss you…' Patrick paused for effect as Emma looked up from her napkin notes to see how serious he was. 'And Katy can't make strong tea to save her life.' Under pressure, he'd lightened the tone. 'I mean you'd probably—'

'I'd love to.' Emma's answer got lost in his sales pitch.

'—only have to do a few days a week.' Patrick couldn't resist a grin as he heard her, a few seconds later. 'Well, that's that, then. Let's order another bottle...'

'But you know I can't.'

Patrick crossed his arms and allowed his shoulders to slump.

Emma wondered whether all men were still boys bluffing maturity. 'Come on, we both know you can't always have what you want.'

Patrick stopped in his tracks. Had that been a come on? Or merely the timely use of a proverb?

'Anyway, enough about me. How about you? Mrs Robson number three being lined up yet?'

Patrick sighed. 'That doesn't sound good, does it?'

'Depends if you're talking to numbers one and two, I'd imagine.'

'No one.' Patrick fiddled with his napkin. 'There was a potential candidate on the horizon, but she slipped out of the race.' Not so much slipped as was pushed. And only himself to blame.

'Had to go to university, did she?' Emma arched an eyebrow.

'Are you never going to let me forget Jo?'

'No way.'

'I admit she was pretty young. Well, pretty and young and looked much older—and I was a man in the throes of a midlife crisis. At the mercy of my hormones.'

'Glad to hear nothing's changed, then.'

'Seriously, Em, I felt like her dad. She hung on my every word as if it were educational and she thought Fleetwood Mac was a type of raincoat.'

Emma laughed and wiped her eyes, before blowing her nose on her napkin and wishing she'd used a tissue.

'Most of my finest wooing moments were down to your ideas.'

'Well, maybe you should set yourself up with a client.

Apparently it's all the rage. Forget PR. Start a dating agency.'

'It seems to have done wonders for you,' Patrick's voice was almost a whisper.

'I still can't quite believe it. And Jack seems to be dead keen on the married life thing—which is, of course, making me more reticent…or maybe just nervous.'

'Women.'

'Yeah, go on. Try and write us off as a flawed race when *you're* the ones with the problems.' Emma paused as her thoughts gathered. 'It's just—well, how can he really know who I am? I mean, what really makes me tick?' Emma wondered if post-marital depression existed. She should have been on top of the world.

'How can anyone?'

'Yeah, but most people meet and date, rather than start dating as a result of a meeting. I mean, what happens next?' Emma asked, not quite rhetorically.

Patrick chickened out and decided to steer the conversation back to shore. 'Seriously, why don't you just do some freelance for me? A couple of days a week? When you have time between facials…and charity functions…'

'I don't think it's what Jack had in mind for me.'

'What about what I have in mind for you?'

Patrick put his hand on Emma's. His skin was hot, but dry, and she could feel his pulse throbbing. Her heart pounded irresponsibly at his touch. Could it be that they'd shared an office when they should have been sharing a…?

'Hello, you two.'

By the time Emma looked up Patrick's hand was nowhere to be seen. Master of illusion. In fact, maybe she had hallucinated the whole moment. She couldn't even remember the last time she'd had her eyes tested.

'Amy. So glad you could make it.' Relieved and annoyed at the same time, Emma poured herself a fresh glass of water and forced herself to drink it as Patrick cocked a brow questioningly

'Patrick, you remember Amy from the wedding?'

'Of course.' Irritated, he folded his arms and leant against the back of the booth. It was his own fault for taking everything so slowly. They'd been there for hours.

Amy slid herself on to the bench seat, next to Patrick and started talking to Emma. 'I'm not stopping for long. I have to collect the kids in a minute. But I was having my annual "where do we go from here?" lunch with my agent when I picked up your message, and I couldn't miss the opportunity to snatch a quick coffee with more grown-ups.' Amy looked around the table for evidence of a coffee-time moment. 'Are you two still on wine? It's nearly four o'clock, you know.'

'It is?' Emma looked at her watch, wondering if her teeth were stained as red as they felt. Hey, she was sure Jack could buy her new ones if necessary. 'We're just catching up. So, how was your meeting?'

'Fine.' Amy caught the attention of a waiter and ordered three coffees. The mother of the party had arrived. 'Basically, the ball's in my court. Either I try and write another book or I don't. And I do it now or in ten years, when I have more time.'

'You can have some of my time if you like.'

'How about I lend you the children for a month or two?'

'I wouldn't know where to start.'

'With hips like yours you'd be a natural.'

Emma smiled momentarily and then retracted it. With hips like hers? So she had curves. Amy had Pilates.

'Look, I'm joking—plus, I wouldn't trade my family in for anything. Getting married was the best thing I ever did,' Amy said.

'Cheers to that.' Patrick winked at Emma as they raised their glasses and the coffee arrived.

'So I guess I've missed all the gory honeymoon details,

then?' Not since she'd been pregnant had Amy felt so behind in the alcohol stakes, although inhaling Emma's breath
would probably get her off to a pretty good start.

'Emma's been playing those cards very close to her chest.'
Patrick smiled to himself. It was the sort of chest that definitely encouraged thoughts of playing.

'Makes a change, I guess.'

Emma gave her best friend a sidelong glance. She'd always
been discreet. And Amy had always been able to wind her
up. Some things were still exactly the same.

The bill was settled, it was getting dark, and Emma was
rummaging in her bag for pre-emptive ibuprofen and something minty for her breath.

'Just come back to the office with me for a minute.' Patrick
was being surprisingly firm as they walked down Piccadilly.

'I'll pop over soon. Right now I just need a cab.' Emma's
shoes had been designed for ladies who lunched, not ladies
who walked.

Patrick stopped. 'I want you to meet Katy.'

Emma sighed. Female irrationality dictated that she was
reluctant to see someone else at her desk. 'Why? Want my
approval before you take her to bed?'

'Don't be ridiculous.' Patrick did his best not to smirk. Katy
had been no challenge at all.

Emma kept walking and Patrick took extra-long strides
until he had caught up with her. 'OK, let's share a cab and
you can drop me at the office on your way home.'

Within seconds they were in transit, and then, just as she
was succumbing to the comfort of her seat, she heard him
give the driver his home address.

'Patrick…'

'Yes?' Now, facing her, he wasn't even looking embarrassed
at his blatant deception. Nor was he looking smug, just hopeful and—something Emma definitely wasn't—in control.

She tilted her head inquisitively, in case she felt more sober at forty-five degrees. 'Working from home these days, are you?'

He took her hand, brought it up to his lips and kissed it. 'Please?'

Please? Patrick Robson—chief executive, chief sounding board, and one of the handful of people on the planet who knew her best—was requesting permission to seduce her a mere month after, at *his* suggestion and as her shelf-life was coming to an end, she had married someone else. Obviously the answer was no. Not that she had managed to utter a sound between the hand kissing moment and now. So apparently not obviously at all.

She beckoned to Patrick to come closer and whispered in his ear. 'You're drunk.'

He nodded unapologetically. 'Dutch courage was required. Mine has proved totally inadequate so far.'

'In a world where timing is everything, yours sucks.' Emma's mind raced as she tried to get a handle on the developing situation.

Patrick nodded culpably. 'I know.'

A joint glance revealed that the taxi-driver was either talking to himself or was on his hands-free mobile phone on the other side of the glass partition. But, both his passengers knew that, if you were even a glint in the public eye, the cab-driving fraternity were best treated with trepidation.

'I can't risk it.'

Emma sat back, analysing her behaviour. Did that mean that, anonymity assured, she was actually saying yes to undercover relations? Was this her first post-marital grass is greener moment? She'd never thought about Patrick as anyone other than her employer—except after one Christmas lunch in the midst of her most barren single year to date, when frankly she'd been finding everyone attractive—even Nicolas Cage. Shaking her head at the absurdity of the situation, she wished she'd drunk a lot more water at lunch.

'Fuck me.' The words just fell out of Emma's mouth. The rest of her was miles away.

Patrick eyes, still focused on her, widened considerably. 'Blimey, I wasn't expecting you to be quite so—'

'It wasn't a command.'

'Shame.' Patrick rested his hand on Emma's and gazed out of the window absently.

She studied the side of his head from the temple down, observing the four-thirty shadow on his jaw and the positively tanned skin on his neck against the crisp white of his shirt. She failed to suppress a smile at the lunacy of her afternoon. The last time she'd shared a back seat with him had been on the way to her wedding.

eight

'Yup, we'll see you on Saturday, Dad.' As his father continued to witter, Jack made himself a fresh pot of coffee. Multitasking was so much easier with a portable phone.

Opening the fridge for milk, he did a double take at the variety of food neatly organised on the shelves. Life had changed. For a start there were two of them. A permanent state of affairs—or, at least so far, a state of *no* affairs. For a finish there were fresh vegetables. As for the influx of tea, he'd never realised there were so many different types. Brand-new leaves for the both of them.

Tuning back into the conversation just at the point a sentence ended, Jack pressed his subconscious for clues as to what was required of him in the way of a response. To his relief, his father started to sign off. Off the hook, scot-free and smiling as he said goodbye and hung up, finally he felt he was doing something right. And his father was keen to spend as much time as possible with his first ever daughter.

Pouring himself a cup of caffeine, Jack punted Emma's enormous inflatable exercise ball out of the way. For the first time in five years his flat was feeling a little on the small side. Wandering back to the lounge area of his riverside loft apartment and sitting back in his favourite battered leather armchair, he kicked his designer trainers off and, socks patchy with sweat, rested his feet on the matching footstool. Sipping his drink, he watched a police boat patrolling the Thames.

He hadn't been down to Greenhill since Charlie died.

It had only been three years, yet most days it felt like a lifetime. And if anyone deserved to be alive it was his brother. Jack might have cheated his way to pole position, yet for reasons of a posthumous pedestal nature he knew he would never come close to winning. The familiar hollowness started to engulf him. In the immediate aftermath he'd run round Battersea Park every day until his lungs had felt as if they were going to explode and all he could think about was breathing. It had been Charlie and Jack for thirty-one years and then it hadn't.

Jack pursed his lips and blinked hard. He knew his father looked at him and wanted to see Charlie. It didn't help that the Carlisle genes had imparted them both with the same hairline, the same thick dark hair and blue eyes, the same laughter lines.

Charles had been a romantic. He'd have loved Emma, but he'd have hated Jack's arbitrary decision to marry. Indeed, he'd travelled to all four corners of the globe in search of true love—if a globe had corners, that was. And then his downfall: a woman in distress. Her knight in shiny Church's brogues had been an inadequate match for a mugger flying high on drugs. A gun. In London. Loaded. Fired. They'd kept him alive. If you could be alive without any brain stem function. And then, three months of PVS later, a decision that no parent should ever have to make.

Jack closed his eyes a moment too late to stop a tear escaping and he wiped it away automatically. The pain was still there every morning, when he realised he was an only child.

He needed distraction. Jack checked his watch. Emma had warned him about Patrick's lunches. But his audition had been rescheduled and he'd ended up having all afternoon on his own. Exhaling deeply, he allowed his head to tip back on to the top of the armchair and stared up at the high ceiling. This was exactly the sort of moment when the drugs had helped. Uppers, downers, the highs, the lows—days and weeks merging until a month had passed, then a year.

Forcing himself to get to his feet, he put on a favourite Marvin Gaye CD and reached for his press file. As he re-read the feature articles and the positive reviews he could feel the pendulum of his mood shifting back to centre and beyond. Approval was the only legal drug that helped him now.

Closing his eyes, he projected an old favourite family photo onto the back of his eyelids. Two boys on the beach at Salcombe, during the hot summer of 1976, slaves to the fashions of yesteryear in matching terry towelling beachwear, slathered in inadequate sunscreen. Their beautiful young mother, vital, standing between them, hands proudly resting on the shoulders of her progeny. He felt a fist of tears welling up in his chest and washed it down with coffee, berating his sentimentality.

It wasn't as if he was alone. Emma had been through the emotional mill too— the yellowing photo of her parents on their own wedding day on her night-table the only clue that she missed them. He admired her self-reliance, her inner strength and her buoyancy. And her breasts.

Silently, Jack had words with his testosterone for the inappropriate timing of that last thought. Both Emma's parents had been taken from her in one evening. Impossible to predict. Yet no one had even told him his mother was ill. He'd been away at school when she'd died, and his father had been abroad on location. Charlie had been sent to explain. No goodbyes. No last messages. If he closed his eyes hard enough he could still conjure up her smell: a mixture of talc, vanilla, roses and something almost buttery.

Waving the remote control in the vague direction of the television, he watched the huge flat screen on the wall come to life. Surfing through the channels that provided him with much needed portals to a plethora of different worlds, Jack relished the escapism available without having to put on your shoes and leave the house. No immunisations, packing or passports required.

His father's Oscar-winning performance was just drawing to a close on a classic movie channel, Schwarzenegger was playing the suited politician on a news programme, and then, a few clicks of the remote later, was starring in an action-adventure flick from ten years ago. The line between fantasy and reality was becoming increasingly blurred. Jack found an old Superman movie playing on an eighties film channel before closing his eyes and promptly falling asleep.

Emma stared at the greying hair on Patrick's chest from her resting position in the crook of his arm, the smell of sex all around them. Her throat was parched from a combination of exertion, the aftermath of arousal, and the surfeit of alcohol over lunch. A shroud of guilt descended to bed level. Acutely aware of her engagement and wedding rings, she attempted to roll away. She'd let herself down.

Patrick opened an eye and stroked her hair tenderly before kissing the top of her head.

'Probably my best lunch ever.'

Not a hint of his usual sarcasm. And Emma had been hoping it was a mutual one-night stand—or, more accurately, a one-afternoon lie. Nervously she faked a laugh. Hell, she'd just faked an orgasm. She needed to make as swift an exit as possible. While the tumbling in to bed had been fun, the tumbling out was making her feel nothing short of slutty.

'Amazing. All those years together in that office and it's only after you leave that I realise what an idiot I've been…'

Patrick was apparently also the king of pillow talk. Emma wished he would just pass out and let her sneak off. Trust her to get the one man who was more awake after sex than he was before it. She, on the other hand, wanted to sleep for ever.

'I know it's a cliché, but you really don't know what you've got 'til it's—'

'Don't, Patrick.' Emma raised her arm to silence him. 'How about, you always want what you can't have…?'

'Or absence makes the heart grow fonder…?'

Emma had no idea what to do with Patrick's direct, if corny, declarations. Instead she busied herself with the urgent matter of underwear retrieval. Finally she clamped her toes round her bra, entwined with the duvet near the foot of the mattress, and, ape-like, brought it up to her hand.

It hadn't been the best sex of her life, but it certainly hadn't been the worst—even with her ever-expanding guilt complex. Maybe she was one of those women who needed more than one man? Emma couldn't help but grin grimly at her misdiagnosis. She'd managed for years without even a whiff of one. Sitting up, she started getting dressed. What had she been thinking?

'Don't you think you should have a shower?' Patrick was propped up on his pillows, watching her.

Emma nodded as she unhooked her bra, this time shyly. It was a very valid point. Men were clearly better prepared in terms of lateral afterthought when it came to matters of infidelity.

Emma was just running her hands over her hair to ensure it was evenly soaked before she realised her mistake. 'Jesus Christ!'

'I swear I haven't touched the taps.'

Emma did her best to take Patrick's presence in the bathroom in her stride. She was pretty sure he wasn't peeing, but she couldn't be sure, and she really didn't want to check. Unfortunately his bathroom didn't have a lock on the door. She kept her eyes closed.

'No, you idiot,' Frustrated by her own mistake, Emma shook her head under the jet. 'I don't suppose you've got a hairdryer here?'

'Erm, no…just a towel or two.'

'In which case I'm going to have wet hair.'

'It'll dry.'

'Eventually. And I'm not sure Jack's going to fall for an "I slipped and fell into an ice bucket" kind of explanation as to why his wife… Crap. I'm a wife. Brilliant. Never two-timed as a singleton, and now I'm married and behaving like an eighteen-year-old. I think I should be put down for the good of the nation.'

Patrick laughed. 'You do make me laugh.'

Blinking, Emma wiped the water from her eyes and scanned the paltry collection of bottles on the side of the bath. Shampoo for grey hair—the consequences of which she wasn't prepared to risk on her blondey-brown, high and lowlighted tresses—and a selection of male-scented shower gels, all with the words 'cool', 'wave', 'ice' or 'water' proudly printed on their labels in assertion of their masculinity.

Damn and double damn. First of all she couldn't arrive home smelling like the Gillette girl. Plus, based on her current performance, she wasn't the best a man could get. Secondly, in the absence of John Frieda serums, her hair would become a frizzball—so much for effortless style. Indeed she was scrunchieless, hairbrushless, dryerless, and late. And at this rate was going to have an afro by the time she got back to Chelsea.

'Have you got anything neutral—less man, more unisex?'

Totally naked, Patrick was standing on the bathmat, his arms folded across his chest as he surveyed his afternoon's work. 'I'm all man.'

Emma did her best to keep her gaze at eye-level. He was

in pretty good shape for his age. To her horror, he lifted a leg as if to climb into the bath and join her in the shower. Taking up as much space as possible, Emma managed to channel a jet of water along her arm, directing it onto his chest with her elbow, and then subtly raised it to face level, hoping to get him in the contact lens.

Stepping back, he reached for a towel. She was safe.

'That wasn't in question. Now, please, how about some soap?'

Patrick handed her a bar of Imperial Leather from the basin. 'Need a hand or two?'

Her life had become a soap opera.

'No, thanks.'

One vehement session of towel hairdrying and the creative use of elastic bands later, all clocks were pointing to seventy-twenty p.m. And she was in Primrose Hill. She had to call home.

Jack was flying around the world at speed, the vapour trails from his cape ensuring the globe was looking increasingly like a ball of string in his dream world, when suddenly his sixth sense picked up an electronic ringing sound. Somewhere in the world, someone was in trouble. A damsel in distress? A minibus full of children teetering on the edge of a cliff? The noise pierced his consciousness again. Opening his eyes, he was transported back to reality. Jack reached for the phone.

'Hello?'

He didn't know if he'd been out cold for five minutes or five hours.

The phone was still ringing. Sheepishly, Jack replaced the remote control he was holding to his ear with the handset still on the coffee table. They all looked the same.

'Hello?' He struggled to focus on his watch. Only seventy-thirty, but he was still alone in the flat by the look of things.

'Jack, hi. It's Amy.'

'Oh, hello there.' Jack yawned and stretched in his chair, feeling his spine extend.

'I didn't wake you, did I?' Amy wondered if he was naked and hastily changed the screensaver in her mind. Talk about Emma landing on her feet. The man actually had a six pack. Or at least he'd had one in the 1999 calendar Tim had found for her on eBay. Emma's birthday present was sorted now.

'I must have dozed off in front of the television. How's things? And how are the girls doing?'

'They're great. Hopefully just drifting off to sleep as we speak.'

'Send them my love tomorrow, then.'

'Will do. Now, any chance you could unchain Mrs Carlisle from the kitchen sink…?'

…or the bedframe. Ovulating, Amy was at the mercy of her hormones today. She'd even thought Patrick was charming earlier. Tim needed to get home from work before nine occasionally.

'I'm afraid she's not back from her lunch yet.'

'Really?' Amy stopped herself. There was bound to be a sensible or not even that sensible explanation. 'Oh, well, there's no such thing as a quick drink with Patrick Robson.'

'So I've heard.'

Jack couldn't have sounded any less bothered. Amy decided to follow suit.

'Can I give her a message?'

'Not to worry, it's not at all urgent. They've probably run into some old friends.' Amy was hoping.

'No doubt she's just enjoying some time on her own. And the press seem to be giving her space when she's not with me.'

'It must be tough.' Amy did her best to empathise, but it was difficult to imagine people being fascinated by her every move. Even Tim didn't seem that interested most of the time.

'Hey, I'm used to it. Comes with the territory.' Jack stopped surfing channels when he stumbled upon the VH1 *Top 100 One Hit Wonders.* They were currently only at fifty-five. His interest in pop music was still adolescent in its fervour. 'I'll tell her you called. Take care.' Rather like Owen Paul, currently strumming his way to obscurity, it was his favourite waste of time.

'And you, Jack.'

Carlisle. Amy put the phone down. She still hadn't quite got used to it.

And what the hell was Emma playing at? Talk about having your cake and leaving it at home. Dialling Emma's mobile, she heard it click straight on to voice mail.

Jack had just retrieved a cold beer from the fridge to accompany his trip down musical memory lane when the landline rang again.

'Hello?' Jack reduced Chesney Hawkes's volume enough to be able to hear his caller.

'Jack. It's me.'

'Hey, me…'

Emma could feel her stomach lurch penitently at his welcoming tone.

Jack smiled, delighted to hear Emma's voice at the end of the phone. 'Good lunch, gorgeous?'

'Yeah, fine.'

'Fine?' Jack clamped his mouth shut before joining in with a chorus. He was the one and only. Far too catchy for its own good.

Standing by his picture window, he stood, feet slightly apart, non-phone-carrying arm aloft, clutching his beer bottle, nodding his head, his silhouette miming to anyone who was looking as he surveyed an imaginary stadium packed with screaming fans.

'Well, you know—lots of banter, lots to catch up on, lots of wine. And then I went to the gym…'

Emma congratulated herself on the perfect excuse for the wet look. Silence in Chelsea.

'Jack?'

He was mid-chorus. If only his real singing voice was as good as the one in his head, he'd have been giving Robbie Williams a run for his money. 'Sorry, I am listening. Hang on—you did say the gym, didn't you…?'

'Yeah, I fancied a swim.'

Emma never ceased to amuse him with her eccentricities. The fact that she danced everywhere—in the supermarket queue, in the driver's seat of her car, in the shower. The fact that she mixed Shreddies with Sultana Bran. That she genuinely liked Westerns. That she could recite every word of dialogue in *Pretty Woman.* That she was happier in House of Fraser than she was in Harvey Nichols. Very few people surprised him, yet he'd married an enigma. A swimming enigma.

'I don't think you're supposed to swim after you've been drinking.'

'I was hardly going to get caught in the undertow at Holmes Place.' Emma froze as Patrick put his arm round her and stroked the small of her back. 'Anyway, just thought I might pick up some takeaway for us on the way home. Can I tempt you with anything in particular?' She'd never been less hungry in her life.

'You mean in the food department?'

Dismissing any possible innuendo, Emma continued with the matter in hand. Much easier, being that everything else was now officially out of hand. 'Why, have you already eaten?'

Jack paused. Had he?

'Jack…?'

'Sorry again. Bit disorientated.'

'Have you been drinking?' Emma wondered how she dared to be accusatory.

'No, no. Just napping, I'm afraid. Not very rock and roll at all.' He swallowed a couple of times to try and jump-start his gastric juices. 'Well, I'm not peckish now. But I'm sure I will be.' Jack checked his watch 'Are you hungry again already?'

Emma balked. It was a valid question. In dinner terms it was still early, and the takeaway detail had really just been there to provide her phone call with a purpose and to see if he was home.

'We can always order in later…or we could go out—there's a new Thai I'd love to try,' Jack suggested.

'I could eat.'

'Did Mr Robson not feed you solids? Or is this a case of hangover avoidance, madam? Careful, or people will be saying you're a bad influence on me…'

Emma laughed. It was the only response she could muster in this frankly ludicrous situation. Patrick was standing behind her, his arms wrapped around her waist, and every hair on her arms and neck was standing to nervous attention. She was surprised Jack couldn't hear him breathing. Her heart was pounding with adrenaline. Like a virgin. Like a mistress. Like a very inexperienced one. No more wine at lunchtime. Ever.

'Unless, of course, you're pregnant already?'

Emma shook herself free and walked into some personal space, ignoring the post-coital heightened awareness between her legs. 'Oh, yeah, you'd love that.'

'I'm beginning to think I wouldn't mind.' Jack surprised himself. Maybe he was growing up? Maybe this was what maturity felt like? After all, he was watching VH1 and not MTV.

Emma pressed 'save' on the situation. She was standing in Patrick's sitting room, discussing starting a family with the man she had shagged less recently. 'It's probably just that post-swimming, vending machine, knee-jerk appetite thing. I only have to immerse myself in chlorinated water and I'm starving.'

'Fuck it, pick something up—whatever you fancy. Just hurry home. Your husband needs you.' Jack suddenly had an image of Emma looking decidedly Bo Derek in a bikini. He'd missed her today. He really ought to take Patrick out for a beer.

'On my way.' Emma hung up and grabbed her coat, ducking and diving as Patrick tried to give her a kiss. 'Enough, enough. I'll call you later—or tomorrow.'

Or never. Emma wondered if the Witness Protection Scheme took American Express. She'd known exactly what Patrick was like, and yet she'd been easier than a Sunday morning.

Emma heard the front door close behind her as she strode towards the main road, forcing herself to look straight ahead. She was convinced her guilt had highlighted her with a neon Ready-Brek glow as she completed the walk of shame to the taxi rank.

nine

Jess reached up to the top shelf of what had until recently been her kitchen cupboard, accessible only by precariously balancing on the retro-American red leather and chrome breakfast-bar stools.

'What are you doing now?' Sarah's irritation wasn't even loosely disguised.

Sarah might not be overtly impressed by her display of cat-burglar agility, but triumphantly Jess retrieved six small items from the back corner and handed them over before jumping down. 'These are my egg cups.'

'You don't even like boiled eggs.'

'That's not the point. Nick told me to take the lot. Something about having enough emotional baggage without physical stuff to boot.'

'Are you sure? Sounds a bit—well, deep for him.'

'Not to leave any of my crap, I believe is what he said.' And she'd be damned if Rosie was going to be eating eggs out of her hand painted Austrian egg cups.

Jess wrapped them in several layers of newspaper at her

packing station on the granite work surface before adding them to the current box and hesitating in front of the stainless steel fridge door.

Her shadow butted in. 'You touch a fridge magnet and you can finish this job on your own.' Sarah's tone was pure Mafia and not to be messed with. 'Firstly, you don't even have your own fridge at the moment. Secondly, we are in the minimalist kitchen age. No tea cosies, no rainbow-coloured plastic, and absolutely no crap stuck on the fridge this side of children.' She knew she didn't have long before Millie would be smearing pots of paint onto huge pieces of paper, creating pictures she would not only have to treasure but display. 'Now, have you finished sorting the CDs?'

Fortunately for Jess, Sarah hadn't factored in any time for sentimentality this afternoon.

'Almost…'

Chivvying her sister into the sitting room, Sarah was amazed by the number of boxes waiting to be sealed. The bookshelves had been decimated, and there were stacks of CDs on the floor. Sarah walked over to begin a site inspection. 'Where are his?'

'On the shelf.'

Sarah glanced at the paltry pile of rejects before taking a step closer and squatting down to sift through a few titles as Jess started filling another box. 'Aerosmith, Coldplay, The Doors, Morcheeba, Jamiroquai, Justin Timberlake, Diana Krall—well, I can believe the last two or three are yours…'

'Whose side are you on? Nick rarely bought any music.'

'These are just material possessions.'

'Well, in case you haven't noticed, we live in a material world. And they're mine.'

'Listen to me, my little Madonna, you were hoping to get Nick back a couple of weeks ago, and now you won't leave Coldplay behind?'

'Why should I?'

"'All that I am I give to you, all that I have I share with you.'" Sarah's delivery was one hundred percent vicar.

'I never said that...' Jess stood up indignantly. 'Fine. I'll leave them all for him. For them.'

'Ah, so *that's* your problem. Jess, you made your bed, now you have to lie in it.'

'For fuck's sake, Sarah, please. That sort of trite bullshit isn't going to help.' Especially as she couldn't even curl up on her own mattress. The bed was staying. Jess wished she could be as semi-detached as the house. She sat down on the floor in a combination of protest and exhaustion.

Sarah leant in towards her sister. 'Don't push me Jess. It's Saturday, Millie is being looked after, and the shops are open. But I'm here, trying to help.' Her patience was wearing thinner than Calista Flockhart.

Jess lay back on the cream rug she'd chosen in Habitat just over a year ago, folded her arms across her chest and did her best not to cry. She was separating their record collection, she was living the cliché. And it was far worse in reality than she had ever imagined. He wanted to buy her out so he could move on. Only she was the one who had to move out.

'Sorry, Sar.' Jess mumbled the apology out of the corner of her mouth as, recomposing herself, she sat up and, leaving the CDs in the hope that they might sort themselves, bravely opened the last cupboard in the sitting room. Alongside their random selection of board games and the occasional removed-from-public-display dud Christmas present, were their photo albums—and then, face down in the corner; the framed photos that had once adorned the bookshelves and the mantelpiece.

Jess turned the top one over. Smiling from within the dark leather frame were a carefree young couple on safari in Kenya at sunset, cans of beer in their hands. Nick still had hair, and a hint of a stomach muscle. Peering into the back of the cupboard, Jess could see piles of photos piled up in their sleeves. His or hers? They had officially gone from 'we' to 'me'.

Sarah had silently traversed the room and, having given her sister a supportive and apologetic peck on the top of the head, was now peering over Jess's shoulder. 'It'll all get easier, but right now you have to go upstairs and finish off there. We've already been four hours, and we promised Nick we'd be out of here by five…'

Eight years of a joint life physically erased in one afternoon.

'Plus, Simon and I are out tonight so I need time to get ready…'

A gem of information. At last Jess could collapse in front of the television on her own—or at least she might be able to if she wasn't still unloading her stuff into her father's loft. Why they couldn't have designed the week to give you a couple of extra hours on a Saturday, she didn't know. The ratio of weekend to weekday was all wrong.

'Just look at this place. He'd get one hell of a shock if he walked in now—'

To Sarah's horror it was, as they say in the trade, perfect timing.

'Ladies…'

Lucy rushed up to her long-lost mistress, her wagging tail polishing a semi-circle of floorboards as she sat down, her master and commander right behind her. Stunned, Jess wished she hadn't decided to wear her oldest, no-longer-fashionable jeans and a security blanket of a skiing fleece. Plus, she couldn't remember if she'd even bothered with lip-gloss, let alone mascara, this morning.

'Nick. Hi. What are you…?' Sarah checked her watch, even though she knew it was only four p.m.—unless, of course, she'd failed to change her watch to British Summertime at the end of March and had been living a lie for more than six months.

'Apologies. Promise I'm not checking up on you, but I forgot my glasses and I'm off to the cinema in a bit.'

Sarah watched his eyes drink in the chaos all around him as he kissed her hello before transferring his attention to Jess, who apparently was glued to the spot, pretending to be totally absorbed by Lucy.

Jess sat in the middle of the floor, marooned, unable to process this twist in her afternoon. Nick. Here. Going to the cinema later. Having a life. She hadn't actually seen him since dinner on the eve of their wedding, and since her return their contact had been perfunctory—always by phone, and nothing short of businesslike. He looked tired. But he looked so comfortingly familiar that she thought she was going to be sick. The same faded jeans, the same Timberlands stained with creosote from their mad gardening afternoon last year, the charcoal-grey lambswool round-neck jumper that she'd bought him for Christmas, his cheeks ruddy from a cocktail of fresh air, emotion and embarrassment.

Sarah excused herself, muttering about sealing boxes, checking the van and summoning Simon for assistance with the loading. While part of her wanted to stay and listen, most of her couldn't get out of that sitting room fast enough.

Sticking to his story, Nick picked his glasses up from the coffee table. Concerned the moment might pass them by altogether, they both started talking at once. An awkward silence followed. Sentimental ebb and flow.

Nick opened the batting. 'You look well.'

'I do?' Jess rubbed at her tan apologetically. 'Thanks.' She didn't feel well. Bloody melanin. But she wished she'd found time to blowdry her hair first thing, instead of feeding Millie.

Nick looked round at his empty shelves, at the absent magazine rack, noted the lack of floor cushions and the exposed picture hooks crudely protruding from his white sitting room walls. 'Well, it looks like I'm going to have to buy a few new pictures for a start. Or maybe I'll hang a dartboard in here and rebel.'

Jess did her best to force a smile and then paused. She

couldn't do small talk. Not yet. 'I wish you'd told me yourself…'

Nick stared at her blankly.

'You know—about Rosie. I mean, what did you think I would do?'

His gaze flitted around the room. 'I wanted to tell you face to face. I thought it was only fair.'

'Bullshit, Nick. You're a coward.' Jess was surprised at the aggressiveness of her tone. There had been two ways to handle this and she'd probably picked the wrong one. Thirty-two years old and still so much to learn.

'*I'm* a coward?' Finally his eye contact was direct—and steely.

'Well, I've been back two weeks, and this is the first time we've actually seen each other. It's not fair to give Fi your dirty work.' Jess made a mental note to be a bit more grateful for her best friend. It was all give and no take in Fiona's world at the moment.

Nick's phone rang and, raising a hand of apology, he turned away. Walking over to the window, he answered it.

'Hey, you.'

Jess froze. It clearly wasn't his mother or his sister. She watched the back of his head as he stared into the garden.

'Sounds great. I'll see you outside at six-forty-five. I've booked the tickets. Perfect. Sweet popcorn for me. *A bientôt.*'

French. He was speaking bloody French. Not that it had much to do with her. Correction: it had everything to do with her.

'Sorry.' Putting his phone away, he turned to face the room. 'Where was I?'

Jess couldn't say anything. She could barely see. And she didn't do jealousy. Or at least she hadn't before. But then, if there had always been one certainty in life it had been that Nick loved her more than anything. But that had been before. And this was definitely after.

Nick sensed the change in her demeanour. 'Look, this isn't going to be easy for any of us, Jess, but we can at least have a stab at being grown-ups about it. It's been one hell of a month. And, not wishing to be childish about this, you started it. This wasn't what I had planned at all. I mean, the quote came back for the loft conversion this week. Not much point now, is there?'

Jess sat there numbly. They'd been expanding. Now they were contracting. Her gaze falling on the antique pine coffee table, Jess decided to let it go. In the grand scheme of things, she had no room.

'But…Rosie?'

'You know we've always got on well.'

'There's well and there's *well,* Nick.'

'Face it, I've seen more of her than I have of you in recent months.'

'That's because she was helping to plan *our* wedding.'

'Which you decided to cancel. Another case when surely face to face would have been preferable to the bloody telephone. You called it off—literally. Don't you think I deserved more?'

'I still can't believe it. I mean rebound, fair enough, but talk about close to home.'

'I don't know how you have the audacity to play the victim this time, Jess.'

Immersed in their own hurt, neither Nick nor Jess could apparently see the bigger picture. Everything was passport-sized in their world at the moment.

Nick fiddled with his watch strap. 'Anyway I'm not sure that it *is* rebound.'

'Of course it is. You just panicked.' Jess was certain.

'I don't panic.'

'Everyone panics sometimes. Have you never suddenly had the urge to shout in a library, or wanted to sprint when you're sitting on a long-haul flight, just because you know you can't?'

Nick paused for thought. 'I don't think so.'

'Well, when faced with the thought of you at the end of the aisle, when staring lifelong commitment in the eye, I suddenly had the urge to run.'

'And the ability, it would appear.'

'I'm trying to explain, Nick. I just needed time to think.'

'On our *honeymoon*? You certainly pick your moments.'

'I hadn't had a minute in years to check I still knew what I was doing. Suddenly it felt like nothing was my choice any more.'

'Rosie says—'

'Rosie has no fucking right to say anything…' Bugger. Jess knew as soon as she stopped for breath that she had just made a grave and intractable error. At least with e-mail you could re-read and edit before pressing 'send', in order to become the best possible version of yourself.

St Nick, on the other hand, just stood there. Calmness and sanity personified. 'Jess, sweetheart, look…' the term of endearment was causing a procession of tears to form an orderly queue '…this isn't just about you. OK, so you say you're ready now. Did you really think everything would just ping back to normal when you got back?'

'Of course not. Not right away. I mean, I was sort of hoping that you would…' *They* hadn't been to the cinema in months, possibly a year.

'What? Turn up at the airport with flowers and beg you to reconsider?' Nick put his hands on his hips. 'You've always only seen everything from your point of view. I've tried so hard over the years to keep up, yet your focus keeps moving. I just dropped off the edge of your horizon and that hurts.' Nick's neck reddened and Jess tried to watch his eyes closely as he began an intensive study of his boots.

Her silence spoke for itself.

Nick studied the woman he'd thought he'd be married to. 'Jess, I loved you more than anything.' Producing a hanky from his jeans pocket, he blew his nose vigorously. 'But talk about blowing hot and cold. Sahara to Siberia in one fucking gust. And it's not like it's the first time. I know this is my fault too. When you ask someone to marry you and they say no, you should leave. Not wait three years and then browbeat them into agreeing.'

'You didn't force me into anything. I love you.'

Nick froze.

'Nick?'

Sitting down on their sofa, he slumped forward and rubbed his temples with his fingers. 'I'd love to believe that.'

'I do. Honestly I do.'

'Yet when you rang me from the villa you didn't mention it.'

'Of course I did.'

'Jess, you didn't. You said you missed me.'

'I did. I'm sure I did.' Jess could feel her breath shortening.

Nick shook his head. His voice was smaller now, but definite. His eye contact was absolute. 'You didn't.'

Boys weren't supposed to remember details like that. Especially when she couldn't even recall the finer ones herself.

'And even if you do still love me, you can't just throw that into the conversation and expect everything to be better. I'm not some sort of puppy, you know. It's not enough.'

'Of course not.' *Why not?*

'You're probably thinking why not…'

Jess nodded. Simply so predictable. Or so it would appear, at least where Nick was concerned. And to think she'd thought that too much knowledge was a bad thing, or at least a boring thing. It was so good to see him. She wanted to give him a hug. She wanted to make him laugh. Yet she had forfeited all rights.

'I know you inside out and you turned me inside out. Hardly fair, is it?'

'No.' Contrite, Jess didn't know what else to say. If she

stuck to answering his questions she hoped to avoid any further trouble.

A semi-sigh as Nick sank back in the cushions. 'You say you love me. You also love blue skies, sunny days, crunchy apples and slightly warm Minstrels. But you're not in love with me. Or at least you'll never be able to give me the one hundred and fifty percent you give to your work, and I can't be with eighty per cent of you. I need to put myself first. I want to have a family…'

Jess nodded. She knew. Trust her to get a man with a biological clock more audible than her own.

'I always thought it would be us. But how could I even have thought about us having children when we weren't spending any quality time together. When was the last time we had a whole weekend together? Or even a lazy morning in bed? Birthdays and Christmas don't count.'

Jess racked her brains… 'Bank holiday Monday, in May.' Admittedly not stunningly recently, but definitely this decade—in fact, less than six months ago.

'You had flu.'

'It wasn't really flu.'

'You were in bed all day. My presence was almost incidental.'

'Look, I know my job involves anti-social hours—'

'Understatement of the millennium.'

'Nick.' Jess could feel her hackles rising. 'It's what I do. It's who I am.'

'And you know how proud I am. I know how far you've come. It's phenomenal, really. People now associate Jessica James with perfect weddings.'

Jess grimaced. It wasn't just ironic. And it would have been in incredibly bad taste coming from anyone but Nick.

'Your profile is rocketing. Business is booming. But I come a pretty poor second these days, don't I?'

Jess couldn't understand his obsession with ranking. But

then she couldn't understand much at the moment. 'You know I couldn't have done all this without you.'

'Well, then, maybe my job is over.'

Jess couldn't believe the calm emanating from her ex-sofa. 'She's brainwashed you.'

'She?'

'You know exactly who I'm talking about.'

'Please, Jess, credit me with my own opinions. I've had to rethink my whole future and I'm tired of being reactive. I need to move forward. I'm not getting any younger. Chris and I have spent many evenings nursing a couple of pints on the subject.'

'Chris?' Jess hadn't even thought about all their friends. 'He and Mel hate me, obviously…'

'Obviously. Come on, no one hates you. Sure, they're disappointed and upset—but for both of us, and for themselves. You did what you felt was right. I'd hate for you to have married me because you felt you ought to. That's not enough. Not for me and not for you. And I know how you feel about divorce.'

So she wanted to do a better job of marriage than her parents had. She was only human.

Lucy yawned and stretched on her haunches before padding over to Nick and sitting on his feet. It was a timely switch of allegiance. At least from where Jess was sitting.

Nick patted his lap and Lucy jumped up into it. 'Jess, we both have to come to terms with the fact it's over.'

Jess swallowed hard. Overdone, overwrought, over-easy—but just over was pretty hard to stomach. It was a case of instant indigestion.

'No doubt you'll be doing more and more of the high profile stuff now. And remember, when you started out this was everything you ever wanted.'

It was?

Nick took a breath. 'And I'm really pleased everything has

taken off for you. Really I am. Obviously I wish things be-tween us could have turned out differently…' Nick's face crumpled and Jess's wasn't far behind.

Sitting up on her knees, Jess shuffled over to where he was sitting and, taking his hands in hers, kissed him on the cheek, her lips soft on his stubble. His aftershave was a new one.

Shaking his hands free, abruptly he got to his feet, a surprised Lucy slithering indignantly to the floor in the process. 'Jess. No.'

Stunned, Jess sat back on her heels before moving on to the sofa. 'What? We're not even staying friends?'

'Not right now. I can't. And I can't see you and Rosie chatting nicely over a cup of tea.'

Jess had definitely had more cups of tea with Rosie than Nick had.

'So she comes first, does she?'

'It's not like that.'

'But you are seeing her—I mean properly?' Jess didn't know why she'd had to ask. Mind you, dignity was hardly her priority at this point.

Nick nodded.

'Well, do say hello from me.' Jess was doing her best to be mature. 'And tell her that she didn't have to resign.'

Yes, she did. Jess's mouth was running away with itself in an attempt to come across as someone she wasn't. A softer, more sensitive, less upset version.

'She's a great girl, as you know…'

Jess noted that Nick at least had the courtesy to blush.

'I mean, obviously it's incredibly early days yet….'

Early days. Implying that there would be later ones. And nights. Which meant Nick had been single for approximately ten minutes. And she was—what? Jealous? Angry? Unim-pressed? Vindicated? He'd wanted to be with her or he'd wanted to be in a relationship?

'And she's very sorry to have left you in the lurch at work. She loved her job, as you know.'

'Hey, *c'est la vie.* Anyway, I have a lovely male replacement arriving on Monday.'

'A guy?'

'Do you have a problem with that?' Jess was embarrassed at her teenage attempt at point-scoring. Nick didn't need to know he was a) called Roger and b) very gay. Mind you, with a name like Roger he probably didn't stand a chance. Nature versus nurture. What had his parents expected?

'Of course not…'

Of course not. Nick wasn't stuck on her rollercoaster of emotions.

'Look, the film isn't until seven, so I can stick around and give you and Sarah a hand with some of these boxes, if you'd like.'

He'd always been the complete gentleman. Unless, of course, he was just checking she was really going.

'There's no need. Simon's coming over in a minute.'

'Well, I'm sure he'd appreciate a hand. You seem to have amassed quite a lot of stuff over the years. I'll stick around, if you don't mind. And it'd be good to see Si.'

Jess just sat there, a guest on the sofa she'd lovingly ordered and waited nine weeks for with the same excitement usually reserved for an expectant mother. This house, not long ago her sanctuary, already felt alien. 'So, you came home early on purpose?'

'I told you, I needed my glasses.'

'You're not meeting her for ages.'

'OK.' Nick held his hands up in surrender. 'Guilty as charged. Part of me might have wanted to see you, just to check you were doing all right. Which I'm glad to see you are…' Nick was wandering amongst the piles. 'Hey, are you taking Aerosmith? Didn't you buy that CD for me?'

'I think you'll find you bought it for me—the week before you took me to the concert.'

'Which you were dreading…'

'And then I loved.'

'You have it.' A simultaneous offer.

'Go on, I've still got it on tape somewhere.'

Nick probably had more semi-obsolete music cassettes in his loft than existed on the market today.

'OK.' Jess accepted his offer knowing that now she'd probably never be able to listen to it again.

'We had so many good times, didn't we?' Nick looked up at Jess as he started taping boxes closed.

'We did. We could…'

'No, Jess. We can't.'

Jess put on her bravest face and nodded.

'Seriously.' He walked over and put his hand on her shoulder. The kindness of his touch threatened to trigger instant tears. 'How could I trust you now?'

Today she didn't even know if she could trust herself. And Lucy's *Lassie Come Home* mournful wet-eyed gaze wasn't helping. 'It's not as if I slept with anyone else.'

'You took my heart and kicked it into touch…'

Jess bit her lip hard and sniffed. Her nose always ran just before she started crying. And she was determined to retain her poise. Although right now she couldn't think of a reason why she needed it.

'What's worse is that you were probably right. You always were the braver one, the risk-taker.'

'How can this be right?' Getting up, Jess closed her eyes and nestled into Nick's chest, in an attempt to burrow out of the real world. As she absorbed the familiar deodorant and body musk combination every nerve ending pricked with nostalgia. Gently but firmly he returned her to an independently upright position.

'Let's at least walk away with our dignity. This shouldn't descend into who did what to who when. You know I'll always love you. And I don't want any bad feeling. If we can just try and be adult about this…'

She'd left him waiting for her at the church and he didn't want any bad feeling. The enormity of her error was starting to dawn on her. She was never going to sleep with him again. Never going to taste his slightly bland Bolognaise sauce. Never going to be subjected to another rant on visible Tampax in the bathroom. She was on her own. And it was her choice.

ten

Emma was jolted back to reality as Jack decelerated from forty miles an hour to a standstill before swinging his car right, through an understated entrance. After a fraction of a second, the electric gate picked up the signal from his car and opened, the sports car barely coming to a halt as he accelerated through with only millimetres to spare.

The start of the driveway was marked by a pair of red brick pillars crowned with lichen-covered ornamental pineapples. Or were they acorns? Emma was sure wild boar had grazed in the forests when the first Carlisles had been stamping their authority on the shires, at which time pineapples would have been a fanciful fruit fantasy of the future, the concept of a Hawaiian pizza a mere twinkle in Mr Pizza Hut's eye.

The gate automatically swept closed across the gravel behind them, and Emma could sense the tension in her husband. He'd been drinking Diet Cokes back to back since the last service station, and his whole demeanour had changed as they'd left the motorway. If he'd bothered to look to his left he'd have noticed she was nervous too. An entire weekend with her father-in-law was a first. And this wasn't any old weekend. Or indeed your average parent-in-law destination.

Peering up the drive, she saw there wasn't any sign of the house yet. Focusing on the view from the car, she removed her chewing gum, which suddenly felt rather urban and uncouth in this verdant setting.

'Darling…'

Emma smiled. Once you'd tied the knot there was apparently no need for Christian names any more. You could pretty much 'darling' and 'sweetheart' it out until you got to being Mummy and Daddy. And Jack was proving to be a master of marital role play.

'Mmm?'

Jack pushed his new Prada sunglasses further back on his head and rubbed his temple. 'Sorry, I completely forgot to tell you that Patrick called yesterday.'

'He did?' Emma would have been reaching for a cigarette at this precise moment if she smoked. Maybe it wasn't too late to start.

'Yup. He mentioned some work—a couple of days a week for him on some charity thing.'

'Oh, right.' Emma did her best to sound as vague as possible. 'Not sure that I've got the time, but it's nice that he—'

'Of course you've got time. And, anyway, he said you could do some of it from home.'

'Did he, now?' And the Not So Hidden Agenda Award for underhand interference in a brand-new marriage goes to…Patrick Robson.

Jack expertly changed down a gear just in time to take a speed bump safely. 'Anyway, I said I'd get you to give him a call when we'd discussed it. You were saying only last week that you missed work.'

Last week. Before lunch. And afters.

'Well, I do—I did.'

'That's settled, then.' Jack found her hand and squeezed it.
'I just want you to be happy. This is bound to be a strange
time for you…'

Not least because her husband was being so attentive. Jack
was behaving like a newlywed—in love with life, in love with
his wife—yet Emma had never believed theirs would be a
normal partnership.

'Hey, it's pretty weird for me, and I'm still living in the same
place, doing the same things.'

Emma stared out of the passenger window. Jack had taken
to marriage like a duck to water. He was caring, he was sharing, he was generous. Emma had to keep reminding herself
that they were no ordinary couple or she really would have
been falling for him. *Pretty Woman* had a lot to answer for.

'Hey, when I say weird I mean it in a good way.'

She nodded. 'I know.'

'You OK? You're being a bit quiet.'

'Just thinking…'

'Sounds dangerous. You don't want to do too much of that.'

Maybe Jack was right. Why couldn't she just enjoy the moment? It was supposed to be all new and exciting, not a time
for over-analysis.

'I have to confess that I am a bit nervous…'

'You too?'

'Well, I've never been down here before. Plus, you know
how much I like your dad, but a whole weekend…'

'Don't worry—we'll tough it out together. Hey, it's my job
to look after you. And it's such a beautiful spot here that it's
hard not to fall in love with the place. I'd almost forgotten.
I haven't been for years. Not since—you know, since Charlie…' Jack's voice cracked.

'I know.' Emma put her hand on his lap. 'We'll be fine.' If
she said it enough times, maybe she'd believe it.

Jack started tapping out an unrecognisable rhythm on the
side of the steering wheel as a new burst of nervous energy

kicked in. He'd procrastinated at the flat for as long as possible. Cleaning out the fridge had become strangely urgent after breakfast, as had descaling the kettle. As a result they had been driving west at speed, racing the edge of darkness as dusk fell behind them.

'You know, we should have Patrick over for dinner with his wife some time.'

Emma wished he would move on. 'Which one?'

Jack raised an eyebrow quizzically.

'Well, at the last count he had two ex-wives and no current one.'

'Yet he still wears a ring?'

'Does he?'

'I think so.' Jack prided himself on his attention to detail.

'Maybe he thinks he makes it look him less accessible and therefore more desirable.' Emma tried to recall his left hand in isolation and zoom in on his third finger. No detail visible. Only his hand in a variety of places it should never have been granted the opportunity to explore. This had to be as much her fault as it was his. Yet, she'd really only ever seen him as a friend. Damn men and their When Harry Met Sally tendencies.

'Now, that's what I call cynical.'

'He's always fancied himself as a bit of a wow with the ladies. Not that he's had much luck recently.' Emma didn't dare pause for breath '…which is a shame, because I think he's finally worked out his priorities and is ready to settle down…'

'Well, let's get him over anyway. In fact, maybe we can invite a woman along for him. You must know his type.'

Emma's stomach looped the loop, and not in a good way. 'It seems to vary quite a lot.'

'We should have some dinner parties. I'm ashamed to admit I own twelve place settings and only ever use six—or at least that's the point when the dishwasher is full and I start all over again. But I enjoy cooking when I get down to it. Let's put some dates in the diary.'

'Let's.' Emma couldn't believe her luck. A good look-ing, successful pin-up of a man, who enjoyed cooking and enjoyed her. Maybe this was her reward for sitting through so many weddings on her own. Jack really was shaping up to be the perfect husband. Unless this was just his latest role.

The rough of the field gave way to a lawn, and the trees that had flanked their route thus far dropped away, revealing, beyond the formal gardens, Great British countryside as far as the eye could see—and in the distance the eponymous green hill.

Emma was just about to move the subject away from Pat-rick when the drive bent round to the left and suddenly there it was. Emma emitted a noise somewhere between a gasp and a squeak. Jack turned to his wife.

'You OK?' To Emma's relief her inadvertent guinea pig sound effect had stolen his attention.

Speechless, Emma nodded. Greenhill was definitely the biggest estate she had ever visited without paying an en-trance fee.

Jack opened the window and poked his head out, taking a deep breath. 'Fresh air. Money can't buy this stuff inside the M25. And I have to warn you, without the pollutants which act as stimulants when they're not killing brain cells, the air here is a lot more tiring. Just wait until we walk down to the lake, or more accurately we are walked down to the lake. The wood is fantastic—although…' Jack peered at the sky '…that might have to wait for tomorrow. You did bring wellies, didn't you?'

Emma laughed gaily. 'Don't be ridiculous. I haven't had a pair of Wellingtons since school.'

Jack peered into the passenger foot well.

'Anything other than trainers?'

'Kitten heels, slingbacks…'

Jack waited for Emma to stop teasing him.

'…and walking boots. I do know the difference between the West End and the West Country. I managed life perfectly well before you came along.' Emma clamped her mouth closed before her independent woman gene took over.

'Well, if it gets really wet there are bound to be a few spare pairs of Hunters in the boot room.'

Boot room. A room for boots. One day she'd like a shoe room, and a handbag room.

Emma relished the crunch of the dark blue Aston Martin on the gravel as Jack looped the car round a circular pond and drove straight past the front door, turning left down the side of the house and eventually into an old open-sided barn. An assortment of Land Rovers of various vintage and condition were parked further down, plus—as incongruous as Jack's sports car—James's pristine BMW.

'Welcome to Greenhill, Em.' Jack leant over and planted a kiss firmly on her lips. 'Seat of the Carlisles—or at least a bed for the night for some of them—since 1687. Home sweet home. You wouldn't believe what we got up to down here as kids…'

'I dare say I can hazard a guess.'

'It was the best place in the world to grow up. I remember every nook, every cranny…'

'…every fanny?' Emma quipped.

'What did you say?' He'd clearly heard perfectly, and yet she couldn't work out whether or not he was cross with her. He certainly wasn't laughing. Silently she scolded herself for being such a guttersnipe.

'Nothing.' Why did she have to insist on lowering the tone?

'I was about to say every nanny…'

'Of course.' Emma sensed a change in his demeanour and adopted what she hoped was caring wife mode. 'Hey, are you OK?'

Jack nodded hard.

Emma wondered whether he'd ever tried to shag any of

the nannies. There she went again. And she'd never thought of herself as the lowest common denominator. Clearly her nerves had short circuited her finesse.

Thinking finishing schools in Switzerland, deportment, and minding her ps and qs, Emma opened the car door onto three eager chocolate Labradors. Her father-in-law was approaching rapidly. A vision in old cords, green wellies and a yellow V-neck under a brown waxed jacket, he was marking each stride with a silver-topped walking cane. Quite the country squire. Suddenly she wished she'd travelled down in a chunky knit jumper rather than her tight-fitting, cleavage-revealing black V-neck. Plus, she'd always been more of a cat person. Less dribble.

James's received pronunciation reached her before he did. 'Finally the two lovebirds descend.' He bent into the car and into her personal space to kiss her hello. 'I'm afraid you'll have to dump your own stuff inside. I sent Sid home early today. Terrible chesty cough. I dare say he'll be back tomorrow.'

'Sid's still here?' Jack leant across from the driver's seat. 'He must be a hundred years old.'

'Only seventy-two, and this is their home almost as much as it is ours. While Elsie still does some of the housekeeping, he's quite happy pottering in the gardens.'

Emma nodded. She didn't know who Sid was, or whether what James was saying was true, but it seemed the appropriate thing to do—and mouth shut was definitely preferable to mouth open at the moment.

'Now, come on, you two—get moving. The boys and I can't wait to give Emma the grand tour, and it'll be dark soon.'

Jack's mobile rang, leaving Emma to start the conversational ball rolling.

Conveying a lot more enthusiasm than she felt, Emma tried not to deliberately knee any of the dogs in the chest as she leapt out of the car. She had thirty-three years of life experience under her belt. She was married. Yet in the presence of a parent she was suddenly feeling very childlike. She wouldn't have been at all surprised if James had asked her to run along and play quietly.

'Jack Carlisle.'

'Hello, mate.'

Jack cupped his hand over his non-phone ear. It wasn't a great line. 'Hello? Jack Carlisle speaking.'

'Jack, sorry to bother you on a Saturday, mate. It's Graham from *CelebriTee*. Is now a good moment?'

Jack closed all the windows and smiled at Emma as she chatted to his dad whilst trying to keep three very bouncy dogs at ground level.

'I've got a minute—literally.'

'Just wanted to give you the heads-up on something.'

'Go on.'

'We got a tip-off. Emma was spotted in Primrose Hill a couple of evenings ago with wet hair, early evening. She was picked up by a taxi driver. In fact he's the one who called us.'

'Right.' Jack did his best to sound unsurprised as he spooled back a couple of days.

'We don't have a photo, but it is going to feature in our "Seen But Not Heard" section on Wednesday.'

'Fine.'

'So there's nothing surprising about that, then?'

Jack listened to Graham casting his line before he laughed flawlessly. 'Honestly, you guys. She'd just been to the gym.'

'Thought as much. Nice one.'

'Still happily married, I'm afraid.'

'Thanks for setting us straight.'

'Appreciate the call, though.'

'No problem. You've been good to us, Jack, and we appreciate that. Don't forget us when you want another cover story or have another exclusive. You know we're the best in the business.'

'Of course. Have a great weekend.'

'And you.'

Jack hung up just as Emma tapped on the window and beckoned for him to join them.

'Get down, boys. Down. Harpo, Groucho, Zeppo, *now*.' Despite the authority of James's tone, none of the dogs paid the slightest bit of attention to him. 'Sorry, Emma, they just want to say hello. They're so excited to see you. I've been promising them this W.A.L.K. since breakfast, and we've probably only got another hour of daylight at the most.'

An hour. Emma smiled, humouring James, and turned her attention to the three noses investigating her at waist height.

'They're just adorable.' Emma grabbed and re-routed the head of the most mischievous as his nose strayed to her groin. 'Aren't you, boys? If a little high-energy.' Eyeballing the culprit, she made sure he knew she knew who he was.

After over two hours on the road she'd been hoping for a cup of tea. And a home made Victoria sponge. Or a scone. A moment round the Aga. And the opportunity to change. She was currently in her smarter jeans, the ones she was hoping *not* to get caked in mud. And there were already a few pawprints in evidence. She was sure they'd dust off when they dried.

'I had been hoping you'd make it down a little earlier today.'

'Oh, that'd be real life getting in the way.' Emma made their excuses as she pushed down hard on the crown of Zeppo's head. Actually, it could have been Harpo. 'You know what it's like.' It was about time Jack got off the phone. Emma tapped on the car window again as she continued talking to James. 'People always call at the worst moments. It's like they can sense you're in a hurry and then choose to take absolutely no notice. If anything, it encourages them to be as long-winded as possible.'

James nodded empathetically, which amused Emma as, today aside, he was the main culprit.

'But timekeeping has never been Jack's forte.'

'I heard that, Dad.' Jack and James embraced with a hearty exchange of back slaps which Emma found strangely touching. 'And don't forget I learnt everything from you.'

'Good journey down?' James watched as his son effortlessly unloaded the luggage and wished he was twenty years younger.

Finding a stick and flinging it as far as she could, to give herself a moment of personal space, Emma dusted herself off and started helping her husband as the men began a mind-numbing discussion of roadworks and bypasses. Checking her mobile out of habit, she was relieved to see that, out here in the barn at least, her network had no signal.

WILL YOU TAKE THIS MAN
TO BE YOUR HUSBAND?
WILL YOU LOVE HIM, COMFORT HIM,
HONOUR AND PROTECT HIM AND,
FORSAKING ALL OTHERS, BE FAITHFUL
TO HIM AS LONG AS YOU
BOTH SHALL LIVE?

eleven

Jess pressed the snooze button again.

A few metres away, in the master bedroom, Sarah was ready to explode. 'That was the ninth bloody time. Why can't she get up? Or at least set her alarm for later than normal? And she only got in at one a.m....'

They might not have noticed if she hadn't turned all the lights on, or had bothered to take her heels off before clattering up the bare wood of the stairs. Stair carpet was a luxury they were waiting to afford.

'It's bad enough not being able to have sex on a Sunday morning without her ruining a rare lie-in too.'

Simon pulled Sarah in for a hug. Her body was stiff with tension. 'We can have sex.'

'Yeah—quietly and without moving.'

Simon stroked his wife's naked body under the duvet, his hand wandering from her neck via her breasts along the outside edge of her body to her hip, before re-routing to her tummy button and heading south. Sarah wrestled with arousal as he kissed her temple before brushing his lips against hers.

'We could try.'

'She's my older sister…'

'You're hardly fourteen years old. We're married and everything.'

Sarah smiled at her husband. Nearly three years and counting. For better, for worse—for ever didn't seem nearly long enough. Remembering she was in a bad mood, Sarah reached for an extra pillow and took her book off the bedside table before folding her non-novel-holding arm across her chest.

'Well, I can't. She's just there. And if she presses that effing snooze button one more time I might join a rifle club this afternoon instead of coming to Pete's.'

'I'll speak to her.' Simon rolled out of bed.

'I'll go.' Sarah made no attempt to move as Simon reached the door.

'Don't be ridiculous. I can't let you loose in there now.' He waited a moment for his erection to subside.

'You're so bloody good.'

'Hey, it's all part of the deal. Love, honour and protect you…and I think you'll find clause 64(b)(i) of the small print specifically details obligations relating to small alarm clocks and sisters-in-law.'

'Thank you. And, Si…?'

'Yes, darling?'

'Boxer shorts. I mean, I know we're all family and everything…'

'Excellent point.' Simon separated yesterday's boxer shorts from yesterday's jeans and pulled them on before opening the door. 'Love you.'

'Love you more.' Sarah turned over and planted her face in Simon's pillow, inhaling his musky morning smell. Patience was a virtue. Just not hers.

Across the corridor, Jess was deep in semi-conscious analysis. Well, it sure beat getting up on a Sunday when you had absolutely no plans and your best friend was indulging in start-of-a-relationship non-stop sex in Paris. She missed Fi. Of course she was happy for her. But she missed her.

Simon knocked on the door before poking his head round.

'Yes?' Jess propped herself up on an elbow. Privacy was no longer an option. She had even started wearing pyjamas to bed again.

'What's going on with the all-morning alarm calls?'

'Can't be arsed to get up.'

'Then switch it off and leave it off, will you? Sarah and I keep jumping to attention and it's Sunday. Day of rest. Remember?'

'You have a one-year-old daughter who doesn't know what day of the week it is.'

'Who is staying with my parents for at least another hour, so can we lose the alarm every nine minutes from now on?'

'Sorry.' Jess said it with as much feeling as most petulant teenage boys muster when told to take their trainers off the sofa.

Apparently Simon hadn't finished yet. He was still standing there, hands on his love handles. He'd never used to have those. More exercise and fewer biscuits required. But what now? She was sure she'd flushed the loo and rinsed the toothpaste residue out of the basin.

'Yes?'

'Look, Sar and I are going over to some friends for Sunday lunch. Why don't you come along? I mean, if you're not busy or anything.'

'Hmm, let's see… Third wheel, spare part, gooseberry for dessert. No, not sure I will, actually.'

'Go on—we've hardly seen you recently, and there'll be loads of people there.'

'I really ought to pop to the office. I need to put some sample menus together. It would appear that marriage is very much in vogue, despite all the rumours to the contrary…'

Simon's brow was furrowed as he observed the specimen

in his study-cum-spare room. Confused, he scratched his head as he observed his files and PlayStation games under two feet of Jess's clothes and personal effects.

'Don't worry, I'm more positive with the clients.'

'Glad to hear it. Look, don't hide behind your desk. Have a day away from the office. Come with us and I promise I'll sit on one side of you…'

A moment of hesitation.

'…and I won't put Millie on the other. Excellent.'

'Hang on, I haven't said yes yet. And how do you know they won't mind? Simon? You didn't already say yes for me, did you?'

'Well, I said I'd have to check…'

'You're unbelievable. You're not even my husband and you're organising my diary. Thank you for reminding me of one good reason why I said no to Nick. I was just beginning to start regretting it all over again.'

'Really?'

'I'd have been fine after my shower. Thank God for them. Deep cleansing in every sense.'

'It'd do you good to get out.'

'This isn't one of your Jewish husband conspiracies is it?'

'Well, the feeding you element might be. But I'm not trying to marry you off, if that's what you're thinking…'

'I don't know what I'm thinking.'

Simon gave her the look, the one normally reserved for small children and puppies, and Jess thought she was going to cry.

'Don't worry—it'll all sort itself out.' Perching awkwardly on the foot of her bed, he tapped her leg under the duvet in what Jess presumed was an attempt to be supportive.

'Do you think I've made a mistake?'

'What would I know? I'm a mere male mortal.'

'Well, you know me, and you know Nick, and you always seem to be so sure of everything.'

Simon was reluctant to proffer an opinion which no doubt would be held against him at an unspecified point in the future. 'I guess—although to be honest there haven't been many heavy discussions between Sarah and I.' He almost sounded apologetic.

'I know, I know. The perfect couple. I, on the other hand, seem to over-analyse everything in my personal life to the point of destruction.'

'Don't be so tough on yourself. You don't have to justify your decisions to anyone.'

'That's the problem.'

'Look, I'm no expert, but a bit less thinking and a bit more getting up might be a pretty good start.' Leading by example, he returned to the safety of the doorframe.

Jess didn't want to mention the only place in their home she could be on her own was in bed.

'I know it must be hard for you not to have your own space.'

God, he was good.

'Look, we're heading off to my parents to collect Millie in a bit, and we'll be about an hour. Then we're coming back to get you.'

'For lunch?'

'Exactly. So wait until you hear the front door close and then, as Depeche Mode once said, enjoy the silence…'

'Until you said that I was going to say that sometimes I think you might be the sanest person in the world.'

'Well, I doubt that. I married your sister.'

'I heard that.' Sarah's voice sailed through the wall as Simon and Jess shared a silent smile. But from the lightness of her tone Jess could detect her sister's upswing in mood. She wasn't a smug married, but she *was* a happily married. And somehow that was worse.

twelve

Jack rolled over and rested his head on her breasts, the lowering of the duvet allowing an icy gust of air into the bed.

'Christ.' Emma pulled the duvet over their heads.

'Help! Help!' Jack was doing a pretty good impersonation of Penelope Pitstop. 'Somebody—anybody. My wife is trying to smother me.'

'I'd say you were trying to smother yourself.' Emma wasn't in the mood for playing. 'And in the process I'm clearly supposed to freeze to death.'

Jack's mood matured accordingly. 'It's bracing.'

'It's fucking arctic. Tell me the Carlisles aren't Amish. Tell me they believe in central heating.'

'Of course we do.' Jack's voice slurred as he did his best to slip back to sleep.

If Britain had a national sleeping team, Emma was sure he'd be selected.

Holding her breath as she moved the duvet from her head for a moment, Emma peered around the room. She could only see one slip of a radiator—to her disbelief located under a rattling window—and a dark, empty fireplace, no doubt channelling chilled air from outside and displacing what little warmth they had generated themselves.

'One tiny radiator?'

'They didn't have heating when this house was built.'

'No, but they probably had maids who came and lit a fire before anyone expected you to venture out from under the counterpane.'

'Fine. You want a maid? I'll get you a maid. Anything else you'd like while I'm at it? Good to see you're settling into the idea of having staff. It hasn't taken you long.'

'I don't want a maid. I want a convection heater.' Emma shivered and Jack rubbed his hands along her goosebumps, each one melting away at his touch. She also wanted a clear conscience. Not something he could help her with.

Jack laughed. 'You're funny.'

'Don't sound so surprised.'

'Seriously, you really make me laugh.'

'Maybe you need a new sense of humour.'

'You should write.'

Internally, Emma shone at the compliment. Outwardly she remained deadpan. 'I did write.'

'Really?'

'Press releases, cheques, notes for the cleaner…'

'See?'

Emma placed a rapidly cooling hand on Jack's chest. 'I don't believe it. To add insult to injury, you're boiling hot.'

'Your fault, Mrs Carlisle. You are far too sexy. And obviously you'd be warmer if you'd packed pyjamas.'

'I don't think I've had pyjamas since…probably for as long as I've been welly-free.'

'Well, I love you welly much.' Jack closed his eyes again.

Emma stared at the underside of the duvet. That was a first. And…?

Ruffling his hair in what she hoped suggested consensus,

she let Jack reach above his head for her hand, bring it down to his lips for a kiss and hold it there.

If it hadn't been for Thursday it would have been a perfect moment. Mind racing, she closed her eyes and pretended to be dozing. As if. The room was silent, except for a new knocking from the radiator, suggesting that the one potential source of heat in the bedroom contained more air than hot water. And now the moment had been and gone and she'd said nothing. Did she love him? It might have helped if she was feeling a bit more affectionate towards herself.

Jack opened an eye. 'Em?'

'Still here.' She rested a cold hand on his chest to prove it.

'Did you have lunch in Primrose Hill on Thursday?'

What? Emma wondered if she was dreaming. She knew she shouldn't have had brie after supper last night. Staring at Jack's navel, she decided to go for bold. 'Yup.'

'Cool.'

'Why do you ask?'

'Just wondered—you were spotted out that way.'

By who? Emma's heart quickened in her chest as she deployed humour to get through the next few sentences. 'Are you having me followed?'

Jack sniffed his contempt at the suggestion. 'Of course not. It's just that someone called yesterday because they'd thought they'd seen you out and about.'

'Which is quite possible.' Silently Emma cursed her new profile. Just as long as he'd forgotten she and Patrick had been due to lunch in St James's.

Somewhere in the arctic tundra of their clothing Emma's phone beeped, and immediately Patrick wandered into Emma's mind's eye, a smug grin plastered on his face. She needed to talk to him before there was an emotional pile-up. She wanted the one she'd married; she loved the other one not.

★ ★ ★

Nick started a third lap of the village green, much to Lucy's delight. As he walked, slightly hunched, fists in his pockets, he watched his feet, barely aware of life around him. To call or not to call—that was the question. Fiona had said any time, but she deserved a break. And she was in Paris. He was old enough to deal with life on his own. Some mornings were bound to be tougher than others. Besides, Rosie was waiting for him back at the B&B. Whistling to Luce, he turned back and headed towards the car.

It was a perfect cold, crisp, alpine day as Fi and Mike left the Louvre courtyard behind them and strolled along the Seine.

Mike laid his arm across her shoulders. 'So, what do you feel like doing next? I've booked us lunch somewhere, but otherwise I am totally at your disposal.'

'A disposable boyfriend?' Fiona laughed.

She was her own worst enemy. Rationally, what aspect of her single life was she so afraid of losing? The takeaway for one? Custody of the remote control? This weekend was going really well. Making a total of five consecutive great weekends. Which probably meant she had a boyfriend. And, more to the point, a relationship. Then again, he'd had lots of girlfriends before, so maybe this togetherness was standard behaviour for him.

Mike shrugged his shoulders in mock defeat. 'Well, if that's what you want…but I was sort of hoping I'd be allowed to stick around for a bit.'

'A bit of what?' His assurance was infectious and there was no doubt about it—she hadn't felt this relaxed in anybody's company since for ever. Fi kissed him on the cheek. 'I'm having a lovely weekend.' Travel was definitely a lot more fun when you had a hand to hold.

'That was the plan.' His grin was honest. Mike was a game-free zone.

Fi wasn't sure she'd be able to cope if he changed his mind. She'd been hoping for this moment for years, yet now she was feeling as if she wasn't quite ready. But she was thirty-two years old. Just how ready did she want to be?

As they neared Pont Neuf Mike raced ahead, reaching for his digital camera, his cheeks and lips a matching crimson with cold. Fiona hesitated, suddenly self-conscious, as he stopped, turned, and watched her via his screen. Lowering her head slightly, she glanced across at the Left Bank before smiling at him as she approached. All she needed was a beret and a black and white film. Suddenly she was feeling very Audrey Hepburn—well, a size twelve to fourteen version, with highlights—and very in love.

Impatiently he waited for her to reach him, his light brown hair combed by the breeze, and kissed her hello as if it had been hours rather than seconds since they'd last seen each other.

'I love you, Fiona Seaton.'

'You do?' Fiona was sure that wasn't the line he'd been hoping for.

'I do.'

Staring into his eyes, she leant in and kissed him back before taking his hand and letting him lead her across the bridge. Nothing troubled about the water under this one. Just the communication skills of the woman currently crossing it. She might have been struggling to admit it to herself, but she'd fallen for him in that first fortnight and to her delight he had apparently fallen right back. And yet the familiar doubts had started to appear in the wings, rhetorical questions that no one could or should answer.

Now her nose was running. Squatting down, she rummaged in her bag for a tissue. 'I love you too.' Admittedly she was muttering into her coat, but she had proved she could say it out loud. One, two, three, with gusto. Or maybe just one final practice.

'I don't suppose you've got any chewing gum in there, have you?' Mike squatted down just as Fiona was having her last rehearsal.

'I love you too.'

Mike rubbed his gloved hand across her shoulders, the friction causing a band of extra warmth to ripple through her.

'Excellent news.'

Fiona felt herself blushing. 'I was going to say it to your face.'

'Just practising?'

She nodded as she blew her nose.

'How about practising at being a fiancée?'

'Hmm? What?' Her hearing had been impaired by the clearing of her sinuses. 'Pardon?'

'Well, more specifically, *my* fiancée. Will you marry me, Fi?'

Mike went from squat to bended knee, and irrationally Fi stood up, before squatting down again, as she stuffed the tissue in her coat pocket and wiped her hand dry on her jeans. This was a moment she wanted to remember. Her first ever proposal and not at all indecent.

'What? Already…?' OK, she needed to work on her responses. He was so laid back, and genetically she wasn't.

'I'd been hoping for the more traditional yes. Feel free to practise with your handbag if it helps.' His eyes were shining.

Fiona wanted to giggle childishly. 'Don't you think it's very soon?'

'Well, we could move in together for a couple of years, and all our friends can grill us every time we return from a weekend away, but face it—we're not getting any younger. I know me and I know what I want. The question, I guess, is do you?'

Apparently not just a whim, then. And if he wasn't getting any younger, she was practically prehistoric.

Mike stood up. Fiona mirrored his movements, relieved to be upright before pins and needles ruined the moment. No one had stopped and stared. Clearly the French thought he'd just had a tricky shoelace moment and didn't want to draw attention to it.

'So…?' Mike did his utmost not to sound too hopeful.

'I think there's something you should know.'

'What?'

Fiona watched Mike's face change as he began to fear his proposal might have been a little premature.

'Well, in light of everything that's just happened, and actually irrespective of that, I don't want a big wedding. In fact I'd like a very small wedding.'

Relief washing over him, Mike exhaled. 'So long as we're both there, I don't care where *there* is… I'm sure Jess will organise whatever you ask her to.'

Jess. Of course. And Nick. Suddenly the whole marriage thing seemed even more hasty than it had a few moments ago—even if the non-thinking part of her body felt like a teenager in love.

'I realise it's been a tough year for Jess, and for your brother, but this isn't about them.'

Fi nodded. He wanted to marry her. Just a regular fact-stating sentence. I want Shepherd's Pie for lunch. I want Fiona to be my wife. Michael Benson. Fiona Benson. Fiona Seaton-Benson. Fiona Benson-Seaton. That was sounding like a yes, then. And talk about alphabetical promotion. After years of languishing in the S doldrums of the register, she was going to be a B. Yes.

Slowly Fiona started to grin. 'OK, then. Yes. *Yes.*'

She was getting married. To the kind, generous-spirited, talented, pretty good-looking man she loved. And who loved her back.

As Mike kissed her gently Fiona felt her insides fizzing. She hadn't been this excited since—since… Well, for a very long time.

Pulling back, Mike tucked a tendril of Fiona's hair behind her ear.

'Hey, let's not tell anyone until we get back. There'll be plenty of time to celebrate with everyone else when we get home. This should be our moment.'

'Deal.' It suited Fiona's way of thinking. Why face up to anything today when this evening would do nicely?

Walking across to the Left Bank, Fiona felt her phone vibrate in her handbag and ignored it. She was engaged.

thirteen

Emma rattled the door handle several times before managing to coax the swollen wood into granting her access to Jack's old room. She was on a mission.

Crossing the threshold was tantamount to taking a step back in time, with the wintry sunlight casting an almost ethereal glow across the musty childhood bedroom of one Jack Carlisle. A neatly made single bed lay along the wall under the window, its thin mattress slightly sagging in the middle, a faded *Star Wars* pillow case protruding from under the bedspread.

Jess walked over to the chest of drawers. Her primary and official objective was to find warm socks. The secondary, undisclosed yet overriding one: to have a good old nose around.

'Make sure you close the door behind you when you're done in there.' Jack's voice ascended the staircase as he descended to make a pot of tea.

'I will.' Even if she had to remove it from its hinges and plane a couple of inches off first.

Her eyes couldn't register items fast enough as she tried

to absorb every nuance of the bedroom. A framed snapshot from the seventies stood on top of the drawers, a photo of two boys arm in arm, dressed in yellow knitwear and brown corduroy trousers with a slight flare, matching toothy grins dwarfing their faces and the straightest of fringes framing their unmistakably blue eyes. A stitched leather football lay on the manicured grass in front of them, and out of focus in the background was the distinctive brickwork of Greenhill.

She'd never had a sibling, but she'd been at boarding school with Amy for long enough to be able to imagine what it would have been like to have one, and then not.

Emma opened the middle drawer in search of ski socks to make up the difference in size between her feet and the boots James had conjured up for their walk—the need for specialist footwear in her opinion was not a good sign. As she pulled the handles towards her a vintage cloud of sports liniment escaped, evoking a nostalgia for locker rooms and hockey practice, and for days when the epitome of stress was forgetting your gym kit.

Sitting on the bed, she pulled the socks on, determined to make use of the extra layer before she lost the feeling in her toes. The walls of the room were a fusion of RAF-blue, warship-grey and the washed out hues of hospital corridors, no doubt faded by years of sunlight. Assorted trophies were collecting dust in a huddle on the top bookshelf, and expensively framed team and year photos adorned the walls, the names of their members inscribed on the mount in majestic calligraphy. Hockey, rugby, tennis, football—she had married Mr Jack Of All Trades. Above his small desk, signed photos of several well-known faces grinned suavely. And an original *Grease* movie poster covered the wall at the foot of his bed.

Detective Inspector Emma had learned more about Jack in the last ten minutes than she had in the last ten months.

Breakfast time. But, staring at the bedside cupboard, she

wrestled with her conscience and her curiosity. If she was going to honour, protect and be faithful to him for the rest of her life, or at least from now on, she had to be allowed access to all areas. She opened the door gingerly.

This Pandora's box was apparently spring-loaded, and the first items to fling themselves to the floor were a couple of contorted threadbare teddy bears, surfing their way to freedom on the covers of a few faded magazines. Emma hurriedly gathered the items together and assessed the non–existent space available for their return, smiling as she noticed a selection of first generation digital watches and, completing the leaning tower of nostalgia, a newer blue shoebox.

Opening the lid as tentatively as if it belonged to the Ark of the Covenant, she was instantly rewarded with a stash of ordered yellowing newspaper and magazine cuttings, secured with an elastic band rigid with neglect and close to perishing. At the bottom, the edges of a dog eared photo protruded and, extracting it carefully, Emma found herself gazing at the head and shoulders of a beautiful woman, captured for all eternity in black and white. Her kind eyes smiled at the photographer, her dark hair tied back loosely from her face with a ribbon fell seductively onto her shoulders. Underneath, an order of service from her funeral had been carefully stored. Helen Judith Carlisle, beloved wife of James and mother of Charlie and Jack.

Transferring her attention to the bundle of newsprint, it didn't take her long to realise it must contain every article pertaining to Charlie's death filed chronologically, plus a well- thumbed notebook, its leaves curling from the pressure of their contents. Flicking through a few pages, Emma was moved by the rawness of the emotion they contained.

She could only have been sifting for a few minutes when she realised she was no longer alone in the room. The chill now spreading through her had nothing to do with the draught.

'So you found the socks OK, then.'

Jack's voice was normal—or at least Emma couldn't detect any anger. Standing in the room, feet slightly apart, he looked larger than life, the mug of tea steaming in his left hand, emitting wisps of steam, suggesting he had appeared genie-like from within it. In the midst of so many mini-Jack images his adult presence was somehow forebidding and vitally three-dimensional, in stark contrast to the faded scene surrounding them.

Emma pointed a thickly covered toe and nodded, before attempting to put the lid back on the box as nonchalantly as possible. Apparently it had shrunk in the last few minutes and no longer fitted. He watched her struggle for a few seconds.

'What do you think you're doing?'

'I was looking for more socks.' That was her story and she was sticking to it.

'In my nightstand?'

Emma ignored him and, leaving the box on the bed, attempted to stuff everything else back into the small cupboard.

Jack stepped over and managed to put the lid on first time. 'You should know that a shoebox is a man's private domain.'

He wasn't shouting, but Emma knew she was in the wrong. Blinking back a couple of guilty tears, she couldn't believe she'd been caught red-handed.

Jack noticed the telltale glisten at once. 'Hey, no need to get upset.'

'I shouldn't have been—I do respect your privacy—I was just curious and I wasn't expecting this room to be such a shr... I'm sorry.' She *was* sorry, and then again she wasn't. She'd married a man who harboured more life laundry than his superficial playboy persona suggested, and for that she couldn't have been more delighted.

Jack stroked the top of her head. 'Well, at least I guess it prevents me from having to go through it all again.'

Retreating, Emma sat cross legged on the bed and gathered up the bedspread, wrapping it around herself. 'It shouldn't feel like I was snooping. I just wanted to know more, to know everything, and being here…' She faltered.

Jack nodded, encouraging Emma to continue, relieved that she was vocalising something he couldn't.

'It's difficult with you—you know, to find out what's really going on inside there.' She continued to roll herself up, a human Arctic Roll in the making.

Standing awkwardly in front of her, Jack put his free hand in his pocket. 'I'm not sure how much there is to know. I guess you could say I've made a career out of being other people. I've never had a burning desire to change the world. To stand up for anything. I could always see both sides of every story. Not like Charlie. Your tea's ready, by the way.'

'There you go again.'

'Look, Dad's going to be at church for another hour at least. Bring the box, we'll have breakfast in the den, and you can ask me anything you want…'

Ten minutes later Emma had drunk most of her tea at scalding point, hoping to transfer most of its latent heat to her core. Jack had lit a fire, but as yet the den wasn't quite warm enough to sustain comfortable life—although at least it was small. Stationed on the sofa, she was using her empty mug as a hot water bottle. But, disappointingly, it was cooling rapidly.

Jack was a different man today. Sporting faded jeans with a straighter leg than had been fashionable for many years, an old and worn light grey jumper and a day's worth of stubble, he looked softer, more youthful. Emma watched him try to make sense of *The Sunday Times* crossword from the armchair adjacent to the nascent fire before deserting his post to prod the logs and employ the bellows. Once he was satisfied that the flames were strong enough to sustain themselves, he turned to face his wife, now devouring the cuttings.

'Sorry, Em. I just assumed you'd know more. It was all over the news at the time.' Jack sat back on his heels.

Emma put a finger on the paper, so as not to lose her place. 'I must have read a few articles—I even pulled a few out for Patrick in January—but, and please don't take this the wrong way, it was just news. A tragedy, nonetheless, but a week later everyone was talking about something else. Obviously if I'd even had an inkling that one day I'd be married to you I'd have paid closer attention.'

Jack chewed on his thumbnail. 'I still don't really like to talk about it…'

Emma nodded empathetically, encouraging him to continue.

'I think about him all the time. Well, not all the time, but whenever I'm not thinking about anything else. You must know what I mean.'

Jack was as vulnerable as she had ever seen him.

'Of course. For the first few years after my parents died I used to wake up feeling fine, and then a couple of seconds later it would hit me like a left hook. They were dead and I wasn't.'

Jack hadn't felt closer to anyone since Charlie. 'I'm sure. How old were you when they, you know, died?'

'You can say it. I can. They were killed. There.'

'Murder or manslaughter?' He couldn't believe he hadn't asked her about this before.

'Manslaughter. I was nine. I had no idea it was so perma-nent. I thought there might be ghosts or something. Then again, if you'd asked me if there was anything after death I'd have said a funeral…'

Jack smiled. Children were so much more pragmatic. And honest. Adults spent far too much time over-complicating everything, and asking question after question when they al-ready knew or didn't even want the answer.

'I don't think it really hit me until about four years later, when it finally dawned on me that they were never coming back, that a whopping great bough had been lopped off the family tree. And then came the pressure of being the only one left to carry on their branch. Of living up to their expectations.'

'And you say we're different?'

'Well, if we're talking genealogy, bank balances, property ownership, fast cars…'

'Hey, your Lupo's pretty nippy. But we could definitely get you something more fun, if you like.'

'Look, it's mine, and to be honest it's all I need. And nice try. That was almost a perfect subject change. From heartbreak to brake horsepower. Typical.'

Jack laughed as Emma returned their topic of conversation to the straight and narrow.

'You're the Jedi master of denial. So much more guarded than I am. And much more angry.'

'It was just such a waste of a life.'

'As opposed to my parents?'

'Sorry, I didn't mean it to come across like that.'

Emma wasn't like any of other women he'd dated. She was witty, attractive, intelligent, capable. Neither a gold-digger nor a bunny boiler. And he'd married her without knowing the half of it. Clearly everyone else knew what was best for him and Jack didn't. The story of his life.

Emma was determined to finish this conversation. 'At least Charlie helped someone in the process.'

'But Charlie wouldn't even have been in Brixton that night if I hadn't insisted that he came to the bloody wrap party. And one good turn deserves another—not a fatal gunshot wound. Not only did I deprive myself of a brother, I killed my father's first born son.'

'You didn't kill him. He was shot—fact. He was in the wrong place at the wrong time—fact. He saved a woman's life—fact.'

Jack rummaged in the drawer of the coffee table for a cigarette and lit it quickly, taking a long drag before answering as Emma did her best not to be irritated by the smoke.

He exhaled. 'I'll probably always feel that it should have been me.'

'Well, that's very constructive. How do you think the woman he saved feels? If you don't mind me saying, you're being a touch self-indulgent about all of this.'

'I can't help it. I was the pretty boy who liked partying, the one who had an unhealthy need for approval—be it that of fellow actors, audiences, awards committees or Dad himself. Charlie would never have gone into the "family business", as he put it. He was a geologist. Far more down to earth, far more intelligent, and yet incredibly supportive of everything I did. I don't think I even attended one of his lectures. Bit late now.'

'Look, I could have been in the car with my parents when they had their accident. I if had been I almost certainly would have died. Would that have been better? At times it might have been easier, but I'm certainly not going to be a third victim. The guy who was driving the other car was in prison for all of ten minutes. And he was four times over the legal limit.'

Jack searched Emma's eyes intently. She really was amazingly calm. He envied her clarity of thought. He moved over to the sofa.

Emma rested her head on his shoulder as they sat side by side, watching the flames flickering. Jack was the first to break the reflective silence.

'We're pretty similar, you know.'

Emma scoffed. 'What? You mean we both like Starbucks and—?'

'Seriously. You're doing better than me, but you've had longer to get over it.'

'You never get over it. You just deal with it. You have

to move on or you get left behind. And I've never been a quitter.'

Jack kept silent. He had a horrible feeling he might have been in the past. Too much money wasn't always a good thing.

'You know, it might help you to talk to more people about it? Survivor's guilt is pretty common.'

'Are you saying I'm common?' Jack's accent was suddenly pure Cockney as once again he jogged away from the intensity of the moment.

'Yeah, mate, course you are. Dead common.'

Jack smiled at Emma's attempt at Estuary English as he got up and flicked the rest of his cigarette into the fire. Her whole demeanour had changed for the performance. Her head was askew, her shoulders had dropped, and they were moving from side to side as if she was swaggering from the waist up.

'To be honest, I'm not sure talking would be much use.'

'It might be good for the people who think your life is perfect to realise that you're just like they are.'

'Maybe.' Jack didn't sound convinced.

'You'd be helping people. Take this diary, for example…' Emma proffered the notebook from the box.

Jack looked embarrassed as he returned to the settee. 'It was cathartic. I just had to get stuff out of my system. But it was just for me. Now I can barely bear to tell people I had a brother. Only, every time I go for an interview, or do something new, it's brought up again. I can't move on.'

'Of course you can.'

Emma took Jack's hands and placed them between her palms.

Tipping his head back, he addressed the ceiling. 'I have thought about writing a memoir, or even a play, but I've always been scared of too much time on my own with my thoughts. And I don't think Dad would see the funny side.'

'Who says there's going to be a funny side?'

'Of course at the time I found another way to deal with

my feelings. Blimey, if I think back now Dad's lucky he's got one son left, really.'

'I can imagine.'

'You can't.' Jack shook his head, appalled at himself. 'I just wish I'd had a smidgen more will-power at the time. It would have saved a lot of heartache all round.' Jack reclaimed his hands and combed his hair with his fingers, visibly calming himself down. 'Look at that.' Jack pointed at a photo of his mother with her two sons dressed in suspiciously pristine grey and red school uniform, socks pulled up to the knee, caps straight, brown satchels slung diagonally across their shoulders. They were all beaming at the camera, Charlie with a protective arm around his younger brother's shoulder. 'Just think—there'll never be another photo of us together now. And you'll never meet him—or Mum, for that matter.'

The emotion was causing his voice to falter.

Emma lay down on the sofa, resting her head in his lap. 'Why don't you write something? Even if it ends up only being read by a few people it might help you…'

She stared at the fire as she thought back to her days of creative writing at school after the accident, one dark piece after another. The phase had lasted for months…

'And I'm sure your agent can whip up more than a bit of media interest if you decide you want to go public. I can proof-read stuff, if you like.'

'It's not going to make light reading.'

'We'll cope. And it's not like I don't have any spare time at the moment.'

Jack gave Emma's shoulder a squeeze. 'I want you to know everything.'

'Good.'

Jack stroked her hair affectionately. 'And, by the way, it's too late to run. We're married now.'

'Run? Me?' Emma could have done a half marathon without even blinking. Or maybe half a Snickers without leaving the sofa.

'You've handled this whole situation incredibly well.'

Emma smiled as innocently as she could.

'I know we started off on a strange footing, but I really want us to be happy and I think we're doing a pretty good job so far.'

Emma nodded her assent on the basis that if she wasn't speaking she couldn't be lying.

'And I know this has got to be hard for you. You've had to put up with far more changes than I have.'

Emma pulled a mock grimace. 'Well, it's been tough. New credit card, facials, shopping on Bond Street…'

'Seriously, Emma.'

'OK, it has been pretty strange. And I felt like it was all a big joke at first. But as long as I don't feel I'm alone in this marriage I'm sure—'

'Do you?'

Emma forced herself to tell the truth. 'Maybe a bit. Well, at first quite a lot. I mean, we spent lots of time together but there was hardly a connection. The closer we get, the easier it makes everything.'

'If you think this is close you ain't seen nothing yet.' Jack leant down and kissed her. 'I know this is the wrong way round, but I really am falling in love with you, Emma.'

'Good.' Good? It was excellent. Against all conventions, her situation was looking very promising indeed. Just one loose end she needed to tie up and it could all be perfect.

'I just want you to be happy.' He kissed her again. 'Speaking of which, have you called Patrick yet?'

Emma stiffened and her stomach lurched, launching a thousand intestinal fireworks, their detonation causing an audible whooshing. Give her death of a parent over the behaviour of her previous employer any day of the week.

Jack addressed her midriff—or at least the area where her

midriff would have been, give or take three layers of clothing. 'You OK in there?'

Damn. Emma had been hoping she'd been the only one who could hear her tummy.

'I'm fine…'

Well, almost. Patrick had already sent a couple of text messages, which she'd accidentally picked up in pockets of signal inside the house before finally switching her phone off. These advances in communication weren't always a good thing.

'I will call him.'

'Promise?' Jack kissed her lightly on the lips.

Emma nodded. She couldn't help feeling she'd spent the last few months making pledges of a not inconsequential nature.

'It's just if I'm going to be busy writing, I don't want you getting bored. You can set up a study in one of the spare rooms.'

'Fab. I'll sort it out.'

There was sharing and caring, and then there was truth economy. Total honesty was the end goal. But one baby-step at a time. Forsaking all others, she had every intention of being faithful to Jack. Starting today.

WILL YOU, THE FAMILIES
AND FRIENDS, SUPPORT AND UPHOLD
THEM IN THEIR MARRIAGE NOW
AND IN THE YEARS TO COME?

fourteen

Jess studied her reflection one more time in the mirror of her compact. Pale and interesting, or shades of panda? Washed up or washed out? In less than a month she had apparently managed to wash the tan off her face, which was now a whiter shade of pale and a total contrast to her bronzed tummy—which unfortunately, due to the chill of autumn and her new single status, had only been observed by her and a couple of people in the changing rooms at the gym.

'Everything OK back there?' Sarah wrestled with her seatbelt before peering back between the front seats to gurgle at her daughter and give her sister a supportive smile 'Stop gilding the lily. You look great, Jess.'

'Reading glasses. That's all I can say to you.'

'Only when I'm tired, or the print is very small. Seriously, you look fine…smile and you'll look great.' Jess had looked better, but make-up was far too superficial for the job and she didn't want her sister to arrive at lunch looking like Aunt Sally.

Pulling a fake smile, Jess felt like a second child as she stared out of the back window and Simon accelerated on to a faster road. She probably should have driven herself for quick getaway purposes…and for maximum self-confidence…but at least she'd made the effort—unless wearing eye shadow was too much for a Sunday lunch in Surrey? She needed a drink.

The myth of the fantasy of freedom versus the reality of a relationship was already beginning to fade around the edges. She should have known better. A lot better. But, Jess reminded herself, had she and Nick stayed together today she'd have been trying to lure him out of the house, further afield than Homebase or the local pub.

From now on she was going to be thankful for every small mercy. If her bed was made, so be it. But she didn't intend to lie in it alone for ever. And everyone always said that you meet new people when you least expect it—although now she'd had the thought maybe today didn't count any more, in which case an afternoon in front of the television wouldn't have gone amiss.

In the absence of a soulmate, she needed a playmate. She smiled at Millie. And one who was out of nappies. Jess sighed. She and Fi hadn't even managed to co-ordinate one day of simultaneous singleness, and now Mike had whisked her away for the weekend. Nick hadn't whisked her anywhere in years. Except perhaps to Tesco for a late night supermarket sweep. Which was why she was on her way to meet new people. The world was her playground. In which case…

'Maybe I should go and live and work abroad for a bit?'

On her way to work yesterday she had realised that her life had become a bus ticket. One adult single. So perhaps it was time to change the final destination. In a civilisation where bulls needed to be taken by the horns, there was nothing to prevent Jess from relaunching her life right now.

Simon and Sarah had been chatting in the front seats, but Jess's opener silenced them immediately.

'I mean, people need wedding planners all over the world.

And indeed barmaids. Maybe I need a change?' Jess could feel herself getting quite fired up.

'Run away if you like. He'll still be here when you get back…'

Sarah, on the other hand, could have been a professional firefighter.

'As for being a barmaid, you've never pulled a pint in your life. Plus, far be it from me to state the obvious, you have your own company. Jessica James has responsibilities and a reputation to maintain. You have clients to satisfy.' Sarah wasn't mincing any words.

'Darling, you're making her sound like a prostitute.'

Sarah shot her husband her best 'not-helpful' silencing glance, which he missed completely as he was concentrating on the road instead of his wife's facial expressions. Jess, however, caught it perfectly.

She sighed. 'Trouble is, Simon, I am just that. I'll do anything anyone wants for a fee—'

Sarah interrupted. 'Rubbish. You've got skills—a real talent.'

'Like what? I'm organised, and I look pretty good in a suit. Wedding planning is hardly rocket science.'

'That's quite enough self-deprecation. You have a career and that's that. It's not like David Beckham can wake up one morning and decide he'd rather have a go at playing golf for a year or two.'

'She's right, you know.'

Jess raised her eyes to the heavens as Simon added his support. What did Sarah know about risk anyway? She'd got married to her first serious boyfriend. Admittedly he was probably her soul mate, but anyway…

Sarah wasn't finished with her yet. 'You can't just throw it all away. Now, more than ever, it's your security you're toying with. I bet you don't even have a pension…'

Everyone knew pensions were a rip-off and that you never saw most of the capital. So Nick had been her pension, but from now on she would start saving. And she was going to buy somewhere to live just as soon as she got her money from the house. It was official. She was chequing out of their relationship. She'd even given the ring back. He hadn't wanted it at first, but she'd insisted.

'So you're having a few tough months? I mean, I'm sure there are days that Tony Blair would like to be a barman in Sydney, but he can't just up sticks and leave.'

'It's different.'

'Not that different. You're an adult. You have responsibilities.'

'I don't answer to the electorate.'

'But you do have to answer to yourself.'

Jess bet Sarah was an excellent teacher. Emotional blackmail. The ultimate weapon. The old letting yourself down line. Always a killer.

'Sar, I'm drowning in orders of service. Everywhere I look there is a happy couple. Part of me wants to be them, part of me is jealous, and part of me wants to tell them to run as fast as they can. Dress designs, seating plans, bands versus DJs, roses versus gerberas, John Lewis versus the General Trading Company…I create perfect days for people. Yet I just can't do it for myself.'

'Maybe you need to see a therapist?'

'In fact forget planning weddings. I should clearly start an introduction agency. Rosie, Mike—not only am I fabulous boss, but I will find you the perfect partner from my very own address book.' Jess couldn't promise that she wasn't going to burst into tears. A swirl of emotion had taken hold, and yet she'd felt so positive when they'd left the house half an hour ago.

'Just a couple of sessions. It might help to have a neutral sounding board. Your life has just done an enormous U-turn; you're bound to be reeling with the aftershocks.'

'Yeah, that's it. I'm nuts. I'm Woody Allen. If only I was

as funny as Woody Allen it wouldn't be as much of a problem. I don't even have an adopted child to run off with.'

'You know Mum's been seeing a therapist for years.'

'Literally.'

'OK, so their relationship progressed. But there's nothing to be ashamed about in asking for a little help from time to—'

'Hey, you're not saying I'm like Mum… Hang on, you *are,* aren't you?'

'I'm not suggesting you sleep with yours. And she's our mother. It wouldn't be such a coincidence if you had a few similar character traits.'

'I'm nothing like her.' Genetic defensive reaction.

'I'm so glad she can't hear you. Granted, she's slightly eccentric…'

Jess waded in before Sarah thought her idea was being accepted. 'She's got more issues than the average edition of the *Economist.* She is the least happy person we know.'

'She's not unhappy.'

'She's been a mistress for fifteen years.' Jess tried to keep her voice from soaring.

'Which she loves. Best of all worlds—living life on her own terms…'

'That's just rhetoric. The bottom line is she's selfish.'

'You've always been very tough on her, Jess. She just wants her independence, and above all she doesn't want to compromise. Any of this sounding familiar…?'

Silence might have traditionally been golden, but right now it was also stony.

'Anyway, all I'm saying is that maybe you should talk to her.'

'I do talk to her.'

'You haven't—not properly, not since the wedding. We had a long chat while you were away.'

'She's always preferred talking to you.'

'That's not true. I just call her from time to time. You two lock horns before you've even said hello.'

'She liked Nick more than she likes me.'

'He just talked to her. And listened. And I think it might do you good to speak to someone who isn't me or Fiona. I mean, we're hardly objective…'

'And Mum *is*?'

'How much harm can one call do?'

'I guess.'

Jess didn't like to admit it, even to herself, but she'd been in a relationship and running her own business for so long that with the exception of Fiona her wider social circle had evaporated. At first she'd thought that old friends would always be there for her, yet one by one her university and schoolfriends had dropped off her social radar. Regrettably, it was her own fault. There was clearly no such thing as a maintenance-free friend. They needed to be checked on regularly and taken out every now and again for a coffee or a bottle of wine to top up their fluid levels.

'And I'm sure your work environment isn't helping.'

'Actually, it's fine. It's good to be needed. And it's busy. We're almost completely booked up for the summer now.'

'Well, it's a shame you and Rosie fell out.'

'*Fell out?*' Jess reined herself in. Boiling point was not an option so close to a social engagement. 'Nick is sleeping with her.' *She* wasn't the one being unreasonable. She knew she wasn't. It was everyone else.

'It's just maybe you could have handed over to her for a couple of weeks—you know, given yourself a chance to—'

'I've just had a holiday.'

'You've had a honeymoon. And you've had a life change. Stop trying to be the toughest woman on the block. You can't handle everything.'

'Sorry to break up group therapy, girls, but you might want to think about lightening the tone when we go inside.' Simon pulled up alongside a shiny four wheel drive and proceeded to reverse park at impressive speed. 'Jess, all you need to re-member is that she's called Chrissie, the baby is called Harry, he's called Pete and we were at school together. They ski and sail and love Italy, so any conversation in those areas is a guar-anteed winner. And they've just had their kitchen redone, so do a bit of cooing over units and floor tiles and you'll be well away.'

'Got it. Thanks.' Jess was grateful for the inside track as she followed Simon up the path, determined to be the life and soul of the afternoon and wishing she'd made time for break-fast. She was starving.

James leant back in his chair and patted his small pot belly contentedly. 'There is still nothing like one of Elsie's enor-mous Sunday lunches to get you buying a pair of looser trou-sers. Right, now, who's for a quick game of Scrabble before our walk?'

'Why not?'

Emma hoped Jack wasn't allergic to board games. She wasn't sure her word power was up to it, but she was in no desperate hurry to clomp through a succession of muddy fields in boots that didn't even fit her.

'Excellent.' James lifted his gaze above his gold-rimmed half-glasses. 'Do you know what? I think you'll make Jack a fine wife.'

'Well, that's good to hear, as we've been married for five weeks now.'

He laughed heartily. 'I think you're the first girl he's dated in recent memory, possibly ever, with more than one A-Level and your own breasts…'

'Dad…' Jack wondered whether if you had two parents they were less embarrassing than one.

Bemused by his discomfort, Emma gave Jack's thigh a playful squeeze under the table. And to her surprise he took her hand gratefully in his.

* * *

Jess's fake smile was fading. Her arrival had definitely triggered a momentary silence as the other guests had exchanged tacit 'oh-she's-the-one-who-left-her-long-suffering-boyfriend-at-the-altar-then-wanted-to-try-again-would-you-believe-it-and-he-said-no-quite-right-too' glances. Red wine was her new best friend.

The last time she'd been single everyone had been fresh out of university, determined to take the world by storm, and lunch parties had been bring a bottle, not bring a baby. Yet apparently now her generation had become self-centred career bores and home-makers.

She'd gone through the motions, taken a heroic interest in everyone else and talked about bread makers, buggies (at least she had a niece), schools and sailing before attaching herself to Simon until nature called him away, at which point Chrissie had immediately introduced her to someone she had missed on her earlier circuit of the sitting room.

"…lovely Josh. Great friend of ours…" Whereupon her hostess had adopted a stage whisper. "Just split up with his girlfriend, actually."

Despite his introduction, he'd been nice enough. A singer-songwriter when he wasn't managing a wine bar, no wife, no baby, no girlfriend, no halitosis and not even unattractive. However, she'd just been contemplating an extended trip to the bathroom for some personal space when Chrissie clapped her hands and twelve people stood to attention. God forbid there should have been an odd number. Noah was alive and well and living in Cobham.

'Right, everyone, time to sit down.'

Jess managed to leave Josh with Simon and walked over to the table with Sarah, hissing furtively as she went. 'We don't have to stay long do we?'

'We haven't even eaten yet.'

'I mean after lunch.'

'I would have thought no more than a couple of hours…'

Jess wanted to burst into tears. Should have driven, should have stayed at home, should have married Nick. That always seemed the sensible option after a few drinks. But at least today she hadn't felt the need to dial any of his phones and hang up before he or the machine answered.

'It's just Simon hasn't seen Pete for ages…'

'Right.' Jess swallowed hard.

'Are you OK?'

'Fine.'

'Pissed?'

'No. Of course not.' Jess's denial was far too emphatic and her tongue was far too blue. But pistachios weren't nearly absorbent enough. 'Pissed off, but not pissed.'

'Pissed off?'

'No wonder people get married. At least then you can stay at home all weekend without anyone asking awkward questions.'

'Have people been giving you a hard time?'

'Not directly, but they are all so patronising.'

'You're just being paranoid.'

'They all think I'm desperate to meet a man. What no one appears to have taken on board is that I've just called off a wedding because I didn't feel the need to be a wife.'

'Who cares what anyone else thinks?'

'Harriet said that single men in their thirties were as rare as prize-winning ring pulls on Coke cans. She was unbelievably smug.' Jess flashed a smile across the room at her through gritted teeth. 'Oh, and Chrissie's trying to set me up.'

'Right, Jess.' Chrissie's voice sailed over. 'Why don't you come and sit over here, next to Josh?'

'Lovely.' Jess beamed at her hostess before giving her sister a look as she sat down. 'Lunch smells delicious—and can I just say, fabulous kitchen?'

Chrissie blushed so deeply at the compliment it was as if

she had sanded every cupboard door herself, rather than just paid someone a lot of Pete's money to remodel and refit it. Pulling in her chair, Jess vowed never to be a woman who took compliments about her kitchen to be more important than her life itself.

Emma stared at her selection of tiles before moving them around on their little shelf, waiting for inspiration to strike. It would have helped if she'd spent the last ten minutes preparing for her turn rather than staring round the drawing room. But to Emma's delight she had spotted a photo of their wedding day in pride of place on top of the piano. In the same room as James's Oscar, no less. She had arrived.

'OK.' Emma went through her options. Dabble. Baby. Bad. Cab. All roads led to her burgeoning guilt complex.

She could feel James watching her. 'You can exchange your letters if you're prepared to forfeit your turn.'

Emma's focus returned. 'No need.' She laid her tiles out. 'Dabble—eleven.'

Turning the board for James, Emma looked over at Jack, who was absently scratching his head in a Stan Laurelesque indication of concentration. Glancing out of the double doors, she watched a pheasant stroll across the ha-ha beyond the terrace just as one of the Labradors started snoring at her feet. It was cold and crisp out there, but thanks to a blazing fire quite toasty indoors for once.

James placed his letters on the board. 'Arson. Double letter under the R and double word—twelve.' With a flourish of his fountain pen, James updated the score sheet. 'Jack, your turn.'

His son looked up. 'Remember the fireworks parties we used to have down here?'

'Chaos.' James reached into the bag for his replacement letters.

'Chaos? They were fantastic.'

'I mean you should play chaos. Triple word sc—'

'How can you see my—?'

'Reflection in the piano…'

Emma couldn't believe James was cheating.

'Merely using my initiative.'

'If that's what you want to call it.' Although now, looking at his choices, Jack could see that frustratingly his father was right.

'Have I taught you nothing? Never leave yourself exposed. As to Bonfire Night, as far as I remember, from the occasions when I wasn't away filming, there was always a terrible mess the following day.'

'Come on, Dad, you have to admit the year Charlie organised the display over the lake it was awesome.'

'Really?' Emma, like most girls, was a sucker for a bit of fireworks–over–water action.

Jack nodded. 'And we always used to have a serious bonfire. It was like a beacon. You could see it for miles.'

'Cool.'

'So how about another one?'

Emma hadn't seen Jack this enthused all weekend. Nor had she seen James any less excited.

'Patience, Jack. It's just the sort of thing the grandchildren will love.'

The grandchildren? Emma was taken aback at her father-in-law's not so subtle indication of what was on his Christmas list.

Jack took no notice of him. 'OK, I've got a better idea.'

James sighed, shaking his head slowly. 'Why doesn't that surprise me?'

'We have a party for Emma's birthday and throw a couple of fireworks in? Face it, you're unlikely to acquire any grandchildren in the next few weeks. Even Harrods don't stock them.'

Emma was grateful for his intervention. She was a new wife, not a walking ovary.

'Next few months?'

'Dad, please. We've only just got married.'

'I know. It's just—you know, I don't know how long I've got left.' A timely cough from Carlisle Senior, the drama king.

'You're the fittest sixty-four-year-old I know. Come on, let's have a party in November. Why not?'

While she knew it was ludicrous to admit it, Emma was impressed that Jack knew when her birthday was. 'Have you been swotting up, darling?'

'So when are we talking, exactly?' James hadn't said no, but he hadn't said yes either.

'Fourth of November—which, if I'm not mistaken is a Friday. So how about the weekend of the fifth and sixth?' Jack turned to his wife. 'What do you normally do for your birthday?'

'Supper with a few friends and a couple of bottles of wine—or a weekend with fireworks at an almost stately home. Pretty interchangeable, really.' Emma was starting to get excited. Although she'd have to tell Amy to bring ski-wear for the girls, just for them to sleep in.

James was hesitant. 'I don't know. This place needs quite a bit of work, and you're only talking a few weeks' time.'

'I'm not talking about anything formal. Just a weekend down here with some friends. We're all far too old and bor-ing to think about trashing the place and climbing the rose arbours, or the wisteria, for that matter. I'm thinking twenty to thirty people, not two hundred, and this place is perfect as it is.'

'OK, what the hell? Why not?'

Emma was sure James was enjoying his moment of power as he granted their wish.

'Now, concentrate. It's still your turn.'

James turned to his daughter-in-law. Emma reminded him of Helen in some ways—not that he would tell Jack that he'd married someone like his mother. It just wasn't what sons wanted to hear. 'Now, what you probably don't know, Emma, is that Greenhill was originally built for entertaining. Records go back as far as—'

'Dad...' Jack's tone was a warning one. He was sure Emma wasn't ready for the unabridged family history.

'Don't you "Dad" me. I'm just educating my daughter-in-law a little further. And go on, Chaos. You know it makes sense.'

'OK, OK.'

Emma pulled her chair in and eagerly leant towards her father-in-law. She hadn't had a dad in nearly twenty-five years. Her capacity for boring anecdotes had barely been tested.

'Well, I hope you're proud of yourself.'

Jess opened an eye and closed it again. Sarah had very unsportingly switched on the main light, which was directly over her bed and in danger of precipitating a migraine. She put her arm over her eyes—her eyelids were nowhere near effective enough—before rolling on to her side and pulling a pillow over the top half of her head.

'I thought it would be better to quit while I was ahead.'

'More like off your head.'

'I just wanted to leave before—you know—Josh got the wrong idea.'

'The right idea being that you are a neurotic alcoholic who is "so single you wouldn't believe it".'

Jess grimaced as the sentence took on a dim familiarity. 'Chrissie sat me there on purpose.'

'She thought it might be useful for you to have a singer-songwriter on your books.'

'Personally or professionally?'

'Honestly, Jess, you both just happened to be there on your own.'

'Which, I'd venture, wasn't an accident. And Simon promised me.'

'You're going to have to lighten up. No one was planning anything. And talk about making an exit…'

'Was it very embarrassing?' Jess pulled the duvet up, covering her head completely.

'What? When your sister stands up mid-dessert and announces that she's just remembered a meeting and has to leave urgently, when she is obviously three sheets to the wind and barely able to make it to the front door, and then has to ring the doorbell to ask which way it is to the nearest tube?'

It had been a schoolgirl error. Cobham was far too twee to have a tube station. Jess folded the duvet back to chest level. Suddenly she was having a hot flush.

'I got the train. I was fine.'

'I take it you know you're still in your clothes?'

Details. Details. Although that would probably explain the sharp pain in her side. Jess moved herself, alleviating the pressure on the zip of her knee-length skirt, which had obviously rotated round her waist by forty-five degrees at some point since she'd got back. At least she'd taken her boots off.

'So what time is it now?' The longer Jess was conscious, the worse she was feeling.

'Seven-thirty.'

'You all stayed there until *now*?'

'It was a fun afternoon. It's good for Millie to play with other children, and I was hardly in a hurry to rush back here and hold your head over the toilet bowl.'

'I haven't been sick.' Jess swallowed. Granted, her breath was unusually minty, but she was sure she hadn't. 'I do think the wine was a bit dodgy.'

'I doubt it. It just wasn't meant to be consumed in half-pints. I think you'd better drink some more water—and you might want to call Josh some time…'

'Yeah, right.'

'To apologise.'

'What? For not fancying him?'

'For presuming that he fancied you in the first place.'

'You're just trying to make me feel bad now.'

'So "Don't even think about asking me out. You're all the same. You just want a wife and kids…" That was just a joke, then?'

'I didn't…?' Jess's normally robust voice was barely audible.

'Oh, you did.'

A picture was coming into focus in Jess's mind's eye, and it wasn't a pretty one.

'Oh, shit. It was his fault. He said he wanted to have children.'

'Presumably he didn't suggest he had them with you?'

Jess dragged herself into an upright position, despite the fact she knew she must look awful. The room stank of stale alcohol and she felt terrible, yet she was decidedly giggly. Hysteria was setting in. Sarah was standing over her, proffering a pint glass full to the brim with water, in a pose owing everything to the Statue of Liberty.

'Drink this. You'll feel better later…and you might want to think about getting undressed.'

'Might do. Might not.'

'Jess, you're behaving like a child. Everyone knows you've had a hard time of it recently.'

'Everyone thinks I've lost my marbles. I made an unpopular decision, that's all, and now I just want to—I just *need* to get on with the rest of my life.'

'You are.'

'But without all this scrutiny. And reaching normality seems to be taking a bloody long time.' Jess laid herself back on the pillows and attempted a sip from the glass.

Water ran down her neck. Flicking as much of it away as possible, she put the glass down on the floor. Sarah was still standing there.

'What have I done now?'

'Nothing. Um…this probably isn't the best time to tell you, but if Nick is buying you out of the house, maybe you should start for looking for a new place.'

Jess groaned.

'I mean, we're not evicting you, or anything, and you can stay as long as you like, but I'm sure you'd like more space—and Simon is missing having a study.'

'Funnily enough, I'm missing having a home, and a dog.'

'I mean, in the very short term we're OK, but…' Sarah was finding this much harder in reality than it had been in her head on the drive home.

'Don't worry. Message received loud and clear. No one wants a spinster living in their not-that-spare room… One maiden sister will start flat-hunting first thing tomorrow.'

'It's not like that.' Guilt highlighted Sarah's expression.

'Look, I still have a sense of humour. And if I'm going to get over Nick I'll need some serious retail therapy. What better than having to buy somewhere to live? Just think of the Habitat and Ikea spin-off trips. Not to mention the DIY I'll be doing.'

'I'm happy to help.'

'Thanks.' Jess was grateful for the offer. Her first month as a single girl about town had been hugely overrated. 'And I'm sure I'll be able to lure Fiona out when she's stopped spending every evening and weekend having start-of-rela-tionship sex.'

'That's not fair. Mike's a great guy. I happen to think they are very well suited.'

'You just want everyone married off.'

'Come on, Jess. Marriage isn't a four-letter word, nor is it a sentence—life or otherwise.'

'I know.' Jess castigated herself for her bitchy tone. 'But I'm allowed to miss her, aren't I? I mean, this weekend they've gone all the way to Paris to have a shag…'

Sarah winced.

'At least if they were in North West London then I might have been able to meet her, or at worst *them,* for a coffee.'

'You know I hate that word.'

'What? Coffee?' Jess grinned. 'You're such a schoolteacher. You're lucky I haven't etched my initials into the dining room table.' Sarah brought out the absolute pupil in her. 'And if I'd been off having coffee with them I wouldn't have bloody well been at Sunday lunch in Smugsville with you.'

Somewhere in the house the phone started to ring, and, observing the empty base unit in the study, Sarah left in search of a handset. Each ring cycle fractured Jess's skull into a thousand headaches. Unfortunately she was sobering up, yet it was far too early to go to bed for the night. As if on cue, Millie started crying in the next room. Even the duvet was failing to muffle everything.

'Jess?' Simon shouted up the stairs and round the corner. 'Jess!'

His footsteps clattered towards her, echoing ominously on the bare pine floorboards. Thrusting the portable phone at her as she emerged from her undercover position, he went to resettle his daughter, shouting over his shoulder as he exited the room. 'It's Fi.'

Speak of the devil. Jess glanced at her alarm clock as she answered. Nice of Fi to squeeze her in this weekend. Maybe Mike had fallen asleep on the return Eurostar.

'*Bonjour,* my love. Was Paris gay? Your life is so jet set. Make that train set.'

Fiona laughed. It didn't take much at the moment for her to make the transition from perpetual grin to belly laugh. 'That sounds a lot less glamorous.'

Jess reminded herself that she was supposed to be happy for her best friend. 'Well…I didn't mean…it's lovely that he…'

Fi didn't seem to need any positivity; she was practically effervescent. 'Paris is such a wonderful city.'

'So it's safe to say you had a good time, then?'

'Excellent. Fab. Really, really good. And I'm definitely more in love now than when…' Fi trailed off.

'Fi? Are you there?'

Silence. Jess was going to count to five and then hang up. She only got to three and a half before Fiona rejoined her sentence.

'I just don't quite know how to…' Fiona took a deep breath. This was her moment and this was her best friend. 'Mike asked me to marry him.'

Irrational tears sprang to Jess's eyes and she blinked them away. She needed to keep as much water in her alcohol-tainted system as possible at the moment.

'It was perfect, and…and… Jess?'

'I'm here.' Jess cleared her throat. 'Go on.'

'I said yes.'

'Wow. Great. That's great.' Jess was doing her best to muster a small whoop in her delivery, but as yet nothing. In fact she was feeling positively cardboard. Hopefully Fi would just think it was a bad line. 'Congratulations. You must be over the moon. Scratch that. He must be over the moon. What a catch you are.' Jess noticed Sarah standing in the doorway again. So now she couldn't even have a phone call in private?

'I'm feeling pretty lucky myself. I know it's soon, very soon, but it just feels so right. And I know that's the cheesiest line in the world, so feel free to make a retching noise.'

Jess decided against it in case her pickled body thought she was method acting. 'So where are you now?'

'We've just got in to Waterloo. We wanted to keep it a secret until we got back…'

We. *Oui*. Fuck a duck. Fiona was getting married.

'…and I wanted to tell you first.'

'I'm first?' Jess's chest swelled a little at the compliment. 'What about your brother?'

'Nick?'

'Is there another one I almost married?'

Fiona didn't laugh. 'He was away this weekend too…'

Away? Jess felt a stab of jealousy as she imagined him taking Rosie to all their old haunts.

'And I figured the parents could wait until later—or tomorrow. And it goes without saying that we'd really like you to plan our wedding for us.'

'Of course.' Jess praised herself for mustering an appropriate level of enthusiasm. 'That sounds like a definite possibility.' Jess knew she was sitting on the fence, but there was only so much a newly single girl could take in one conversation.

'We're thinking early next year.'

'Well, with that sort of timescale it's going to have to be diary permitting. Unless you don't mind getting married on a week-day, or they've developed the technology for me to be in two places at once.'

'Jess, are you stalling me?'

'Of course not.' Oh, the disadvantage of having friends who knew you far too well. 'It's just…'

Jess was starting to wish she organised funerals, not weddings. Starting with her own.

'Well, don't you think it's all…?' How was she going to put this. 'Quite soon?' Some things were definitely best left unsaid, and Jess couldn't help thinking that might have been one of them.

'I know it seems fast, but when you know, you *know*.'

'Or you know and then you forget for the crucial seven days you really should remember before becoming as sure as he is unsure.' Jess knew this wasn't the time to be talking about herself.

Fi wasn't playing. This was her moment and no one was going to tarnish it. 'There's always going to be an element of timing. I mean, look at Jack and Emma Carlisle.'

Jess sighed. Frustratingly, she couldn't divulge any details. 'Oh, yeah, because they're so normal.'

'What's normal these days? And anyway we—well, I only want a small wedding.'

'I'm sure we'll be able to sort out the perfect day for you…' Jess could already foresee one slight problem. As microscopic as Fiona's wedding might be, Nick was going to be there. And he was the one person she didn't need to see at a wedding for many years—if indeed ever. However, for Jessica James there were no options. Life was a two-way street—well, most of the time, in an ideal world, when they weren't laying a gas main… 'And of course I'd love to do it. Big hugs and kisses to you both.' Jess congratulated herself. That was sounding much better.

Sarah was now perched adjacent to her sister, pretending to flick through an old magazine, desperate to make a contribution. As the conversation progressed without her she started bouncing up and down, and the seismic waves rippling through the mattress were making Jess feel very nauseous. She waved at her sister to stop.

'Can I say hello?' Sarah grabbed the phone before Jess could stop her.

'Fi? It's me. Fantastic news, darling. A million congratulations from me and Si.'

Jess lay back on her pillow and listened. Sarah was in seventh welcome-to-the-wonderful-world-of-marriage heaven.

'Brilliant. Of course. Exactly. You can't predict these things. Of course. Of course. How romantic. Perfect. I'm so excited for you. It's just the best, the most exciting time…'

Sarah was showing her up now. Ten times more effusive. Damn. And she hadn't even finished yet.

'We can't wait to see you. In fact, where are you now? Why don't you come over for a glass of champagne? Of course…ask him… Either way it's fine. We're in all evening. I'll pop a bottle in the fridge just in case.'

Sarah handed the phone back to her sister, who was determined to be better at gushing the second time around.

'Go on—come over.' Jess wondered if Fi would notice if she had a glass of Ribena instead. Maybe if she mixed it with sparkling water and decanted it into a flute she could pretend it was a Kir Royale. 'And then we can start planning right away… Your wish is my command…as long as I think it's a good idea, of course.' A laugh, just like before. Things didn't have to change. Although she was currently talking much faster than normal.

'We were thinking intimate.'

'There's no doubt about it. Small is beautiful.'

'And maybe Paris.'

'Paris?' Jess repeated the city name as if it was a newly discovered planet in the solar system. 'Well, of course it's up to you two. But the French make you jump through a hundred hoops and there's a potential residency issue. Almost easier anywhere else.'

'Oh…'

Fiona sounded disappointed, and it was pretty much all her fault. Jess wanted to get herself off the phone. She needed to regroup. 'Look, don't rule it out yet. Let's sit down and discuss all this properly.'

Sarah had started doing the nervous energy thing again. Clearly she had something to add. All in good time.

'And, by the way, you two had better come over or Sarah might explode with excitement.'

Jess heard Fi talking to Mike. That figured. Fi was going to have to get used to checking everything with her fiancé. Jess couldn't help herself. She needed a slap.

'Please, thank Sarah for the invite, but we're going to head home. I've got to be at work first thing tomorrow morning, and we've had a fair bit of champagne already today. Plus, as you can imagine, we have a few phone calls to make. But let's meet up soon—maybe Tuesday evening?'

'Sounds great. Call me at work and I'll check the diary.'

'Done.'

'Love to you both.'

Jess hung up just as Sarah succumbed to her next bout of excitement. She stood up, she sat down, she stood up, she sat down. She was a single-handed Mexican wave in the making.

'Sar. Please. Go and tell Simon, or something. Just—I need a moment, if that's OK.'

'Of course. Fine.'

Sarah pulled the door to behind her and Jess stared at the phone keypad before dialling the familiar number and waiting.

'Hello, I'm sorry I can't take your call at the moment. Please leave your name and number after the tone and I'll get back to you as soon as I can.'

He'd changed girlfriends and the answer-machine message. He had officially moved on.

The tone came and went. 'Nick, hi, it's me. Jess. Just calling to congratulate you on being Fi's brother. Hopefully she'll have spoken to you by the time you get this.' Jess paused as she wondered what on earth she was doing. 'Anyway, great news. Erm, hope all's well with you and—'

Jess couldn't bring herself to say her name.

'…hopefully we can catch up soon?'

Jess clicked the button to cut the connection between her and her old home and held the handset to her chest. Where was her dignity? Her self-control? Her sense of purpose? She'd never used to be a jealous person.

Gingerly she reassumed the horizontal position, so as not to upset her hangover further. Probably just as well he was out. She missed him, and it would have been just as dangerous as going food shopping on an empty stomach if he'd been there. But Sunday night was television and tidy-up night. It had been for as long as she could remember. And what about *Top Gear*? He'd never even learnt to set the video.

fifteen

Patrick sat at Emma's old desk, searching the Internet for answers that even Google couldn't provide. Unless you needed to find a cardiologist, the information superhighway was ill equipped to deal with matters of the heart. It was only ten days since she'd told him to back off, yet by removing herself from the emotional equation she had thrown down an invisible gauntlet which he was wrestling with his conscience to leave well alone.

Her marriage of convenience had become an inconvenience, but he really didn't need a new relationship. Been there, done that, got the decree absolute. Twice. But since when was modern life about need? Self-employed, self-motivating, selfish, focused, fucking successful—call it what you like—Patrick Robson was used to getting exactly what he wanted.

At the moment he really just wanted a chance to talk. But not on the phone, not about work, and not in Jack's flat. He knew Emma would never agree, however—Patrick consulted his watch to confirm the date—it could well be time for a progress meeting.

Fiddling with his shirt cuffs, he dialled Emma's mobile number on speakerphone.

'Hello?'

Her voice echoed round the office before Patrick could pick up the handset.

'Mrs Carlisle.' Patrick feigned being relaxed. Thanks to him, a missed opportunity had become a Mrs opportunity. 'How's it going?'

'Manic. Not quite sure when I ever had time for a full-time job.' Emma laughed semi-hysterically. Patrick on the phone. Not ideal. 'Don't worry, rest assured I'm getting your stuff done too…'

'I got the e-mail—thanks.'

'Good.'

'You could have called.' He knew she was definitely avoiding him. And he was definitely missing her.

'I thought it would be easier for you to have it all in front of you first. Anyway, I look forward to hearing what you think. Meanwhile, I've only got about a week to organise a fireworks party—money no object, but venue miles away, and I have no clue about the finer details of rockets or Catherine wheels. I have a vague recollection of launching rockets from milk bottles as a child, only clearly they're pretty rare these days, and I'm not sure a plastic carton is going to be quite so effective.'

Patrick stretched out in her chair. 'Call me old-fashioned, but surely this is Jack's department?'

'So you'd think. But he's very busy this week.'

'Busy?'

Emma hesitated. None of this had anything to do with Patrick. But this was information Jack would gladly hand over himself. 'Jack has decided to be a writer.'

'A writer?'

'Indeed. Plus, he's just got wind of an audition for the lead in a potentially huge film, so he's spending a fair bit of time at the gym.' Emma stopped herself a few words too late. Patrick absolutely did *not* need to know that she was regularly home alone.

'At the gym?' It would appear that Patrick was only capable of questions this afternoon.

'He'd be playing a boxer.'

'With his perfect looks?'

Emma smiled ruefully. 'I know, but he couldn't be more excited about a real character part. We now have a punch bag suspended from our ceiling, and he's practising talking with a lisp. Slightly irritating, and he's spitting a lot. Not attractive…'

Suddenly Patrick really wanted him to get the part.

'Why is it that so many boxers have lisps…and nuns for that matter? Interesting that men respond to being picked on at school by making a career out of thumping people and women go the convent route. There you have it in a nutshell—the difference between the sexes. Anyway, you'd better watch your step, mister, because my husband will be able to knock your lights out very soon indeed.' Emma was only half joking.

A grunt from Patrick's end of the conversation.

'Look, I'm sorry, but I'm going to have to run.' White lie. Emma was doing civil, she was doing chatty, but she wasn't interested in doing prolonged. And so far there was no point to this conversation.

'Just before you go, I've got a favour to ask.'

Emma braced herself for the worst. 'Go ahead.'

'I really need you to come in for a meeting.'

'Right.' She bet he didn't. 'When?'

Patrick marvelled at her normality. 'Tomorrow? I know it's short notice, but the clients only called this morning, and I'd really like you to be here seeing as Give Mum the Night Off is really your baby.'

Flattery, Patrick had learned, got you everywhere.

'Any chance we can make it the afternoon? Say fourish?'

'Sure.' Patrick realised it supposedly wasn't just up to him. 'I'm sure that'll be fine. I'll check with them and let you know.'

'Great.' A few more weeks and then she'd be out of there for good. If only Jack hadn't insisted she took the job. 'So I'll probably see you tomorrow, then?'

'Yup.'

'Cool. It's all looking pretty good. I've finalised the wish-list, and I've got a couple of suggestions for the ads. All we need are a few key faces involved and we'll be laughing as hard—hopefully—as the audience.'

'Sounds like you've been busy.'

'Life's much more fun that way. I am becoming a master juggler.'

'Careful with all those balls, young lady.'

Emma flinched. It was never going to be a good time for innuendo on that front. But to her immense relief, and almost disbelief, since she'd bitten the bullet the whole incident seemed to have blown over. Sometimes it was great being an adult.

Patrick noted the silence. 'Well, I'd better get on. Loads to do.' He looked round the deserted office. 'I'll call and confirm later.'

'Great. Bye.'

'Bye.' Patrick replaced the handset, sat back and closed his eyes. Meeting sorted. Now all he had to do was work on the agenda.

sixteen

'Cheers, Fi.' Nick raised his glass. 'Congratulations. I'm sorry it's taken so long to organise this face to face, but I really needed to get away for a few days.'

Fiona watched the traffic snaking around Hyde Park Corner from their table at the Windows on the World restaurant. For once London was at her feet.

'Well, you've certainly made up for the delay with this venue. So long Pizza Express. And it's not like I've been short of a decent meal recently. At this rate I'll be rolling down the aisle, the first spherical bride ever…'

'I doubt it.'

'You have no idea how much champagne I've been forced to drink. And then I've been far too hungover to go to the gym before work.'

'Am I supposed to be feeling sorry for you?'

Fiona smiled. 'Of course not. And, in case I haven't mentioned it recently, Mike is just fantastic.'

Nick was still adjusting to his sister's unbridled excitement.

'Does this mean you're not going to need your older brother any more?'

'I'll always need you—if only to tell me I'm being flighty/unrealistic/self-absorbed—just delete where applicable…'

Nick nodded.

'Feel free to jump in and correct me.'

'I will—just as soon as you say something that's not true.'

'Look, you, I've only been engaged for ten days or so. And it feels like ten minutes. There's been so much happening.'

'Ten days or so?' Nick faked being wistful and pretended to twiddle a bit of hair he hadn't had for nearly ten years. 'Surely you mean ten days, twelve hours, seven minutes and three seconds?'

Fiona would have hurled a slice of freshly baked walnut and raisin bread at her brother if it hadn't been so delicious.

'Sorry, but it's not every day your sister gets engaged. In fact, it's not every day your sister has a new boyfriend—or at least this sister at any rate. And I have to say that this time there wasn't much of a gap between the two. But I know, I know…' Nick adopted a slighty more breathy tone than normal. '"He's just, well, perfect."' He ended his sentence with a little sigh.

Fiona giggled. 'Have I become the most boring woman in the world?'

'No…' Nick hesitated. 'But you might be in the running for the most excited one. Which is great. Mike seems like a great guy. I mean, he should really have asked my permission for your hand in marriage…I'd have set him a few challenges, interviewed a couple of previous girlfriends, suggested a suitable fee, brokered your dowry—that sort of thing.'

'Nick.'

'Remember, I know what boys are like…maybe I'll take him out for a few beers.'

'Don't put him off, will you?'

'I think it's going to take more than a babbling property developer to do that…'

Fiona smiled. 'I really was beginning to think this day would never come.'

'What rubbish. We all knew you'd be fine…'

'*We all?* I didn't realise I had a board of governors.'

Starting to heat up from the inside out, Nick pulled his jumper off and took a sip of water.

Fiona just stared at her brother who, it appeared, was wearing a black shirt with white collars and cuffs. 'Where the hell did you get that shirt? Have you joined the Mob?'

'Rosie bought it for me. No good?'

Fiona pulled a face. 'Not you at all.'

'It's some designer. Italian, I think.'

'I don't care who it is…' Fiona took another sip of champagne '…it's revolting.'

'OK. Well, I haven't got another one with me, so you're going to have to live with it for tonight.' Nick toyed with the idea of putting his jumper back on. But he was far too hot. 'Now, back to you—or rather back to Mike. I'm guessing the man may need a few pieces of inside information…like the fact you used to kiss your Duran Duran poster goodnight every evening.'

'That's a lie.'

Nick arched an eyebrow.

'It was only Simon Le Bon.'

'And…?'

'John Taylor. Come on, Nicholas, there's no need to start airing my dirty laundry. How about that Sam Fox picture you used to have hidden in your atlas?'

Nick blushed. 'I'm sure Mike will be very understanding.'

'Anyway, you have met him a couple of times.'

'I have?'

'He took some photos of you.'

'Oh, then…'

'Come on, Nick. Sorry, but it's nearly two months now.'

'Seven weeks, four days and...' Nick's shoulders slumped.

Fiona watched her brother carefully. He'd never been a very good actor. Or even a mediocre actor. 'You're being serious, aren't you?'

'The thing is, we really were great together. I mean before we started taking each other for granted and I started applying pressure—and not even for any good reason. It was a total fuck-up.'

'It wasn't that bad.'

'Women have just got harder and harder to read. Once upon a time they were itching for their men to propose. Now they want to be proposed to spontaneously, but only at a time to suit them and without giving any overt clues.'

'Maybe you just grew apart.'

'Maybe.' Nick didn't sound convinced.

'You were together for a long time. You just had a marriage without a wedding, that's all.'

'People rescue their marriages all the time. But communication is key and she went silent on me.'

'She said she needed space.'

'On the day of our wedding? Fortunately I can no longer remember all the details. My mind has kindly blanked them out—along, unfortunately, with meeting Mike. I'm sorry. Anyway...' Nick raised his glass. 'Thank goodness for you. Love you lots. Congratulations. And who'd have thought you'd beat me to the altar, eh? It's a funny old world sometimes.'

Fiona studied her napkin apologetically for a moment. She didn't know why. None of this was her fault. Well, apart from introducing them in the first place.

Nick hadn't finished being chirpy yet. 'And the parents are over the moon. You've single-handedly rescued their year and given them something positive to put in the Christmas cards.'

Fiona took her glass and clinked it with Nick's.

'You'll be fine—honestly.'

Tipping their heads back, they both drained their champagne glasses.

'So, come on. I know I've had the telephone version, but I want it all…' Nick refilled their flutes from the bottle. 'The down-on-one-knee, widescreen director's cut. It's weird, you know—maybe it's one of those psychic sibling things—but I tried to call you that Sunday. Around midday, in fact. Clearly I could sense your allegiance shifting to another man…'

Fiona laughed. 'You're mad. But my phone did ring.'

'And you didn't answer it, so proving my point.'

'I didn't want to ruin the moment.'

'Charming.'

'I didn't know it was you, did I? And you can imagine the scene: *Middle of Pont Neuf. Paris. A cold but sunny day. A prospective fiancé is on bended knee.* "Will you marr—" *A phone rings. His intended rummages in her handbag.* "Sorry, I'd better take it. Won't be a second."'

Nick laughed at her am-dram role play. 'Did I call right at that moment? Spooky.'

'OK, that was artistic licence. But it was only moments afterwards.'

'You weren't—you know—um…consummating your engagement or anything?'

'Nick! Have you not listened to a word I've been saying? We were on a bridge.'

'So? Some people don't care where they are.'

Fiona blushed. This was not the sort of conversation she wanted or expected to have with her brother.

'So, what did you want?'

'Pardon?'

'When you called?'

'Oh, nothing.'

'Really?' Fiona folded her arms.

'I shouldn't really have called you anyway, but it was either that or…' Nick started chain-nibbling olives.

'Or…?' Fiona's eyes searched her brother's. 'Or call Jess?'

Nick looked sheepish. 'I was having a bad day and, well, you know you said I should just call you instead… It's just sometimes—well…' It was his turn to inspect his place setting now. 'I just can't help wondering—' he addressed his fork '…if—well, I was angry and hurt when she got back. Call it what you like: temporary insanity, self-preservation. I wasn't thinking straight, even though I thought I was fine.'

'But what about Rosie?'

'Don't get me wrong. She's been great. And she was just what I needed.' Nick grinned.

'You don't say?'

'What's that supposed to mean?'

'You've been wielding her like a Samurai sword. You've taken her everywhere with you, like a human comforter. What is it they say? Attack is the best form of defence?'

'I've just been having some fun. Hell I deserved it. But eight years plays nearly eight weeks. And I'm realising more and more that she's not—well, she's lovely, but she's not Jess. Obviously.'

'Jess was upset, you know.'

'*Was* upset?'

'Was upset.' Fiona continued to tiptoe through the minefield, wishing she hadn't drunk two glasses of champagne already.

'About Rosie?'

'Of course…'

Nick brightened.

'Don't forget she was a great assistant.'

Fiona watched her brother's face fall. 'And, you big idiot, because she was hoping… But she couldn't just say she'd changed her mind and expect you to come running.' Fiona had no idea whether any of this was helping or not. She was an accountant, not a diplomat.

Nick rested his chin on his hands pensively. '*Was* upset or *is* upset?'

'Oh, you know—she has her moments.' Blood brother versus soul sister. Fiona was definitely piggy in the bloody middle.

Nick nodded.

'But you two have to be realistic. Things have changed.'

'Too right. I don't have any decent CDs, for a start.'

'Nick.'

'Sorry, it's just that—'

Fiona interrupted. She almost didn't want to know exactly what he thought. 'Just remember the easiest option is not necessarily the right one.'

'Whose side are you on?'

'Mine.' Fi really wanted to move on now.

'And who said anything about Jess being easy?'

Fiona laughed. 'Fair point.'

'Anyway, I'm still not… Maybe I've given her too many chances already. And she's not exactly knocking down my door, now, is she?'

'Perhaps because Rosie might answer?' Fiona shook her head. The male perspective was unique.

'But Jess was going to be my wife.'

'Look, officially—no comment. Unofficially—just go carefully. Human lives are at stake. And remember you are the man who drank far too many pints while Jess was away and told me you didn't believe you could ever go back.'

'How about sideways?'

'You said it could never be the same.'

'I don't want it to be.'

'Well, just take a good look before you even think about leaping.'

'Have you swallowed a whole book of those?'

Fiona placed her hand on top of her brother's. 'Remember, pride comes before a fall.'

'What the hell is that supposed to mean in this context?'

'Absolutely no idea.' Fiona studied the label on the champagne as she retrieved the bottle from the ice bucket and refilled their glasses. 'You'd better ask Mr Heidsieck.'

Nick smiled apologetically. 'Sorry, Fi, I didn't mean to hijack your evening.'

'Don't be ridiculous. We haven't even got to the main course yet. Prepare to be Michaeled.'

Nick leant forward on his elbows. 'I'm ready.'

'I was actually thinking maybe he could meet us for a drink afterwards.'

'Cool.'

Fiona giggled.

'What?' Nick paused. 'OK, Fi—how long have we got until he gets here?'

'About an hour and a half.'

'Thought you'd be bored with me by then?'

'Thought you might like to meet him.'

'Do you always get your own way?'

'Of course not.'

'Just as long as he knows what he's letting himself in for.'

'And maybe if you could put your jumper back on?' Brothers. Best enemies, best friends and best left at home sometimes. But not when they were buying you dinner.

FOR BETTER, FOR WORSE;
FOR RICHER, FOR POORER;
IN SICKNESS AND IN HEALTH...

seventeen

Emma waved her magic wand and wished it would transport her somewhere else. Over the years she'd missed loads of things: television programmes, buses, parties, deadlines, the occasional friend's birthday…but never a period. And in a minute she'd know whether her hunch was going to be a human being.

Boiled, scrambled, poached, free-range, barn-laid, white, brown, speckled, chocolate, fertilised. Eggs were everywhere. And until recently the only ones not having a good time had been hers. Thanks to the Pill she hadn't ovulated for nearly fourteen years, and while she'd been hoping that her body hadn't lost the 'How to' instruction booklet in a miscellaneous kitchen drawer, this was on the verge of being one of the fastest conceptions on record for a woman of her age.

The bathroom was silent, bar a sporadic drip from the showerhead, and, crossing the tiles carefully, Emma locked the door as quietly as she could. Her caution was absolute. Jack had left the flat first thing for a meeting or something—she'd been too semi-conscious to care—but their cleaning lady was due in less than half an hour.

And there it was. Emma blinked a couple of times to make sure it wasn't an optical illusion. The fine line. The thin blue line. Or perhaps the waving had simply caused the ink to spread. No such luck. Emma stared and stared some more as a wave of elation at her fertility rose within her—shortly crushed by the descent of a cloak of panic.

Light-headed, Emma sat on the loo and rested her forehead on the adjacent sink, the cool ceramic proving to be a calming influence. It wasn't that she wasn't ready for the children thing, but this month she'd had a husband and a lover and they weren't the same person. Emma grimaced as she checked the stick one more time. She couldn't believe she'd made such a potentially expensive mistake. Eggspensive. Her imagination had never been more fertile, or more pessimistic.

Putting all the paraphernalia into her sponge bag, she walked into the bedroom as nonchalantly as possible before hiding the evidence in amongst her gym kit for anonymous disposal later. Climbing back into bed, in an attempt to hide from the reality of the rest of her day, Emma was dismayed at her behaviour. She was a mother behaving like a child.

If you were basing your calculations on the number of ejaculations that might be responsible, statistically it was much more likely to be Jack's. But biology textbooks and shocking tabloid articles on teenage pregnancy recurred in full view: it only took one bloody-minded sperm. She felt like a character from *Eastenders*. She was pregnant and she couldn't be sure who the father was. At least as an orphan and an only child she didn't have any close family to disappoint. But Emma couldn't believe it. For years she'd been single and virtually celibate; now she was married and a slapper. Talk about mistimed maturity. One afternoon. That was all. It wasn't much consolation, but at least she'd never seen a grey-haired baby.

Emma did her best to be rational. It couldn't be Patrick's; there'd definitely been a condom. Well, eventually. Curling up on her side of their bed, she eyeballed the floor. She was suffering with morning sickness of an irresponsible nature. It had to be Jack's.

Emma flicked on the television in the bedroom and turned the volume down to minimal, allowing just enough of a burble to break up the silence and her focus. She only half watched the tanned blond host introduce another guest to an explosion of studio applause. And there he was, her husband, at the end of her bed, a mere six inches tall. Scrabbling for the remote to increase the volume, Emma sat up and waited to see what he had to say for himself.

'Good morning, Jack.'

'Morning, Katie.'

'Great to have you here, and thank you for getting up so early.'

'My pleasure.'

'So, tell me, how come you look so good first thing?'

'That'd be your make-up artist.' His trademark laugh. 'Seriously, I have no trouble getting up these days.'

'So married life agrees with you, then?'

'Most definitely.'

'And will Mrs Carlisle be watching this morning?'

'I doubt it. She sees quite enough of me already. I'm sure she's got far more interesting things to do.' A laugh and Katie did her best to join in. Emma was frozen in her viewing position.

'So…' Katie clasped her hands on her lap, crossing her legs to accentuate the tight cut of her skirt '…do tell us about your latest project. You're writing a book, is that right?'

'Yup, that's it. In my spare time. In fact at the moment most of the time.'

Since their weekend away, Jack had spent most of his days typing, in a cloud of smoke, at the computer in the corner

of the sitting room overlooking the river. Emma was unsure
if the extra smoking was all part of his perceived image of
a writer or whether the nicotine was really helping to focus
his mind.

'And it's an autobiography?'

'Not exactly. It's pretty much an account of the worst year
and a half of my life.'

'Fantastic.'

'I'm not sure that's the word I'd use.'

Emma laughed. Served Katie Fletcher right for flirting
with her husband.

'Of course. I'm sorry. I'm sure it was an incredibly difficult time for you.'

'To say the least. But I'm hoping that overall the exercise
will do me more good than harm.'

His agent had certainly assured him that the financial re-
wards would be substantial.

'And do we have a title?'

'Not yet.'

'Riiiight.' Katie did her best to take instructions from the
producer in her earpiece whilst struggling to come up with
something pertinent to say. 'Cool. Great.' Only from Katie's
delivery it was clearly none of the above. 'So, when should
we expect to see it on the shelves?'

'Oh, not for another six months or so—depends, really, on
what else comes up in the way of the film projects, and
whether the muse has any holidays booked.'

'But it's factual?'

'Very much so. And autobiographical. I know there are
plenty of people who've been through similar experiences,
and hopefully it'll help them to know they are not alone.'

'Well, I for one—and I'm sure the audience here in the
studio—' the camera panned along rows of nodding heads
'—and at home will all be rushing out to buy their copy. Are
you finding it draining to write about Charlie?'

Jack nodded soberly as a picture of his brother filled the screen for a few seconds. 'For the first couple of days I could barely put anything on paper. It just somehow felt disloyal. If that makes sense…'

'Totally.'

Emma doubted Katie knew what she was even agreeing too. Yet her brow was furrowed with pseudo-sincerity.

Jack didn't seem to have noticed her interjection. 'But I have to thank Emma for this idea. For the last couple of years I'd really been going nowhere emotionally, and thanks to her I am making real progress.'

'Really? That's fantastic.'

Jack nodded. And so did his wife, as she tried to remember whether he'd mentioned this television appearance at all.

'Anything you'd like to say to her?'

Emma stared at the screen as Jack expertly turned to the camera and winked before returning to his interview.

'I didn't tell her I was coming along this morning and, no, she knows how I feel.'

'She's a lucky woman.'

'Oh, she knows that.' Jack laughed. 'And I'm a lucky man.' Nearly a million housewives up and down the country wept into their cleaning products, praying for just an iota of glamour in their lives—or, failing that, a little appreciation from their husbands.

'So, any films in the pipeline?'

'I've been in talks about a couple.'

'Rumour has it you might be donning a pair of boxing gloves for your next role?'

'We'll see. Although I could do with a reason to go the gym a little more regularly.' Jack pinched an invisible roll of fat. 'Writing isn't exactly an aerobic activity.'

Katie laughed again and flicked her hair. Jack kept his gaze steady, his famous smile a little lopsided, as he sat back on the sofa and ran his hand through his hair.

'But, wife or not, we're still going to see you around?'

'Of course.'

'Excellent.'

'This year has been all about change for the better.'

Emma exhaled. Apparently she'd been holding her breath. And now she was supposed to be providing oxygen for two. Breathing deeply, she returned her attention to the small screen.

'Good, good. And now, I'm sorry to have to ask this personal question...'

'Fire away.' Jack crossed his legs and sat back on the pastel sofa.

'...but there has been some speculation over the fact that Emma might be pregnant.'

The blood drained from Emma's face as she wondered if she'd hallucinated the last sentence. It was uncanny. Unless her fallopian tubes had access to an outside line.

'You guys really shouldn't believe what you read in the tabloids.' Jack was a pro. He hadn't skipped a beat.

'So no truth in the rumours?'

'None at all. Although, being a man, I guess I'm likely to be one of the last to know.'

A laugh from the audience at this well-rehearsed self-deprecation.

'Do you mind me asking if you are trying for a family?'

'Do I have a choice?'

One of the four pictures that had appeared in *CelebriTee* of Jack and Emma on their wedding day appeared full screen.

'I don't want to seem defensive or evasive, but why is it that as soon as you get married everyone expects you to have children? Speculation is a mug's game. I know it sells a lot of papers, but really...'

The picture faded into a blurry shot of them walking along the river clutching takeaway coffees. Not a good hair, face or clothes day for Emma. She still hadn't got used to never leaving the house without make-up on. And she really hadn't looked as bad as she looked on screen right now. She'd bet Katie had selected that picture herself. There'd been some pretty good ones of the two of them, and that wasn't one of them.

'If it happens it happens, and we'll be delighted, but right now we're just adjusting to being Mr and Mrs and we're having a lovely time.'

Emma hoped he was ready. Clean sheet. Clean sheets. She couldn't believe what she'd done. And in a worst case scenario how, or indeed why, would you leave Britain's best loved man? She only knew one PR guy well enough to ask, and in this case that was definitely not going to be a good idea.

For better, for worse. Her vows definitely hadn't made any provisions for accidentally having a fling. One hundred per cent culpable and one hundred per cent unwilling to deal with the consequences. Absently she stroked her still flattish tummy. This was supposed to be a euphoric moment in her life, and yet all she could think about now was damage limitation. Until September all her options had been open. And now they weren't. A child. Next summer. With no twenty-eight-day exchange policy if it didn't fit or suit her. Options were dropping off the spectrum faster than lemmings off a ledge.

She needed Amy. And fast. Dialling her number, she sank into the goosedown pillows and sent a silent prayer to the ceiling. She didn't have long. Her husband had just left the studio to whoops and rapturous applause, and no doubt an executive car was waiting to whisk him home.

eighteen

'So, are you going to sell your flat?' Jess cradled the phone between her neck and her shoulder and ripped open the most interesting-looking of her mail packages.

'I think we'll probably just let it out at first. I can move into Mike's for now, then we can sell both and buy somewhere bigger when we're not paying for a wedding.'

'Don't tell me—you've got the spreadsheets to prove it?'

Fi smiled. 'Of course. And as it is he's got two spare rooms. Well, one and a study.'

'Nursery.' Jess squeezed the stress toy in the shape of lucky horseshoe which *domeafavour.com* had sent her. There was apparently nothing they couldn't manufacture for the wedding table. Jess had a good mind to set them a few challenges. Maybe a liquorice ball and chain, an edible noose or inflatable handcuffs. She was feeling much better, but clearly was in the wrong job at the moment.

'Study.'

'It's good that you're keeping your own place.' Jess flicked through the accompanying brochure before filing it in the bin.

'What? Just in case?'

'Exactly.'

'Honestly, Jess, we're getting married. This isn't a fling. We're not sixteen and playing at being engaged. It's a flat, that's all. Four walls, a roof and an enormous mortgage. I love Michael. Not that I intend to be a kept woman.' Fiona looked around her sheepishly, suddenly aware that the hot-desk she'd selected that morning in the very quiet open-plan office was central enough for everyone to be listening.

'I'm not doubting you for a second. But what about—did he, you know, live with anyone else in the flat he's in now?'

'I don't know, and it's not really any of my business.'

'Hello? Fi, you're marrying him, hopefully for ever. *Everything* is your business. Didn't Jody live there with him for a bit?'

'Does it matter?'

'Only because you told me that he'd said he didn't really believe in living with anyone before marriage.'

'I think Jody was why. And we *are* getting married. That's the point.'

'So why not buy somewhere new together? Start afresh.'

'It seems silly to sell up for the sake of it.'

'Whatever.'

'Don't "whatever" me, Jess. I've thought through it all. And by the time all my stuff is there and I've hung a few pictures it'll be different. I refuse to be insecure about this. You've got to live for the moment, and for the future.'

'Speaking of which, any more thoughts about where you might want to get married?'

'Mike had a Slovakian grandmother, and apparently there is a beautiful castle in—'

'I don't care if there's a Buckingham Palace. It'll be a total red-tape nightmare. How about…let's see…' Jess faked contemplation. 'London?'

'We want to go away.'

'OK, then, Brighton?'

'How about Spain?'

'Don't tell me. Mike's got a pair of shoes from Spain?'

Jess could sense the wryest of smiles from Fiona.

'Try a Spanish uncle with a lovely big house in Mallorca.'

'Thinking of larging it in a nightclub? Maybe a wet T-shirt competition before we cut the cake?'

'It's not a timeshare in Magaluf. Carlos has a huge place on the north coast, near Valldemossa. Apparently it's beautiful, and very quiet off-season.'

'Sounds perfect.'

'Jess?'

'I'm not being sarcastic.' For once.

'Cool. So shall I get him to e-mail you the details?'

Jess was being thawed by Fiona's unreserved enthusiasm.

'Definitely. If you're serious. It can take eight weeks for the application to be approved, and then prepare for the translation games to commence. Were you thinking of having a civil or a religious ceremony?'

'Gosh, it all sounds quite complicated already. Is it really that big a deal?'

'What? Getting married? No. Not really. You just have to make sure you do the right thing. Personally I'm still not sure whether love and legality go together—I mean, maybe it's just an unrealistic merger of business and pleasure... But you're OK, aren't you? I mean really?' Jess berated herself for being a little self-centred of late. From now on she was going to be the best friend in the world.

'I guess.'

Jess softened her tone. 'It's totally normal to have a few doubts, you know. Especially when you've been as single for as long as you have. It's a huge change in outlook.' She could sense a flatmate on the horizon.

Fiona's tone was suddenly defensive. 'Not doubts *per se.*

Well, not that would register on the Jessica James scale of second thoughts.'

'Yeah, yeah. I guess I asked for that.'

'But…' Fi relaxed as she confessed to feeling a little uptight '…perhaps a slight increase in pulse when I think about the reality of it all. It just seems so…so final.'

'Hurrah, so you're a normal twenty-first-century, until-recently-single woman. But nothing needs to change. I mean, your name might—if you want it to. But don't think you'll be having sex three times a night or indeed three times a week—for more than a month or two.'

'You're really selling it so far.'

'Seriously, eventually the need to sleep kicks in, and there isn't time to wash your hair every day, buy new underwear every week, or indeed hand wash the expensive stuff. But that's development, progression. Suddenly you have an ally. Someone who is there for you above all others, who laughs at your jokes, who is bemused by your foibles, intrigued by your CD collection and pretends to be interested in your day. You just have to embrace the changes.'

'Blimey, Jess. You know, you're bloody good at this.'

'All part of the service.' Jess really didn't understand why learning lessons always had to be about hindsight. What about *during*sight?

'For a minute I'd forgotten how excited I was. Insecurity Fi rides again.'

'Calamity Jess at your service.'

'That was Calamity Jane.'

'Says who?'

'Hey, how are you doing?' Fiona asked seriously.

'Me?'

'Yes, you, braveface—who might be finding all this wedding planning a little bit hard but would never dare to say so. Or not to me at least.'

'I'm great. Much better. I'm fine, I guess.' Jess stopped

herself. Reflection was not a good thing, especially when it was much easier to hide amongst practicalities. 'I need to find somewhere to live. Can't think about buying until Nick thinks about selling—or remortgaging—or I win the lottery. Which statistically would be one hundred per cent more likely if I ever got round to actually buying a ticket.'

'Why don't you move into my place? As long as you cover the mortgage you can stay as long as you like.'

'Minutes ago you were telling me you needed the extra income.'

'Go on. You can have a bit of space and I can have a spare key.'

'And peace of mind. And a bolthole.'

'I'm not bolting anywhere.'

'Well…' Jess could feel herself getting excited about some space of her own. 'Maybe just in the interim. If you're sure you don't mind? Until I get the money through… Have you seen—? I mean, is he well? Sorry, you don't have to answer that.'

'Nick's fine. Totally fine.' Not the whole truth, but Fi wasn't ready to be a go-between. 'Call him if you like.'

'Best not. We've both got to move on now.'

'You're probably right.'

'I wish I wasn't, but I think I am.' Jess sighed.

'So, come on—take my place. Tell you what, we'll even go to Ikea and get you some more shelves, then you'll be able to unpack all your boxes.'

Jess struggled with the concept. 'You do realise Ikea is Swedish for Hell on Earth?'

'It is?'

'No, but it should be. Or a direct translation of Queue for Hours. Look, Fi, it's a really kind suggestion, but let's do Habitat instead—plus, I'm happy to buy the stuff myself. I'm bound to need it sooner or later. You know, when I can afford to buy a little window box of my own.'

'You'll have half a house to spend soon.'

'Believe me, I can't wait to buy a flat—although it will mean a return to single-storey existence.'

'I can almost hear the violins. Honestly, these are exciting times, Jess, It's exactly what you wanted. And just remember—no rugby DVDs, sport channels or Play Station games.'

Jess laughed. Life wasn't all bad.

nineteen

'Me—me again.'

Pippa clapped her hands and kicked her legs with sheer excitement as she watched herself on the television screen. Georgie was also wholly absorbed, but in an almost reverential silence.

As the vows ended, Amy duly skipped back to their arrival at the church.

'Thanks for bringing this over, Em. Georgie hasn't stopped asking to see the "bideo"—actually, the "DBD"—since we got home from that weekend… Although how, at five, she knows about DVDs I have no idea.'

'I think they're born with a different hard drive these days.'

Emma watched herself getting out of the Bentley for the third time in half an hour. Her insides tensed as she watched herself taking Patrick's arm and observed him watching her as she straightened her veil. She should have known.

Amy was starry-eyed. 'You looked stunning.'

'Jess did an amazing job.'

Jess. Of course. Emma couldn't believe she hadn't thought

of her earlier. She was exactly the person to speak to: neutral, trustworthy, and someone she'd promised to call weeks ago.

Finally exhausted by her repeated television appearance, Pippa leant her head heavily against Emma's side and started sucking her finger noisily, the warmth of her presence suddenly mading her feel more than a little maternal. Amy approached, brandishing a J-cloth, and her children barely batted an eyelid between them as she wiped the remnants of chocolate crispy cake from their fingers, nailbeds and the corners of their mouths. Emma could feel her eyelids getting heavy. A certain case of narcolepsy under fire. She could only anticipate the barrage of questions heading her way on the subject of Mr Jack Carlisle.

The wedding was still on in the background as Amy started tidying Barbie-sized outfits into an old empty ice-cream tub. 'We're getting old, you know.'

'Speak for yourself.' Although today Emma felt pretty prehistoric. And not even that pretty. It was a rare sighting of the DoYouThinkAnyoneKnowsOrSaurus.

'Look at us. Both married, and I've got two kids, neither of which I can call a baby any more.'

And I've got one on the way. It would have been the perfect moment, but Emma let it pass. 'I wouldn't write us off yet. I'll know I'm old when I start buying Ronan Keating albums because he's such a pleasant, polite fellow with such a nice voice.'

Amy smiled. 'And, by the way, I am never going to be your typical housewife, even if my stay-at-home career has yet to take a foot off the ground. So, how's your new life of leisure? Bored yet?'

'Haven't had a chance to be, really. A few weeks of shopping and finding my feet, and then of course Patrick stepped in. And there's never a dull moment with him around…'

Was it her imagination or could Emma feel a tug in her abdomen? Probably pure projection on her part; surely it could only be a microscopic ball of cells at the moment? Definitely time to buy a book and mug up on hair, nails and teeth-growing factoids. But that would mean admitting she was pregnant, which wasn't a bad thing *per se,* but…

'Earth to Emma?' Amy was standing in front of her.

'Sorry, I was miles away.'

'So, what are we doing for your birthday this year?'

Emma wasn't sure she was worth celebrating at the moment. 'Haven't I mentioned my birthday party yet?'

'No.' Amy sighed disappointedly. 'That must have been your other best friend. And you promised you wouldn't forget about me when you were married.'

'Don't be stupid, Ames. Clearly the fewer things I have to remember, the less my brain can be bothered to try.'

'Well, it doesn't matter. Don't take this personally, but I'm not sure that Tim and I are up to some Soho nightspot any more. Plus, babysitters have started charging the earth after midnight.'

'Soho nightspot? I don't think so. It's a whole weekend thing at Jack's dad's place. A bit of tea, fireworks and supper on Saturday, and then lunch on Sunday. Nothing major. And there's plenty of room for you all to stay.'

'Let me just refresh… You're inviting us to the stately home of an Oscar-winning British legend for the weekend and it's no big deal? Good God, Em—reality check, please. When was the last time you got on the tube, for example?'

Emma hesitated. Not since she had got married. It was quite ridiculous, really. Tomorrow she'd buy a Travelcard.

'I mean, will we have to dress for dinner?'

'I'd suggest a fleece. OK, the house is big, but it's pretty shabby and *very* cold.'

Amy clapped her hands with unmasked excitement. 'That's so upper class. Threadbare carpets and cold noses go hand in hand with *Kind Hearts and Coronets…*'

Watching Amy, Emma wondered if she'd ever have

enough energy to be left in charge of children. Today she wasn't even sure she was responsible enough to look after herself. And she was absolutely exhausted.

'You remember the classic Ealing Comedy? Alec Guinness?'

Emma shook her head. She'd never been a fan of black and white films. They somehow just seemed so gloomy and so—well, *old*.

'Anyway, they're all the same. Posh families, I mean. Why do you think they all drink so much, huddle round the Aga and wear shoes at all times? So when is it?' Amy leapt to her feet.

'The weekend after this one.'

Amy started flicking through the diary by the phone. 'As for your laid-back attitude—well, clearly you were destined for greatness. Excellent...' Amy had found the right page, '...we can make it. Georgie will have to miss a swimming party, but...' Amy was practically rubbing her hands with glee '...we'll be there.'

'Brilliant. Really, it wouldn't have been nearly the same without you.'

'Good job I reminded you, then.'

Emma smiled. 'Thank you.' This really wasn't the time to start becoming a bimbo, and her highlights weren't any blonder than they had been before she was married.

Amy looked up from scribbling in the diary. 'Make us ninety-nine per cent definite. I'd better double check with Tim first. Apparently I'm very presumptuous or controlling or something. I prefer organized—although I guess he does have to work for all of our livings. I hate not having a salary. As soon as Pippa starts going to nursery I'm going to plug the laptop back in.'

'They'll see sense eventually. Someone told me it's ten per cent inspiration and ninety per cent perspiration.'

'Maybe my deodorant is just too damn effective. If all else fails I might just head back to recruitment.'

'Jack's doing a bit of writing at the moment.'

'Great. He'll probably get a trillion pound advance any day now.'

'It's not fair, is it?'

'Em, publishers want to sell truckloads of books. A mere mention of Jack's name on the cover of *Hello!* magazine sells thousands and thousands of copies. Even if he can't spell his own surname they'll be banging down his door, and they'll just get a ghostwriter in if necessary.'

'Mmm…' Emma had been distracted by her husband currently going through his vows again on the small screen. As the camera panned round her attention was suddenly stolen by a man who had apparently arrived late and was just taking his seat at the end of a pew at the back. She peered at the screen. 'Who's that?'

'No idea, but he's on Jack's side. Do you know all his friends?'

'Of course not.'

'Well, then.'

'I guess, but…this guy's wearing odd socks.'

'Bound to be an old Etonian, then.' Amy laughed. 'Anyway, a weekend at Greenhill…' She'd had quite enough of the TV. 'So, who else is going?'

'How did you know it was called Greenhill?'

'It's a pretty well-known fact.'

'Really?'

'Well, to anyone who has Googled Jack Carlisle.'

Emma raised an eyebrow.

'Look, I was doing some research and I needed a break.' That was Amy's story and she was sticking to it.

'Research, my arse.'

Amy stood her ground. 'Everything starts with a Google.'

'It used to start with a kiss.'

'That too.'

'Well, it'll make a change from white wine and whingeing on my birthday.'

'And I guess fireworks are only fitting. Your life has certainly been going with a bang this year.'

Emma did her best to look pleased. 'Look, I'd better go.'

'Already?' Amy looked at her watch incredulously. 'Have you got to go and bake a cake for Jack's tea?'

'I've got to go in to the office for a meeting.'

Emma actually had three hours to go, but she needed some headspace, and some entertainment that didn't involve her wedding day. Jack. Patrick. Jack. Patrick. It was enough to make her want to leave the country. And she'd only been back for a month.

twenty

'For God's sake...'

Jess was ranting to herself. Out loud. Thanks to an illiterate printer, she had just taken delivery of two hundred menus, each promising chocolate *mouse* for dessert on Saturday. And it was Thursday afternoon.

Picking up the phone, Jess could feel herself smarting at falling standards. Back to basics, back to school. She had officially become a Victorian. And woe betide them if the next set came back as 'chocol8 moose'. In her current mood she was certain that text messaging was going to bring about the end of civilization—or spelling. Next she'd be claiming rap music led to violence.

Resisting the ageing process, she inserted Eminem into her CD drive and dialled the printer, head nodding as she let the beat take over, promising herself she wouldn't lose her temper with whoever was unlucky enough to answer the phone.

'Don't let secrets ruin your life.'

Emma stiffened as Jack's voice filled the car.

'*The One that Got Away.* A new drama, starting tonight on 6.'

Disadvantage #85 to being married to a household voice as well as name. Turning the radio volume down, Emma reached for her mobile and, barely looking, dialled the number which for most of the year had been her almost personal helpline.

'Thank you for calling Jessica James. We're sorry, but due to an increased volume of calls at the moment all our operators are busy. Please hold the line and we will put you through as soon as we can.'

Emma sat in her inconspicuous car a hundred yards down the road from Amy's house. No way was she letting Jack buy her a sports car. Her ability to blend in was her greatest asset. She clearly wasn't interesting or glamorous enough without make-up to turn heads everywhere she went. And that was just the way she wanted it.

Looking up from her diary, Jess jumped involuntarily. Roger had managed to reach her desk in total silence, and her body reacted seconds before her mind identified the figure casting a shadow on her in-tray and her day.

'So sorry to disturb you…' Roger waited patiently as his silent 'but…' followed.

Jess hung up on the printers, who'd failed to pick up the phone in twenty rings, before hitting redial in an attempt to catch them out by pretending to be a new call and in the hope that this time she would be able to coax them into answering.

'What?' Her heart-rate had yet to return to normal.

'I've got someone on the other line who wants to talk to you.'

'Can't you take a message?' Surely that was what she was paying him for? Come back Rosie, all was forgiven. She couldn't afford to lose her man *and* her career.

'I can—of course I *can*…' Roger was sounding weary.

'Good.'

He was still standing there.

'But…?' Jess was doing her best to retain her patience.

'But you see I said I'd put her through—and then—I mean now—you are, or you were, and now you are again—on the phone, so I've put her on hold.'

'So?' Jess's tone was exasperated.

'Well, I promised to put her through to you.'

'So she's been listening to Frank Sinatra. She'll be fine.'

'Frank Sin…? Oh, no. I changed the music.'

'You did what?' His days were numbered.

'Love & Marriage was so dated. I replaced it with a voice message. We sound much more efficient now.'

'Look.' Jess did her utmost not to shout. 'I liked the music. And without wishing to be rude—' actually she wished to be very rude '—it's my company and I'd appreciate it if you'd ask before you just went ahead with stuff like that.'

Jess gave Roger her best withering look. From an employer's point of view he was the worst possible combination of enthusiastically semi-incompetent and thick-skinned, with a penchant for taking his often misguided initiative.

'Who's holding, anyway?'

'Emma Carlisle.'

'For God's sake, Roger. Go back to your desk and put her through immediately—before she loses the will to live on hold without any music.' Jess hung up on her call as Roger made himself scarce. In seconds the other line flashed into her office.

'Hello? Emma? Sorry about the delay.'

'Who's Roger?'

'The new Rosie. Only a tad less efficient.' Jess raised her voice pointedly.

'What happened to her?'

'She left.'

'I'm sorry. Gone to the opposition?'

'I suppose you could say that.'

'Shame. She seemed lovely.'

'Hmm.' Almost too lovely.

'Look, I 'm really sorry it's taken so long for me to get round to giving you a call. I was full of good intentions and then…I fucked up.'

'No worries.'

'No, really—I did.'

'Believe me, I know the feeling,' Jess consoled.

'Plus, the last month has just whizzed by.'

Jess's days had not so much flown as crawled. 'So, how are things?'

'Fine, fine—well, actually, I was hoping to pick your brains. I really could do with a confidential shoulder…'

'Of course.' Jess had apparently become dial-a-mate. Increasingly, people were calling her in a quiet moment of their day for advice and a quick catch-up—and yet her social diary was a flatline of activity.

'Fire away.'

'Actually…' Emma hesitated and stared out through the windscreen. She knew walls had ears, but did cars? 'Would it be OK if I popped in to see you?'

'Sure.' A human being in the office that wasn't Roger. Jess might even be tempted to crack open some complimentary champagne. 'When were you thinking of coming in?'

'I know this is super-cheeky, but how about later today— if you're not too busy?'

'Today?'

'Actually, I could be at your office in twenty minutes.'

'Twenty minutes?' Jess couldn't help feeling that her role today was a reactive one.

'I have to be in Soho in a couple of hours, but I've definitely got time for a coffee or something.'

Jess wondered who Emma thought was doing who a favour here. But she wasn't that busy. Or at least not 'no time for coffee' busy.

'By all means come in. But you'll have to take us as you find us. The office is a bit of a mess, but only because a con-fetti bomb has just emptied itself all over the carpet.' She re-ally should have kept the sample intact and shoved it up the printer's arse.

'Confetti bomb?'

'Yup. It's the latest thing, apparently. A weapon of mass repulsion.'

Emma laughed. 'For single people to fire at the bride and groom?'

'Not exactly…' Jess smiled as she conjured up an image of a row of ushers lined up in their morning suits with ba-zookas held to their shoulders. 'Apparently they are for dec-orating the tables. To help your party go with a bang, no doubt…' Maybe she could fire one at Roger—by accident, of course. 'Come over whenever you like. I'm office-based all afternoon, dealing with various items of administrivia.'

'And you'll have to tell me what's going on with *you*.'

'I thought you said you only had a couple of hours spare?' Jess was fine. But if she stated that out loud it immediately sounded as if she wasn't, and she really didn't want to have to keep harping on about it. Her other line was flashing. 'Em, I've really got to go. See you later—or sooner, even.' Jess ended one call and started on the next. 'Good afternoon. Jes-sica James.'

'Jess?'

It might have been nearly two weeks, and she might have been subject to the evils of alcohol when she'd heard it last, but the voice definitely belonged to Josh.

'Speaking.' Jess pronounced the word as slowly as she could to buy herself some time. Time for what, she wasn't sure. Was the man brave or foolhardy? It was difficult to tell from one syllable.

'Great. Thanks very much for your message.'

Silently Jess bit her lip. Under duress, and with Sarah at her elbow, she'd called him at work a couple of days later to apologise—but only at eight-thirty a.m. when there was absolutely no chance he'd be there.

'I just wanted to check you were, you know, feeling better…' Josh was edging his way into a conversation.

'I'm absolutely fine.' Jess meant it.

'I mean, obviously I know you never want to date again—like, ever…'

Josh had adopted a sorority falsetto for the sentence.

'Really, I can't believe I said that.' Jess tried and failed to keep a straight face.

'It's pretty much a direct quote. And there are plenty more. The most unexpectedly entertaining Sunday lunch party I've been to in a long time.'

Jess slumped back in her chair and rubbed her eyes. 'OK, so I was quite stressed that weekend. It's been a horrible couple of months, and I'm afraid you were really were just in the wrong place at the wrong time.'

'Well, I was hoping that today I might be in the right place at the right time. I hope you can excuse the short notice, but I'm in your part of town today and wondered if you fancied a drink later.'

'Are you a masochist?'

'No. Can't see the point. Life's painful enough.'

'Then it must be National Spontaneity Day or something…'

'Sorry?'

'Never mind.' She'd lost him already. Only apparently not.

'If today's no good for you, we can always arrange another time—if you'd like to, that is.'

'What on earth have I done to deserve a second chance?' Jess balked at her choice of phrase. Everyone of her generation knew that no meant no, but only if you vocalised it.

'Well, like I said, you certainly made lunch a whole lot more entertaining. I couldn't give a stuff which schools are performing well, or how much it costs to have three cars on a resident's permit at the same address…'

Jess chipped in 'Or indeed which bread maker was given four stars by the *Sunday Times*.'

'Exactly. So what do you say to a drink?'

'A drink would be fine.' Jess heard herself answer. It would? Getting up, she paced the length of her desk.

'So, shall I come and fetch you later? Say seven?'

'You know where I work?' This was not a good sign. She had clearly agreed to have an alcoholic beverage with a professional stalker.

'You gave me your card.'

'Right.' Jess had another vague flashback. And to be honest, anything was possible. Yet again, she wasn't coming across as the best version of herself. Jess consulted her appointments diary. 'Yup, seven works for me.'

'Great. See you then.'

Flustered, Jess hung up—only to find herself face to face with Roger once again.

'What now?'

This company was rapidly becoming not big enough for the both of them.

'Emma's here.'

Jess didn't care that she had clearly travelled at Mach 1 speed to get there. Distraction had arrived, and not a moment too soon.

Despite a couple of tears, undoubtedly attributable to hormones on the verge of a nervous breakdown, Emma was already feeling better. She drained her mug of tea. 'I really appreciate you listening.'

'You've certainly managed to put my so-called crisis in perspective.' From now on Jess was abandoning her navel-gazing. Plus, Josh wanted to go for a drink. A slightly random invitation, but if she was going to re-enter the dating game she was going to have to adopt the right attitude. No more being dismissive at first sight. Second sight? Maybe.

Emma had had enough of talking about herself. 'I'm just so sorry to hear you've been having such a tough time. It must be difficult—especially with your day job.'

Jess nodded, grateful for the empathy, but in her new, three-second-old frame of mind, she didn't want to dwell on it. Instead she focused on her former client. 'So, what are you going to do?'

Stalling for time, and an answer, Emma busied herself turning her mobile phone back on and noticed the clock on the display. 'Shit, I'm going to have to go.'

'Where next?'

'I'm due in the office for a meeting.'

'The office? As in…?'

Emma nodded. 'I know. I know. Don't say it, but I promised to help out on a project.'

'With Patrick?'

'Right. Actually, probably not at all right. The initial idea was to give me my own client—a focus, something to help get me out of bed in the mornings.'

'And clearly into someone else's.'

'Hey, that was only once.' But to Emma's relief they were laughing. 'Obviously this goes no further.'

Jess mimed zipping up her mouth. 'Goes without saying. And if you want a new hobby, you could always come and work for me. Seriously…' Jess reduced her voice to a whisper as she nodded in the direction of the other room '…he's not going to last. And you'd be perfect.'

'Because I'm doing so well at being married so far?'

'Because you love weddings. You knew exactly what you wanted and you kept your cool throughout.' It made perfect sense.

'If I hadn't been so desperate to have a big white wedding I'd never have let Patrick talk me into marrying Jack.'

'Regrets?'

Emma sighed. 'Actually, no—not at the marriage, just at my behaviour since.'

'Maybe you panicked?'

'Do you think that's what you did?'

Jess remained circumspect. 'I don't know. I'd always believed in The One.'

'So how do you know Nick wasn't The One who got away?'

Jess paused for thought.

'Don't tell me—he didn't live up to your invisible tick-list.'

Jess twisted awkwardly in her chair. 'He did at first, and then... I don't know. I took my eye off the ball. I took him for granted. And I can barely bring myself to admit this, but for some insane reason a few years in I started to think that I was somehow superior, that I could do better...'

'Isn't that just human nature?'

'Plus, I just couldn't make a leap of faith. Leave faith out of it. I couldn't make a leap of commitment.'

'And now?'

Jess sat up straighter in her chair. 'I think you have to move forward. Things happen for a reason. I've never really been able to visualise my own wedding day. But maybe that's because I couldn't imagine marrying him?'

Emma nodded thoughtfully. 'It's funny, I'd always wanted to get married. It was a bit like going to university—just a life stage I didn't want to miss out on. I wanted a wedding, a husband—a partnership—and children. They were all on my "to do" list.'

'Well no-one can fault your efficiency. Time to start a new list.'

Emma smiled grimly. 'But just look at me now.'

'You're looking pretty good to me.'

Emma raised an eyebrow at Jess. 'Don't try and flatter your way out of this one. I know I've screwed up.'

'I'm sure it'll all work out. As long as you know what you want out of it all. That's the important bit.'

Emma nodded sagely. If she could turn back time. She and Cher, of course.

'I've got to run, but if what you suggested earlier was genuine, I'd love to help out here... Although I'm not sure this is quite what Jack had in mind for me—not that I seem to have been too worried about what he'd think recently...'

'Sit with it for a few days. I do work almost every weekend, but you could just do one weekend a month if you like. Or you could just take care of all the office-based stuff, Monday to Friday.'

'I don't have any wedding training.'

'And I have? You've worked in an office. You've co-ordinated high-profile events. You understand confidentiality. You can enthuse about all things marital. You're organised. You're down to earth...'

Jess's business head was swimming. Emma Carlisle—now, that was an assistant. Just having her name on the headed paper would bring in more clients. Maybe they could even develop a product range. It was perfect.

'You had the dream day...you're living the dream.' Jess was in sales mode.

'I'll talk to Jack. Actually, what are you doing the weekend after this?'

'Pampering a happy couple?' Jess clicked on her computer diary. 'Nope, it would appear to be a Blue Moon. Either that or the Guy Fawkes wedding has yet to catch on. Or...ah, yes. That explains it...'

Emma cocked an eyebrow inquisitively.

'England are playing a football World Cup qualifier, kick-off at three p.m., so most grooms will have selected an alternative date rather than risk an annulment because they're caught sneaking off to watch the game when they're sup-posed to be at the church or in the receiving line.'

Emma laughed. 'Well, not that I'm exactly in the mood, but Jack's organised a very informal birthday party for me down at his father's place—fireworks, food, and feel free to bring a friend. There's plenty of room if you want to stay. You know Amy and the girls, and there's Jack, of course—and you've met his dad, haven't you?'

Jess nodded. 'I might just have to take you up on that.' Secretly she was delighted. She wasn't going to have to pretend to be having a lie-in, hide at the gym or wander round the shops for hours. She could face up to the reality of being a single woman in London at weekends another time. 'In fact, I'd love to.'

'Brilliant. Call me next week—let me know who you're planning to bring…'

Fi? Sarah? Fi? Sarah? Jess had a new problem on her hands.

'Meanwhile, I'll talk to Jack. Obviously I'll probably be on maternity leave before I've even started…although I could do some work from home. Your clients wouldn't need to know we're not in the same office. I can put them through to you from pretty much anywhere.'

Jess was impressed. Roger couldn't even put calls through from fifty metres away.

'Well, let me know and if you need to chat any time, you know where to find me. Best of luck with it all.'

'I'm not sure that luck is going to come into this. My mess. But I'm going to sort it out right now.'

Emma took a step towards the door. One small step for her, one huge step for womankind—and, as ever, this time it was personal.

twenty-one

Emma strode into the office brimming with energy. She'd been listening to dance music at full volume in the car all the way from West London and she was ready to roll.

Patrick looked up from his desk. 'Bad news. I'm afraid they've had to cancel.'

'Why didn't you call me?' She could have gone for a drink with Jess. She could have driven off into the sunset…if it hadn't got dark. And now it was just the two of them. Far too cosy for comfort.

'Well, it's not such a disaster, is it? I mean, we haven't had a face-to-face catch-up for a while…'

'Were they ever even coming?' Emma's volume increased as her mood swung. Emma Jekyll was Emma Hyde. Frustrated, she walked over to the window, every clicking step she took in her boots giving a Hitchcock feel to the tension she now realised she'd brought with her.

'Of course…' Patrick sensed danger and did his best to look sincere. But at least she'd arrived. There was no time like the present, and no presents or prizes for bottling out.

Trying to control her rising blood pressure, Emma stared at the roof of a bus as it stood in a traffic jam several floors down and wondered how it was that in action films people just jumped onto hard metal surfaces and a) lived, b) didn't bounce straight off and get run over by the car behind, and c) weren't sued for the damage they caused.

Patrick interrupted the strained silence. 'And now that you're here we might as well have a quick meeting anyway.'

Emma watched a mother pushing a buggy along the pavement. 'Sure.'

'But first would you mind typing a couple of e-mails for me?' He had an idea.

Patrick's audacity knew no bounds. She'd used to think it was a spelling thing. Now she realised it was more of a power thing and a laziness thing. 'Why don't you ask your secretary?'

'Katy had to leave early—doctor's appointment or something.'

A few e-mails and then she was on her way. And once Give Mum the Night Off was in the bag she'd go and help Jess. She'd never been more decisive.

Patrick was still jabbering away. 'Oh, and Jack called to check I was coming down to Greenhill for your birthday weekend.'

'He did?' She really needed to talk to her husband about this burgeoning friendship. He had other people he could hang out with. Loads of them.

'So, I guess you forgot to mention it?' Patrick tried and failed to disguise his acutely miffed state. The less bothered Emma was, the more he wanted her. And he wanted her anyway.

'I was going to mention it today. It's all been quite last-minute.' Emma waited for a lie detector to start ringing.

'I take it this is what all the fireworks are about?'

'Exactly.'

'Well, I'm really looking forward to it. Jack's promised me a bit of tennis action too.'

'Great...'

Just what she needed. A love match. Emma slipped into her old chair and automatically adjusted the lumbar support to suit her. Patrick stood up and took the vacancy at the window, staring down into the hectic world of W1 below to steady his nerve. It was just like old times—except she was wearing a wedding ring, designer jeans and very sexy spiky boots. Clearly in a world without public transport everyday footwear could take on very different dimensions.

'Fire away.' Emma stared at the screen, the link between her ears and her hands intact, her mind miles away pondering genetics. Both men were dark and of a similar build. Or they would be if Patrick went to the gym more than once a month.

'OK, first one is to Peter Smythson at PSPG.'

Emma's fingers danced across the keys without any conscious thought as Patrick dictated. Once a secretary always a secretary, and general servitude didn't require her brain to be on anything other than standby. She'd had years of practice.

Dear Peter

Many thanks for lunch. It was great to catch up with your plans for the agency and I have no doubt that the next six months will prove to be very interesting for us both. (New para.) I look forward to a further meeting when you have compiled the figures and...

As he paused, so did Emma's fingers over the keys. Patrick stole a glance at the object of his desire and continued.

Emma, will you marry me?

At the sound of his voice she started typing again and then stopped, awaiting further instruction. A few seconds passed, with Emma's hands hovering in the ready position. Ostensibly she was up to date. Patrick was disbelieving. But he continued.

Best wishes

It was as if she was voice-activated.

With kind regards...etc. etc...

Still nothing except the tapping of her fingers on the keys. 'Now, if you could read that back for me?' Patrick sharpened a pencil as she began to speak, her voice a monotone.

Emma stared at the screen. She'd been reading aloud since she was four years old but this was a first.

Stealing a glance at Patrick, she saw to her horror that his grin was all-encompassing—and, unless April Fool's day had been moved under some European directive, this was clearly not a joke. Emma's mouth was dry. As she rummaged in her bag for her bottle of water, almost in slow motion Patrick dropped to one knee, still clutching his mug of coffee.

'Marry me...'

His desklight shone through his silver hair, giving him an uncanny and unfitting halo. He was proposing with an instant coffee. And his charcoal-grey shirt was tucked into his too-black jeans. Emma took a long swig of water. It had never felt less refreshing.

'OK, it wouldn't surprise me if you weren't going to take me seriously, but—and believe me I have given this a great deal of thought—' well, a couple of days at least '—but I would really like—scrap that—I would *love* it if you would agree to be my wife.'

Emma couldn't move. Frozen, spellbound, or hoping to have a heart attack. The office was silent. And, irritatingly, she was still breathing.

'Are you out of your creative mind?' Emma's reaction was beyond her control. And that was a total relief. 'I'm married. It was your idea. You were there.'

'I know.'

'So?'

'I've been desperate to ask you since—'

Emma didn't want to know. 'You are desperate, period.'

'I'm desperately in love.'

'Oh, please. Do me a favour.'

'Emma, you know I can't lie.'

'Can't lie? You are a PR wizard, a spin surgeon. You live in a world of your own creation. In fact, maybe that's the problem here.'

'Come on, that's unfair. You've known me long enough to know that I can't help but follow my heart.'

'You love the excitement but you hate the reality. And above all you hate it when the opportunity isn't yours to take.' Harsh, but fair, and right now Emma didn't want to leave any room for misinterpretation.

Sheepishly Patrick got to his feet and, dusting the knees of his trousers, perched on the edge of his desk. It looked like he'd be eating at Gordon Ramsay on his own tonight. And he'd had to beg, borrow and steal for a table.

'So I'll take that as a no, then?' Patrick was doing his best to be flippant as his hopes for the day cascaded like a Domino Rally.

'Look, you know how much I respect you, Patrick—and we've had a great time working together. But marry you? Aside from the fact that I'm already hitched, it simply wouldn't work.'

'But with you I'm different. I'm more relaxed—more me.' Patrick didn't like the whiff of desperation that had crept into his voice. It was so *not* him. It wasn't as if he hadn't been turned down before.

'What the hell is that supposed to mean?'

'That you're not expecting me to be anything except who I am.'

'I was never expecting to be with you beyond office hours every day.'

'Emma, I'm being serious.'

'So am I.' Emma's delivery was slow and considered. 'I'm sorry, Patrick, but my future is with Jack.'

'Come on, Em, you barely know the guy.'

'I'm getting to know him better every day.'

'OK, how about some fun on the side, then? We'd be good together.'

'So the vacancy has changed from wife to mistress in two minutes? I propose you fuck off.'

'I only want what's best—'

'For yourself.'

Patrick shrugged. It was a dog–eat–dog world. 'But Jack's not making you happy.'

Emma barely hesitated as she realised she knew the answer. 'Yes. He is.'

They both jumped as the office phone chirruped into life. Clearly still in shock, Patrick answered his own phone.

'Patrick Robson…Hi, Jack.' Patrick looked round his desk, wondering if he could impale himself on his Cartier fountain pen. He'd never been more embarrassed in his life. And he was going to be walking away empty-handed—he could feel it. 'Hello? Yup, I can now. Sorry— terrible line.'

Her knight in shining Aston Martin. Emma silently praised Jack's impeccable timing. He'd just made her very happy indeed.

'Fine. That's fine. We're almost done.'

Emma shuddered. To think, if Patrick had had his way

again they'd no doubt have been in some sort of clinch at that precise moment.

Patrick replaced the receiver slowly. 'Jack's on his way up. He was driving past.'

No point mentioning that she had her car until she was safely out of the building. All the signs were pointing in the direction of Leave Quietly.

'That's fortunate.'

'Not for me.'

'Look, Patrick, I'm really flattered that you have feelings for me…'

'No need to let me down gently, Em. It's far too late for that.'

'Look, it's been a mad few months for all of us. Let's just leave it. Remember, you always want what you can't have.'

'Well, if you change your mind…'

'It was one afternoon. Sharing an office and sharing a life are completely different.'

'But we had great…' Patrick's expression said it all.

'It was a shag. And you should be ashamed of yourself for letting it happen. Jack's your client.'

'I couldn't help myself.'

'Don't be ridiculous.'

'Well, I didn't see you begging me to stop,' he challenged.

'It was a moment—a mistake. We need to move on. And I really don't think you should come down to Greenhill…'

Patrick hated being told what to do. And he hated being turned down. It was turning into a really shitty day. He didn't have a Plan B for this evening either. His fault for sending Katy home early. He hated to see a good table go to waste.

'And once Give Mum the Night Off is in the bag, I think we should call it a day.'

'What? Surely you don't have to stop working? It was a stupid mistake. It won't—'

Emma was amazed at how calm she was feeling. 'It's probably all for the best. Jack and I are bound to start trying for a family soon. You need to find someone who's going to stick around.'

'Women do manage to work and have babies at the same time, you know…'

Emma gave him a wry smile.

'Probably not Carlisle women, of course…'

'What about them? Knock-knock.' Jack poked his head round the door before entering. 'Evening all. So, who fancies a drink?'

'To be honest, I'd rather head home. I'm knackered.'

'OK, gorgeous.' Jack walked over and gave Emma a kiss before acknowledging Patrick.

'Sorry, Patrick, but when the good wife says time to go, it's time to go. You know how it is…'

Patrick wished he did.

'It's one of the unwritten vows. One of the many I'm learning about. Come on, you. Let's go and have a quiet night in.'

As Patrick watched Jack rest his arm across Emma's shoulders he had to admit they looked happy. And his ego wasn't sure whether to choose elation at his professional prowess or depression over his rejection. To add to the confusion, Emma came over and kissed him on the cheek.

'Bye. Good meeting. I think we know where to go from here.'

'Yup.' So much to take on board, and no words to help him now. To love and to cherish was way too much work. To love them and leave them was much easier. And if he wanted more permanent companionship, maybe it was time he got a dog.

'Don't forget Saturday week—tennis and Bonfire Night.' Jack slapped him on the back before following his wife to the door.

Emma turned momentarily and glared at Patrick from the crook of Jack's arm.

'I'm not sure I can make it…' Patrick fiddled with his pen.

'Of course you can.' Jack was adamant.

'Seriously, I've got loads on.'

'So just come for the day.' Jack was insistent.

'I'll have to see.'

Patrick waited until the office was empty before sitting in Emma's chair. Finally it was quiet, just a couple of sirens cutting through the ambient traffic noise outside. A grey and blue box appeared on the computer screen: System Error. For once, he could relate.

twenty-two

'I know things haven't been easy, but, trust me, I can change. We have to put the past behind us before it destroys our future.'

'I'm tired of being underwhelmed.' A tear welled in the corner of her eye, threatening to test the waterproof properties of her mascara.

Taking his ex-girlfriend by the hand, the man in faded Levi's got down on one knee without any concern that the brick-red earth of Arizona might stain his trousers. 'Marry me.'

Curled up on Sarah's sofa, in the not very wild west of London, Jess took another sip of her tea and checked her watch. Fi and Mike were due any moment. Her hand hovered over the remote control.

'What on earth are you watching?'

Bollocks. Silently, her stealth sister had made it to the doorway, her arms full of shopping, Pampers and child, and Jess nearly spilt scalding tea in her scrabble for the 'off' button—or at least the 'something-slightly-less-embarrassing' button. She wasn't nearly quick enough on the draw.

'Oh, just flicking around…you know…' Jess feigned nonchalance as she gestured at the screen. 'This made-for-TV movie is almost as crap as my made-for-me life.' Jess winked, to demonstrate that she really had rediscovered her sense of humour.

'Well…' Sarah peered at the screen. 'He could be a lot worse-looking.' Readjusting Millie on her hip, she smiled to herself. She couldn't believe she'd caught Jess watching such slush when she thought no one was looking. There was still hope for her.

'Here, Jess, take your niece for a moment. She's getting far too heavy. So, how was your day?'

Jess lifted Millie onto her lap and jiggled her about until she smiled—or burped. Either way, she looked happy enough.

'Well, another loved-up couple have made it to the altar, through lunch and to their first dance without a hitch. And Fiona and Mike are on their way over to talk about their wedding plans, so feel free to stick your oar in.'

'Charming.'

'Come on—you know you love having more nearly-marrieds to play with. And the kettle has just boiled.'

'Sure I can't tempt you with anything stronger?'

'Are you saying that you think I need a drink?'

'The wedding planner, she protesteth too much. Have a gin and tonic. I'm going to have one before I give Millie her bath, and I hate drinking alone.'

'OK, then—just a small one.' Jess had tried to make it a new policy of hers not to drink before seven p.m. But it was a Saturday.

Sarah wandered through to the kitchen as Jess returned her attentions to the TV, shouting after her, 'You guys really need to get cable. It's either this, horse racing, rugby league, a cartoon, or a documentary on steam trains.'

'We've got plenty of kiddie videos in the cupboard.'

'Please…' Jess lifted Millie up and down a few times to work her triceps, and stared as she gurgled placidly and blew a saliva bubble. Surely she should have been feeling just a little bit broody? Maybe she was missing a gene?

Sarah returned with the hard liquor. 'Here you go.'

Jess took the glass as Rob Reddy took his sweetheart by the hands and promised to love her for ever.

All three fell silent as Eva, siren of the South, in a floaty white dress, had her turn. For some reason her cascading dirty blond curls failed to stick to her lipgloss. Hollywood had a lot to answer for.

'I take yo to be my husbaynd.'

The director trained the camera on her face. And if he'd been able to pan to Jess on the sofa he'd have seen that her expression of inane wistfulness appeared to be catching.

'For better for worse, for richer for poorer, in sickness and in heyalth.' Her southern accent was adding syllables all over the place.

Rob winked at his almost-wife, his eyes an iridescent blue against the dirty tan of his weathered cheeks.

'To love and to cheyrish…'

Their profile became a silhouette as a golden sunset began behind them.

'Till deyath us do part.'

A swirl of incidental music built as the credits started to roll and the camera pulled back.

Jess could barely contain herself. 'So, what? Now she's Eva Reddy and she'll live happily Eva after? Who the hell writes this shit?'

'First of all, don't swear in front of my daughter. Secondly, at least try and suspend your disbelief. Maybe if they rewrote the wedding vows you'd find the whole concept of marriage a bit easier?'

'What…? ' Jess sipped her G&T contemplatively. 'I'll have a go with this man for a bit, as long as he treats me right, as long as I don't get bored, and as long as he lets me do what I want when I want to do it...? Actually, you're right. That does sound a lot better. Shame it'll never catch on.'

Sarah found a bit of hair at the nape of her neck that was long enough to twiddle. 'I have to confess that's the one thing I regret about my wedding day...'

'What? Agreeing to a life sentence with no parole?' But Jess was paying close attention. Sarah had never admitted her day had been anything less than perfect.

'Ha-bloody-ha. Seriously, though, there were no vows. Not in the traditional sense. We had an official translator, but basically we just said yes when we were told to.'

'And all because you were in Bali.'

'Thank you once again for stating the obvious. Face it, we were never going to have a traditional church wedding here...not unless Simon fancied becoming a Christian first.'

'He is the least Jewish Jewish person I know.'

'But still too Jewish as far as the vicar was concerned. And converting is stating a preference for one organised religion over another. You can't go from Jewish agnostic to Protestant agnostic, or vice versa. In our relationship the power of prayer has always been reserved for sporting fixtures and the Indian takeaway still being open at one in morning.'

'You could have written your own vows and had a civil ceremony here. Just a handful of guests: family members—me, basically—that sort of thing...'

'It was all pretty spontaneous.'

'Yeah, I always pack my birth certificate, just in case there's an opportunity of a nuptial nature.'

'Look, it's not as if we booked a weddingmoon.'

'I'd never have let you live that down.'

'And we're happy—surely that's the most important part? There's no point having a picture-perfect day if you can't stand each other by the morning. Any couple can have a wedding, but not everyone can have a successful marriage.'

The doorbell rang and Jess, eager to escape the six o'clock sermon, chucked Sarah the remote control as she leapt to her feet. 'For God's sake change the channel. And the subject.'

Jess drained her second gin and tonic and flicked through the pages of her paper diary. 'If you're set on February, that doesn't give us long.'

Mike had his diary open too. 'It's four months away.'

'Four months takes us to the end of February and you know as well as I do, in the world of weddings that might as well be next week. Plus, February is Valentine's month.'

Fi folded her arms. 'I trust you're this accommodating with *all* your clients?'

'Why, of course.' Jess bobbed a half-curtsey from the waist up. 'But if we're talking Spain there's a lot to organise. It's actually much harder to get married in Europe than it is in the States and some parts of the Caribbean.'

Michael took Fiona's hand. 'I was thinking Hawaii might be fun?'

Fiona's eyebrows shot up almost as far as her hairline. And, Jess took a guess, not in a good way. 'Flower garlands, bikinis and hula-hula—I don't think so. Next you'll be suggesting Vegas.'

Mike remained unfazed. 'They're both pretty kitsch.'

'As are Perspex coffee tables. Doesn't mean I want one.'

'I can really recommend Bali.' As predicted, Sarah was determined to contribute.

'Yeah, because that worked so well for Mick Jagger and Jerry Hall. We want to actually *be* married.' It was a definite no from Mike.

'Meaning?' Sarah's tone was tetchy.

'Their ceremony wasn't recognised as legal under British law. They didn't even have to get a divorce, just an annulment. So I guess it just goes to show that money can't buy you love or a marriage.'

Jess watched as Fi played with Mike's hand affectionately. She was shaping up to be as much of a romantic as she'd previously purported not to be. But right now Jess had to change the subject, before Sarah got over-defensive.

'Fi, what are you doing next weekend?'

'If Mike has his way, no doubt I'll be shopping for a grass skirt and a surfboard. Why?'

'Emma and Jack have invited me to a fireworks bash. Want to come along?'

Fiona's demeanour changed entirely. 'Hello? Does Ross Geller like dinosaurs? Does the Pope wear a funny hat? By the way, did you see that fantastic photo of Jack in the *Mail* today?'

Jess shook her head. 'And, by the way, jokes like that last one and you definitely can't get married in Spain—or Italy, for that matter.'

'Thanks for asking your sister and landlady.' Sarah got up from the sofa, ready to strop off to the kitchen.

'I didn't think you would want to come. You don't even buy *Hello!* or *Heat* magazine.'

'I read then in the staffroom.' Sarah's voice rose a couple of octaves. 'I would have loved to go.'

'You can go if you like, Sar. Really, I don't mind.' Fi, ever the diplomat, attempted to save the situation. But it wasn't her moment to rescue.

'No, no. I wasn't asked.' Sarah glared at her sister.

'Well, I wasn't asked to your wedding.' *Touché*. Jess retrieved the reins of the conversation.

Fiona watched the verbal ping-pong unfold. 'Look, really, I don't mind…I could even look after Millie for you if you like.' Fiona couldn't believe she'd just volunteered to look after a child who was still in nappies. Her oestrogen levels must have been sky-high.

Exasperated, Jess sighed. 'Fine. Just work it out between you.'

Sarah was stunned. 'How can you leave it up to *us*?'

'Because I love you both, and if I could take two people I would, but I can't. It's hardly a night at the Oscars.'

'It's the closest we'll probably ever get,' Sarah was muttering as she took her empty glass to be refilled.

'We could toss for it?' Fiona was happy to put her faith in probability. She had definitely been on a winning streak recently.

Mike produced a coin from his pocket. 'Best of three?'

Jess re-read the section on Bali, her concentration challenged by the activity all around her. She inserted a Post-it note for later.

'You go.'

Fi had won the toss, eventually the best of seven, but was deferring to Sarah.

'No, you won.'

'Which gives me the choice, and it's you.'

'Look, I don't mind—honestly.'

Jess was bored with spectating. This contest of politeness wasn't exactly riveting—or resolved. 'Fi, you won, you come. Sarah, you're my date next time—OK?'

Nods of submission from both parties.

Mike looked relieved. 'So, Jess, where are we on Mallorca?'

Fiona intervened petulantly. 'She said it was difficult.'

'Actually, what I said was that there'd be a fair bit to organize. First you two need to decide if it's what you definitely want, and then, if you're serious, how about we go over there for a couple of days and take a proper look?'

Fiona's face lit up. 'Jess, you're a star.'

'No problemo.' Sheepish, Jess pretended to note something down in her file, avoiding direct eye contact. Over the years, Fiona had earned the platinum level of friendship, and for once Jess was in a position to give her what she deserved. Plus, travel was always good for the soul—if not for the waistline.

★ ★ ★

The happily engaged couple safely on their way to a dinner party, and Millie bathed and in bed, Jess and Sarah had returned to the sitting room. Sarah was prone on the sofa, while Jess had taken over Simon's armchair, her feet slung over one side. Both girls were reading.

'Where's Si tonight?' Jess really would have liked him to be here for this next conversation.

Sarah didn't even look up from her magazine. 'Brighton.'

'What's he doing there?'

'Smoking drugs, pretending to be young enough to go to a nightclub, watching strippers, drinking shots.'

'Stag weekend?'

Sarah nodded. 'Although why they have to leave London is beyond me.'

Jess had re-read the page on Bali again and again. Chewing the cuticle at the side of her thumb, she skimmed it one last time. It was a question of scruples.

Sarah propped herself up on her elbow. 'Are you memorising that page, or something?'

Jess shut her file assertively. 'Fi and Mike are good together, don't you think?' She needed a little more time.

Sarah nodded heartily. 'They're so relaxed with each other. And Fi is just glowing…'

'Yup.'

Sarah failed to notice Jess's curtness.

'Not that I'm surprised. Just imagine the Paris backdrop, the Seine flowing beneath them. Si proposed to me in bed. I mean, not immediately after…' Sarah blushed. 'Not in the heat of the moment, at any rate. Nick proposed in Mum's garden, didn't he?'

Jess wondered if Sarah had forgotten they hadn't got married.

'The first time. The second time was much more romantic. But still not quite Paris.' And both had been quite a long time ago.

'So Fi wins?'

'If it was a competition. But moments don't have to be abroad to be special.'

'I guess I'm just a sucker for the traditional.'

'Says the woman who ran off to paradise to get married as a barefoot bride…' Jess couldn't wait any longer. And maybe it was better if Simon wasn't there—at least initially. 'Just out of interest, what religion did you tell them you were?'

Sarah stared at her sister. 'Who?'

'The Bali wedding people.'

'I think we told them we were English, and we had to sign an affidavit to say we were single, and have some photos taken…that's about it. Why?'

'Well…' Jess hesitated for a second before spitting the sentence out at breakneck speed. 'According to my information, both parties have to be of the same religion, and neither of you are allowed to be Jewish.'

'That's ridiculous.'

'So is the fact that the groom has to be on the right-hand side of the photos you submit with your application. I don't make the rules.'

Sarah hesitated. 'They organised all the paperwork for us at the hotel.'

'Oh. I'm sure that's fine, then.'

'Yeah.' Sarah pointed the remote at the television, but even with Saturday night programmes distracting them Jess could hear her sister's mind whirring.

Sure enough, a few minutes later Sarah hit the 'mute' button and sat up, hugging a cushion for support, tucking her legs beneath her. 'What if they just assumed that we were Protestant or Catholic and we're not?'

'Well, it's such a technicality—I mean, it really doesn't

have to matter. Who's going to know? Presumably you own a translated version of your marriage certificate?'

'Of course. And I'm sure there's no mention of religion anywhere on it.' Sarah's eyes widened. 'Bloody hell, Mike was right. Wasn't he?'

Jess tried to sound as calm as possible. 'Plenty of people get married successfully in Bali. And no one's going to try and trip you up on this. I mean, you've managed to change your name, your passport, credit cards...'

Sarah nodded.

'So it's fine, then.'

'But not if our marriage isn't legally binding. If their laws are different...'

'Look, everyone thinks you're married. You're wearing a ring. Nothing's changed between the two of you...'

'But what about—?' Sarah nodded at the baby alarm monitor and mouthed Millie's name. Sarah's face crumpled. Tears were right on cue.

'Look, I'll get us another drink. Don't panic. I'm sure there's something simple we can do.'

Sarah nodded hopefully. 'Better make it vodka. Gin's a depressant.'

'Vodka it is.'

Jess was starting to feel like a cracked record as she went over the basics with Sarah again.

'You live together as man and wife, you love each other, you respect each other, and you would run through fire for each other. What more do you need?'

'Millie is illegitimate.'

'Not according to her birth certificate. Although if someone contested your marriage I guess on paper she might be...but there's nothing you can do about that now.'

Sarah shook her head in disbelief. 'You're either married or you're not. Right?'

Jess shrugged. 'Only in the eyes of the law.'

'What? As opposed to in the eyes of the Post Office? Be as diplomatic as you like. You know I'm right. And we're not. Or at least not according to anyone in the UK.'

'Actually, probably more in the eyes of the UK than in the eyes of the Balinese.'

Sarah got to her feet and started pacing. 'Maybe we can sue the hotel?'

'What's that going to achieve?'

'We paid for a wedding.'

'You know what they say—money can't buy you—'

'Will you stop trying to pretend this is all a joke?'

'I'm not. I'm trying to keep you sane. You paid for a wedding; you had a wedding.'

'But we're not married…' Sarah wailed.

'Maybe not techn… Effectively you are. Nothing has changed in the last hour—or the last three years…'

'You don't get it, Jess. It's already all different.' Sarah was practically panting.

'Calm down, please. None of this is hard to remedy. Worst case scenario, you need to have a quiet civil ceremony here, and if you let me investigate that option then that'll be the easiest way to find out whether you are in fact married or not.'

Sarah wasn't listening. 'People gave us presents. What will everyone think?'

'No-one else needs to know—apart from Simon, of course.'

'I want him back here.'

'He'll be back tomorrow.'

'I need to talk to him *now*.' Sarah picked up her phone.

'You probably don't want to let him know he's not married at the moment he's about to head to a nightclub.'

Sarah raised an eyebrow and put the phone down again. 'That's not funny.'

'You've got to laugh.'

'I think I'd rather cry.'

'If you do have to get married again, you can just tell people you're renewing your vows. No one will suspect a thing.'

Jess watched her sister sort apples according to size as Sarah harnessed her nervous energy to rearrange the fruit bowl.

'We might not have even been married for a day...'

'A teacher who hasn't done her homework, eh?'

Not even a smile. Jess changed tack faster than Ellen MacArthur.

'Come on, Sar. You two were married long before you had a bit of paper to prove it. You're the one who always tells me it's all about teamwork, about attitude. Think Starsky and Hutch, Cagney and Lacey, Batman and Robin, R2D2 and C3PO... When push comes to shove, they're all invincible partnerships.'

'The last two were droids. And in fact all those examples are of same-sex couples.'

'Look...' Jess rubbed her temple and reminded herself to be nice. 'I almost wish I'd never started this. You're just the same. A marriage certificate is just a piece of paper. The ceremony is only an official seal of approval. Marriage is a way of life, not a series of vows you repeat.'

Jess moved her hand to her neck and wished she knew which area she had to pinch to pass out instantly. She'd been trying to lighten the tone. However, Sarah's expression was darkening by the second—and, if she wasn't mistaken, there was a storm front approaching. Time to throw in the towel. Take a shower. Leave the house. She got to her feet.

Sarah watched her incredulously. 'Where do you think you're going? This is my hour of need.'

'Hey, don't shoot. This messenger has a date.' Jess had never been more grateful that Josh existed.

'A date? You?'

'I know—impossible to believe.'

'That's not what I meant.' Sarah was back-pedalling furiously. 'It's not like you to be all Secret Squirrel about this stuff. I just didn't think—I didn't know there was anyone on the horizon…'

'Well, I guess you don't know everything.'

'You think I don't know that right now?'

'Got to shower. Got to preen.' Got to escape. Jess made a mental note to check her eyebrows. Frida Kahlo might have led a revival of curiosity in the monobrow, but it was never a good look, date or no date.

'A Saturday night date, eh? Sounds serious.'

'Sounds like dinner.'

'So, who is he?' Sarah clapped her hands gleefully, the state of her marriage apparently forgotten. 'Do I know him?'

To lie or not to lie. That was the question. 'Sort of.'

'It's not Josh, is it?'

Jess barely started to nod.

'It bloody *is*. God, I'm good. Si is going to be over the moon when I tell him you've got a boyfriend. Maybe I'll text him now. *Fantastic.*'

'Please calm down before I have you put down. Number one, it's dinner. We had a drink earlier in the week and it went better than our first meeting. This is just natural progression.'

'So this is a *second* date?' Sarah was playing with fire. Jess failed to acknowledge her interruption and continued.

'Number two, at this non-existent stage I would appreciate absolute discretion. I'm not just here to entertain, to provide you with interesting stories to tell your settled friends. And, number three, I don't have a boyfriend. You have.'

OK, so that was a bit below the belt. But she had to get ready. No further questions asked. The great escape was underway.

twenty-three

As the waiter cleared their dessert plates Jess sat as far back as her chair allowed, wondering when she was going to learn that it wasn't always necessary to order three courses when someone else was paying, and how long would it be before someone invented skirts that were comfortable to eat in.

Josh placed his linen napkin on the dark wood table, being careful to keep the cuff of his expensive date-shirt well away from the candle, which had almost burnt down to its base but was clearly determined to end its life at full flame. 'So, what now? Coffee? Liqueur? Or do you fancy going on somewhere for a cocktail and maybe some dancing?'

Jess wondered if she was hearing things. She had never been out with a man who liked dancing. 'Really?'

'If your heels permit.' Josh peered under the table and Jess congratulated herself for finding the time to shave her legs before she left. There was only a narrow strip of leg exposed between the top of her knee-high boots and the hemline of her skirt, but thankfully it was a hair-free zone. 'I'm always up for a bit of a boogie.'

Boogie. Jess did her best to skip over the Seventies vocab, which was suddenly making her think that perhaps her image of the rest of the evening was a little less sweaty than his was. Idly she wondered if she could stop somewhere on the way to have her stomach pumped, before she literally became a barrel of laughs.

'Me too. I'd love to.' Sore feet tomorrow was a cheap price to pay for a sashay tonight. 'Provided, of course, that you're not using dancing as a euphemism for something else?'

Josh smiled at her. 'I'm beginning to understand the correlation between aggression and alcohol consumption as far as you're concerned.'

'I'd prefer assertive to aggressive. And, face it, at school and university discos men only asked you to dance so they could snog you or push themselves up against your groin.'

Josh laughed. 'I guess that might be true.'

'Might be true? Believe me. It was totally the case.'

'Well, I spent a few months travelling in South America, and now I can never resist an opportunity to swing my hips.'

'So you're quite a mover, then?' Suddenly Jess had an image of him in tight black trousers, a partially unbuttoned white shirt and Cuban heels. It must have been the dark triangle of hair visible under his trendy brown and beige striped shirt. And the wine.

'I wouldn't go that far…'

Jess hoped he was being self-deprecating. Nick had never been a natural dancer. He'd had to literally be dragged onto the dance floor—at which point the moment, or the favourite song, had usually passed by altogether.

'Well, I'm game if you are.' Jess hoped that hadn't sounded too overtly sexual. It really *had* been a long time since she had been on a date.

'OK, sounds like we have a plan to me.'

'Let's get the bill and then I must go and pee.' Jess stopped herself a word too late. She'd just said pee. On a date. She could feel herself blushing.

'I'll get the bill. Go on—go powder your nose.'

Josh was rapidly notching up reward points. At first she'd been pretty taken aback to find he'd booked a French restaurant that she and Nick had frequented many times, but as a gesture of exorcism Jess had ordered completely different dishes. More importantly, he was far more interesting than she'd realised. Well-travelled, a good listener—as she already knew—and far from conventional. Not really her type. But then who knew what that was any more?

Jess caught sight of an older version of herself in the mirror as she was washing her hands and proceeded to paw at lines around her eyes that she had never noticed before. Thank goodness the lighting in the restaurant was romantic. She wondered if she'd have time for some sort of dermatological peel before their third date. Third date, eh? She was obviously having a better time than she'd realised. Taking a couple of steps back, away from the harsh lighting over the mirrors, she looked much improved.

She needed a good night's sleep—and, no doubt, some expensive face cream. But the dancing venue was bound to be even darker. Jess road tested a couple of dance moves as she dried her hands. She was ready.

Her head held high and her stomach held in, her new lacy first-date-with-a-sliver of-potential underwear feeling much less itchy than it had when she'd set off from home, Jess strutted back to the table. Trying to avoid having to stare at Josh all the way back, she casually cast a glance over a few other diners and then wished she hadn't. Whipping her head round as fast as she could, she prayed Nick wasn't wearing his contact lenses. However, judging by the sound of chair-legs scraping to her right, he was.

'Jess?' Nick could barely disguise his surprise. She wasn't at work on a Saturday night. And she was stunning.

'Nick.' Jess did her best to pretend she hadn't seen him moments earlier. A second glance confirmed that Rosie was next to him and that they were both drinking champagne. Nick didn't even like champagne that much. Or maybe that had always been her. Jess managed a semi-smile and a wiggling-of-fingers half-wave at Rosie—who, she noted, was wearing a top that revealed her ampler-than-Jess's cleavage. Maybe it would have been easier if he'd been dating a total stranger.

'Why don't you join us for a drink? And bring—' Nick was craning his neck and scanning the restaurant to see who Jess was with.

Jess cut him short. 'We're just leaving, actually.' She flashed a smile. Nick was wearing a very un-Nick shirt, but the rest of him looked much the same. 'We're off dancing.'

'Great.' Nick's face was tense. 'You love dancing.' His tone was flat.

'Indeed I do.'

'What is it with you girls? Rosie loves salsa…'

If Jess had been Rosie she'd have been bristling at being talked about as if she wasn't there.

'The dancing, that is. Not the tomato stuff.' Lovely laid-back Nick was sounding incredibly awkward.

'Actually, she loves both.' Jess's smile was rictal as she remained determined to keep the upper hand. 'So, have you had a good meal?' For some possibly sado-masochistic reason she was apparently determined to drag the conversation out. Although what point she was trying to prove was beyond her.

'It's been excellent. But then to be honest we've never had a bad meal here, have we?'

To Jess's childish delight the 'we' definitely referred to her and Nick, and not to Nick and Rosie.

'I guess not.'

'And you're looking great…I mean well. Well—both, actually.' Nick struggled to keep everyone happy.

'You too. You two, in fact.' Jess wondered if that quip worked aurally. 'Lovely to see you both. Rosie, we should get together some time—for lunch or a coffee at least.' Determined to keep the upper hand, Jess forced eye contact. 'Drop by the office if you like.'

Rosie nodded awkwardly.

Jess knew she had to leave now, before something weird happened. And Josh was advancing with her coat.

'Your coat, madam?'

'Thanks, Josh.' Jess thanked her lucky stars for providing her with an attractive date. 'Come on, let's go.'

Nick was on his feet again, his hand extended. 'Josh, was it? I'm Nick…'

Nick towered above him.

'A pleasure to meet you. This is Rosie.'

Jess watched him giving Josh the once-over and knew he'd be noticing his full head of hair. She hadn't had nearly enough to drink for *any* of this.

'Nick?' Josh glanced at Jess to check if it was 'the' Nick—which, from Jess's behaviour, it clearly was. 'Good to meet you, too.' Josh put his arm across Jess's shoulder and she didn't shake it off.

Nick was still standing. 'Seriously, why don't you join us for a quick drink?'

Luckily for Jess, Josh was as keen not to stay as she was. 'Unfortunately, I think we have to go. We won't get in to Rio if we get there much after midnight.'

There was nothing unfortunate about it. Jess turned to Nick. 'Bye, then. Give Lucy my love.'

'Will do. Bye.' Still shell-shocked, Nick sat down and drained his glass.

★ ★ ★

'Thanks for walking me to the front door.' Jess was very hot, still slightly sweaty, and incredibly thirsty—due in no small part to the multitude of Caipirinhas consumed. She could taste sugar and lime every time she swallowed.

'All part of the service, madam.'

Jess noted that Josh had his hand on her hip just at the point when he swung her round and swept her up into what was a surprisingly ardent kiss. Josh pulled away first.

'Well, I guess I'd better get going.' Josh tucked a tendril of damp hair behind her ear. 'Thanks for a great evening.'

'No, no—thank you.' Jess tilted her head slightly in what she hoped was a coquettish fashion and waited for her brain to adjust to the new position. She really was very drunk. 'I don't think I've ever met a man with such natural rhythm.'

Josh kissed her again. 'Believe me, you ain't seen nothing yet.'

Jess giggled. She felt as if she was sixteen years old, and it was a welcome relief. She missed the responsibility-free days of having an allowance, exams to revise for and an encyclopaedic knowledge of song lyrics. Adulthood was waiting for her on the other side of the door.

'Sure you don't want to come in for a coffee?' Jess watched herself run a hand across his back underneath his shirt before disentangling herself as naturally as she could.

Josh wasn't sure what to think. 'Blimey, you've changed your tune since I met you.'

'Female prerogative.' Jess really wanted to sleep with him. It was probably a side-effect of all the gyrating and all that Cachaca, but she was sure he'd be great in bed.

'I'll call you tomorrow.' Josh set off down the path and got into the cab which was waiting patiently, its driver undoubtedly enjoying the floorshow.

'Yeah, right—you will.'

'I will. You'll see. Trust me, all men aren't bad.'

Jess nodded. Actually, thinking about it, she hadn't met a

bad one since before Nick. She really didn't know what she was complaining about.

Josh waved as the cab did a U-turn, and Jess almost fell through the front door as it opened for her.

'What sort of time do you call this?'

Sarah was still up, dressed, and sounding very sober.

'Bedtime? It's very late, you know.'

'I thought you'd be Simon.'

'I thought he was dancing the night away in Brighton.' Jess shimmied past her sister.

'He's on his way home.'

'I told you not to call him.'

Jess used the hall wall to guide her to the downstairs toilet. As she tottered into the small room she caught sight of herself in the mirror. Her eye make-up was all over the place. She giggled.

Sarah was right behind her. 'He called *me,* actually, to say goodnight.'

'Oh.'

Sarah watched Jess as she pulled her boots off, shortly followed by her tights, and sat on the loo, her face in her hands as a hiccup ricocheted through her.

'Looks like someone had a good night at least. You were giggling on the step like a teenager. Goodnight kiss, eh?'

'Were you spying on me?'

'You were both shouting.'

Jess noted that Sarah was indeed sounding very muted. Bloody nightclubs were so noisy these days. 'I'd better get to bed.'

'Not so fast, you. So, what was he like?'

'Josh? Very nice, actually. Nick wasn't looking so good, though.'

'Nick?'

Jess heard a key in the lock and pulled the door closed for some privacy. 'I'll fill you in later.'

Simon's voice filled the downstairs. 'Hello, my darling.' Any consternation was diluted with kindness. 'Don't you worry, we'll sort this little mess out in no time. Love you so much.'

'Love you too.'

Jess felt her head loll in her hands and forced herself to her now throbbing feet before splashing some water on to her face, drinking from the cold tap and then wiping her smudged mascara on the hand towel. Opening the door gingerly, she checked the coast was clear before tiptoeing past the half-open sitting room door to the kitchen, to get a pint of water and a handful of Nurofen. She had just downed her first glass when Millie started crying. Wheeling, Jess shushed at the red lights on the baby monitor before realising that it wasn't two-way. Turning the monitor off, she grabbed her glass and left the room.

'She's one year old. She doesn't know what's going on.'

Jess hesitated outside the living room, wondering whether to interrupt Simon.

'Someone will tell her.' Apparently Sarah's main concern was her daughter. Only she was crying upstairs and she didn't know.

'Not if nobody knows.' Simon, as ever, was the voice of reason.

'Or she'll remember.'

'I doubt it. Do you honestly think she'll even remember her first birthday party? We were the ones that drank champagne and ate cake. She just had milk and her normal mush. But if you don't want her there, Mum can babysit.'

'And where are we going to tell your mother we are?'

'Out. Anyway, get Jess to check this out. We might be fine.'

'I want it sorted.'

'It will be, darling. And we don't have to tell anyone.'

'Isn't that dishonest?'

'Do you think anyone is that interested? And it's not like anyone is going to ask.'

'It would make a great story.'

Jess was tired of waiting for an appropriate moment and popped her head into the sitting room before her niece got any more agitated.

'Sorry. Evening, Si. Just wanted to say I'll settle Millie on my way up.'

Sarah looked appalled at herself. 'Oh, my goodness, I didn't hear her.'

'That's because I turned the monitor off when she started a moment ago. I'm on my way.'

'Thanks, Jess.' Simon was poring over their wedding certificate.

'You turned the monitor off?' Sarah was doing her best to keep calm.

'So turn it back on. I know what crying sounds like. I didn't need to hear more than a few seconds of it.'

Sarah was on her feet.

'Sit down, please. And I'm really sorry about all this. Not that it's my fault, but I promise it'll be sorted in no time at all. And no need to tell a soul. I mean, Millie will probably be in therapy by her fifth birthday, but…'

'Watch it.' Jess could tell Simon was amused and only supporting Sarah. 'Anyway, Jess, I could have sworn it was just gone three in the morning…'

Jess checked her watch drunkenly. 'Indeed it is. Now, shhh—you two sit tight and I'll go and sort Miss Millie out.'

'Do me a favour?'

'Anything for you, Si—brother-in-law and landlord extraordinaire.'

'Don't breathe on her.'

'Yeah, yeah.'

'And don't think I won't want the lowdown in the morning.'

'Can't a girl just go on a date any more?'

'Not when she's living in my house, she can't.'

Jess pulled the door to and staggered towards the staircase, water sloshing out of both sides of the pint glass as she climbed to the top floor to check on her niece. One year old and she had a bigger room than her aunt did.

Jess lifted Millie out of her cot and put her over her shoulder, rubbing her back. Immediately the volume of her discomfort dropped and Jess walked round in circles in the dark, admiring the space in the loft conversion.

'Now, what's all this noise about, eh?' Tummy ache? More teeth? Boy trouble? 'I saw your uncle Nick tonight—well, he might have been your uncle Nick if Auntie Jess hadn't fucked up quite so royally. Oops, forget I said that word. Don't tell Mummy.'

Millie gurgled. Jess had always thought she understood more than she let on.

'Good, that's much more like it. No more screaming. I've got quite a headache on the way, and if you cry you'll get one too.' Jess continued with the jiggling and rested her cheek on Millie's back. She smelt lovely and clean. 'Anyway, tonight Auntie Jess went on her first date in…' Jess tried to work out how many years it had been '…in a long time. And Josh is nice. He's really nice. *Nice.* Not the sort of word you'd want someone to use to describe you, but anyway, he's funny—sort of—and kind, and he can dance. He can definitely do that. And apparently he can sing, which must be a good thing. So we'll see. I mean, he's not Nick. But then that was my choice. And the trouble with that is I've only got myself to blame for all of this. Oh, well, one step at a time. Eh, Mills?'

Jess peered at her charge. Fast asleep. Holding Millie's head, Jess carefully lowered her into her cot.

'You've got no idea how lucky you are. A mummy and daddy who love you very much—which I do too, of course—and your whole life ahead of you. Maybe one day

I'll be mature enough to produce a friend for you. First of all, though, I have to get on with my life. I can't be in love with the past. Night-night, sweetheart.'

Jess watched Millie sleeping and felt her eyelids drooping. Tiptoeing down the narrow stairs to her bedroom, she reminded herself to get undressed before passing out.

twenty-four

Emma stood at the upstairs window. As she warmed her hands on the waves of warmer air curling up from the radiator she watched her party shaping up below and relished a much needed moment of solitude. She felt decidedly nauseous. Either morning sickness was frustratingly *not* confined to the hours before midday, or her body clock needed resetting.

'Well, well, well—aren't you a hard lady to track down?' Jack, incongruous in tennis whites and a cricket jumper, and panting slightly at the exertion of the last few stairs, entered the bedroom.

Emma turned to face him, away from her view over the cold, grey, but thankfully dry garden. Some time in the last week his hair had gone from slightly unruly to foppishly long. He needed a haircut. Her day had suddenly become a little too *Brideshead Revisited*.

'I'm sorry, is it 1930s fancy dress?'

'Don't you like it?' Jack puffed his chest out and swung

his incongruously modern Wilson tennis racket before checking his ensemble in the full-length mirror.

'Where's your striped blazer?'

'Yeah, yeah.'

'Are you not cold?'

Emma already knew the answer to that question. The hairs on his calves were standing to attention, a pair of old rugby socks slouched at his ankles.

Jack kept a shiver at bay. 'Of course not.'

Machismo was best left to its own devices. Emma was sure he'd lose a toe through frostbite rather than change now.

'I'll be fine when I start running around. You know I hate being too hot.'

'No danger of that.'

Jack laughed. 'Finished? Right, now I'm totally undermined. Thank you. And what, pray, is the hostess doing, standing up here all by herself?'

'Just psyching myself up for being the centre of attention.' Normally the life and soul, Emma had always had her shy days—and usually only on occasions when it was simply not an option. Today being one of them.

'You are funny, my lovely. And you're *always* the centre of my attention. I've been looking for you for…well, for minutes. In fact I'm almost running late.' Jack checked his watch so fast that he had to check it again, this time remembering to actually interpret the hands. 'Here—I've got something for you.'

Awkwardly stuffing his hand into the pocket of his baggy shorts, Jack produced a Tiffany box. Emma's eyes widened. If they hadn't already been married, this would have been the moment she'd been waiting all her life for.

'Happy Birthday, darling.'

'But you gave me a present yesterday.'

Emma wasn't sure she deserved whatever it was. Guilt did funny things to a woman's capacity for gifts.

'Consider this the official one.'

'You shouldn't have. You didn't have to.'

'I know, but I wanted to. Aren't you at least going to look at it?'

Emma opened the eggshell-blue box slowly, prolonging the moment of mystery.

She'd barely clapped eyes on the contents when Jack, peering over her shoulder, gave her an enthusiastic kiss on the cheek.

'Do you like it, then?'

His excitement was infectious.

Nodding, Emma did her best not to burst into tears as a platinum band studded with diamonds winked back at her. It was stunningly simple and incredibly beautiful. What the hell was she going to get him for *his* birthday? The jumper and a couple of DVDs solution was no longer looking like such a good idea.

Taking the ring, Jack placed it on the third finger of her right hand, where it nestled perfectly. No wonder celebrities wore sunglasses all the time. Vital to protect themselves from the glare of their own jewellery.

'I love you, Emma Carlisle.' Jack's gaze was intense, and Emma's first instinct was to close her eyes and go in for the kiss—but, like a cat playing a game, she wasn't going to be the first to look away. The moment had a power that she intended to harness.

'I love you, too.' One of these days she was going to say it first.

Holding her tightly, he kissed the top of her head and Emma congratulated herself for bothering to rewash her hair after their morning walk, even though it had looked fine from a distance. 'You know, since we got together everything has picked up and I'm going forward again.'

'I don't think that's all down to me.'

'Em, please—you're so quick to self-deprecate. Face it. You're good for me. And I just want to say thank you. You should hold yourself in the highest esteem. I do.'

Maybe it was time for her news.

'Anyway,' Jack kicked his right heel with his left toe. 'I hope you like it.' Suddenly sheepish at his grand declaration he was having an attack of the fidgets. 'Better dash...'

Emma smiled to herself. She was married to a man who said 'dash'. And who bought her lovely jewellery. She was sure they had years of happiness ahead of them.

'Only I'm due on court. I promised Patrick a game of tennis before it got dark and we haven't got long left.'

Emma's perfect mood crumbled to dust. 'I thought Patrick said he couldn't make it?'

'That was last week. But I called by his office yesterday on my way back from lunch and persuaded him to come down. He took a bit of convincing, but when I told him I knew that you'd be really disappointed if he didn't make it...'

'You didn't?'

Jack grinned. 'A bit naughty, I know. But it seems to have done the trick. And it wouldn't be the same without him, would it? In fact, without him there wouldn't even be an "us". I, for one, am forever in his debt.'

'Brilliant.' Emma hadn't meant to verbalise that level of sarcasm. Not that it had any impact. Jack took the praise on the chin.

'Excellent...'

The trouble with an egotistical husband was that, hard as he tried, he only really had one perspective—his own. Jack's world really must have been a much simpler place...

'Come and watch, if you like. I get the impression that Patrick's quite a player...'

Emma nodded grimly.

'And you haven't seen me on court yet.' Jack bounded over

to his wife and gave her a kiss before taking the stairs at speed for his descent. 'See you down there.'

Emma closed her eyes and sat down for a second. She had married an over-excited, adorable puppy. And the world was watching.

Jess and Fi were lost. Well, not *lost* lost. They'd arrived at the party in one piece, said hello to Emma, helped themselves to a drink, and then Fiona had spotted a pond—or so she'd said—and off they'd trotted. Now there wasn't a guest in sight, although they could still hear other people milling around, so they must at least still be in the right Ordinance Survey square. But Jess was running out of patience.

'Come on, Fi, let's get back to the party. It's rude.'

'We're *at* the party. And you still haven't given me the full lowdown on Josh yet. Hey, look at the size of the Koi Carp in this pond. And…' Fi broke into a jog as something else caught her eye '…check out this summerhouse.'

'I think it's a gazebo.' Jess walked as briskly as she could without running. Her gait had become that of an Olympic walker—her legs resembling an egg whisk as her heels and toes worked her legs from the calf up.

'I think you're pedantic,' Fi shouted over her shoulder as she jogged on, completing a lap of the inside of the glass and wrought-iron structure.

'OK, Liesl.' Jess was puffing at the entrance. 'You're far too old for *The Sound of Music* now.'

'Speak for yourself. I'll always be sixteen going on seventeen.'

'We're pushing thirty-five.'

'And I never wanted to be Liesl. Having said that, Rolfe was pretty perfect. Blond and handsome, a messenger…'

'…a Nazi. And a telegram boy.'

Fi folded her arms. 'Where's your sense of romance? Actually, don't answer that.'

'I'm romantic.' Jess knew she was. Or at least she had been. Once or twice.

'Don't think I've finished with you yet, but…' Fiona almost sighed as she surveyed the gardens and the house '…do you think Emma realises how lucky she is?'

'Jack's only a man…with all a man's limitations.'

'So can I take that to mean it's not all going well with Josh, then?'

'What?' Jess wasn't altogether comfortable talking to Fiona about her dates.

'Well, you know… Drinks. Dinner last Saturday. Cinema on Thursday. I'd say it was moving along quite nicely. He's even met Nick.'

'Don't remind me.'

Fiona wished they'd been dining in separate restaurants. It had taken Nick over an hour to get it out of his system the following day, and he'd called her almost every day since. 'I'd say you were seeing him at least.'

'I suppose we're dating. And he's OK.'

'OK? Well, that's a start, I guess.'

'On paper he's probably great. He's attractive, independent, kind, non-demanding of me, keen, even. I'm just not sure how I feel.'

'Have you shagged him yet?'

'Fi!'

'So that's a no, then?'

'Well, it's all so soon. And so new. He's pretty cute, actually, and a great dancer.' Jess listened to herself. She sounded as if she was describing a teenage boyfriend, not a suitor in her thirties. 'I don't know—somehow at our age the stakes are higher. It's almost as if when you agree to a fourth date you are tacitly agreeing to marriage. Take you and Mike, for example.'

Amused, Fiona shook her head. 'We're hardly representative of a trend. Glad to see your hang-ups are going from strength to strength.'

Jess smiled. She could definitely see the funny side. She just couldn't do anything about it.

'Somehow…it feels disloyal.'

'Disloyal?'

'To…you know…to Nick.'

'Right, that's it. I'm having you put down. He's happily going out with Rosie. To dinner, to the cinema, to bed.' Or maybe not so happily now.

Jess flinched. 'Subtle. Thanks.'

'Pleasure, treasure. You've just got to stop thinking so hard about everything.'

'Oh, yes. That's rich, coming from the doyenne of over-analysis. We're women; it's what we do.'

'So he's not the one? At least have a bit of sex to check.'

'I'm just not sure that it's going anywhere.' Jess repeated herself in the hope that this would be the sliver of information that made it back to Nick.

To Jess's relief Fiona was now looking around. She prayed for a subject change.

'Do you think this summerhouse is the size of my sitting room?'

'I think that'll be *my* sitting room.'

'Not for another few weeks. Now, come on—let's go and see if we can spot Jack.'

'Emma said he was playing tennis.'

Fiona jumped down the three steps to grass level. 'Why didn't you say so?'

'Does it matter?'

'Jack Carlisle is playing tennis and I'm pretending to be in *The Sound of Music*…of course it matters. We're wasting precious time.'

'No wonder you didn't want Mike to come with us.'

'There's no law against window shopping. You don't think that if Denise Richards and Kylie were playing beach volleyball right now *we'd* get a look in?'

Jess smiled ruefully. 'I guess my only trouble is I haven't seen anything I want to buy in ages.'

'To be honest, I'm impressed you even went on a date.'

'You are? Why?'

'You can unfold your arms now.'

'I was chilly.'

'And defensive. You know you'll meet someone when you least expect it.'

'Honestly, Fi, Barbara Cartland must be whooping from her grave.'

'It's what you always said to me.'

Jess shook her had. It probably served her right. There were lies, damn lies, and there were platitudes.

Emma stood behind the green netting surrounding the court, half chatting to James as she fiddled with her new ring. Watching what was apparently a friendly game, Emma secretly raised the stakes. If Jack won the next point she'd tell him tonight. If Patrick beat Jack maybe she'd leave it a bit longer.

Patrick placed a volley deep in the backhand court which left Jack for dead.

Emma changed tactic as the men changed ends. It would be far more exciting to make it the best of three. To her left, James had just launched into the story of the history of the tennis court at Greenhill when, to Emma's total relief and distraction, Jess appeared at her side.

Her manners had never been so instant. 'James, you remember Jess?'

Slightly miffed at the interruption, James stopped his story. 'Ah, yes, the wedding girl.'

Jess brightened. Having hated it throughout her twenties, now she was firmly ensconced in her fourth decade she loved being called a girl.

'And who, may I ask, have you brought with you?'

'James, may I introduce Fiona Seaton? Fiona, this is James Carlisle.'

Fi resisted the urge to pass out or bob a curtsey as James dipped his head and kissed the back of her sheepskin glove.

'Do you play?'

Emma wondered whether all fathers-in-law were so flirtatious.

'I've been known to swing a racket.' Fiona was rising to her moment—although Jess wasn't sure how many more times her best friend would be able to flick her hair without giving herself a form of whiplash.

'Not since the late Eighties,' Jess whispered to Emma as they started to half-watch the game. Taking Emma's arm in hers, Jess gave it a supportive if imperceptible squeeze.

'Well, your husband certainly looks the part.'

'When doesn't he? A graduate of the method school of acting, I suspect. But I think Patrick seems to have more shots in the bag.'

'Let's hope not.' Jess smirked and Emma stiffened. 'Sorry, Em.' She turned to check Fi and James were still deep in conversation before speaking to Emma out of the corner of her mouth. 'Does he have any idea?'

'Nope.' Emma's lips barely moved.

'Any plans to rectify that?'

Emma replied under her breath. 'I'll probably tell Jack later.'

'Tell Jack what?' James was leaning in under the privacy radar.

'Nothing.' The tips of Emma's ears reddened

'Hey, we're all family now.'

Emma's mobile started vibrating in her pocket and she answered it whilst walking away from the danger zone. Serendipitous timing. Amy had arrived. Emma walked towards the house without looking back. The great escape might have been amateur, but it was underway.

★ ★ ★

The dogs were chasing sticks. Georgie and Pippa were chasing the dogs and Tim was trying to avoid harm coming to any of them. Fi, meanwhile, was sucking up to James, enabling Amy, Jess and Emma to sneak off into the kitchen alone.

The three of them gathered round the Aga as they waited for the water to boil. Actually, strictly speaking only two of them—since her arrival Amy had apparently become a fully fledged inspector of the Kitchen Cupboard division of Scotland Yard.

Emma was retrieving three mugs from the dresser when Amy grabbed her most recently adorned finger.

'New?' Her tone was accusatory.

'This old thing? Hang on, is that a new top?' Emma did her best to deflect the attention from herself.

'Shut up. And it's fantastic. Birthday present?'

Emma nodded, suddenly embarrassed by her husband's bank balance.

'Do make a point of showing it to Tim. Last year I got a new dishwasher, and if I get a matching fridge this year I may have to leave him.' Amy spooned coffee generously into a cafetière she'd found moments earlier.

Jess nudged Emma inconspicuously. 'Wouldn't you'd rather have green tea or something?'

It was a good point. 'Actually, Ames, I'll have a peppermint tea.'

Amy wafted the coffee scoop under Emma's nose 'But this is going to be amazing coffee.'

Emma stood up a little straighter. 'Right to choose herbal tea being exercised by Citizen Carlisle—if that's OK with you?'

'Sometimes you make absolutely no sense.' Amy closed the tin, suddenly swivelling to eyeball Emma. 'How about a glass of wine?' Her tone was mischievous.

'Now?' Emma pretended to be baffled by her best friend.

'Now…or later?'

Emma wished Amy's mind was a little less sharp. She'd had two children, for goodness' sake. She was supposed to be a shadow of her former self. 'Well…'

'You *can't* be. Already?'

Emma tried to look as vague as possible.

'Em.' Amy was visibly irritated. 'I can't believe you, of all people, are keeping secrets from me.'

'It's not like I wasn't going to tell you.'

'When? At the bloody christening?'

Emma hesitated and glanced at Jess, before returning her focus to Amy. 'I've only told you two so far.'

'You've only told one of us. The other one found out.'

'Please, Ames, keep your voice down. I was going to tell you when I came over last week, but—'

'You've known for a whole *week*?' Amy's voice soared as she tried to harness her indignation and disappointment. 'I don't believe it. That's it. I'm filing for divorce.'

'I haven't told Jack yet either, if that makes you feel better…the thing is, it's not quite as—'

Emma stopped. Either there was a rat the size of an elderly lady in the utility room or…

The door opened. 'Don't mind me, girls.'

'Elsie, I didn't realise you were here today.' Blood rushed up the back of Emma's neck as she tried to assess the damage so far.

'Emma, my dear.' Elsie's beady eyes were twinkling with newfound information. 'I was just doing a bit of ironing. James asked me to pop by this afternoon, and it gets me out from under Sid's feet for a couple of hours when the football's on. I didn't mean to interrupt.'

More like overhear.

'Would you like a cup of coffee or tea, Elsie?' Amy was in natural mother mode, regardless of the fact she had only been in this kitchen for ten minutes—ever.

'Ooh, no thanks, dear. I'll be fine. Got to be off.'

Emma raised her eyebrows imperceptibly.

'Sid will be wanting his tea soon.' Her soft leather bun-ion-accommodating shoes shuffled across the tiles to the side door. 'Bye for now.'

Emma waited until she'd heard the outer door open and close. Elsie couldn't even *spell* discreet, let alone define it. Maybe she hadn't heard. Maybe Graham Norton was straight.

Out on centre—well, the only—court, using his home advantage and against the overall standard of play, Jack had used a couple of cracks in the playing surface to sneak a match-taking winner past Patrick. James and Fi, unofficial officials and now self-appointed companions, congratulated the players as they departed for hot showers.

James slapped Patrick on the back as he passed, sticking his tennis shirt to his skin, before transferring his attentions to his son.

'Good game. We must play again together some time.'

Jack rose to his father's compliments.

'And, better still, this means Emma's got something to tell you.'

'What are you on about?' Jack pushed his hair back out of his eyes, using his cooling sweat as impromptu styling gel.

'Fiona, here, will back me up…'

Jack proffered his hand. 'Nice to meet you. You're Jess's friend, aren't you?'

Fiona nodded, the power of speech temporarily deserting her in the face of a slightly sweaty sex symbol.

James hadn't finished. 'Emma was talking to your wedding planner earlier. Um, what's her name…? Jane, was it?'

'Jess.' The correction came in stereo.

'Yes. Jess—that's her. Strange, I never used to forget a name. Then again I never used to forget why I'd gone to the fridge. Anyway, that's all irrelevant.'

'It so often is,' Jack muttered to Fiona, who did her best not to laugh at her host while he was standing next to her.

'Anyway, Emma said to Jess that if you won she'd tell you later.'

'Tell me what?' Jack couldn't have sounded less interested.

'This a good year for us.' James's eyes were shining with excitement.

Jack dried his temple with the inner part of his upper shirtsleeve. 'I still don't know what you're talking about, Dad.'

'Don't be a fool...'

Jack's hackles rose.

'Come on—what could a new wife be waiting to tell her husband?'

'That she's having an affair? That she's overspent on her credit card? That she's crashed my Aston Martin?'

'Jack.' James's tone was impatiently paternal.

'Dad, whatever it is, butt out.' A shiver ran through Jack as the sweat evaporated from his skin faster than his body could heat it. 'I'm going inside to shower and change. I'll see you later.'

Clean, refreshed, and sartorially back in the twenty-first century, Jack found Emma chatting to Jess and Amy in the drawing room. The fire was blazing, Georgie was playing with an antique Fuzzy Felt game, Pippa could be loosely described as colouring—mostly the paper and a little of the rug—and, parenting duties suspended for the moment, Tim was dozing in an old battered leather armchair.

Jack leant in and gave his wife a kiss before perching on the edge of the sofa next to her.

Amy was the first to react to his arrival. 'Good game?' Giving him her sidelong attention as she wrestled a hot pink felt-tip pen from her daughter's fist, she could see why the camera loved him.

'Great, thanks.'

'So, who won?'

'I did, of course.' Jack's chest swelled visibly.

'Of course?' Patrick lowered his broadsheet newspaper, revealing his presence to his on court rival. 'It was pretty hard-fought, I'd say—and it's always good to have a runaround.'

Emma couldn't help but find a double meaning in every sentence at the moment.

'Right, first things first—who would like a drink?' Jack got to his feet. 'Patrick? Tim? A whisky?'

Two nods. Tim clearly he wasn't as asleep as his closed eyelids suggested.

'Bottle of white for you girls?'

Emma answered without skipping a beat as Amy and Jess simultaneously shot her a look. 'We're still on tea and coffee.'

'Well, it's your birthday. And I won't tell if you don't.'

Jack poured two generous whiskies before looking up from the decanter 'Em?'

'Yes?'

'Dad seemed to think you had something to tell me.'

'He did?' Emma did her best to look baffled, and wondered why it was only mothers-in-law who were traditionally accused of being interfering.

'Probably just a misunderstanding. Typical of the old man. Now, Jess, what can I get you?'

'Actually, I'd love another coffee—but don't worry, I can get it myself.' Jess took a step towards the kitchen as Emma sprang up, desperate to leave the room. 'Seriously, I insist. It's your party—relax. And anyway, you shouldn't be rushing around all the time.'

'Why not? I'm thirty-three, not eighty-three.'

'Thirty-four now, actually.' As Patrick piped up from behind his paper Emma wondered why on earth a party had seemed like a good idea. There were too many sides to every story, and they were all in the same room.

'OK, that's still thirty-four and not one hundred and four.

Plus, I have excellent coffee-making and carrying skills. Patrick can certainly give you a reference.'

An affirmative rustle of the paper. 'She's pretty competent.'

'She's a whole lot more. But, look, I'll go.' Jack took Jess's empty mug. 'You girls carry on chatting. It's about time I made myself useful. I mean, what are husbands for these days? Tea, sympathy, opening jam jars and conception.'

Emma closed her eyes in silent prayer and wished hers had been immaculate.

'Hello, you.' Jack put his hands on Emma's hips as she joined him in the kitchen. 'I can be trusted to make coffee and toast a crumpet.'

'I know. There *was* a time when I wouldn't have trusted you with a crumpet, but…'

'Believe me, there was a time when I wouldn't have trusted myself with one either. But that was in the bad old days…you've changed that.' Jack kissed her tenderly and, momentarily forgetting the news she was carrying, Emma lost herself in the moment.

They didn't pull apart until the old-fashioned kettle on the Aga started to whistle.

Composing herself, Emma walked over to the central island in the kitchen, using the work surface as a lectern from which to address her audience of one.

'You know, I think your dad is great, but he can be an interfering old gossip.'

'Welcome to the family.'

'There *is* something I wanted to talk to you about. But in private.' Emma could feel a tear or two on the way. Bloody hormones. She couldn't think when she'd last cried as a singleton. Except with empathy at *Bridget Jones's Diary* and during a particularly poignant moment in *The West Wing*. But these days she was on the brink more often than not. Swallowing hard, she recomposed herself before her voice started to falter. She'd never been a chicken and she wasn't going to start now.

Jack was watching her, coffee forgotten.

'I wanted to be a hundred per cent sure before I said anything. It's very early days, and it's not really safe to tell people at this point, but—well, I think we might be pregnant.'

'Really?' Jack's blue eyes were shining. 'Are you sure?'

'As sure as I can be. But I hadn't been planning to announce it yet.'

'Not even to your husband?'

Emma smiled at him. 'We're probably talking five or six weeks at the absolute most.' Emma crossed her fingers out of sight. 'And I think it's important that we get everything, you know, checked out before we tell the world. Statistically there are plenty of dangers at our age.' So she wasn't going to tell him the whole truth, then. Apparently not. Her instinctive peacekeeper had taken over.

'OK. Absolutely. You're in charge of this one.' Jack kissed his wife gently and pulled her up against him for a hug. 'Great news, darling. Um, so how on earth does Dad know?'

'He must be half-guessing. I was talking to Jess at the tennis court and I think he put two and two together and got seven. Only in this case seven is clearly the right answer.'

'I'll tell him to keep a lid on it.'

'Will you? Thank you. That would be great. Tell him he's got it wrong, if that's easier. It's just, to be honest, I'm quite nervous, aside from anything else.'

'I'll go and find him in a minute. God, you're clever. His first grandchild—the man will be over the moon.' Bending down, Jack kissed Emma's stomach through her jumper. ' I love you already.'

'I'm not having it in there, darling. I don't think there's room.'

'Oh.'

'Lower.'

'You're so naughty.'

Emma chuckled nervously. 'I know.'

'It's unbelievable. I've got a lovely wife, a bestseller in progress, and a child on the way.'

'We.'

'Of course. Of course. Without you I wouldn't have any of it.'

'Now, then, before I light the touch paper…'

James was building his part by the minute. Emma was enjoying the undoubtedly toxic scent of the burnt out sparklers which had served as pyrotechnic foreplay to the main event, nostalgic for her childhood and glad that the invention of fleece clothing had occurred since her days of Guy Fawkes Nights at the local cricket club, when she'd been made to wear so many clothes that her arms had practically been at right angles to the rest of her body, her mittens dangling from the sleeves of her coat on improbably thick elastic which had made actually putting them on an exercise in contortion.

'…on behalf of Emma and Jack, I want to thank you all for coming this afternoon. I haven't had the privilege of having Emma in the family for many months yet, but it is my great pleasure to be able to host my daughter-in-law's first birthday party here at Greenhill. If you would raise your glasses, may I propose a toast to the newest member of the Carlisle family?'

A selection of drinks were held aloft as Emma's blushes were spared by the darkness.

'Now—and it's not official yet, but as you are a hand-picked selection of friends I'm sure you can be trusted to keep this next piece of news close to your chests—it is my great pleasure to let you know that by this time next year I am to be—*finally,* I might add—a grandfather. So, let's drink to the health and happiness of you all, and especially to Emma.'

Patrick's previous sip of whisky stuck in his throat as he stared through the handful of guests from his carefully chosen, slightly remote perch on the terrace wall. He found her in a moment.

Emma glared at her husband.

'I haven't even spoken to him yet.' Responding to Emma's silent accusation, Jack hissed a reply through a gritted smile as well-wishers started to make a gradual move in their direction.

'You must have done.'

'I promise, Em, I haven't had a chance.'

'Why not?'

'Apparently he was giving Elsie a lift home, and then… Look, leave it with me. I'll talk to him.'

'Well, he can't exactly *un*tell people now, can he? This isn't *Men In Black*, you know.'

'He can say he made a mistake.'

Emma bowed her head in the hope that it would be easier to collect her thoughts if they all fell to the front.

Jack shook his head. 'The man is a liability. He only had a hunch. He has no actual idea. And, take it from me, he's never been a master of sensitivity. The night he called me to tell me that Charlie had been shot he blamed me for being at my own party and not with my brother when it happened. I know it was heat-of-the-moment stuff, but—'

'Congratulations, you two.' Tim led the back-slapping and Emma endured a few good wishes before making her excuses—just as the first rockets soared into the night sky. The trails of light and smoke ensured they resembled, to the birthday girl at least, giant spermatozoa, with wiggling smoke tails exploding into red, green and golden showers of fertile light high above the fields.

Emma had almost made it into the safety of the kitchen when out of the dark, and away from the masses, Patrick appeared.

'Well, well, well.' His tone was mordacious. 'This little

news item would go a long way to explain your reluctance to accept my proposal. Why didn't you just say something?'

Emma stood her ground. 'It wasn't the only factor.'

'OK, sometimes I wish you were a smidgen less honest. But at least there was a reason.'

Emma buttoned her lip. She couldn't believe she'd been sleeping with two people. Admittedly not simultaneously, but contemporaneously was quite bad enough.

'Could it be mine?' Patrick's voice was controlled but firm.

'No, it's mine.' Emma realised she hadn't prepared herself at all for this moment, and she had absolutely no idea how to play it.

'How can you be so sure? We had sex.'

'We had protected sex. Once.'

'We had a few problems with the condom, though. Don't you remember?'

To her embarrassment Emma couldn't recall much about any of it. 'It's highly unlikely.'

'But not impossible?'

'Highly improbable. I'm sure I was probably already pregnant that afternoon.' Emma was consumed by a wave of nausea at the thought of her misdemeanour.

'Only probably?' To his surprise Patrick was enjoying Emma's moment of discomfort.

'Almost certainly.'

'Interesting how life imitates art.'

'What do you mean?'

'Well, if you're not careful you could wind up being a single mother too. Good job you're raising a shedload of cash for lone parents. You might just need it.'

'A week ago you want to marry me and now you're plotting my demise?'

'I didn't say I was going to say anything.'

'I should bloody well hope not.'

'It'd be front page news, though…'

'Just for the record, I don't like the way your mind works sometimes.'

'It's not my mind you need to worry about. It's the media's.'

'Look, as soon as I've seen a specialist they'll be able to tell me exactly how pregnant I am, and then you can put your sordid mind at rest.' Perfect. She was thinking more clearly in the heat of the moment than she had been all week.

'I take it Jack doesn't know about us?'

'Of course not.'

'Of course not.'

'Don't just repeat what I say for effect.' Emma could feel her pulse quickening. 'And if you're trying to unnerve me, it's not working.' It was.

'We'll talk about this later.'

'I don't really see what there is to discuss.'

'I don't really see what I'm doing here. Jack said you wanted me to come along. So if this is your idea of fun, don't worry—I've got the hint.'

'It was his idea to ask you, not mine.' Emma softened as she saw Patrick's jawline stiffen. 'You're upset?'

'Thanks for the compassion. Good to see you're not having any trouble being detached about all this.'

'I just didn't think that you were really...you know. Look, I'm—' Emma stopped herself. What was she? Sorry? A bitch? Confused? 'It was Jack's idea to ask you today. I'm sorry if you got the wrong idea.' Emma was glad to see her years at boarding school had stood her in good stead on matters of manners if not of morals.

'I think I'd best go. Tell the proud father that I had to go back for some work-related something. Anything.'

'Are you sure you should be driving?'

'I've only had a couple of whiskies.'

'Exactly. You know how sensitive I am about—'

'You don't get to tell me what to do.'

'Patrick.' There was no messing with Emma's tone. 'Drive carefully—or, better still, drive tomorrow.'

'Might do.'

'Stop behaving like a twelve-year-old. I'll call you next week.'

'If you can find the time.'

'We've still got a job to finish.'

Patrick wrapped his hand around her wrist and gripped it just a little bit too hard. 'I'll see you.'

Emma watched, emotionless, as Patrick strolled across the gravel, hands in pockets, shoulders hunched under his jacket. Instead of falling in love and getting married she had championed the reverse process. And yet it seemed to be working.

Standing in the doorway to the kitchen, Emma watched the rest of the fireworks alone as a carefully timed succession of rockets, comets, torches and roman candles lit up the sky with neon showers. As the last rocket screeched and soared into the blackness before dissolving into a silver cascade she stared so hard she could see the traces of smoke trails long after they had disappeared into nothing. And then a polite round of applause signified it was suppertime.

'Emma, darling girl. Here you are…and all alone.' As James strolled over and gave her a hug Emma could feel herself shrinking into herself. He was the last person she wanted to see this evening. 'Did you enjoy the display?'

'It was fab. Thank you.' Courtesy under fire.

'My pleasure. Anyway, we're all heading inside for hot dogs now. You should get indoors. It's freezing. And remember you've got to look after yourself in your condition.'

'James…' Emma's tone was a warning one.

'What? Are you not feeling well? They say the first few months can be very tough.'

'I feel fine.' Emma sighed. 'Or at least I did. But I really didn't want everyone to know yet. It's so very early. It's unlucky. Statistically there's a very good chance that… I haven't even had a scan.'

James shifted his weight in his Wellington boots. 'I'm sorry. Jack's just had an almighty go at me. But when Elsie told me I couldn't wait. I was just so excited.'

'So Jack didn't tell you?'

'Jack? Tell me anything of importance? Don't be daft.'

Irritated that she had underestimated her husband, Emma snapped at her father-in-law. 'For God's sake, is no one allowed to have a private life any more?'

'Not if your surname starts with a C and ends with an E. We haven't had a private life for years my dear. I thought you knew that?'

Emma sighed. She did and she didn't.

'Speaking of your public, I do believe it's time for a photo op.'

'Damn.' Emma had totally forgotten about Jack's promise to *CelebriTee*.

'Tell them I'll be there in a second.'

Emma snuck through the kitchen entrance and up the back stairs. She needed a moment with her make-up bag. Millions of people were not going to be seeing her with pink eyes, blue lips and a red nose.

twenty-five

'Fiona?'

'Hi.' Proffering a hand for shaking, Fi sincerely hoped a name to match the face would follow—and sooner rather than later—but as yet nothing. This was one party where she really hadn't expected to meet anyone she knew. The stranger in question smiled as if the exposition of a couple of teeth was going to help the recognition process.

'It's Graham. I was at college with Mike. We met the other week in that wine bar in—'

'Richmond.' Her mental filing cabinet reordered itself just in the nick of time.

'So, what are you doing here? Friends of the family?' Graham's bushy eyebrows rose into his hairline in a display of incredulity.

'Not exactly. I'm with a friend of mine who knows them pretty well. She's single, so I'm her hot date.'

'Cheating on Mike already, eh? Does he know?' Graham had the sort of ruddy complexion that suggested a combination of too much time spent outdoors, too much alcohol, and total ignorance of the range of products known to the rest of the western world as moisturisers.

'What? That I'm here or that I date women?' Fiona relaxed into her verbal stride.

Graham's laugh was dirtier than Fiona's boots.

'Of course he does. So, how do *you* know Jack and Emma?'

'The same way the rest of the nation does...'

Fiona must have looked as clueless as she felt.

'Through papers and magazines.'

'Oh, right.'

'But I'm here on business...' He gestured at the two flight cases of camera kit just under the window and the portable steel freestanding lights in the drawing room. 'To take a few photos for *CelebriTee.* The public just can't get enough of these two. And I've been invited today, which makes a pleasant change. Sure beats hanging around in the freezing cold outside flash restaurants, waiting for people to go home so I can grab a photo on the off-chance they've had one too many or leave with someone they didn't arrive with.'

Did Mike know a real paparazzo? Did she know *anything* about her future husband?

'Did you always want to do this? When you were growing up, I mean?'

'It's not exactly what I set out to do when we all left college, but it pays bloody well...'

Fi tried to look as non-judgemental as possible, but her lousy poker face must have given her away and Graham set about defending his work.

'It's basically a case of supply and demand. If I don't take the pictures someone else will.'

'Doesn't the demand come from you guys?'

'The magazines only sell if people buy them. I've been in the game for about seven years now, and it's doing me very nicely, thank you. No point in taking arty photos of bridges if you want to drive a fast car.'

Fiona wondered whether Graham had always spoken like an understudy for *Eastenders* or whether it was all part of the job—along with jeans (even if they were Paul Smith ones), a leather jacket, and a watch on a chunky metal bracelet.

A door opened and closed further down the corridor, emitting a snapshot of party bustle, and Jess appeared holding two hot dogs.

'Ah, so here you are.' Jess marched up to Fi and handed her one. 'We're supposed to be in the kitchen. This is a restricted area for now.'

Graham took a step back. 'Well, nice to see you again, Fiona. Give my best to Mike.'

'Will do. Hope the job goes well.'

Graham leant in. 'Piece of piss. Or at least it will be when the wife finally gets here. Stay and watch if you like.'

'Really?' Fiona got in before Jess could swallow her mouthful and shoo her away.

'Take a seat at the back there and keep quiet. You should be fine.'

Jess followed Fiona to a discreet corner of the room. 'And he is…?'

'Graham. He and Mike were at college together.'

'He seems very familiar.'

Fiona shrugged. 'Well, I've only met him once, a couple of weeks ago, and you weren't there.'

Jess watched him check his camera and hoped for Emma's sake that he'd been inside setting up for the last hour, well out of earshot. Good news might travel fast, but celebrity gossip would have given Concorde a run for its money.

'Here she is.' Jack strode over to the sofa as Emma walked in, picture-perfect.

'Are we doing this sitting down?' She was faking relaxation like a pro.

'Can do.' Jack winked suggestively, a new burst of energy

accompanying the selection of telephoto lenses in his presence. He looked at her approvingly and reduced his voice to a whisper. 'Boy, were you worth the wait.'

Emma was preoccupied with the set-up—and the number of people standing around. 'I thought you said it was just one photo…'

'I dare say they'll take a few.'

'What? "Jack and Emma Carlisle at the family home for the celebration of her thirty-fourth birthday"?'

'Something like that.' Jack took her hand in appeasement.

'Do they have to mention my actual age?'

'Does it matter?'

'I guess not. And there'll be no mention…' Emma's eyes searched her husband's.

'Absolutely not. Don't worry, darling. Everything is going to be just swell.'

'Did you just say swell?'

'I could have said phat.'

Emma's gaze remained steely.

'Not funny?'

'I've heard better. I could have decided to have a nap, you know.'

Jack laughed 'Honestly, Em. I love you. Now, let's get this over with.'

Emma had endured quite enough of Jack's buoyancy. He was floating and she was drowning. 'Come on, then. Let's do it. Where's the photographer?'

'Over there.'

Emma narrowed her eyes slightly to get a better look. She really ought to schedule a trip to the optician before she developed some nasty lines in the eye area. The last thing she needed was the press speculating that Jack Carlisle's wife was going blind or suggesting that she'd had plastic surgery every time she wore a hat or scarf to go shopping.

'I know him.' Emma was watching the man with the camera, waiting for the penny to drop.

'I don't think so.' Jack took her hand and started to massage the tension away from the area between her thumb and forefinger.

'Are you sure?'

Jack nodded.

Jess watched Graham intently as Fiona demonstrated an impressive new knowledge of camera parts and lenses.

'OK. We're ready.' Jack addressed the room and everyone jumped into place. A man knelt at his side, just out of shot, holding a circular silver reflector as Graham adjusted lights on their stands.

'This won't take a minute. Chloe, love—powder, please.'

A waif-like teenager with less meat on her than on Jess's frankfurter appeared, to powder their noses and pull the wrinkles out of jumpers and shirts.

Graham was acting ringmaster. 'Right, you two. Let's get this done and then you can get back to your party. Emma, love, over this way. Bit more. Chin up a bit.'

The camera flashed repeatedly.

'And a fraction more. Perfect, Jack. That's lovely... Now, look at each other...'

All Emma could see were gold-edged circles of black from the flash.

'Great. Super.' Graham paused and checked the small digital screen on the back of the camera. 'Right, let's have you on your feet—just a couple more. You haven't got a dog handy, by any chance? Or a piece of birthday cake?'

Chloe scurried off in search of props, both animal and cholesterol.

'And let's have you over there, in front of those photos. Brilliant. Just a fraction to the right. In front of the wedding photo. Stop there...' His shutter clicked repeatedly. 'Look at me, look at each other—fab. Super. Great. That's perfect. Now, if we can get Oscar in too…'

As he danced around his subjects, Jess suddenly realised where she'd seen him before. She didn't forget a face. And his had been the only unidentifiable one. His hair was shorter, but…Jess narrowed her eyes to hone her focus. It was definitely him.

Nearly ten minutes of superlatives later and they were done. Jack chatted animatedly to Graham as he started packing his equipment away—Jess seized her moment—and her former client.

'Em?'

'So, how do I look?' Emma shifted her weight from one hip to the other before jutting a hip provocatively and mockingly. 'Up a bit…a bit more…perfect…to your left a touch…' It was a perfect impression.

Jess smiled. 'First of all, you look absolutely beautiful.'

'What's second of all?'

'As long as you've really absorbed my first point?'

'Got it. Thanks.'

'And that's a gorgeous top. Now…'

'Is this the second thing?'

Jess nodded. 'Do you know that photographer?'

'Well, I thought he looked familiar but Jack says not. Then again, I see so many photographers these days…' Emma interrupted herself. 'Good God, will you just listen to me? Please take me outside and slap me. Next I'll be demanding someone carries my bags at all times and that I only fly First Class.'

'So Jack says he's never met him before either?' Jess rubbed her chin. 'Interesting.' She accentuated every syllable.

Emma furrowed her brow.

'Well, take a look at Jack now. Total strangers? I think not.'

Emma had to admit that it looked decidedly as if Jack and Graham were sharing a joke. 'So?'

'I could be way off target here, but the more I look at him, the more I'm certain that he was at your wedding.'

'Yup—he was the groom.' Emma laughed at her joke, but noted Jess's total lack of reaction. Moving on as swiftly as she could, Emma adopted what she hoped was a suitably concerned expression. 'Are you saying Graham was?'

Jess nodded. 'Swap those jeans for a morning suit. Add a couple of inches of length to his hair and a bit of a tan...'

Emma stared at his profile, made mental adjustments and took in the general picture. Nothing. 'Sorry, Jess, not ringing any bells with me. But then again I don't know most of Jack's friends.'

'Exactly.'

'I still don't get it.' Emma wondered if this was because she was pregnant. It was bad enough that she was going to get fat, but she really didn't want to get stupid.

'OK, put it this way—if Graham is a friend of Jack's, why wouldn't he just tell you?'

'I don't know.'

'Unless, of course, you're not supposed to remember Graham. Because he wasn't supposed to be there.'

Finally, somewhere, a penny dropped. 'You think Graham gatecrashed the wedding?'

'I'd go so far as to say that security wasn't so much breached as flouted...' Jess didn't know why she hadn't gone straight to the man in question—or at least the man she wanted to question. Instead she simply nodded as Emma started to understand. 'I think the wedding photo mystery may well be over. Get him over here if you can.'

'Darling?' Emma beckoned to her husband.

Jess sighed. Not her first choice of summons.

'Yes, lovely?' Jack wandered over.

'Jess wants to pick your brains about something.'

Emma left to talk to Fi, in order to check Graham out from a selection of other angles in case it jogged her memory. Right now it felt as if her processor was way below Pentium speed.

'Jess? Enjoying your weekend so far, I hope? So, how did it look from where you were sitting? Pretty good photos, I think.'

'I'm sure they will be. So, how do you know Graham?'

'I don't. I mean I've seen him around a few times—you know, a face in a crowd.'

'So he's not a friend of yours?'

'Well, I mean, you want to get on with the people in charge of your image, don't you? But "friend" would be pushing it.'

'Not the sort of man you'd invite to your wedding, then?'

Jack stalled. It was only a second, but Jess noticed the delay straight away.

'It was Graham who sold the photos, wasn't it?'

'How would I know?' Jack's fake nonchalance only irritated Jess further.

'Because you invited him.'

'So what if I did?' Jack's voice was quiet, but penetrating. 'It was my wedding. It could only have been positive coverage.'

Jess's cool was on the verge of deserting her. 'Even though we decided, along with Patrick, that there would be no photos for the press?' Her delight at having found the perpetrator was fading fast. 'How the hell did you get him in?'

'I just sent him an invitation.' Honestly, sometimes Jack wondered why everyone thought he wasn't as bright as he actually was. 'I used the proof—the sample invite you sent us from the printers for approval. He arrived a little bit late for the service, dressed in all the right kit, and they obviously didn't check the list of names properly. It was Patrick who wanted total secrecy, not me. My childhood was one photo op after another, and I really couldn't see the harm. Far from it. '

'Are you addicted to attention-seeking?' Jess's irritation was tinged with relief. At least the breach in security hadn't come from within her own staff.

'There was no harm done. No one died. No one pulled a trigger.'

'Don't tempt me.'

'Has your business suffered?' The way Jack asked it was almost a rhetorical question.

'See—no harm done. And if people are happy to pay to see a picture of me, it's just plain market forces.'

Jess couldn't understand where his ego ended. Unless… 'Did you make money from this?'

Jack looked away.

'*Did* you?'

'Does it matter?'

'Of course it bloody matters. Does everything in your life have a price?' Jess interrupted herself. 'Actually, don't answer that.'

'I don't see what could possibly have gone wrong.'

Jess barely had to pause for breath. 'Well, apart from Graham telling the world that you were in on his scam and taking money from the proceeds of his visit.'

'Look, I did him a favour and he returned it. That's all. Nothing bad happened. Panic over.'

'So you trust him?'

'He's a good guy.'

'Even with the news that Emma is pregnant?'

'Keep your voice down.' Jack's response was snappy. 'He was inside. They all were.'

'You don't think he or one of his minions might have overheard? It's the top topic of conversation in the kitchen now.'

Jack paused. 'I'll make sure I tell Graham it's off the record. Emma is absolutely firm on this one.'

'So he *does* know?'

'How would I know? I'm just covering my back.'

'Do you really have no idea of how big a scoop this would be for a magazine like *CelebriTee*? You're going to end up being shopped by your own precious market forces, and if it wasn't for Emma in all of this I'd say you deserved it.'

'Do me a favour and drop the Miss Marple stuff. You were invited here this weekend as a guest. Graham is here today to take a couple of photos for Britain's bestselling weekly— all on the record, all above board. That's it.' His outward demeanour might be remaining intact, but inside Jack was starting to worry.

'So, does Emma know about your predilection for photographers?'

'She trusts me.'

'Well, I guess someone has to. You're not going to start letting her down now, are you?'

'Of course not.'

Effortlessly Jack broke into an instant smile as Emma arrived back. Not even noticing him put his arm across her shoulder, she hissed at Jess.

'OK, I'm pretty sure he's the missing link. I was watching the wedding DVD with Amy the other day, and she pointed out some guy in the pews that neither of us recognized. I think this might be him. Having said all that, there were hundreds of people in the church.' Emma's doubts were resurfacing.

Jess volunteered the statistics. 'Two hundred and ten. Actually two hundred and eleven with our Graham.'

Emma glanced over to where Graham was kneeling on the floor, packing his kit away. His jeans were riding up a little, to reveal one light grey sock and one darker one. 'I'm sure it was him. Well, pretty sure. But I don't remember seeing him later on.'

Jess raised an eyebrow accusatorily at Jack. 'I imagine he didn't stick around for long.'

'OK, so you've found your man. Case closed. Now, please,

let's move on. I'll write you a letter for your files if you like.
Put me down as a client reference. That should help.'

Jess walked off. Collecting Fiona, she led her to the kitchen
to garner more support for her outrage from her best friend.
And more hot dogs.

Emma watched Jess and Fi leaving the room and observed
Jack chewing the cuticle at the side of his thumb. 'What's
wrong with her?'

Jack shot her a silencing look as Graham sauntered over.

'We're off, mate. Time to leave you guys to a bit of peace
and quiet. Thanks. Great shoot. Great stuff.' Graham winked
at Jack and slapped him on the back heartily. 'Hope to run
into you again some time.' He doffed an invisible cap at
Emma. 'Happy Birthday.'

'Thanks so much—to all of you.' Jack flashed a smile at
all the assistants as they started to file out, laden with kit.

As Jack walked Graham to the door, deep in conversation,
Emma nibbled at a spare hot dog and, enjoying the moment
of peace, waited for his return. Moments later, Jack flopped
onto the sofa, tilting his head back to rest on the narrow edge
of the cushions. Staring at the ceiling, he moved his jaw as
if he were chewing invisible gum. She could see the tendons
flexing under his skin.

'Jack?' Emma's tone was inquisitive as she went to close
the door to secure their privacy. 'What's up with Jess? She
was fine a moment ago.'

'She's developed some half-baked theory that I invited a
press photographer to our wedding so I could take a cut of
his profits…'

'And did you?'

Jack made eye contact with his wife. 'Does it sound like
something I would do?'

'Well…' Emma danced with diplomacy. 'You were never
convinced that we should be so secretive about the whole
thing. And maybe back then…'

'So you believe Jess?'

'This isn't a competition. I'll believe whatever you tell me is the truth.'

Jack paused. 'I just didn't see what harm it would do. I figured if I didn't see to it then someone else would. And it was still a great day.'

'So she was right. And you can see why she was upset...'

Jack shrugged and looked around the room, hoping to avoid another reprimand.

'Come on—it was meant to be a press-free zone, and then someone gets in and—more to the point—gets out with photographs. Why on earth were you tiptoeing around behind everyone's back? What if Graham had decided to turn you in?'

'Why would he have done that?'

'Because you're Jack Carlisle and it would have been a great story. You know how offended the public are at tales of the rich getting richer—especially at the tabloid buyers' expense.'

Jack hated to admit it, but Emma might have a point. 'So I didn't think it through...'

'And you didn't tell me either.'

To Jack's discomfort, Emma looked more disappointed than cross as she continued.

'I may not be particularly well qualified, but PR is something I do know a little bit about.'

'Sorry.'

Emma had experienced more genuine apologies. 'Did you think *us* through?'

Jack sat up immediately. 'What is that supposed to mean?'

'Why did you marry me, Jack?'

'Because...' Jack reached into the ether.

'You wanted a wife? You needed a wife? You needed a new image?'

'Well, I admit that...maybe initially. But now it's different.'

'Different? You really know how to bowl a girl over. And I thought you were a romantic.'

'I am—and I do love you, Emma.'

'You'd better do, because against all my better judgement I bloody well love you, too.' Emma realised she'd just come out with it. As a matter of fact. For the first time without really thinking about it.

'So it was a gamble that paid off?'

She wasn't even sure he'd been listening. 'There you go again, Casanova.'

'And Jess has done OK out of us, so no harm done? Right?' Jack was hopeful. He really wanted Emma's approval.

'That's not the point. Jess did a fantastic job. She makes dreams come true on a weekly basis, and those dreams aren't any less important if the budget is half or a quarter of what ours was. She needs to inspire complete trust.'

'I didn't think about all that.'

'Clearly.'

'I'll apologise properly.'

'Good. In fact, I was thinking about giving her a hand when I'm done with Patrick's project.'

'Why?'

'Because she's a friend now. Because I want to.'

Jack nodded. He knew better than to try and change women's minds.

'I'd get paid. And she thinks I'd be great at it.'

'I'm sure you'd be great at whatever you were doing. But don't you think you'll have a lot on your hands?'

'Women with children do work, you know. I'm not going to get a full-time job, but believe me, you don't want me at home all day.' Emma was terrified by the prospect of having her right to roam taken hostage.

'Well, I'm sure it would do her business the world of good to have you working for her.'

'Just because *you* are so pecuniary don't think everyone's mind works the same way.'

'Look, so I didn't think it all through properly, but people cash in on me all the time and money doesn't grow on trees. I'm sorry.'

'We have more than enough. Plus, if it's an official photo shoot, we always get a fee.'

'Which we donate to charity.' Jack countered Emma's argument with a flourish.

'Listen, public image is just as important as profile. I'd rather see the occasional positive column inch than pages of criticism. Just promise me, Jack, you'll be straight with me. We don't stand a chance if you're leading a double life I know nothing about.'

'Roger that.' Jack performed a mock salute. 'All that I am I give to you, all that I have I share with you—secrets to be included from this day forward.'

Emma exhaled. This all felt much more normal.

'But total honesty works both ways, Em…'

Her relief was in the midst of a U-turn. Emma swallowed hard.

'So, while we're having a confession session, anything you want to share with me?'

'No.' Emma's demeanour was intact. There was no way Patrick would have said anything.

'Are you sure? It's just I received a call a few weeks back that made me think otherwise.'

A few weeks ago? 'Well…' Emma closed her eyes to focus her nerve. A direct question deserved a direct answer. No bloody secrets. She was about to be hoist by her own petard.

'There was someone else, wasn't there?' Jack's blue eyes went from inviting to icy.

Emma double checked the room for privacy and started a nod. Or at least her chin fell to her chest and stayed there as she felt her poise come crashing down around her.

'I was going to tell you. It's just it was over before it had begun…it didn't mean anything. It really shouldn't have happened at all.'

Emma couldn't believe it. It was as if she was reading from a bad script—only in a soap opera the credits would have started rolling by now, giving her at least twenty-four hours of reprieve whereas she currently didn't even have twenty-four seconds.

'What shouldn't have?'

'There was a thing. I had a thing. It was just a one-off. I honestly didn't see it coming.'

'Powerless to resist, I'll bet.'

His arms were folded and disappointment radiated from the sofa. She couldn't bear it.

'I swear it will never, ever happen again.' Emma had never felt more penitent.

Jack nodded as if to convince himself, and he rose from the cushions and walked over to the window, his hands clenched into fists in his pockets. He stared out into the darkness.

'How did you find out?' The charade now over, she had to ask.

Jack turned to face her. 'Graham owed me a favour. A taxi driver called *CelebriTee* with something for their "Seen But Not Heard" section. You were spotted with wet hair. Welcome to my world.'

'I was probably on my way back from the gym.'

'In Primrose Hill?'

Emma gasped. She couldn't help it.

'How many swimsuits do you have stashed in lockers all over the capital? I might be egocentric but I'm not stupid. It was Patrick, wasn't it?'

Emma was floored. She fell into the nearest armchair. 'Oh, my God. You've known the whole time.'

'Well, since the weekend after. Graham called when we had just arrived down here. Turns out he's more valuable than I realised.' Jack paced the perimeter of the room like a big cat in a cage before sitting down opposite his wife.

Protected on three sides by the armchair, Emma closed her eyes under the misguided preschool assumption that if she couldn't see him maybe he couldn't see her either.

Jack sat on the edge of the sofa and waited. He had all the time in the world.

Emma opened one eye, and then the other. 'I'm so sorry. Anything I say is going to sound pathetic now. It was so— so stupid. I felt so alone. That's not an excuse. Well, it is. But it isn't. I was naïve. I panicked…' Emma pressed her palms together in an instant emergency prayer. So help her God. She could see a vein throbbing in Jack's temple, his appearance otherwise eerily calm. 'It was a terrible mistake. Just one afternoon. I promise it will never happen again.'

'Too fucking right it won't.' Finally, and to Emma's relief, Jack erupted. 'What the hell were you playing at? And what the hell was *he* playing at? It's not like he didn't know you were my wife.' Jack strode towards the door.

'Where are you going?'

'There are some things that men have to settle themselves…'

'Stop it, Jack. Not now, not here, not ever. Look, I'd had a few drinks. We both had. It's history.'

'I could kill him. Well, actually, I couldn't. I'm far too squeamish. But I could hire someone. Or I could ruin his business.'

'And he could ruin your reputation.'

'Damn. You're right. Again.'

'And it's my fault, too.'

Jack sat down again, the wind removed from his sails. 'And mine, too. I know I'm difficult to live with.'

'Actually, you're really not. The whole thing just took a lot of getting used to.'

'Do you want me to leave you?' Jack asked.

Emma couldn't tell if he was being serious. But she couldn't afford to take any risks either. 'No. I'm praying that you won't want to leave me.'

'And you don't want to divorce me?'

Emma was surprised at Jack's apparent vulnerability. 'Of course not.'

'So I guess this is what marriage is all about? For better, for worse…' Jack ran his fingers through his hair. 'I mean, are we really going to let one night ruin the rest of our marriage?'

'It was one afternoon, actua—'

Jack held up his hand to stop her. 'Just make sure it stays that way. One last thing on the subject—'

Emma interrupted him. 'Anything.'

Jack fiddled with his wedding ring nervously. 'Any chance that…' Jack was staring at Emma's as yet unaffected waist-line. He couldn't bring himself to even say it.

Emma took her life into her hands. 'No.'

Jack's sigh of relief was heartfelt.

'Are you not jealous?'

'Emma, please, don't push me. I'm not delighted.'

'But you're being so rational, so calm…'

'If it was a genuine one-off…'

Emma nodded vehemently

'And it was a few weeks back… Plus, I don't know, things between us have been too good to fake. Maybe I'm just not a jealous person?'

'You're just a good actor.'

'That, too. And it's not like I've been a saint in the past. I know how easily things can get screwed up.'

Emma had no idea why she had been pardoned. She'd had her life on a plate and then she'd gone in search of an alternative menu. She must have been mad. 'So how come *CelebriTee* didn't run with the story?'

'I covered for you.'

'You did? Why?'

Silence from her husband.

'Jack?'

'Instinct, I guess. It had been a weird couple of months.

We were both adjusting. I'm not an easy person, but you're breaking me down and I really want us to work—more than anything. I love you.'

Emma was stumped. 'Even now?'

Jack nodded. 'More every day. How many times do I have to tell you?'

'It's just that you keep saying it…'

'Exactly.'

'Which somehow devalues it.'

'So, would you rather I didn't tell you?'

'Of course not.'

Jack put his hand on his heart. 'I swear, I will never, ever understand women.'

'Seriously, though, do you know how many times you've told women that told you love them?'

Jack looked genuinely puzzled.

'The love-interest in every film and mini-series I've seen of yours, for a start. Not to mention, I'm sure, the numerous women you've dated over the years. How do I know being a doting, understanding husband isn't just your latest role?'

'Granted, love is just a word.'

'Exactly. And love wasn't part of the deal for us, was it?'

'Well, it just goes to show there are some things that you can't plan.'

'But how do I know you're not acting now?' Emma crossed her arms. Defensively? Defiantly? Protectively? Because she was cold?

Jack shook his head in frustration. 'I know I've screwed up in public time and time again over the years, but forget about what you've read, what you've heard. Look at who I am, who you know I really am. I can count the number of women I've genuinely told I loved, on the fingers of my left hand. And one of them was my mother.'

Emma was speechless.

'When you walked down that aisle we didn't really know

what lay ahead for us. And, yes, it could have gone one of two ways. We're just lucky it's working now.'

Emma nodded, her vision temporarily obscured as tears of regret mingled with tears of relief. Hell, it was her party, and she could have a good old cry if she wanted to.

'For the record. I do love you, Jack Carlisle. Very much.'

To Emma's delight Jack's joy was childlike in its exposed honesty. 'Now, that's the important bit.' Squatting down next to her armchair, he stroked the back of her head affectionately and kissed her lightly on the lips. 'Here's to us. From this day forward.'

Emma smiled and then grimaced as an unusual cramping seized her. Bending over, then standing up, hands on her hips, she hoped to find a comfortable position. Another wave of pain ripped through her. She sat down, suddenly dizzy.

'Emma?'

'Bloody hot dog.' Emma clutched her abdomen. It definitely wasn't wind. Looking up, she saw her concern reflected in Jack's expression.

'Em…darling…what is it?'

'I don't know.' Emma did her best not to panic, and yet she could feel herself on the verge of tears.

'Is it the baby? Is something wrong?'

Scared, Emma gritted her teeth as, gripping Jack's arm, she hauled herself to her feet and instinctively tensed her pelvic floor muscles as best she could. 'Get me upstairs and then please find Amy.'

twenty-six

Patrick took a long drag of his cigarette and watched the paper burn orange close to the filter, before stamping it out on the cobbled floor. He hadn't smoked in five years. And now he'd smoked five in ten minutes. He turned up the collar on his coat for a layer of extra warmth before reaching in his pocket for the packet he'd swiped from the sitting room.

'Hello?' Amy's boots crunched across the gravel drive as she walked to her car, scarf wrapped tightly round her, torch in hand. 'Is there anybody out here?' She was sure she could smell cigarettes, yet she couldn't see a soul. It reminded her of prefect duties at school.

Patrick moved into the glare of the torch and Amy, startled, gasped at the sight of another human being.

'Sorry.' Patrick held his hand up apologetically. 'I come in peace. Or maybe that should be pieces. I didn't mean to scare you.'

'What are you doing hiding out here?'

'Emma and I had an argument. I was leaving an hour ago, only I'm still here. How about you? Running away?'

'Pippa can't sleep without Snoppy. And Snoppy is missing, presumed lost in foot well.'

'Snoppy?'

'Yup.' Amy rummaged on the floor of the BMW X5 and produced a very battered, very grey, clearly adored, once plush Snoppy.

'You mean Snoopy?'

'I'm afraid in our house it has always been Snoppy.'

Patrick played along. 'Brother of the world's favourite beagle?'

'Just his long-lost mispronounced cousin, I think.'

Patrick smiled, enjoying the banality of the conversation. Amy studied him. 'So, are you coming back in?'

'Nope. I'm definitely going home.'

'You had a bit of a nerve coming along in the first place, didn't you?'

'What do you mean?'

'Do you really think Emma hasn't told me?'

Patrick didn't make eye contact. 'I was invited.'

'Look, you walked her down the aisle and then you walked her to your front door. You can't just sleep with whoever you like. She didn't want you here today.'

'I love her.'

'What crap.'

Patrick recoiled at Amy's directness.

'You just can't have her,' Amy continued.

'I'd be good for her,' he insisted.

'No again. Open your eyes. See how happy she is.'

'She was.'

'She *is*. Since when did the course of true love ever run smooth? And, speaking as a totally biased observer from Emma's camp, overall it's going well.'

'He doesn't know her like I do.'

'He will. And you only see what you want to see.'

Patrick cupped his hands and blew hot air into them. He was starting to feel numb. 'I want to be with her.'

'It's all in the thrill of the chase for you. You had years to make a move. And now, say you get her, you'll get bored and she'll be left with nothing. It's just a game for you. Remember, I'm a mother. Therefore I know everything.'

'That's quite a claim.'

'OK, then, what did she say when you asked her to marry you? A fact which, incidentally, she's only just told me about. For some stupid reason she wants to protect your image.'

Patrick took the last cigarette from the packet and lit up. 'She said no way.'

'That sounds like a pretty clear answer to me.'

'She was confused, and she doesn't know how lucky she is. She ought to be careful. After all, I'm not the one carrying a fatherless child around.'

'Hardly fatherless, now, is it, Patrick?'

'It could be my very first child.'

'But it's not, is it?'

Patrick raised his eyebrows in surprise at Amy's audacity. 'How can you be so sure?'

'Remember, I know everything. You may also recall that Katy came to you through my former recruitment company.'

'So?' His throat constricted a little. He had genuinely forgotten that Amy had placed Emma in her job in the first place.

'So Katy's a friend of one of my ex-colleagues—a good friend—and women talk…'

Suddenly Patrick could feel an increasingly rapid pulse in his neck.

'And, thanks to Emma, I'm seen to have an inside track on Patrick Robson PR, which is why, I guess, I received an interesting e-mail one morning…'

'You did?' Patrick was shifting his weight from foot to foot, decidedly uncomfortable.

'Apparently Katy's boss has seduced her.'

Patrick felt himself blushing and stepped back into an area of at least semi-darkness.

'Not only that, but they've apparently had sex on several different occasions and at a number of different destinations. Her boss told her that she didn't need the morning after pill because he'd had a vasectomy...'

Patrick's blink was prolonged as Amy continued relating her story.

'It being the twenty-first century, and the age of enlightenment, Katy—unsurprisingly—was also concerned about the risk of STDs. At which point he told her not to worry as he'd been single and celibate for months, and also that she shouldn't tell anyone about their affair if she wanted to keep her position... Any of this sounding familiar?'

Patrick had always hated e-mail, and now he knew why. 'Does Emma know about any of this?'

'Unfortunately I had to promise Katy total confidentiality. Plus, Emma was confused enough about you already. When father figures go wrong...'

Speechless, and defenceless, Patrick just stood there waiting for his ordeal to end. Whatever happened next, in four and a half hours today would be over.

'Nor can *you* tell Katy we had this conversation.'

Patrick nodded silently.

'The company offered to move her to another client, but she was keen to stay. I think she genuinely believes there is hope for the two of you.'

'Shit.' Patrick didn't know where to look.

'Anyway, what you get up to you in your sordid little private life really holds little interest for me. Except for one thing. I'll bet Emma doesn't know you can't have children.' Amy didn't have time to beat round any bushes.

Patrick kicked a small stone across the barn floor.

'Does she or doesn't she?' Amy persisted.

'I don't think... No.'

'And yet you asked her to *marry* you—when you know how much she wants to have a family, and probably when you were sleeping with Katy at the same time?'

'She's made her choice now.'

'She made her choice a long time before you decided to stick your oar in. You even helped her make it, for God's sake. You work with her for three years but then you wait until three weeks after she's married to make a pass and only present her with a hand-picked selection of facts.'

Patrick rubbed his eyes. 'Shitty, huh?'

'Yeah. And some…'

Patrick took a last drag of his cigarette and exhaled languidly in an attempt to keep his head together.

'Luckily you've been trained to clear up this sort of mess.'

'You want me to tell her *now*?'

'Can you think of a better time? She's a pregnant woman, Patrick. There's a small chance that it could be yours, or at least she thinks there is, and she certainly doesn't need any extra stress.'

'I can't believe you didn't tell her.'

'Well, I can't believe she slept with you. My hands were tied. Besides, it's definitely not my job to do your dirty work.'

'I'm supposed to have left.'

'You're supposed to be a nice guy.'

'Amy? Are you out there? Amy?' The footsteps on the gravel were closely spaced, a torch beam jumping. *'Amy?'* Jack's voice filled the open-sided barn as, running, he reached it. The torch beam searched the row of parked cars urgently as he caught his breath.

Amy stepped out from behind the boot of her car. 'Over here.' She waved the soft toy in the air before turning to Patrick. 'Looks like I'm needed.'

'You'd better go, then.'

'And *you'd* better do the right thing.'

twenty-seven

Patrick pulled into a passing area halfway down the drive before turning off the headlights, slipping into neutral and applying the handbrake. Sitting there in the dark, he replayed the conversation with Amy in his head, wondering whether to turn the MG round and head back up to the house. But Monday seemed quite soon enough to speak to Emma. He didn't want to ruin her party any more than he had already.

A wall of headlights dazzled him via his rearview mirror and forced him to squint in order to identify the large car speeding away from Greenhill. Moments later the X5 overtook him, Amy at the wheel, and what looked like the golden couple in the back seat, Jack apparently on the phone. Patrick's car shuddered in their wake. Turning his key in the ignition, he watched the four-wheel drive turn left on to the main road and, giving them a few seconds, he decided to follow. As Amy had told him in no uncertain terms earlier, there was no time like the present.

Jack sat at Emma's empty bedside and waited for her return from Theatre. Amy had gone on a coffee run—not that he was going to need any artificial stimulants to keep him awake tonight, but he'd desperately needed a few minutes on his own. Blinking away a few tears, he looked at his watch again. Surely Emma should be back by now? What if there had been complications? As a young child he'd always believed that doctors could cure everything. But he hadn't been to this hospital since he'd come to see his mother, just after she'd died.

Jack stared at the wall, seeing nothing. *One of those things.* The doctor earlier had been unequivocal. Spontaneous abortion. No one to blame. In the last hour the miscarriage self-help leaflet had been folded and unfolded, read and re-read. What to expect? It didn't come close.

They'd both been peering at the ultrasound monitor, hoping to make sense of the pattern on the screen. The consultant had pointed out the head, a leg. And then the moment Jack knew he would never be able to erase: the silence. No fluttering heartbeat had filled the consulting room. And then the screen, along with their first child, had faded to black.

The door swung open as a couple of orderlies wheeled Emma in and transferred her into a bed. There was an IV in the back of her hand, and a nurse was busily administering a drip, checking her chart. Emma seemed so fragile and Jack had never felt less powerful.

'So, um, Nurse, how is she?'

The young Scottish girl beamed at her good fortune to be working for a patient with a celebrity next of kin. 'Well, she's a bit groggy, but she'll be just fine. The doctor will be along shortly. Don't you worry. She'll be back to her best in no time.'

Jack sighed with relief.

The nurse smiled at him. 'Really, a D&C is a pretty common procedure.'

The doctor entered the room, still in his scrubs.

'Mr Carlisle, just to put your mind at rest, there were no complications. Mrs Carlisle is in perfect working order and there's no reason why you shouldn't start trying for another baby in four to six weeks—provided you both feel up to it, of course. She'll be a bit sore for a week or so, and hormonally she could be a little up and down, but I'm afraid this is such a common occurrence that it isn't even considered medically significant until you've had three in a row—and there's no reason why that should happen in your case.'

'Great.' Jack nodded, doing his best to remember the doctor's exact words.

'I'm only sorry I couldn't be the bearer of better news.'

'That's the way it goes, I guess. But thank you for all you've done, and we really appreciate you coming out—especially at this hour,' Jack told him.

'No problem. Actually, you saved me from a pretty dire dinner party.'

The two men laughed as Emma opened her eyes a little groggily. 'Jack?'

The doctor took a step towards the door. 'I'll leave you two to catch up. Elaine…?'

The nurse returned the chart to the end of Emma's bed and followed the doctor out of the room, closing the door behind her.

'Hello, darling.' Jack took Emma's hand in his and sat beside her, gently stroking her hair with his other.

'Hello, you.' Emma's lips were dry. She looked around for some water.

'How are you feeling?'

'Thirsty. Sore. Empty.'

Jack passed her a beaker of tepid water from the jug next to the bed. Emma took a few sips before sinking back into the pillows.

'And my back hurts.'

'That's because they had to give you an epidural. You'd eaten far too recently to be able to have a general anaesthetic.'

'That bloody hot dog.' Emma tried to laugh, but found herself on the verge of tears. 'I lost the baby.' She started crying.

'*We* lost it, Ems…' Jack pinched the bridge of his nose to try and stop himself from joining in. He needed to be strong—for her, for them.

'Remember what the doctor said. It's purely chromosomal— Nature's way of making sure an unhealthy foetus doesn't get to full term.' For once Jack was grateful for his photographic memory. At least his career had proved useful for something. 'One in twenty pregnancies end in a miscarriage. It's just that often they take place so early that women didn't even realise they were pregnant in the first place.'

Emma nodded. 'I know what he said. I'm just so very sorry. And very, very sad.'

'The most important thing is that you're OK. This isn't your fault; it isn't anybody's fault. While you were in there I kept thinking that maybe without that confrontation earlier…you know…'

'It died two weeks ago.'

Jack nodded. 'At seven weeks. Which means we conceived on our honeymoon.'

Emma was totally shell shocked. She knew the statistics, but there was nothing routine about any of this in her mind. And at least it had definitely been Jack's. She took his hand and, bringing it up to her lips, kissed it. 'We're going to be OK, though, aren't we?'

'We're going to be great. Parents, grandparents—we've got the rest of our lives ahead of us.'

Patrick finally plucked up the courage to walk into the Bath stone building. From the outside it looked like a large private residence, but a closer inspection of the brass plaque at the front door revealed it was a very private hospital. He'd been for dinner and then strangely he'd returned. It was late. The place was almost deserted. Walking past an understated security guard, he went to the small reception desk.

'Good evening, sir.' A beady-eyed receptionist peered over her half-glasses at him.

'Good evening. I'm here to see Emma and Jack Carlisle. I believe they checked in, or rather she was admitted, earlier.' It was an assumption he was going to have to make.

'And you are…?'

Patrick felt as if he was trying to get in to see an 18-rated film as a fifteen-year-old. 'Patrick Robson.'

'Relation?'

'Friend.'

'I'm afraid they're not taking any visitors. If you'd like to leave a message I'll see that they get it.'

'Of course.' Patrick didn't know what he had been expecting. 'Erm, is she…am I allowed to ask if they…if she's OK?'

'I'm afraid I can't give you any details.'

'Of course not.' Patrick took a pen and paper and sat down on one of the sofas, wondering what on earth he was going to write. He should have gone straight home.

Amy walked into the lobby with two steaming coffees, strode straight past the front desk and called the lift.

'Amy.' Patrick sprang to his feet and, as the doors opened, forced his way into the lift behind her.

'What the hell are you doing here? *Jesus.*'

Apparently having beamed himself across the lobby, the security guard appeared at the lift door before it closed. 'I'm sorry, sir—if you could come with me…'

Patrick ignored him and continued to focus on Amy. 'What's going on? Are they—is she OK?'

'No thanks to you.' Amy's reponse was terse.

The security guard placed his enormous hand on Patrick's shoulder. 'If you could step out of the lift now, sir?'

Patrick put one foot in the lobby as a gesture of co-operation but continued to obstruct the beam that kept the door from closing. 'What is that supposed to mean?'

'Sorry, that was unnecessary. It's just been a horrible few hours. They're fine.'

'What happened?'

'Like I'm going to give *you* any details.'

'Please, just tell me—is she OK?' Patrick begged.

'Emma lost the baby. And if you breathe so much as a consonant, let alone a clue, to anyone—press or otherwise—you will wish you hadn't. Got it?' Amy looked at the security officer. 'That applies to you too.'

Patrick nodded. 'I'm only here because you told me I had to tell her tonight.'

'So you thought stalking her was reasonable, did you?'

'You all drove past me. I was leaving, dithering, and then...' Patrick hesitated.

'Well, there's no point adding to her woes now, is there?'

'I guess not. So I'm off the hook?'

Amy nodded. 'You're out of here. Goodnight, Patrick. And drive carefully, won't you. I'm sure Katy would like you in one piece. More fool her.'

YOU MAY KISS THE BRIDE

twenty-eight

A pre-Christmas Wednesday to most, a second official wedding day for others. And as the James-Joseph micro-wedding party emerged from the town hall Sarah and Simon stopped for a kiss on the steps while Jess dodged shoppers, mothers with pushchairs and workers in suits, determined to find a prime photograph-taking position on the pavement.

Simon took his wife's hand as they descended to Jess's level. 'So, Mrs Joseph, when would you rather celebrate our anniversary? February or December?'

Sarah only hesitated for a split second. 'Why not both?'

'What? Two cards to forget? Two meals out? Two presents?'

'Hey, what's mine is yours.'

'And don't I know it?'

'Careful, that includes me.' Jess brandished her digital camera menacingly. 'Smile.'

Sarah barely registered the office workers on their lunch breaks as she walked away from the town hall, for once happy to follow her sister, no questions asked. Today she was safely encased in a marital snowglobe, impervious to anyone but herself and Simon. Smartly dressed in suits, with no give-away wedding paraphernalia on display, the secret was all theirs.

Simon hugged Sarah firmly to his side, and Jess noted they were walking so closely together that they could have been competing in a three-legged race. 'Thanks for agreeing to be my wife. Again. I love you.'

'I love you too, Si.'

'Oh, come on, you two—that's quite enough of all that.' Jess couldn't take this level of slush so early on in the day. Or indeed at any time of any day. 'This is your second wedding, and you've been together for a billion years. Let's just get to lunch…and congratulations, by the way.'

'That's more like it.' Simon punched his sister-in-law playfully.

'You know what they say: first the worst, second the best…'

'Don't push it. Now, what's all this about lunch?' Sarah was sounding much more like her old self again. 'I told you not to go to any trouble. Simon has to go back to work this afternoon—business as usual, remember?'

'First you get married without me, then you get married *with* me, but you still won't let me buy you lunch?'

'Well, one minute we're too together, too old and too boring to have a kiss in broad daylight, and now suddenly I'm not allowed to go back to the office?' Simon was playing with Jess. 'We got married three years ago. We only have sex a couple of times a week these days.'

'La-la-la-la—not listening.'

'Of course it was easier when we didn't have a lodger.'

'In a couple of weeks it'll all be back to normal, then. You're not seriously going to the office are you, Si?' Jess was shocked.

'Of course not.'

'Really?' Apparently Sarah wasn't.

'Darling, I don't do absolutely everything I'm told. I've

taken today and tomorrow morning as holiday. It's the end of term for you, and…' he kissed his not-so-new wife '…we're going to a hotel tonight.'

'We are?'

'This is a moment for celebration. I've booked a suite at The Savoy.'

'But I haven't got any stuff with me. And what about Millie?'

'All taken care of.'

Sarah grinned. 'Marry me.'

'You're on.'

Jess waited for a pause in their moment. Forget green and prickly, she was feeling grey with tiredness and the beginnings of a cold—plus, now she had to move all her stuff over to Fiona's. Sleigh bells weren't ringing so much as clanging in her world. However, as she led Sarah and Simon to the Italian restaurant round the corner, Jess could see that, for her sister at least, this was an extraordinary moment in what for most people was just an ordinary day.

'To Jess.' Simon got to his feet as he announced the toast.

Eight wine glasses and one bottle of warm milk were raised as all parents and one small, now one hundred per cent legitimate daughter, toasted the organiser.

Sarah joined him at the head of the small table. 'Obviously we told her not to go to any trouble, and actually she was instructed not to tell anyone, but I guess we should all know by now that she'll just do whatever she wants.'

'Cheers, Sarah.' Jess took a sip of her drink. 'I think.'

'To the best sister-in-law I could have hoped to inherit.'

'Thanks, Si.'

'I mean it. Mum, Dad…everyone…' Simon did his best to take Sarah's four parent figures in his stride. If they could all get on well together, then he didn't want to upset anyone by giving them the wrong titles. 'Thank you all for joining us today to celebrate what Sarah and I really regard as a renewal of our vows.'

Murmuring affirmatively, the handful of guests in the private dining room all took healthy sips from their glasses of wine.

'And, Jess, I have to hand it to you—to get my folks here without so much as a whisper from them is an incredible achievement. When we dropped Millie off with them a couple of hours ago they were dressed for gardening—and now look at them.'

Jess grinned. 'All part of the service.'

Simon ground to a halt before his next sentence. 'Hello, hello—I think I've met this next guest before...'

Jess turned and raised an eyebrow at Josh where he stood, laden with bags, in the doorway to the private room. He was early. But she couldn't help but smile at Sarah's face as she identified this latest arrival to her party.

'Well, well...' Simon got up to greet his friend of a friend and Josh winked at Jess before starting to set up in the corner.

'What's *he* doing here?' Sarah hissed across the table, barely able to contain herself.

'A favour. For me.'

'Oh, really? What sort of favour?'

Jess blushed. 'You'll see. He insisted.' She'd actually done her best to put him off, in light of the fact her entire nuclear family were going to be present. 'It's for you guys. Not for me.'

'I thought you weren't sure about him?' For once Sarah's concern was sisterly.

'What do you mean?' Jess didn't recall having had any detailed discussion with her sister about Josh. Sarah had been far too preoccupied of late.

'Walls have ears, you know. Or at least babies do—and monitors.'

Jess had no idea what Sarah was talking about.

'That night when you fell home? I heard you talking to Millie from the kitchen.'

Jess blushed as she tried to remember what she might have said that was clearly incriminating her now. 'Yeah, well, I was drunk—very drunk. And Josh is a decent bloke, don't you think?'

'He is. But that's not the point. You have to follow your heart.'

'Because that's worked a treat for me so far,' Jess responded sardonically.

'Well, you know what they say—"in vino veritas".'

'What are you trying to say, Sar?'

'Just do what you want to do. Fuck everyone else and their opinions.'

Sarah hardly ever swore. A by-product of working with small children.

'It's your life—remember that. I love you.'

Jess didn't know what to do with this rare moment of genuine sisterhood. Luckily she didn't have a chance to think about it as Simon returned, grinning widely. 'I didn't know you were seeing Josh—I mean, *properly*.'

Jess did her best to play it down. 'We've been on a few dates, that's all.'

'That's *all*? That's fantastic.'

'It's very early days, Si. I'm still not sure it's really going anywhere.'

Sarah tried to catch Simon's eye, desperate for him to stop.

'She says all the nicest things, you know,' Josh butted in as he approached, and Jess chastised herself for talking so loudly and so openly as he kissed her hello. There was nothing wrong with Josh's hearing.

Simon did his best to smooth things over. 'Just so long as you're both having a bit of fun. Sorry, Josh—blame me for goading her and applying juvenile amounts of pressure.' He changed the subject as fast as he could. 'Now, Sar, I hope you can dance in those shoes.'

Relieved to be out of the spotlight, Jess squinted at her sister's heels.

Sarah looked down at her 'something blue' suede pointed feet. 'Don't be ridiculous. These are cab shoes.'

Jess shook her head. 'He's being serious. Josh is here to sing us a few songs. As I have recently discovered, he's a bit of a lounge singer.' She still hadn't decided whether the fact he could sing was very sexy or a total turn-off.

Josh gave Jess a kiss on the cheek before leaving to introduce himself to everyone on his way over to his microphone. To Jess's relief he was describing himself as simply 'a friend' of hers. Not that her mother believed a word of it, she could tell. She was sure the Spanish Inquisition wasn't far away.

Dressed in smart jeans and a black suit jacket, with a white T-shirt underneath, Josh was looking more Don Johnson in *Miami Vice* than Harry Connick Jr today. As he mumbled into his microphone and tested his keyboard to ensure it was in piano rather than electronica or Dalek mode, he caught Jess watching him and winked at her before pulling up a chair. Sarah's mother and father and their not-so-new replacement partners were rapt in their attentions. And unfortunately they were Jess's parents too.

'Good afternoon, ladies and gents…'

As silence descended, all the hairs on the back of Jess's neck stood to attention. An invariable by-product of someone performing live in her vicinity, independent of whether or not she was sleeping with them.

'I'm just here to do a few numbers for you to celebrate Sarah and Simon's nuptials. I had the mixed fortune of sitting next to Jess at lunch a couple of months back, and— well, here we are.'

As he played a few chords Jess could hear a murmur of approval from the olds. And she had to admit Josh's keyboard dexterity was impressive. He didn't even have any music. She had only ever managed *Chopsticks,* and that was after a lot of practice.

By the end of 'Can't Help Falling In Love With You' the applause at the final chord was far greater than you would have expected from an audience of nine. Josh dipped his head in acknowledgement before crooning deftly into his next performance, a specially customised version of an old Billy Paul number…

'Me and Mrs Joseph…'

Jess smiled. They weren't the only ones with a thing going on. As Sarah and Simon got to their feet for their first dance as man and wife, Jess sat back and observed Josh casting his spell over all the couples in the room, and wondered whether she would remain immune for ever.

twenty-nine

Fiona and Mike were oblivious to their audience as they kissed by the fountain in the old town square. The moment was sealed by a wave of spontaneous applause as the locals put down their shopping bags to observe the marital spectacle taking place and to gawp at the men dressed in waistcoats and tails.

The sun filtered through some passing cloud cover, and a strip of glittering sea was visible over the old stone wall, where the square gave way to a steep bank of trees tinged with the orange and pink rays of a sun which had peaked for the day and was definitely warming up for the spring. The air temperature had hit a flukey sixteen degrees Celsius—six degrees above the seasonal average for February—and, if you were that way inclined, it was a sign—either of global warming or a tacit blessing for the bride and groom. Whichever your theory, the Mallorcan sunshine was having a universally positive effect on the select group of sunlight-deprived attendees, who had been overjoyed at having an excuse to leave the cold, wet and windy shores of Britain, for a long weekend of celebrations.

Jess's mood was light as she sipped a glass of cold white wine, and she wondered if perhaps she was solar-powered and ought to consider moving to a Spanish island where the sun shone regularly and the food and drink cost a fraction of London prices. Plus, Spanish was such a beautiful language—at least when *she* wasn't speaking it. Of course there'd be the small matter of having to earn a living, although going on Emma's current levels of efficiency she could almost think about taking time off without anyone noticing. Well, at least a couple of days' holiday.

Mike's uncle, Carlos, was approaching rapidly.

'It was fast, this, no?' His voice was testament to years of cigars and fine wine and as rambunctious as his stature.

Jess nodded. 'Fast. Yes.' She wondered why she was choosing to reply in basic English monosyllables when she had a full command of her mother tongue, and she proceeded fluently, if more slowly than usual. 'The day always goes fast. Months of planning gone in minutes.'

'I mean the couple, not the day. How do you say? A tornado affair?'

Jess nodded, correcting him automatically. 'A whirlwind romance. But the speed you enter marriage doesn't necessary correlate with the speed you exit it—unless, of course, you are Britney Spears.'

Carlos nodded and smiled, and Jess wondered if he had understood a word she'd been saying. Pretending to be busy keeping an eye on proceedings, she watched Mike checking the digital screen on the wedding photographer's camera. Sarah and Simon were strolling around the perimeter of the old cobbled square hand in hand, enjoying a Millie-free weekend, while Fiona's and Mike's parents were chatting politely. Nick was standing just to their left, watching his sister with affection, and then, before Jess could look away, suddenly he was watching her.

Feeling her ears redden under her hair, Jess rummaged

in her bag for an invisible item, not daring to meet his gaze. She was grateful that he had elected to come alone, but, dressed in the tails he had bought for their wedding, his dark pink waistcoat a perfect match for the silk flower on her red suit jacket, his presence was both magnetic and overbearing.

They'd done polite hellos and air kisses at dinner last night, but, being in charge of proceedings, Jess had conveniently been able to engineer a seat well away from his, so avoiding any difficult conversations that might have detracted from the only two people who mattered this weekend. It had only been a few months since they had last seen each other, but going on their previous frequency of sightings it felt like years.

Nick raised his bottle of beer as he observed her attempt at coyness, and as she raised her glass back, and took a sip, he watched her through the bottom of the brown San Miguel bottle from the other side of the fountain.

Under strict instructions from Fi he had stuck to formalities with Jess. Of course she was right, in the infuriating way that sisters often were, that unless he was one hundred per cent sure of his feelings he shouldn't say anything. And the truth was that he had only been about ninety per cent sure— that was until he had seen her again. So now his emotions were shaken and stirred, and a moment of privacy was out of the question. It was all a mess. He'd been able to hear his mother sucking air between her teeth when he'd kissed Jess on the cheek as they'd arrived at the church. He didn't want his parents to think any less of her than they had a year earlier, yet it felt as if everything was out of his control.

Nick saw Carlos check his watch, and moments later Jess produced a taxi as if out of thin air, for him to make a head start, as the horse and cart arrived for Fiona and Mike.

Taking a step forward, Nick stopped himself. Was San Miguel the patron saint of second chances, or was this feeling merely circumstantial romance? He imagined wind, rain, grey skies and concrete tower blocks. Jess in tracksuit bottoms, her hair tied back in an unwashed knot instead of swept up off her collar, stray tendrils teasing her neck. But, however grim the setting, Jess remained in the picture.

He watched her as she guided guests to their taxis, and then finally it was the Seatons' turn. He felt his mother's hand on his arm.

'Come on, darling.'

'I'm ready.'

Jess beckoned them over with a warm smile. Nick took an audible breath.

'Are you OK?' Like most mothers, Maggie Seaton was very protective of her children at all times, even when they were in their mid-thirties.

'Of course. Doesn't she look beautiful?'

'I've never seen her so happy. And Mike is such a lovely chap...'

Nick decided not to correct his mother's assumption that he'd been talking about Fi.

'... so different to Fiona, and yet so good for her.'

'I know.' Nick put his sunglasses on to deflect the glare from the sun—and his mother. 'It's a perfect day.'

'I'm sorry, love.' She rubbed his arm affectionately.

'Mum, it's OK. It *is* a perfect day. And don't forget, it's all because of Jess.'

'Well, she's clearly better at everyone else's weddings.'

'Mum, please.'

'I just don't know why you insist on defending her the whole time.'

'Maybe she was right. We weren't ready. Our eyes were wide shut. We were on a marital treadmill—a road to nowhere. It was probably all a blessing in disguise. I do wish you'd forgive her.'

'You can't tell me what to do, love.'

'Don't I know it?' Nick complained.

'I'm just saying, be careful.'

'Of course.'

'So I'm right?'

'You're my mother. You're always right.'

'Right about what, then?'

'About Jess.' Nick was determined to tell someone how he was feeling, and his sister was a bit busy at the moment.

'What about her?'

'Watch what you say. I don't know that this is over yet,' Nick warned her.

'I had a horrible feeling you might say something like that.'

'Mum!'

'I worry. That's what happens when you have children—you worry. You're proud, so proud, and you worry.'

Nick gave his mum's hand a squeeze and she turned to him, her eyes moist. 'I know you still love her, darling.'

'Mum. Leave it. We'll just have to see.'

'Fiona seems to think Jess has been missing you, too.'

'What am I? After-dinner conversation?'

'My phone calls are free after six p.m. Anyway, we're a family—we're concerned.'

'You're gossips.'

'Look, Rosie was a lovely girl—you knew that; we knew that. But at the end of the day she wasn't what you wanted—you knew that, we knew that. Simple.'

Simple. Or maybe that was just him.

Jess was tumescent with paella, good wine and good spirits as Mike got to his feet to make his speech.

'On behalf of my wife and I—'

A hearty cheer rose from the inebriated guests. Sixty people were sounding more like six hundred.

'First of all, a huge thank you to Carlos—for marrying my auntie, bringing her to such a beautiful country, for having such a wonderful home and for letting us use it. Thanks also to the weather, for excelling itself, and to all of you for coming over. It was Fiona's dream to have a small…well, small-ish wedding in the sunshine, and here we are. So if we could all charge our glasses and drink to my wife. To Mrs Benson!'

Mike was still standing.

'I'm afraid I'm not done yet…'

Mike left a pause for hecklers, but everyone was too busy drinking.

'A big thank-you to Jess, and to Emma, manning Jess's office back in London. Today has gone without a hitch, and I know there has been a great deal of organisation, gentle persuasion and Spanish translation going on behind the scenes—speaking of which, *muchas gracias* to our official translator, Beatriz, thanks to whom I'm pretty sure I just agreed for Fiona to be my wife.'

A laugh rippled through the guests.

'Now, back to Jess…For those of you we haven't bored with the story, if it hadn't been for her, Fiona and I would never have met…and there never would have been the tale of how a high-flying accountant came to marry a cheeky-chappy photographer like me. A special thank you from us both. To the gorgeous Jess.'

Jess blinked back a champagne tear and deliberately kept her gaze locked on Mike and Fi as the others got to their feet and drank to her good health. Simon, sitting to her right, patted her shoulder proudly.

In a symphony of chair-scraping, everyone returned to their seats. Almost everyone.

The groom was still upstanding.

'I also owe a big thank you to Maggie and David. Firstly for raising such a fantastic daughter—a woman I intend to make the happiest woman in the world, or at least in Valldemossa—and also for your generous contribution to today, for singing so loudly in the church and, to David, for agreeing not to make a speech.'

Jess laughed and the crowd cheered. David was well known for not being able to say hello in under half an hour.

'Now, you may be starting to think otherwise, but I *am* going to keep my speech short…'

Another cheer.

'…however, I couldn't possibly sit down without saying a word or two about my beautiful bride. I had never even come close to getting married before I met Fiona, yet within a few weeks—some might say too quickly…'

Jess fiddled with the flower arrangement on her table.

'…I just knew. Not only is Fiona a kind, warm-spirited, generous, loving…'

Mike turned to face his wife.

'Sorry, darling, I can't read your writing. Does that say "beautiful"…?'

Fiona laughed and the room laughed with her.

'Seriously, she is all of the above and a lot more. Thank you, Fi, for saying yes, for agreeing to be my wife, and for making me the happiest man in the world.'

Jess sighed inaudibly. There must be stiff competition at the top. *All* grooms couldn't be the happiest men in the world. It just wasn't possible.

'I don't know what life has in store for us, but I can't think of anyone else I would want to be embarking on this adventure with.'

Mike kissed Fiona as a murmur of approval wafted in their general direction and a lot more champagne was swigged. After what felt like a teenage amount of time, eventually they pulled apart for fresh air.

'Apologies for the overdose of sentimentality, but I figure a man is allowed to gush on his wedding day. Follow your hearts. Drink to my wonderful wife, and then let's dance.'

Mike led Fiona to the allocated dance floor area just as the music started—and Jess thought of Josh. She needed to get out.

Jess filled her glass with cold white wine before wandering on to the balcony. Dusk was falling. The air was sweet and cooling rapidly as birds sang the remnants of the day away. As she leant on the stone balustrade she watched the colour slowly seeping out of everything around her. And then, as the music seemed to fade, she had an acute sense she was no longer alone. Turning, she saw that Nick was standing with his back to her, pulling the doors to the reception room closed behind him. Jess didn't flinch. She had definitely been hoping this would happen.

Nick turned to face her, his pink waistcoat highlighting his now rosy cheeks, his white shirtsleeves surprisingly uncrumpled for this stage of a wedding reception.

'Hello, Jess.'

'Hi.' Jess flicked her hair to remove any possibility of a centre parting ruining what she hoped was going to be a moment she wanted to remember.

Nick stood next to her and silently they observed the same view. Intimate strangers surveying an unfamiliar scene. On the horizon a few flashing lights became visible, no doubt marking hazards further along the rocky coast. But there was nothing warning him of the nearest danger of all. And at any moment she could walk back inside and the opportunity would have passed him by altogether.

'So, how's things?' It wasn't the most scintillating opener, but at least it required a response.

'Good, fine…' Jess didn't know where to start.

If only a brief answer.

'You?' She didn't want him to leave now.

'Not bad.' Nick wondered how long they could sustain this masquerade of mundanity.

A synchronised sipping moment as they recognised that they were barely keeping their heads above water in the small-talk round.

'Great day.' Nick realised he was going to have to try

harder. If he was failing to keep his own interest in the conversation he could barely expect Jess to endure much more of this.

'Thanks.' Jess smiled as genuinely as she could. Although the fact she was thinking about it probably meant that it didn't look even remotely natural.

'I'm finally beginning to understand why it's so difficult to get a date with you…'

'It's not that hard.' It was supposed to be her best flirty tone, only to her horror Jess realised that while she flirted convincingly with suppliers, IT support, parking attendants and security guards—in fact anyone to get her own way—flirting with the man she still loved wasn't something she had practised recently.

'I mean for weddings.' Nick couldn't help but smile at her awkwardness.

Jess blushed. 'Of course. Well, most people prefer weekends, and there are only fifty-two every year…' She stopped and composed herself before she revealed that there were seven days in a week. 'Can I let you into a secret?'

'If you like.' Nick couldn't have been more delighted.

'I never felt this adrift when we were together.'

'You feel adrift?' He was sure Fiona had told him that Jess was still dating Josh.

'Not every day. I mean, I can hold anything together if I have to.'

'I wouldn't doubt you for a second.'

'I doubt myself sometimes.' Jess smarted at the uncharacteristic frankness of her admission.

'You shouldn't.'

'But…' Jess hesitated. Vulnerability wasn't her thing. 'Well, to think I thought I'd be better off alone. The trouble is I had it too good for too long.'

'Blimey.' Nick did his best to disguise a grin. Pursing his lips together, he thought he probably looked like a frustrated flautist. 'Next you'll be telling me you took me for granted.'

'I did.'

'Hey, look, I wasn't perfect.'

'Who said anything about perfect?'

'Good…' Nick was confused. He could have done with a time-out to consult his *Idiot's Guide to Women* before he screwed everything up again. 'Because I don't want you building me up into something I can't live up to.'

Jess turned her head to meet his eyes. 'What do you mean?'

'Look, this probably isn't the time or place—but then it probably never will be… What the hell…?' Nick paused. 'Hang on.' He remembered the fly in the ointment. 'Fi mentioned that you were still dating that chap I met very briefly at the restaurant.'

'Josh.' Jess blushed for no apparent reason.

Nick nodded, pretending he had forgotten his name. 'Josh—yup, that's it. So that's been going on a while?'

Jess returned her gaze to the horizon, nervously rubbing the palm of her non-glass-carrying hand on the slightly rough surface of the balcony balustrade.

Nick took the silence to be an affirmative response. 'He looked OK. What's he like?' He didn't really want to know. And then again he did.

'He's fine. He's nice.' Jess was experiencing a hybrid of emotions. Today's specials so far: embarrassed, disloyal and awkward. 'We only see each other a couple of times a week at the most.' She didn't know what she was trying to prove. 'We're passing the time…having some fun.'

'Right. Well, why not?' Nick could think of quite a few reasons.

'But he's not a long term prospect for me. And, I guess most importantly of all—well, he's not you.' Jess balked. She'd never to her knowledge said anything so saccharine before in her life. But it was true.

'I would have thought that was a huge point in his favour.' Nick stuck to the humorous approach.

'Oh, it was. It is.' Jess was joking. She hoped Nick knew that.

Nick paused, resting his forearms on the balcony wall and leaning forward, looking down over the edge. 'I was thinking the other day about that holiday we had in Turkey.'

'That awful one when we had no money and they hadn't even finished the hotel yet?'

'It didn't matter, though, did it? We were together. It was an adventure.' As the blood rushed to his head, he raised it again.

'It certainly was.' Jess hadn't seen mosquitoes that size before or since.

'But we were just happy to have each other. I think I forgot that later on. I wanted our life *my* way.'

'Steady on, you're beginning to sound as selfish as I was.'

'You weren't selfish, you were focused. You knew what you wanted to do and instead of encouraging you I was cross...I was sulky...I'm sorry.'

'Things went wrong. It happens.'

'It does. Look, I was thinking...' Nick dared himself to continue. 'If this is going to work, we have to be realistic.' He paused.

Five seconds of stunned silence ensued, which felt closer to five hours.

Jess turned to face him for the first time 'If *this* is going to work? Have you lost your mind?'

'I'm pretty sure I packed it yesterday.'

Jess smiled, and as they allowed their eyes to lock for the first time in months she forced herself to blink, to dilute the intensity of the moment. An army of questions started to assemble, shuffling themselves according to rank and urgency.

Nick found his verbal feet first. 'Lucy misses you.'

'Rubbish.'

'She does. She spends more time sleeping outside your old wardrobe than she does anywhere else.'

'Don't play the animal card. That's not fair.'

'OK, she's not the only one. You miss me too.'

'And don't put words in my mouth,' Jess scolded.

'How about your numbers in my phone?'

'Now you've lost me.'

'Missed calls. I've had a few, and all from your numbers.'

Jess blushed at her transparency. 'I was in mourning. It was just a phase I was going through.'

'Well, I was almost sorry when it ended. But obviously then Josh came along and rescued you.'

'Since when did I want rescuing? At least I wasn't pounced on.'

'It wasn't like that.'

'Come on, Rosie had been single for ages.'

'We had lots in common,' Nick insisted.

Jess was so focused on her bitchy repartee she hadn't noticed him tense. 'Drinking champagne and salsa dancing?'

'Other stuff.'

'So it's still going strong?'

'With Rosie?'

'Blimey, Nick, is there more than one?'

'No.' He shook his head. He couldn't believe she didn't know. 'It ended.'

'It did?' Fiona was lucky it was her wedding day. Very lucky. There had clearly been deliberate withholding of information of a semi-urgent nature. 'When?'

'Nearly a month ago now. Last week of January. I thought Fi would have told you.'

'Yuh. You'd think. It wouldn't have been an unreasonable assumption to make. So what went wrong?'

Nick frowned. 'Nothing, really. It just wasn't feeling that right either. And I suppose the whole start-of-a-new-year thing really got to me. I missed you, and it wasn't fair on her—or on me.'

Jess nodded, wishing she could come back with a similar

story. But New Year's Eve with Josh had been very alcoholic and, surprisingly, a lot of fun. More fun than they'd managed ever since, in fact.

'Look at this view.' With one command, Nick rescued her from introspection.

'It's perfect, isn't it?' Jess watched a cloud of tiny birds moving across the sky. 'But life is just life, wherever you are, and however glamorous the location.'

'Ah, yes, Dr James. The pop psychologist returns. I'd forgotten about your philosophical side.' Nick winked at his ex-girlfriend—his ex-life. 'It's certainly all about the cast of characters. The rest is literally just wallpaper.'

'Reality doesn't have to be boring, right?' Jess put her glass down and, using her arms, gently raised herself onto the edge of the balcony, legs swinging. The ledge was wide enough to lie on, but Nick still found himself edging closer protectively.

'Of course it doesn't.'

'I thought not.' Jess wasn't thinking about Josh any more. 'The thing is, you can never go back, can you?'

'Right, right…' Nick returned his focus to the horizon. A couple of boats, their sails minuscule, inched their way from right to left as they tried to out run dusk. 'But then again…' his eyes brightened as he thought of a new spin, '…there's always second time lucky…'

'And that's different how?'

'I'm not sure. Anyway, who said anything about going backwards? Why can't it be sideways?'

Jess nodded, endorsing his analogy. 'I guess…'

'It's all a question of perception, and—well, hypothetically at least, you could argue we haven't been forward yet.' Nick rubbed the palm of his hand up the back of his neck, over the crown of his head and back again. He missed his hair.

'But it didn't work last time.'

'No.' Nick hesitated.

'I stalled.' Jess furrowed her brow.

'I noticed.'

'I'm sorry. I'm still sorry. I think I'll probably always be sorry.'

'Hey, no regrets. Things happen for a reason.'

Jess was grateful for the warmth of his gaze. 'Not necessarily.'

'You always said they do.'

'It's just something people always say.'

'Well, I think people have a point. I just thought I was right about what we wanted, what we needed, and that you'd come round eventually. I wasn't even pretending to listen carefully. I couldn't spell empathy. We would never even have been able to have this conversation. And yet now I can see your viewpoint perfectly. I mean, why bother with the getting married thing? It's only a bit of paper, really.'

'My career is just a piece of paper, eh?' Jess had a mischievous glint in her eye.

'Hopefully lots of pieces of paper—with the queen's head and the number fifty on them…'

'Seriously, Nick, you're Captain Marriage—well, at least the concept of it.'

'Maybe I was just Captain Conventional, kow-towing to what my parents expected of me—or at least what I *thought* they expected of me. Now Fi's gone and got married out here, ten minutes after meeting someone, and they're cool about it. Maybe I got them all wrong.'

'They like Mike, though?'

Nick pulled himself up to sit next to her. 'They love him. To be honest, he's difficult not to like—and Fi hasn't looked this happy in ages, even *ever*.'

'True…'

Together they swung their legs.

Jess nodded. 'I'm still not sure about all this organised stuff.'

'You are the most organised person I know.'

'I mean in terms of religion. I don't see why we, or indeed anyone, has to say the same things as everyone else.'

'I guess it's just tradition,' Nick reasoned.

'It's like everyone suddenly wants to conform.'

'We could just *not* get married.'

'Or we could write our own vows. Hey, why not? Let's do it.'

'Jess, don't. I can't deal with… Don't play with me.'

'Really, Nick, I mean it. And, well, I can't rent a flat from your sister for ever.'

Nick was silent.

'Clearly I'm joking at an inappropriate moment, yet again.' Jess wondered if it would be easier to tip herself backwards off the balcony and put herself out of her misery. She had such good intentions—and such poor execution.

He turned the upper half of his body to face her. 'Really?'

'You're going to have to be a touch more articulate than this if we get married.'

Nick sat on his hands and looked down at his feet. 'I can't go through this again, Jess. The soaring up, the crashing down.'

Jess slid off the balcony and stood herself between Nick's legs, recognising the waft of aftershave as one she'd chosen for him. 'Me neither.'

He looked searchingly into her eyes. 'Are you sure you're sure?'

Jess didn't blink. 'Never been surer.'

'Not just panicking about dying alone or with a club singer?'

Jess slapped his arm playfully. He clearly knew far more about Josh than he'd let on.

'No, just panicking about dying without you.'

'I had no idea. You should have said.' Nick slid down to join her and put his hands on her hips. Jess shivered.

'No, I shouldn't.'

Nick pulled Jess in for a hug, and as he did she kissed him.

Excitement rushed through her body, tempered with a familiarity which made her want to laugh and cry all at the same time. And he'd always been a fantastic kisser.

Jess pulled back first. 'We definitely have to do more kissing this time around.'

'You bet. I'll take you, to have and to hold, and to kiss…' Nick stroked the exposed nape of her neck as their lips met again. 'Just practising…'

'So—' Jess squeezed her eyes closed '—I guess I'd better give Josh a call.'

'I'd better take the house off the market.'

'No, leave it there.'

'What?'

'We should start again.'

'We *are* starting again. It's our home.'

'It *was* our home. It was our life. And this is a new one. Or at least the next instalment.'

Nick smiled, doing his best to keep up. 'It's like the Nick and Jess trilogy.'

'Like the *Lord of the Rings*?'

'Or in our case no rings.'

Jess laughed 'So far…'

'OK, my precious. In which case this must be the happy ending at the end of part three.'

'Or the happy beginning.' Jess was feeling incredibly relaxed.

'Exactly.'

'So how about next week? Next month? Let's seize the moment.'

'What? Before you change your mind?' Nick folded his arms across his chest.

'I'm not going to change my mind this time.'

'If you could just sign here…' Nick produced his folded menu from a trouser pocket and pretended it was a contract.

'My word is my bond—or it will be this time.'

'But what about everybody else?'

'What about them?'

'You don't think there's going to be lots of tut-tutting in our direction?'

'Sod them. We'll win them over.'

'Of course we will.' Nick sounded a lot more positive than he felt. She had no idea what some people had said.

'Just by being ourselves.'

'You do realise this is the greatest U-turn in relationship history since Elizabeth Taylor married Richard Burton for the second time?'

Jess rolled her eyes. 'She married loads of people. You always were prone to a smidgen of exaggeration.'

'Moi?'

'Toi.'

As Nick and Jess kissed again, the handle of the balcony door turned and it opened a fraction.

'Fucking hell.'

It closed again.

Jess and Nick wheeled to see Fiona and Mike peering at them through a pane of glass. Nick beckoned encouragement, and in seconds they had joined them.

'What are you two doing out here?' Fiona wasn't wasting any time.

Nick put his arm across Jess's shoulder. 'Clearing the air.'

'Clearing it? You were pretty much stealing each other's.'

'It's OK, Fi.' Jess linked arms with her best friend.

'Oh, is it?'

'Yes.' Nick smiled as he pecked his sister on the cheek. 'It is.'

'So, what? They all lived happily ever after?' Fiona grinned.

'Excuse me, Madame Paris Engagement.'

Mike clapped his hands excitedly. 'This is fantastic. It was all down to my speech, wasn't it?'

Jess smiled. 'Probably not *all* down to your speech.'

'Fucking hell.' Fiona's vocabulary had disappeared in her shock.

'Fi, the swearing doesn't sit well with the virginal look.' Nick kissed his sister on the forehead. He was suddenly kiss-stastic. Mike had better watch his step.

'Seriously, Nick, Mum's going to flip.'

'Mum's going to be great. She knows more than you think.'

Fiona was blinking a lot. 'And you're both really OK?'

Jess and Nick nodded, and Jess was secretly delighted to be part of the collective 'both' once again.

'Well…bloody hell.'

Mike rescued her. 'That's brilliant.'

Fi regained control of her emotions—and her sentences. 'I can't believe it. Congratulations. And, Jess, no funny business this time.'

'Are you joking?'

'I hope so. Come on, then—group hug. And go easy, Jess. No make-up on the dress, please.'

Nick was the first to regain his composure. 'Anyway, you two, what do you think you're doing, sneaking away from your own party?'

'We just wanted a moment alone. To let it all sink in. To watch the sun go down. But it would appear the best spot has already been taken.'

A new tune started playing in the main room. Nick took Jess's hand and led her inside. 'Want to dance?'

'You hate dancing.'

'I used to hate dancing.'

Jess raised an eyebrow. 'What? You bought natural rhythm? Were they auctioning it on eBay?'

'I took some lessons. Plus, Rosie dragged me to salsa a couple of times.'

Jess stiffened.

'Look, no secrets. I dare say you slept with Josh a couple of times.'

'I dare say.' At the mention of his name Jess flinched. The

poor guy had done nothing wrong except be the wrong person.

'So we're going to have to be grown-ups.'

'OK.'

'At least some of the time.' Nick swung his hips in mock *Dirty Dancing* style and Jess giggled. 'And, for the record, I hate salsa.'

'Oh.' Despite herself, Jess was disappointed.

'But the general stuff's OK, and I *am* trying.'

'Oh, so trying…' Jess echoed.

'No, that's you.'

'Is it, now?' Jess put her hand on her hip.

'See—we're already sounding like an old married couple.' Nick couldn't have sounded more delighted.

'Less of the old.'

'So what about Josh?'

Jess grimaced. 'I'll call him tomorrow. Or tell him face to face on Monday—what do you think is kinder?'

Nick appeared pensive. 'You're asking *me*?'

'Well, you're a guy. Would you rather have a phone call or a drink?'

'Depends.'

'On what? I feel really bad. He's been lovely to me. I mean not *lovely,* obviously, but nice—and kind. And just when he thought he was breaking down my defences.'

Nick paused. 'I think face to face. But lunchtime, not evening.'

'Is that protocol?'

'Actually, I took Rosie for dinner to tell her. But it was terrible. She'd bought a new outfit, had her hair cut and basically made a monumental effort. Apparently it was our four-month anniversary. Not that I'd noticed.'

'Oh, Nick.'

'I know. Can you imagine…? And it's not like we hadn't had a fun few months.'

'You had?'

'Is that going to be a problem?'

'Of course not.' Jess wondered if she was lying.

'So you're not jealous?'

'I didn't say that. But if you can get over me leaving you on the morning of our wedding, I'm sure I can deal with you shagging my assistant.'

'It wasn't just sex.'

'You could at least try and help. Just a little bit.'

'Shut up. Come and dance with me.' Nick started walking towards the dance floor.

Jess was about five centimetres behind him, scanning the room for familiar faces. 'What? In public?'

Nick took Jess by the hand and together they started moving to the beat. Nick smiled. 'I give Mum twenty seconds…'

Jess grinned back. 'What? Before she shoots me? Careful. Sarah and Simon. Dancing at two o'clock.'

'Calm down. I thought we were leading by example.' Nick deliberately led them in her sister's direction.

Jess was buzzing as they danced together—their eye contact absolute, his rhythm immeasurably improved. In less than a minute the music had been faded down. Someone had entrusted Carlos with a microphone.

'*Hola*. Please, ladies, gentlemen, it is time for the cutting cake. Please follow me to the outside and, um, Jessica…?' Carlos winked at her. 'If you could…?'

'Damn.' Jess pulled back

'What?' Nick tensed. Second thoughts he could deal with. But not third or fourth.

'I'm supposed to be running this show, not rubbing up against my ex-lover on the dancefloor.'

'Ex?'

'Sorry. Current.'

'Current?'

'What's wrong with that?' Jess asked.

'It just sounds like there might be another one tomorrow.'

'OK. How about the love of my life?'

Nick's grin couldn't have been any broader. 'Much better.'

'Good, because I've got to go to work now.'

'Hurry back.'

Jess strode to the cake-cutting area, cunningly sidestepping Maggie and David Seaton by collecting the bride and groom from their quiet moment *en route*.

Fi was very pleased to see her on her own.

'What's going on?'

'Your cake is ready to be cut.'

'No—what's going on?'

'A song by Marvin Gaye?' Jess grinned.

'What's with the Olympic question deflecting? With you and Nick?'

'It's all fine. In fact it's better than fine. It's going to be perfect. Certainly nothing for you to be worrying your bridal head about.'

'Really? Just like that?'

Jess nodded confidently. For once as confidently as she felt.

'So basically you put me through hell, and now it's all going to be OK?'

'I put myself through hell too. And to be honest I don't think Nick had the best time, either.'

'Are you sure you know what you're doing?' Fiona had so many questions and so little time.

Jess nodded. 'I do.'

'Save that for him,' Mike intervened, and kissed Jess on the cheek before leading his brand-new bride to their cake.

A rose-tinted sunset bestowed a warm glow on proceedings as sunlight as rosé as the glasses of pink champagne the guests were clutching highlighted the courtyard. All attendees were in their jackets, but determined to make the most of the great outdoors as the cake was cut.

Jess couldn't help but smile at Sarah and Simon's combined expressions of frustration when, doing their best to wind their way towards her, Nick appeared at the dessert table first and slipped his arm around her waist before they'd managed to get anywhere near close enough for direct questioning.

Nick grinned at Jess. 'Hello, you. So, what? Now my sister gets to have her cake and eat it too?'

'Were you always this funny?'

'Were you always this sarcastic?'

Jess kissed his cheek. 'Always.' Out of the corner of her eye she could see Sarah, nodding at her.

'You know, I think you're all I need.'

Jess scoffed. 'What on earth is that supposed to mean?'

Still smiling, Nick shook his head. 'When Jerry Maguire told Dorothy she completed him she didn't ruin the moment by asking how that was physiologically possible. Honestly.'

'Sorry. You see—this is doomed.'

'I prefer fated.'

'But if I'm irritating you already…'

More tapping on the microphone as Carlos milked his unofficial role as master of ceremonies and interrupted them for a second time. 'Now, please, Fiona is going to throw her flowers to Jessica.' Carlos laughed as he realised he had repeated the bride's instructions perhaps a little too verbatim.

'Did he just say what I think he—'

Nick smiled. 'Yup, petal. Go play.'

'What on earth is your sister like?'

'I think we both know the answer to that question. And, by the way, she's about to be your sister, too,' Nick couldn't resist reminding her.

'Great—an interfering sister-in-law. What more could a girl want?'

A voice from above interrupted them. Either Jess was having her first ever spiritual moment or…

'I heard that. Now, for God's sake, catch these.'

Fiona lined up her target from the balcony before tossing her bouquet in Jess's direction, and as the hand-tied flowers tumbled, head over stalk, towards her, Jess mentally prepared herself to make the catch of her life.

New from Ariella Papa, author of
On the Verge and *Up & Out*

Q: What are the two most dreaded words that a single
girl can hear from her married best friend's mouth?

A: We're trying.

And that's just what Voula's best friend, Jamie, tells her,
quickly ending their regular drinks-after-work tradition.
So with Jamie distracted by organic food, yoga and
generally turning her body into a safe haven for her
impending bundle of joy, Voula sets out in search of a
bundle of joy to call her own—an apartment. In the
New York real estate game, though, she's more likely
to stumble upon an immaculate conception than an
affordable one-bedroom....